MADE TO RULE

MARIANNE A. SCOTT

MADE TO RULE

Your mental health is important! Please beware of the following while reading this book:

Torture

Assault

War, violence, death

Death of a parent

Death of a family member(s)

Sexually explicit scenes (MF) that include anal play and the use of sex toys

This is the final book in the Made from Magic Series and DOES have a happy ending!

PROLOGUE

Lowell

WHY IS IT THAT cities always smell of urine? The air in London is mostly permeated by exhaust and gasoline, but even so, the faint smell of human waste lingers like a bad aftertaste. It's partly why I avoid urban areas. Tonight, there's no other option.

Clouds dampen the moon's natural light and leave only a flickering streetlamp to illuminate the oppressive gray buildings and garbage littering the alley I stand in. The rain is indecisive, coming down in a tepid drizzle that adds to the chill of the February evening. Cold doesn't affect me, werewolves run warm, but it makes it hard to stand in the middle of a sidewalk without looking suspicious. Luckily, the magic surrounding the abandoned warehouse before me makes mortals avoid this place like the plague, even if they don't understand why.

If I shift forward the slightest amount, the visage of the warehouse pixelates, revealing the expansive lawn and stone wall surrounding the palace of the Kingdom of Magic. I duck into the shadows as patrols of Dragons Soldiers scan the area, the crest of the Kingdom emblazoned on their tunics. The crest paints such a pretty picture of four magics living together in harmony, but it's nothing more than a fairytale.

For now.

When the soldiers round the corner, I resume my position on the curb, fighting every impulse in my body to run straight through the wards and bound over the wall. It's only been a few hours since Katie marched into the palace to make a deal with the crown prince, Archer Baran. Hours since I saw the deal go south and she was strung up in the dungeon as he tortured her with his magic.

Katie believes in our mission to restore the balance in the Kingdom so greatly that she forgets that others won't share the sentiment. In the two hundred years since the Four Kings War, Elemental Witches have learned to fear Dark Witches and Magical Creatures, and to view Light Witches only as healers. If we succeed in our mission to restore the four monarchs, those in power would be admitting to their wrongdoings.

And who wants to admit they've been wrong for centuries?

After I saw her in that dungeon, a strange calm washed over me—Katie calls the feeling her military calm. She named me her second, which put me in charge in her absence, so I formed a plan to get her out. Three days. That's how much time we need to gather enough allies to lay siege to the palace so we can rescue our queen.

It's a good plan. Well thought out, not impulsive or rash, and approved by Adriana and her clairvoyance.

I hate it.

How can I sit still while my mate is tortured for three days?

My fucking mate.

I suspected Katie was my mate from the moment we met, but it seemed so impossible. She's human, and mates are incredibly rare amongst werewolves. I ignored the signs, my inability to stay away from her, the bond between us that let me read her emotions, the fact that every time she entered a room my wolf was immediately on high alert, ready to protect her at all costs. But when she came to me last night and blurted out the fact with such surety, all protests and questions faded from my mind and we basked in the joy of that revelation. She's fated to be mine. My perfect partner, my other half.

And now she's in trouble and I can't do anything about it.

My body trembles with the desire to shift. I'd already be inside, tearing throats until I find her if I didn't think that piece of shit would hurt her before I could get there. But Archer is insane with his desire to claim Katie. He's a wildcard and has an entire army at his disposal.

So I stand here. On a curb outside the façade of a warehouse, willing the mating bond to kick in and give me any sense that the love of my fucking life is alive and well.

I didn't realize how debilitating it would be without the presence of our bond. That constant tug in my gut lets me know where she is and if she's okay. I've grown accustomed to feeling her emotions as vividly as I feel my own. Its absence is driving me insane.

The singular scuff of a shoe against the pavement signals Vlad found me. "You don't need to announce your arrival," I say without turning away from my vigil. Vampires are virtually silent, so that sound was very deliberate.

"I've grown quite fond of having all my limbs," he drawls, stepping up beside me. Vlad's translucent skin somehow glows despite the little light from the alley. Combined with his impeccably tailored three-piece suit, he sticks out in this neighborhood like a sore thumb. His posture is relaxed, as if we frequently stand in an alley in London staring at the palace plotting the murder of the future king.

"Adriana sent me to remind you that you need rest," he says, his deep voice cutting through the din of the raindrops. "You almost died."

I huff out an exasperated breath. Katie's father shot me with Dark Magic during an attempted coup yesterday. But my brilliant, tenacious mate didn't give up on me and guided her sister in the steps to remove the magic from my system, saving my life. I'm virtually healed, werewolves heal faster than humans, but I probably need one more solid night of rest to be back at full capacity.

"How can I stand by and do nothing while she's in there with *him*?" I seethe. Archer has hurt Katie before. It's why her magic has been suppressed for the better half of two months, and why she has a scar down the left side of her chest and arm.

"Ye have little faith." Vlad clucks his tongue. "While you've been camped out here, Misty and I created a backup plan. With Adriana's blessing, naturally."

Misty and Marcus, Katie's mom and stepfather, are our inside connection. They're still generals in the Dragons Army and still technically serve Archer, even if they've been recruiting soldiers to our cause since the new year.

"A backup plan," I repeat, finally turning to look at my friend.

"Tomorrow is the coronation, and everyone will be distracted. But for the plan to work, we need the Dragons to think everything is perfect. Nothing amiss. Most specifically, they can't see a werewolf pouting at the front gates."

"I'm not pouting."

Vlad arches an eyebrow. He's right. I know he's right. I should go back with him to the coven and organize the wolves. My sister is capable, but the wolves will only listen to a Beta for so long. And I need to make sure Edina, Katie's best friend and a recently emerged Faerie Princess, learns how to seal a portal for her half of our escape plan.

My wolf whines, not wanting to leave our mate.

"Adriana also asked me to give you this." He pulls a silver locket from his pocket, the red rubies glistening in the flickering streetlight.

Aldonza's necklace.

The necklace is imbued with were-magic to beat when you've met your mate, mimicking their heartbeat. I snatch the trinket from Vlad's hands, brushing my long hair out of the way so I can clasp it on my neck. I hold the pendant and wait.

It beats, and my chest crumples in relief. The heartbeat is wild and erratic, but it's there.

"See? She's strong," Vlad assures me. "Stronger than any other human I've met. She'll survive."

The heart rate in the locket spikes, and I feel it ricocheting in my very marrow. She's in pain. My canines lengthen as my wolf tries to force his way out. The instinct to protect my mate at all costs is riding me hard as I breathe through my nose and try to stop the shift.

"Do you need these?" Vlad asks, extracting a pair of magic-suppressing handcuffs and dangling them around his finger. I shake my head and shove it all down. I'll need to go for a run to expel some energy tonight, but not here in this cesspool. It can wait until we're back in the Highlands.

"If he hurts her, I will not stop until his head is torn from his body and lying at my feet."

"Love that look for you, but for now, we need to go," Vlad says. And when I don't move, "Don't make me get your mother."

I scoff but turn away from the palace. Vlad pats me on the back, and I let him guide me down the street and away from my little witch.

Soon, Ma Reine. Hang on a little bit longer.

Chapter One

ALL I KNOW IS the searing pain of being burned from the inside out.

Archer's grip on my temples is strong, determined, and no matter how violently I thrash, I'm unable to dislodge him as he sends his magic into my body. His fire courses through my blood, seeking to destroy everything I am. I clamp my jaw down so hard I'm convinced my teeth will shatter, but I'm not giving him the satisfaction of hearing me scream.

I trusted him despite everything he put me through. I believed he would never maliciously hurt me. All my friends wanted to come to the palace with me to discuss this plan, but I refused, knowing Archer would never hear my idea of sharing the throne if I walked in with a vampire, a werewolf, a Dark Witch, and a Fae. I had tunnel vision regarding my mission to restore the four monarchs, and I wanted to avoid war so badly that I ignored all the warning signs, including the fact that a thousand-year-old vampire told me it was a terrible idea to come here alone.

Which makes this my fault. And that really pisses me off.

Another wave of pain tumbles through me and I retreat inside my mind, imagining flying through the clouds, running in the woods behind Vlad's house, and dancing around the bonfire with Lowell. Anywhere but where I actually am.

Because where I actually am, in a cell beneath the palace, suspended to some sort of metal contraption with magic-suppressing handcuffs while my ex-boyfriend tries to remove my magic...it's unimaginable. Unthinkable.

He thinks Dark Witches have brainwashed me and are the reason I ran away from the palace, him, and everything that has to do with the current monarchy. When I tried to explain and begged him to listen, he ignored me and continued with his plan of stringing me up and pumping me full of magic.

After an eternity, the pain stops, and I sag in my restraints. My nostrils flare as I take slow, deliberate breaths and try to calm my racing heart.

"I'm so sorry, love," Archer murmurs, kissing my temple where he held his hands not moments ago. I flinch violently, but his lips remain on my skin.

I peel open my eyes and meet his hazel ones, which at this moment are the dark azure of a swirling storm. The skin beneath them is purple from lack of sleep, and the sharp cut of his jaw tells me he hasn't been eating. His blue-black hair is a mess from his fingers, and I find myself wondering if the visible distress is because of my absence, or if it's because he'll be coronated tomorrow. It certainly seems like he's been in pain longer than the past two days, when my father broke into the palace and killed the king, effectively bumping up Archer's ascension.

"This will work," Archer assures me. "I'm sure of it."

"You can't take away my magic." Venom coats my words. "It'll kill me."

"For a normal witch, yes." The growl I give him has him stepping back. "But your Dark Magic was given to you."

"Your Majesty?" a deep voice rumbles from the shadows.

"What?" Archer and I snap simultaneously. He turns back and gives me a sad, pitying smile.

"Umm...Prince Archer," the voice continues. "There's a matter that needs your immediate attention. For the coronation tomorrow—"

"Right." He trails a finger down my cheek, and I snap my teeth when he's only inches from my lips. Biting off a finger is the least he deserves. He jerks away before I can connect. "I'll be back shortly, my love. It'll get easier."

Turning on his heel, he fades into the dark and leaves me alone with the soldiers who accompanied him to my cell earlier. As soon as he's gone, I let my body sag completely, exhaustion from being in so much pain overwhelming me.

I search for my Mind Magic channels but come up empty. Even my mating bond with my werewolf is dark due to the cuffs. It feels like a piece of me is missing. The constant presence, the reassuring flow of Lowell's emotions, and even the incessant urging to be close to each other became comforting over the past few weeks. I'm remarkably empty without it.

"We're going to get you down now," one of the officers says, approaching me like one would approach a feral dog. "Prince Archer will be back soon to continue your treatment."

"Call it what it is." I laugh mirthlessly. "He's torturing me."

"That's not—" The other officer, the one who hasn't spoken, comes closer. I recognize the voice before I recognize the man. "He means well, Captain," Jacobs says.

Jacobs was one of my men when I was a Captain in the Dragons Army. I always found him kind and loyal. Although, now that I think about it, even on the mission to Sicily, he had Archer's back over mine. Loyalty to the crown over his immediate superior.

"You believe his bullshit, Jacobs?" I ask. "You think the Dark Witches brainwashed me?"

"No offense meant, Captain," he murmurs, reaching around to undo clasps or hooks that attach to my cuffs. *That's a yes.* Guess I can't count on him to help get me out of here.

"You can drop the title." I roll my shoulder once it's released. "We both know I'm not a captain anymore."

"No, I suppose you're not."

My other arm is released, and before I have the chance to punch Jacobs in his stupid face, my hands are bound behind my back with a spell. I chuckle darkly as they play right into my hand; the knowledge that their magic works means the suppressant built into the bars of the cell must be turned off when Archer is in here with me. I file that information away for later.

A flame appears in the other officer's hand. "Don't get any ideas about fighting your way out of here," he grumbles. I swear and flinch back, digging my spine into the metal at my back. Since Archer burned me with hellfire, I haven't been able to curb my fear of open flames. It's how they managed to trap me in this cell, by surrounding me with fire and taking my moment of weakness to knock me out.

The officer keeps the flame too close as he undoes the manacles around my feet. As soon as the second foot is released, I drop to the floor and land in a crouch, ready to run. I pop up just as the bars slam shut. The spell binding my arms fades as the hum of magic suppressant fills the cell.

"Fuck," I scream, slamming my hand against the bars.

This is bad, but I've been in tighter spots before. Maybe.

I just need a plan.

I was a soldier in the Dragons Army for two years before I deserted to join the Dark Witches, so I know how things work in this palace. There won't be any prisoners down here with me, not with the coronation tomorrow. They'd be too afraid someone would break in and free them during the ceremony, especially since my father broke in and killed the king only a day ago. That also means security will be tight for the next day and a half, so I can't count on anyone from the outside to rescue me. My mother might have soldiers who can help, but more likely, I'm on my own.

I fiddle with the cuffs around my wrist, searching for a seam or a lock I can pick, but they're magically fused. It's fine. I don't need my magic to fight. Archer doesn't know I've been without it for the past few months and have trained to fight a werewolf at top speed, so I can best a couple of human officers, even if they have their magic.

Now that I'm not suspended in the fucking air, I can see that I was cuffed to an x-shaped metal cross that sits in the middle of the cell. Chains hang from each post, which must connect to my cuffs somehow, even though I can't figure out how. I kneel on the floor and yank on the chains, trying to pry them from the cross. They won't budge an inch.

Turning my attention to the cot next, I poke around the mattress and look for a loose coil or a way to unbolt the frame from the floor. When that proves fruitless, I check the metal toilet in the corner, looking for any piece that might detach. There's nothing I can use as a weapon. Fucking hell, that means I need to fight everyone off with my hands.

A slot in the bars opens, and a tray of food is thrust inside before it's slammed back down. I'm not particularly hungry, but I grab the plastic cup of water from the tray and sip as I walk around the cell. My fingers trail along the three brick walls, searching for any gap or indication of a hidden door. When I come up empty, I toss the cup aside and lie on the bed to plot my next steps. Even if I overpower Archer and his guards, I still need to get to the portal. There's a stash of brooms in the offices adjacent to the dungeon, but they're behind a magical scanner. If it doesn't recognize me, I'll lose valuable time by running away from the portal. Do I take that risk?

I go back and forth for a bit until my eyes grow heavy and my mind strays to Lowell. My second in command. My partner. *My mate.* I hope he's not too worried; the last time we were separated and I was in danger, my sister had to tie him to a tree to keep him from doing something reckless. I pour calming energy down our bond and silently reassure him that I'm okay. Even if he can't feel it, it makes me feel better.

I roll to my stomach, imagining the hard mattress is my mate's chest and that his strong arms are wrapped around me as I fall asleep.

Fingers brush against the sensitive spot beneath my ear, and I moan, sleepily seeking out my wolf. I nuzzle into the hand at my neck and inhale the scent of cedar and agave.

Wait.

That's not my mate. My mate smells like the earth after a rainstorm, not like some cheap cologne.

My eyes fly open, and the world spins until I clamp them shut again. I try to smack the hand cupping my face away, but I'm restrained again, back on the cross. *How did I sleep through them moving me?* As soon as the vertigo passes, I try to move my head, but that's bound too.

"Open your eyes for me, love," Archer croons. When I don't, he murmurs something to the soldiers about a healer. "Katie, I need to know you're okay. Open your eyes."

Two Archers blur into one as I open my eyes. He smiles and gently tucks a piece of hair behind my ear before his fingers skim along the charred skin of my neck.

"I've missed you so much," he murmurs, and I can't fight the urge to vomit any longer. It splatters onto his t-shirt and jeans before he has time to jump back. The second wave goes all over me, and sharp pain travels down my neck as the head restraint holds me tight to the cross.

"Ow, fucking shit." I don't know what's worse, the acid burning my throat or the pain as my body bucks against the ties.

When my stomach is emptied, Archer steps back in and dabs my mouth with a handkerchief. "Sorry about that," he says. He performs a quick cleansing spell on his clothes and mine, but I'm pretty sure he missed whatever got in my hair. "The Dragons insisted on some necessary precautions."

My head is throbbing, but I still get the implied statement. "You drugged me," I breathe. "You laced my water with a sedative." Archer cups my face in his hands, using his thumb to stabilize my trembling lip.

For the first time since I've been taken prisoner, I'm genuinely terrified for my life. My fight or flight response kicks in. I need to get out of here while I'm still strong enough. I won't get the chance if he drugs me again.

"How long was I asleep?" I ask.

"It's only been a few hours," Archer says. I try to do the math, but it's like my brain is wading through glue. I left just after sundown, and I was out for about an hour before he started torturing me—

"Normally, your sessions would take place over ten days at the minimum," Archer continues, "but we need to accelerate the process before your sister comes for you."

"She's not the one you need to worry about," I mutter.

"I can handle Edina." So he doesn't know about Lowell or any of the vampires. Good, that's really good.

"Did you say ten sessions?" I ask, and Archer nods. "That's my father's notebook, then?"

"Yes. I found it in your mom's office. She doesn't know I took it, though. I didn't want to get her hopes up."

My father used these experiments to give me Dark Magic, like Queen Carman did to Finley two hundred years ago. But can it really be used to take my magic? Archer is brilliant, though he's more book-smart than physically competent. If anyone could modify Carman's original spell, it's him.

There's something I'm missing. Something about this ritual that's evading me. Vlad and I spoke about it recently—

"We have to begin again, love." Archer places his hands on my temples.

A stopwatch clicks, and the pain is instant and so much more intense. My body hasn't recovered, and the magic *burns*. My father did these infusions weeks apart, not hours, and I had my Light Magic to protect me. This time my magic is held hostage by the hellfire from Archer's last attack and asleep from the suppressants.

A whimper escapes my lips and with it, a tear. Archer murmurs apologies and praise, words that should be wonderful and sweet but are cruel alongside the pain he's causing me. When the stopwatch goes off, and Archer releases me, I take my first full breath in ten minutes.

"Again," Archer says, and I gasp. My legs are wobbling violently in the restraints, my knees knocking together.

"Archer, please," I whisper.

"It'll all be over soon." He unleashes his power on me again.

This time, I scream.

Chapter Two

The next day, Archer comes down in full regalia. His cape is thick and red, with white fur lining the trim. His black tux is perfectly tailored to his slim frame, and his raven locks aren't their usual rumpled mess but are slicked down and adorned with a silver circlet. There's also a sword slung along his waist that I'm sure he doesn't know how to use. On the other hand, I have dried vomit in my hair because I spent the night puking. At least today, the guard tied it up in a poor excuse for a ponytail.

Archer caresses my cheek, the cool metal of several large rings leaving goosebumps in their wake.

"You can still call me *your highness* even though I've been coronated." I glare through his attempted joke. "I missed hearing that when you were gone."

"You knew where I was," I respond, rallying my strength enough to lift my head from where it hangs. "You never tried to come and get me."

"I was advised against it."

"You didn't even stay to see if I survived."

"Your father tried to kill me," Archer snaps, and white fire ignites in his hand before he banishes it. "They had already gotten to you.

You came off that *throne*—" the word is hissed, "—and you were a different person. You were using Dark Magic."

I want to tell him I'd used Dark Magic before that day. That I wasn't brainwashed, I was enlightened. But he won't hear it, and my throat is dry.

I wet my cracked lips, and Archer's brow furrows. "You didn't drink or eat last night."

"I'm not letting you drug me again."

"I didn't...last night's water was clean." He snaps his fingers, and someone extends a cup from the shadows. He sips the drink first, proving it isn't laced with anything, and holds it to my mouth. I shouldn't, but it's too hard to resist.

When I've drained the cup dry, he gently brushes his thumb against my bottom lip, swiping away a stray droplet. I'd spit in his face if it weren't a waste of water.

"Your Majesty," a guard prompts. "Your guests are waiting for their king." Archer nods and places both hands on my head.

"I love you so much," he whispers, and the pain begins. I'm not strong enough to hold back my screams, and they slice through the air like a lance. I'm sure I'm loud enough to be heard back in the Highlands, at least by the people celebrating in the ballroom. Not that any of the courtiers would come. Acknowledging screams from a dungeon would ruin their fun.

I try to retreat in my mind, but I can't. I'm stuck in this cell with this pain. The molten fire snakes through my veins and collides with my existing magic, battering it until I feel bruised.

When the ten minutes are up, Archer steps forward and brushes his lips against mine. I freeze, my body stiff as a board. "I have to go to the coronation ball," Archer whispers, kissing my jaw, his breath hot on my clammy skin. "I wish you were coming with me on my arm."

I don't respond. My stomach is rolling, the water I drank threatening to rise and spill all over his fancy shoes. Apparently, my silence isn't the desired effect because Archer sighs and steps away. "I won't be back tonight, but I'll see you in the morning. Sleep well, love."

The cell door clangs behind him, and an ugly, wet sob bubbles up from my throat. The pain is awful, truly terrible. But Archer touching me... my shudder is so intense that the restraints bite into my skin.

"Are you okay?" I recognize the voice, but I can't open my eyes to see the guard it belongs to.

"No," I answer as hands gently lift me off the cross and carry me to the bed. I'm as limp as a rag doll. How am I supposed to last six more sessions of this? It's so much worse than I remember as a child. Maybe it's because Archer is accelerating the timeline, but I literally can't move.

I roll into the fetal position, facing away from the doors and the officers who linger at my back. I hear their hushed whispers. They sound concerned but clearly not enough to take me out of here or summon a healer to hydrate me.

"You should eat something," the soldier murmurs, but I ignore it, and I let sleep take me into oblivion.

"AGAIN," ARCHER INSTRUCTS AS soon as the magic stops.

"No," I gasp right before screams are ripped from my throat. This is the third one today, the second in a row. He was supposed to stop after two. I was mentally prepared to survive two.

My voice is hoarse from screaming. Tears flow freely as panic envelops me, and I struggle for breath. I try to save my energy and not fight against the intrusion, but my body keeps spasming. Blood drips down my palm from where the cuffs slice into my skin. Everything hurts. Every muscle, every joint, every bone throbs as the magic continues coursing through my body.

I must blackout because the next thing I know, Archer is drying my tears and humming a soothing melody.

My stomach drops as recognition slaps me in the face.

He's humming my lullaby.

The song I shared with him in a moment of vulnerability. The song that became our song.

And now he's using it while torturing me.

"I hate causing you pain," Archer whispers between phrases of the melody.

"You're not just causing me pain." I'm winded, my voice croaking amidst short gasps. "You're going to kill me."

"I did my research, love," he says softly. "Using hellfire—"

"You're using hellfire?" I can't breathe. This is my nightmare, my own personal hell. Everything that I've been afraid of for the past few months since I was struck with the cursed magic. He's pumping me full of the same poison currently holding my magic hostage.

It was bad enough when I thought he was using regular fire. *But hellfire?*

I'm going to die in this cell.

"Yes," Archer boasts with a smile. "I found a tutor. A Fae male with hellfire showed me how to use it without letting it control me."

I also had a Fae male tell me all about hellfire. It's not one of the natural elements but was gained through despicable means by a Fae Queen who wanted more power. That queen bestowed the Baran line with this cursed power. It's inherently destructive.

"And he told you it could remove my magic?"

"Not exactly. I consulted Fae healers about the information I learned from your father's notebooks. We devised a strategy. It will work."

It won't. I'm the only person in recorded history that's survived an attack from hellfire, but it didn't leave me unharmed. Archer may have figured out a way from killing me on impact, but there's no doubt in my mind that it is slowly killing me. It's burning me from the inside out.

"Archer, please listen to me," I beg. "I'm weak. I can't keep anything down. I can't stand or even hold my head up. If you ever loved me—"

"I have loved you since the moment we met." He leans into my space and rests his forehead against mine. "I've spent every day since you left trying to find a way to bring you back to me. Back to the way things were. I know I screwed up. I know I hurt you. But I will spend the rest of my life proving how much I love you."

A fresh tear sneaks past my lashes, and Archer leans in and kisses it away. "Three more sessions," he whispers against me. "Three more, and you'll be mine again."

I won't survive three more sessions.

Archer keeps his eyes on me until he reaches the cell doors, and one of the soldiers follows him out. Like I've tried a million times over the past two days, I reach for the tether to Lowell and stroke the mating bond. I don't think they'll reach me in time. They don't have enough people to launch an attack on the palace, and the portal is so heavily guarded. They need more time...but that's the one thing I'm not sure I can give them.

I'm never going to see my mate again.

I should have told him I love him.

I spent so much time waiting, and then I asked him to take it slow because I was afraid. Not of him, but of the enormity of having a fated mate and of how I'd been hurt before. I repeatedly waited even though I know how much danger we face every day.

I plead with any gods who might be listening to let me have one more moment. One more second to see my mate's golden eyes, hear my best friend's beautiful laugh, have Vlad insult me, and let Adriana teach me something.

One more chance to be with my family.

I pour all my feelings into the mating bond and pray he feels them and knows how much I want to return to him, even if I can't.

"I need you to take slow breaths," the officer whispers as he very gently unties my feet.

It's impossible. The only people who could calm me down are thousands of miles away. I'm adrift in a sea of pain and helplessness.

"Katie, look at me." My breaths are coming too fast, too shallow. My head is fuzzy, my vision swimming through my tears. But I open my eyes.

In front of me is a silhouette with blonde hair haloed by the small light coming from the hallway. I blink away the tears. "Deavers?"

He nods enthusiastically. Deavers was the first person besides my family to know I have Dark Magic. I used it to save his life.

"Breathe, Katie," he whispers. "From here." He lays his hand on my stomach the same way Edina does whenever I'm hyperventilating. His hand is warm through the thin layer of my tank top. I take a deep breath. "That's it," he says, and I continue until it feels like my chest isn't about to explode.

"I'm going to move you now." He unhooks my hands and catches me as I fall off the cross. Gently shifting me, he carries me over to the cot and sits, keeping me cradled in his arms.

"Your mom sent me," he whispers in my ear. "We need you to hold on until tomorrow." He offers me water, a pretense for staying in my cell.

"We have a plan," he continues. "Archer is planning on doing two sessions in the morning tomorrow. The suppressant is turned off on the bars when he's in here. We have a distraction planned that will take him away after the first one."

"What kind of a distraction?" I whisper, and Deavers leans in close.

"We have an entire army ready for you, Your Majesty. Your mate is on his way."

Chapter Three

I LET DEAVERS FEED me every morsel on my tray, so he has an excuse to explain the plan. He tells me that my mother has been gathering forces since the holidays, but it was slow going until the O'Malley twins heard my pleas to restore the balance. Word of the Dark Magic Covens' intentions spread through factions of the Dragons like wildfire, and now almost a third of the army secretly reports to Marcus and my mom.

Deavers leaves with the promise that he'll return in the morning. A mix of hope and anxiety has me up all night, my brain running a thousand miles per minute. I just need to get through the morning and one more infusion of hellfire, and then I can see my mate.

But Archer doesn't come in the morning.

That in itself would be cause for concern, but I don't see *anyone* all morning. No officers walk past my cell to their offices, and no one brings me food or water. Something is wrong, I feel it in my gut. My heart pounds in my ears as I lie uselessly in bed, not even strong enough to pace, and I try to take deep breaths, but my lungs feel like they're being held in a vice.

Finally, after hours, Archer storms into the dungeon. I'm usually tied up before he comes in the cell, but today he's not waiting. The expression on his face is downright terrifying, and when he waves his wand, I snap my eyes closed, expecting pain. It's only a cleansing spell, and as the layers of grime and tears coating my skin disappear, Archer's rage morphs into a predator's smile.

"Much better. I'm sorry I'm late." He sits on the edge of the bed. "It's good that you had Deavers to keep you company last night."

Fuck. He saw us. Did he hear us too? I scan the cell, and just outside the doors, there's a very faint blink of a camera. They must have added extra surveillance down here after Adriana escaped back in December. I curse myself for having not noticed.

The officers are standing closer today, not hiding in the shadows. Soto is there as planned, but instead of Deavers, Jefferson is in his place. Jefferson is also on our side, but this wasn't the plan. Why is nothing going to plan?

"I always found it odd that you visited him so much after our mission," Archer continues. His knuckles are white around his wand. "You practically lived in that hospital room for a while." His eyes flash fiery red as he assesses me, waiting for an answer.

"Are you implying something?" I ask carefully.

"Should I be?" Archer reaches for me, and I flinch violently. "Are you *afraid* of me?" he hisses.

"Should I be?" I echo. A muscle in his jaw ticks. "Where is Deavers?"

"He was a traitor."

Was. My mouth goes dry. My brain comes up with a thousand explanations for that use of tense. Deavers was dismissed, and therefore not a threat to the army or Archer anymore. Deavers deserted as soon as he heard that Archer saw him holding me.

But I can't ignore the obvious answer. The one shouting at me, putting me in a tailspin of fear. "What did you do to him?" I ask.

There's no remorse in his voice when he says, "Everything I do is for us." He scoops me into his arms, and my body goes stiff as a board. I bite down on my tongue hard enough to bleed to keep from screaming. "You'll forgive me one day."

He carries me to the cross and hands me off to Jefferson so he can secure me in place. Our eyes connect, and I silently beg Jefferson to tell me I'm wrong. That I misunderstood. Almost imperceptibly, he shakes his head.

Holy. Shit.

Deavers is dead. Archer killed him.

The breath is sucked from my lungs. It feels like someone is punching me in the stomach. "I need to get out of here," I whisper. "Jefferson, please—"

"Plan's on," he responds, and I clamp down on my trembling lip.

"Ten minutes," Archer says as soon as Jefferson secures my feet. He places his hands at my temples. "Begin."

The initial shock of heat feels like a thousand knives, distracting me from the loss of my friend. From the *murder* of my friend. Seriously, how is this possible? How did this happen? Whether my brain is hallucinating from the pain or the grief, I'm not sure, but I can practically hear Deavers' soft voice assuring me I can get through this. That I have one more round and then I'll be out, back with our army ready to avenge him and the others we've lost. Then, as if some invisible force is helping me, the pain...shifts. It still hurts like hell, but it's different. I spend the remainder of the ten minutes trying to identify this feeling.

"I have a gift for you," Archer says as the pain stops and his hands lift off my temples. I pant, regaining my composure as a trembling woman I vaguely recognize as a healer from the

Dragons' Headquarters enters the cell. He brushes my hair away from my unscarred shoulder, the side where my claiming mark lies. "But first, I have a question." His fingers trace over the mark, and I tremble at the wrongness of him touching me there. "Did you know when you sleep, you touch this spot?"

I do know that. It's been the only source of comfort I've had in this cell. "I didn't think anything of it until today," he says without waiting for a response. White flames flicker across his eyes, and his grip tightens. My pulse skyrockets as the pressure digs into my throat. "But then an army of werewolves and vampires laid siege to my palace. You wouldn't know anything about that, would you love?"

His grip turns scalding hot, and I scream. This is worse than the torture. He's melting my flesh, the skin under his hand bubbling, and still, he doesn't let go. "When the wolves arrived this morning, I thought your father must have done some heavy recruiting. But then I recognized their leader."

He pulls away, leaving an angry red handprint where my claiming mark was. Archer snaps his fingers, and the healer runs over, Light Magic already coating her hands.

"Then Jai said he saw the same man leaving Edina's birthday party. Tell me, *love*," he spits, "just how many men were you fucking behind my back? Deavers...the wolf..."

"What?" I gasp. Tears flow freely down my cheeks as the healer runs her hands over my mangled flesh. "I never cheated on you."

"No? That's not why you've been resistant? Why you cringe every time I touch you? Because you've been *claimed* by someone else."

"All done, miss," the healer coos before hurrying out of the cell. The patch of smooth skin is almost worse than the handprint. That symbolized the promise Lowell and I made to each other, even before we were mates. And Archer just erased it like it was nothing.

It wasn't *nothing*. It was everything.

I don't get a moment of reprieve before Archer touches my head and begins another round of hellfire. This time the magic is vicious. It floods straight into my stomach before erupting into my chest. My heart stutters at the force of the hellfire. I can't breathe. I can't think.

"Nothing happened while we were together?" Archer asks, spit hitting my cheeks as his anger cools.

"No," I squeak. Every nerve feels exposed and misfiring. My muscles are spasming, twitching, and jolting. I know the plan is in motion, but there's only so much my body can take.

He nods, appeased by my answer, and when the round finishes, I sag forward, my body beaten, brutalized, and ready to give up.

"Again." The collective inhale is deafening.

"Your Majesty—" Soto starts.

"Again," Archer snaps. "I need the Katie I know back. I need to break the Dark Magic's hold on her mind."

"I can't let you do that." Soto charges, but Archer flicks his wand and slams him into the wall. Soto's head snaps back before his entire body crumples to the ground. I don't realize I'm screaming until Archer stands too close, shushing me and brushing my hair away from my temples.

Jefferson runs over and quickly checks Soto's pulse, nodding when he finds one. He takes a step toward me, the magic coiled in his hand aimed at Archer. "Don't," I whisper, and he halts.

"You'll kill her," Jefferson sputters, and his brown eyes connect with mine. I understand the feeling I see in his gaze. *Helplessness.*

Pain starts again. The taste of ash mixes with the taste of bile as my stomach writhes. "Almost there, love," Archer soothes.

"Jefferson, I need you to get a message to my family." I howl as a fire attacks my brain, making it difficult to think. How is it possible that the pain is worse? Archer starts humming my lullaby. I tune him out.

"Tell my mom I'm sorry for all the shit I put her through," I pant. "Tell Edina I love her most, say those exact words. Tell Adriana and Vlad to stop dicking around and be happy, and tell Lowell—"

My voice breaks as Archer grips my head with excessive force, but I won't let him stop me. I need to get this out. "Tell him it was an honor to be his mate and I'll always love him, even after my last breath."

Smoke puffs from Archer's nose at my admission, and he starts whispering the same words over and over, "You'll be mine again soon."

The hellfire is a tidal wave, destroying everything in its path and clashing with the hellfire blocking my magic. The two forces collide and join and surge back through my body. I can barely hear my screams over the roaring inferno inside my body. Darkness clouds my eyes, and visions of the people I love flash before me.

"Jefferson, go," I croak, hoping he gets out of the cell before I'm dead and delivers the messages. I need them to know.

There's a scuffle nearby, but I can't focus on it. Archer's hands drop, and he bellows, but the pain doesn't recede with his touch. The magic is still raging inside me, tearing me apart. It's all I can do to keep breathing.

The world goes quiet as the air around me turns frigid. Ice trickles over my skin, and I shiver at the abrupt switch from hot to cold. Someone is calling me, a melodic voice that I want to answer, but I can't open my eyes. There's a snap of metal, and the cuffs on my legs and hands spring open. I fall forward into waiting arms.

A dam inside me breaks.

The hellfire holding my magic hostage explodes in a thousand embers, flitting to the darkest corners of myself. My eyes fly open. I'm no longer being held but floating on a cloud of Dark Magic. My Light Magic bursts from my chest, wrapping me in a warm embrace, and lightning dances around my calves where the two intersect.

My magic is back.

Archer broke the hold the hellfire had on it.

A laugh bubbles from my throat as the Light Magic seeps through me, healing my injuries and making me stronger. A cold hand lands on my wrist, and right beside me is my best friend, her wings keeping her aloft, so we're eye to eye.

"*I love you most?*" she shrieks, wisps of her blonde hair floating around her on an icy wind. Her eyes are puffy and red. "You were going to leave me with *'I love you most?*"

We touch down on the ground and barrel into each other. I grip her tighter than I've ever held anyone and bury my head in her hair, breathing her in. "I had to get the last word in," I get out between sobs.

"You're such a bitch." We laugh as we cry. Edina's frozen tears land on my exposed shoulder, soothing my sizzling skin. She pulls away and inspects me, and when she's sure I can stand, I watch as her relief turns to pure rage. "I will fucking kill him."

I spin around, searching the room for Archer, but only finding evidence of the struggle. There are scorch marks by the cell door, and patches of ice on the floor near my cross, which is completely frozen over.

"Where did he go?" I ask.

"Ran off like the little bitch he is," she sneers. "Did you know there's a tunnel?" She points to the solid wall at the back of the cell. The same wall I searched on my first night.

My were-magic unleashes, trickling over the cinder blocks in a cascade of gold, illuminating the outline of a door hidden between the bricks. "I did that already," Edina says as I start battering the wall with my magic.

"Did you know that was there?" I ask Jefferson, who is helping a dazed Soto to his feet. He shakes his head.

"Babes, we gotta go." Edina tugs my hand, but I ignore her and send more magic at the doorway. I am not letting Archer fucking Baran slink off through a secret fucking tunnel after he spent days torturing me. I have a score to settle, and I swear to all things magical— "Kathryn Isabelle Carmichael!" Edina bellows.

"Did you just full name me?" I stop, turning to my best friend, who looks panicked.

"We need to go. Like right now. There are six of us—five since Soto is basically down for the count—and about fifty soldiers on their way."

"Archer sent out a distress signal," one of the O'Malley twins, who must have arrived with Edina, says. "There's a group of soldiers at the top of the stairs."

"And the rest are about to attack the forces outside," the other finishes. "We need to get out of here so our people can flee."

"Why aren't they fleeing now?" I demand.

"Because your mate is a stubborn ass," Edina shrugs. "He won't leave until you're through the portal, and the wolves won't leave until he does."

I huff out my frustration but stop my onslaught of magic against the door, and reach for the mating bond with Lowell. I was so preoccupied since my magic came back that I didn't think to search for it, but now that I'm aware of its presence, I'm flooded with concern, worry, and adrenaline. I pour everything I'm feeling down the bond and feel Lowell's instant relief and joy, just before his emotions turn darker and grow muted again.

"I think they've already started attacking," I tell the group. "Lowell seems...very focused." I'm afraid my mental channels have been compromised, and somehow while using his magic, Archer has found a way to listen in, so I lock those down and refortify my shields. I'll create new channels once we're safe.

"How are you feeling?" Edina asks. "Are you good to fight, or do you want me to carry you?" In response, I call my lightning to my fingers. She smiles widely before coating her arms in ice. "O'Malley, send the message to the forces outside that we're on our way up."

"Done," they respond in unison. Jefferson urges us out of the cell door so we're between both sets of soldiers. Soto is looking clearer than he was a minute ago, but he's still leaning on Jefferson heavily. Edina and I exchange glances, silently understanding the need to protect our injured friend. She casts a torrent of ice to cover the cell's back wall before slamming the bars shut and flicking the lock.

"I wouldn't put it past Archer to wait to attack until our backs are turned," she says in explanation. "Dickwad."

"Yeah, I really know how to pick 'em." I send my Mind Magic out in a web of golden light and when I reach the Dragons' minds, I give them a strong desire to turn around. It affects a handful, but the rest keep charging down the winding staircase.

"Try not to kill them," I instruct as the O'Malley twins throw up a one-sided shield. The soldiers crash into the magic, raining all four elements down on us, but the shield holds.

"Why the fuck not?" Edina asks as she freezes someone to the wall.

"Because we're better than that."

"Are we, though?"

We barrel up the stairs in a clump of six, slowly incapacitating those who stand in our way.

Surprisingly, I feel really good, stronger than I've ever felt. It's like my magic has been waiting for me, accumulating strength, and now that I can use it, it's ready. My stamina doesn't waver, and I can use my lightning, my Dark Magic, and my were-magic interchangeably while my Light Magic continues to heal the damage wrought from my time in the cell.

There's a fourth power too. It's hiding in the corners of my body, begging to be set free.

Not yet.

Edina is a force of nature. Her favorite tactic is using a wave of water to push foes to the walls or the ceiling and then encasing them in ice up to their necks, leaving them hanging like human stalagmites. Her eyes are glowing, and I can tell my friend hasn't even scratched the surface of her power yet.

We finally reach the doors on the main floor, and Edina seals it behind us with ice. We take off at a run down an empty hallway. It's too quiet up here, and our entire party is on edge.

"Any word from outside?" I ask softly. Edina shakes her head.

"They'll be fine. We're in more trouble than they are—"

A ball of hellfire shatters our shield from behind. "Run," Jefferson calls, pushing us forward. I glance over my shoulder in time to see another blast streaking on a direct path toward him.

I will not lose one more person today.

Without thinking, I shove him and Soto to the side and step in front of them with my arms wide. Screams echo in the hallway as I reach into the deep recesses of my body where my new magic lies. I embrace it, willing it to aid me, and it answers my call.

My mouth opens in a scream of defiance, and hellfire rushes from the open cavity. It streams from my hands, forming a wall of white-hot flames and intercepting the prince's fire. Flames engulf the red carpet. Tapestries go up in smoke. "Go," I scream, and I hear the scuttle of feet behind me as they maneuver backward.

The wall continues expanding, eating everything in its path. Smoke fills the corridor and the heat has me sweating in an instant. I try to banish the fire, but it only surges higher. "My turn,"

Edina says and places her ice-cold hands atop mine. A deluge of frozen water attacks the hellfire, extinguishing it, and leaving only blackened remnants.

Archer stands across from us, his hands limp at his sides and his mouth opening and closing like a fish. "Looks like your Fae friend lied," I say.

"You knew I was giving you magic and not taking it away?"

"I thought you would kill me before it could take, especially once you told me you were using hellfire."

Edina doesn't give him a chance for a rebuttal before she throws up a wall of solid ice between us. "Time to go," she says.

"You belong here, Katie," Archer calls, his voice muffled through the barrier.

"Not anymore."

We turn our backs on him and sprint the rest of the way down the corridor with its tacky red carpets and gold accents. Swirling periwinkle mist reaches out for us in tendrils as we close the distance and jump into the open portal.

"Do you know how to seal this?" I ask as we breach the opening. Edina snatches me before I get swept onto the walkway, flapping her wings to keep us near the door.

"What kind of Fae do you think I am?" she chuckles and slams the door shut. Her eyes glow bright blue before she attaches one hand to the doorway, and it disappears completely, leaving only mist in its place. When she's done, we step onto the walkway and go hurtling in the opposite direction of the Highlands.

"Adriana says we can't go back to base yet. In case Archer retaliates," Edina explains. "I'm dropping you off at a secure location and meeting Vlad at his house."

We continue past doors until Edina points at one that's unmarked. The hum of magic surrounding it is the same that protects Vlad's mansion in Northern Italy.

"On three." She counts, and we jump off, flying through the mist and crashing through the door.

Chapter Four

EVEN IN THE DARKNESS, I can tell we're by the ocean. The sound of waves crashing and the comforting scent of salty air permeate the cool room. There's something about the beach that's always soothed my soul. It conjures memories of ditch days at the Cape and carefree summers with Edina on her parents' island in the Maldives. I don't know if my best friend had anything to do with choosing this location, but I can already tell it's exactly what I need.

Edina swears as she fumbles for a switch, smacking the wall until the lights spring to life. We walk down a short hallway into an open-concept living area with clean white walls and exposed navy beams on the ceiling. My bare feet slap against white wooden floorboards as I walk toward a large, white sectional pointed towards a wall of built-in bookshelves that surround a flat-screen television that still has the plastic on. I trail my fingers over a navy afghan thrown over the back of the couch, the brush of the yarn soft against my skin.

It's cozy but very clearly not-lived in.

Edina goes to the kitchen and opens the stainless-steel refrigerator stocked with more food than anyone could need. She grabs a water bottle and tosses it to me, expertly avoiding the white-marble island and the dangling light fixture. I catch it and cross to the sliding glass door, staring out over a cliffside. Waves splash against the rocks below, spraying water so high it's illuminated by the pale moonlight.

"Is this Vlad's safe house?" I ask, tearing myself away from the view.

"One of them."

"The asshole was holding out on us."

Edina chuckles, and I plop down on one of the stools on the island, pressing the heels of my hands into my eye sockets. "Everyone is retreating now," she says, and some tension bleeds from my shoulders. She slides a protein bar across the island and stares at me until I bite.

"My mom?"

"Safe. With Vlad."

"How did everyone get out of the city?"

She laughs. "Vlad collects favors from the Fae and had them build portals in London. There are hundreds scattered in the city...in pubs, libraries, the Tube."

"Why does that not surprise me?" I run my hands through my hair, untangling some of the knots with my fingers. "What if they're followed?"

"Astor is sealing the portals behind everyone. You don't need to worry, babes. We've got it covered. Your man really stepped up."

"Is he okay?" I ask softly. I can feel him down the bond, but it's still frantic. Knowing my mate, it will be that way until he sees me.

"As good as can be expected," she says carefully. "He issued the orders for laying siege to the palace quickly. But within a few hours, he realized he couldn't wait three days and started coming up with alternative plans."

"And Adriana vetoed them?" I guess, and Edina nods.

"The number of times I heard Adriana say, 'and then Katie will die...'" She grimaces. "The only plan she approved was the night of the coronation, and it failed spectacularly. Don't worry. Everyone's fine."

When I finish eating my protein bar, Edina draws a vial from her pocket, and I recognize the mood-stabilizing tonic Coleman prescribed for me. "The healer thought you might need it. There's more in the medicine cabinet in your bathroom."

I nod my thanks and down the contents. "You said Adriana didn't want us in the Highlands?"

"Too many of her visions included an attack." She swipes her hand through her hair. "Most people are going to Vlad's house or Lowell's pack, but a handful are staying to help her move some stuff around. They want to create a new throne room under a different hill since Archer knows where the current one is."

"Why are we here if everyone else is at Vlad's?"

"Well, *I'm* not staying," Edina drawls with a sly smirk. "You're here because this is the only time we see in the future where you'll have a few days to be alone with Lowell." I stare at her blankly. She waggles her eyebrows and says, "This is your honeymoon! Mating moon?" She scrunches her nose. "No, honeymoon."

"Apparently, wolves get all kinds of territorial when they mate and need a few days away from other people. Vlad, Adrianna, and I talked, and we decided we can spare you both for four days."

"E—" I start, but she holds up a hand to stop me.

"Babes, you need time to process everything. You were—" She clears her throat, and the hint of emotion that crosses her eyes is gone before it can settle. "You've been through something unimaginable. You can't jump into queen mode right away; take the time and relax. Or you know...fuck your mate until you can't see straight."

I nod slowly. Not that I'm not excited to see Lowell, but I'm not used to taking time off, even after something traumatic. Hell, the last time I almost died, I was back to work within twenty-four hours.

"I keep waiting for the other shoe to drop," I confess. "It doesn't make sense, but I feel...remarkably okay." I run my fingers over my jagged scar, tracing the ends that reach my jaw. When Archer struck me with hellfire, it sent me into a spiral of depression. How is it that he tortured me for days, and I just feel normal? Like this was any other dangerous mission that I survived.

"Maybe you're in shock."

"Or maybe I just have a high tolerance for bad shit happening to me," I mutter. Edina laughs, but her smile doesn't reach her eyes. "I need to shower." I can still feel Archer's touch on my skin, and I don't want his scent anywhere near me when Lowell comes.

"Your room is the last door on the right," Edina says, pointing down a long hallway. "There's a bathroom attached. I'll stay until Lowell gets here."

I wrap my arms around her middle, carefully avoiding her wings, and she returns the embrace, sinking into me as I hang onto her. "Love you," I whisper into her hair.

"Love you most." We hug for a long time before she ushers me down the hall.

The bedroom is airy, and the gossamer white curtains flutter in the open floor-length windows. The comforter and pillows are stark white, and the only real color in the room comes from the vase of fresh wildflowers on the gray-stained nightstand. I want to burn my clothes, but I settle for dropping them in the hamper next to the bathroom door for now.

Walking into the white-tiled bathroom, I bypass the large jacuzzi tub and step into the shower, waiting until the water from the rainfall showerhead is scalding. It feels fantastic on my knotted shoulders, and I stand for too long under the spray, staring at the blue mosaic tiles.

I take stock of my emotions, searching for anything I'm subconsciously repressing, but there's nothing overtly wrong. I'm tired and a little sad, but I'm not nearly as devastated as I was when I lost my magic.

When my skin is rubbed raw, I turn off the faucet and open the shower door just enough to grab a fluffy white towel. The bond pulls painfully tight, and when the steam from the enclosure dissipates into the rest of the bathroom, I find Lowell standing in the doorway. Concern tightens his stubbled jaw and creases his brow. A simple black tee is stretched taut over his muscles and hangs slightly over his dark denim-clad legs. He runs his hands through his long, black hair, which is already rumpled, probably from running here.

His golden eyes scan me as overwhelming relief washes over me. I start crying, hugging the towel tight to my chest, the material against my skin a reminder that this is real. *Lowell is here.*

He takes a step forward but pauses, unsure. When dealing with the worst of my PTSD, I pushed Lowell away, so I completely understand why he's hesitating and deferring to me. "Little witch—"

I launch across the bathroom, towel discarded, and leap into his arms. My legs wind around his waist, and I bury my face in his neck. He grips me so tight I think I might break, but I don't care.

"I'm so sorry," we say at the same time.

I pull back enough to look into his eyes. "Why are you sorry?" I demand at the same time as he growls, "Don't you dare fucking apologize."

"I shouldn't have gone in alone—"

"I should have come for you sooner—"

"—I should have listened to you."

"—We tried to get in the night of the coronation, but our men were captured."

"Wait," we both say, halting the flurry of strung-together sentences that neither of us heard. I laugh breathlessly, and the sound has the air whooshing out of Lowell's lungs as he pulls me back into a hug.

"I'm sorry we didn't come earlier, *Ma Reine*," Lowell murmurs as he walks us back into the bedroom.

"It's okay, I'm okay," I whisper, nuzzling into him even further. He kisses my neck, right where my mark was. "He burned it off." A tear threatens to fall, so I shut my eyes to keep them trapped. I don't want to give Archer any more of my tears.

"Doesn't change a damn thing." Just hearing the words releases a weight in my chest, and I move so that our foreheads are touching. Lowell brushes his nose against mine before pausing at the edge of the bed. Without ever taking my eyes off his, I perform a quick siphoning spell that leaves my skin and hair bone-dry, sending the water into the shower drain.

"You have your magic back," he whispers. I nod enthusiastically and lower my legs from his waist to kneel on the mattress. Relinquishing my hold on him, I coat my skin with my Light and Dark Magic, lightning sparking where they intersect. Lowell stares, transfixed. "Fucking beautiful."

"Wait." A smile blooms across my lips as I call a ball of my were-magic to my hand. The magic swirls and pulses, and Lowell's eyes widen as he reaches forward to touch the golden orb. At his proximity, it quickens and expands, reaching to brush against his fingertips.

"This is..."

"From you." I swallow nervously. "Vlad said it happens when a witch and werewolf mate. It appeared the night my dad hurt you. I wanted to show you, but we got distracted." Lowell's throat works as the magic pools in his palm. Unlike at the coven, it doesn't harden or try to encase him. It's simply there like it innately knows it doesn't need to protect me against Lowell.

"There's more," I continue. "When I was...When Archer..." My lips tremble as images skitter across my brain.

Lowell brushes a strand of hair behind my ear. "We don't need to talk about it now if you're not ready."

"Can I show you?" I ask. "I don't think I can talk about it, but can I show you my memories?"

"Of course, little witch."

I scoot back on the mattress and climb under the comforter, pulling it back and patting the space beside me. "Clothes off," I order. Lowell arches an eyebrow. "I need to feel you." He obliges me, stripping off his shirt first and revealing his sculpted torso before he slowly undoes his pants and slides them down too.

"You went commando to a battle?" I chuckle as he climbs under the covers with me and extends his arm to the pillow beneath my head.

"In case I needed to shift," he says as I curl into his chest, wrapping my arm around his stomach and throwing my leg over his. He kisses the top of my head, and we just lay wrapped in each other's arms for a moment.

"Okay," I sigh and gently caress his mind with my Mind Magic. He has a decent shield erected, and I wonder if that's an innate part of his were-magic. It lets me in instantly, and I send the memories to the forefront of Lowell's consciousness.

His arms tighten as my memories start playing like a movie. I'm able to remove myself enough from the process that I don't see everything, but I have a general idea of what Lowell is seeing. After a minute, Lowell shifts, angling his body, so he's positioned above me. He starts kissing my scarred skin, working his way up my arm, following the path Archer took when he caressed me. He lingers over my cheeks, my ears, and my lips, kissing everywhere Archer touched, erasing the memory of him from my skin.

I know when he hears my goodbye because his breath hitches and a tear falls down his cheek. I brush it away, and he snatches my hand, threading his fingers in mine and pressing a kiss to my palm. His forehead comes to rest against mine, and his weight settles on top of me, the pressure of his body easing some of the tension in my chest. He continues watching, and when I sense the memories are done, he shakes his head, his eyes finding mine.

"I am so in awe of you," he breathes and tips my chin, so I meet his eyes. "You took his hellfire."

"Technically, he gave it to me."

"When we write history, we're saying you took it." He smirks, and I laugh, partially in relief that Lowell doesn't think any different of me now that I have this cursed magic and partially because I'm just so happy to be back with him. "You have all four magics, *Ma Reine*."

"No one can accuse me of being an underachiever," I say, and Lowell laughs so heartily that I feel it in every place where our bodies connect, and I can't help but join him.

I don't know how it happens, but one moment we're laughing, and the next, our lips are crashing together. His tongue dances with mine, slow and coaxing. I thread my fingers through his dark locks and use my grip to bring him closer. Emotions so powerful leave me breathless as they roll through our bond.

"I love you," I whisper, breaking apart just enough to get the words out. "I was an idiot not to say it earlier. All I kept thinking about in that dungeon was that I wouldn't get to tell you."

Lowell pulls me back in, kissing me brutally and turning my body to jelly. I absently realize that he hasn't said it back when suddenly, it's everywhere. Whispered between kisses, flooding the bond, murmured down our mental channel. Lowell tells me he loves me over and over again.

I can't touch enough of him, can't feel enough of his skin on mine. My legs wrap around his waist and I use my crossed ankles to pull his full weight onto me. He hums in approval as I run my hands over his arms and chest and back, relishing in the warmth that radiates into me.

"Katie." My name is a cross between a prayer and a warning, and I tug down on his bottom lip, silently begging for him to give me more. Lowell rolls us so we're on our sides with no space between us, and then guides my head so I'm tucked into his chest beneath his chin.

"Alpha," I protest, but he just tightens his hold on me.

"Not tonight," he insists. "Mating can be strenuous and consuming. You need sleep and food and probably water."

"I'll be fine—" I break off as a wave of exhaustion crashes into me. "Fine," I grumble, fully aware that I'm acting like a brat by not admitting he's right.

"Do you want me to make you dinner?" Lowell asks, and I hum my refusal. "I can get you water—"

"Don't you dare fucking move." I hold my hand out, summoning two bottles of water from the fridge and monitoring their progress with my Mind Magic. One lands in my hand, and Lowell deftly catches the other. "God, I missed my magic."

Lowell chuckles and extracts his limbs from mine, guiding me to a sitting position. I drink greedily, pausing with just a few drops left so I can use a duplicating spell to refill the bottle. Lowell watches me in amusement.

"I've never seen a witch do magic without a wand," he muses.

"Now you understand why I was such a mess without it."

"You weren't a mess." Lowell sips his water, and I arch an eyebrow at him. "Fine, but you figured it out."

"Yeah, once you gave me a sword." My eyes widen, and a slow smile stretches across my face. "Do you think I can shoot lightning out of my sword? How badass would that be?"

"Very badass, little witch." Lowell wraps his arm around me as he settles back into the pillows. He kisses the tip of my nose before wrapping his hand into the back of my hair and pulling me into a passionate kiss. "Try and get some sleep."

"I'm not tired." My body betrays me with a very large yawn, and I concede, snuggling back into my mate. "Lowell?"

"Mmm?"

"Don't leave in the morning," I say, vulnerability sneaking into my voice. "Not even to make breakfast. Just stay with me."

"Forever," Lowell murmurs, kissing me again. "I love you, *mon âme sœur.*"

I'm asleep before I can ask him what that means.

Chapter Five

THERE IS NOTHING BETTER than waking up in my mate's arms, with sunlight streaming through the open windows and a soft breeze fluttering the delicate white curtains. The combination of the salt air and Lowell's rain and earth scent is a balm for my raw nerves. The past few days melt to the far corners of my mind, and I decide to leave them there and be present.

"Morning, little witch," Lowell murmurs, kissing the top of my head. I arch my back, stretching my sore muscles but keeping our legs tangled together. His kisses travel lower as he's granted access until he's nestled right above my breasts, and his very hard erection grinds into my thigh.

"Fuck yes, please," I moan as he moves back up the column of my neck and along my jaw.

"You need to eat," he says in a tone that's all Alpha. I unabashedly pout, and he nips my extended lip between his teeth while I roll my hips, trying to get some friction. "What do you want for breakfast?"

"You," I whimper, skimming my fingers down his rippling abs. His tongue sweeps inside my mouth, and I'm practically panting as I reach the coarse curls above his cock.

"Little witch—" Lowell moves faster than I can anticipate, grabbing my hands and placing them on his shoulders as he positions himself above me. "I can make waffles, eggs..." he keeps listing breakfast food conversationally, like the head of his cock isn't brushing against my clit.

"Pancakes." I wriggle, but Lowell keeps just out of reach. "But American pancakes, not crepes." He chuckles and lowers only his upper body to kiss me sweetly, leaving me wanting.

"Vlad bought clothes for you. They're in the tall dresser." He hops off the bed and grabs a pair of sweatpants from the shorter dresser, putting them on in stride. He pauses and scans my naked body when he gets to the doorway. "Don't put on too much."

My core clenches, and he knowingly smirks as he walks out of the room. I know for a fact I could make him come back here if I wanted to, but my stomach growls, so I get out of bed. After I use the bathroom, I poke around the dresser, trying really hard not to think about the fact that Vlad picked out everything, including the entire lingerie drawer. I find an oversized t-shirt and throw it on before heading to the kitchen.

The back door is open, and in the daylight, I can see the amazing backyard, complete with an infinity pool overlooking the cliffs. The only sound is the squawking of seagulls and the wind tinkling a seashell windchime. It's the definition of peaceful.

"Where are we?" I ask, a little ashamed I didn't think to ask last night.

"Santorini." Lowell is chopping strawberries and blueberries at the kitchen island while pancakes brown on a large griddle.

"It's beautiful," I murmur, hopping up on the counter next to him. I snag a piece of strawberry from the cutting board and extend it to his lips. His eyes don't leave mine as he leans forward and takes a bite, flicking the pad of my finger with his tongue before he pulls away. I run the same finger over his bottom lip, catching a drop of juice that escaped before bringing it to my mouth and sucking it off.

"Stop distracting me unless you want burnt pancakes," Lowell chastises, and I laugh as he returns to the griddle with a very obvious bulge in his pants.

I hold up my hands in surrender and hop down, making my way to the coffee machine. I open random cabinets until I find mugs and coffee grounds and get the process started. I'm about to punch the machine for not working when Lowell reaches around me and flips a lever. The coffee maker whirs to life, and the scent of the life-affirming liquid fills the kitchen. I lean back, and Lowell nibbles the crook of my bare neck.

"Will you reclaim me?" I ask as Lowell goes back to the food.

"If you'd like," he says, his voice careful as he stacks the pancakes on a plate.

"Please."

"Would you like to reclaim me, too?" he asks, giving me his profile. "Since you didn't know it happened when you did the first time."

"Yeah." I turn back to the machine, hiding my smile under the guise of filling two mugs. "Yeah, I do."

His arms wind around my waist before I even realize he's moved. I put the coffee pot down, laughing as he hugs me from behind. I turn my head enough to catch his lips in a light, teasing kiss. His hands drop to the hem of my t-shirt, and he groans as his knuckles skim the curve of my bare ass.

"We need to have a conversation before this goes any further," Lowell says.

"You know I'm not a virgin, right?" He smacks my ass, and I yelp before he rubs the spot, and my pain turns to pleasure. "What do we need to talk about, pup?"

"For starters, you need a safe word."

My mouth pops open. I lose the ability to form coherent words. Lowell chuckles darkly.

"Do you want to have breakfast outside?" he asks.

"Hmm?" I ask, distracted by his info drop and the feeling of his hands on my skin. "Right, sure."

"There's a table down the steps when you walk outside. Take the coffee. I'll bring the plates."

"Yes, Alpha," I murmur. A wave of desire barrels down our bond.

"Good girl," he breathes, nipping at my earlobe. The combination of his words and his teeth against my skin has me clenching my thighs together as he steps away to get breakfast ready. I lean against the counter for a minute, the haze of lust making me dizzy. I need to go outside before I mount Lowell here and now. And he's right. We should talk first. Like adults. For at least five minutes.

I slip outside and skirt around the right side of the pool to a set of white stone steps. At the bottom, a small patio table with an open blue umbrella sits atop a patch of green grass. If possible, the view from the table is even more stunning than from the house. There's nothing but white fluffy clouds, blue skies, and the beautiful blue-green ocean stretching around us. There are other houses nestled in the cliffside, but I get the feeling the property is shielded from prying eyes, just like Vlad's house in Italy. I can feel the magic humming around us, and I make a mental note to add to the protections later.

I sit in one of the chairs just as Lowell comes down the steps. He puts a stack of pancakes the size of my head in front of me and untucks a bottle of syrup from the crook of his arm before moving his chair until it's touching mine.

"Watermelon," I say, spearing fruit from the top of my stack.

"That's a strawberry, little witch."

"My safe word." I flick the fruit on my fork at him. He catches it in his mouth, and I laugh as he smirks and pointedly chews. "Why do we need it?"

"Better to have it than not," he says. "If I lose myself in the moment...I don't want to hurt you."

"You won't," I assure him.

"Just in case, then." He winks. "Do you have any limits?"

I kick the soft grass with my bare toe, keeping my eyes down. "Don't restrain me. I don't know how I'll react since..." I swallow at the memory of being chained to the cross.

Lowell gently grabs my chin and tilts it up. "Of course, little witch." His thumb caresses my cheek, and I lean into his touch, my fears fading with each brush of his finger.

"I don't mind being vulnerable, like at your house..."

"When I had you on my shoulders?" he asks, and a shiver works its way down my spine as I remember the intensity of the orgasms I had that day.

"Yes." It comes out breathy and strained, and I break away to take a sip of my coffee. "And I reserve the right to change my mind on bondage in the future." I wink. Lowell laughs and motions for me to eat.

The pancakes are delicious, fluffy, and amazing. I douse them in syrup and shovel half the stack in my mouth before I come up for air. I didn't realize just how hungry I was until I started eating. We sit in comfortable silence until I'm finished, and the first of a thousand questions spill from my lips.

"Could you see what he was doing?" I ask softly. "Through the mirror?"

Lowell shakes his head. "The feed cut out. But Adriana gave me your locket, so I knew you were okay."

"You wore the locket?" I bite my lip to hold back my smile as Lowell nods around another bite of food. "I'd pay good money to see you running around shirtless with just a necklace on."

"I'll model it for you sometime." He puts his fork down and turns to me. "Little witch, I know Edina told you we're here to mate—"

"She called it a mating moon." We grimace in tandem.

"But if you're not ready, if you need time to recover..." He swallows. "I'm happy just to be here with you. There's no pressure or expectation from me."

God, I love this man. I practically jumped him four times since we've been here, and he's still checking in. I hop out of my chair and cross the small space between us. Lowell pushes back from the table, and I crawl onto his lap, my knees straddling his legs.

"I don't need any more time." Leaning forward, I kiss him passionately. His hands rub my back while mine cup his face before running down his throat to rest on his chest. "Talk to me about the mating bond. What should I expect? I know mates are rare—"

"I spoke with Luna and Cyril when I suspected we might be mates," Lowell says. I tilt my head back, and he trails a line of gentle kisses down to the hollow of my throat, his stubble scratching my sensitive skin.

"They said after we're mated, that we'll feel..." he pauses, searching for the words amidst the waves of lust, "... insatiable."

"More than usual?" I tease.

"It also might bring out my wolf side. I won't shift. I just may be a bit more...primal."

"Like you were on the full moon?" I ask. Lowell grunts his agreement into my flesh. "That's why they wanted us away from the coven. And why you want a safe word."

"Mating also increases a wolf's power," he continues, finally looking up to meet my gaze. "You already have my magic, so it might not do anything to you, but it should make me stronger, even in this form. And I don't want to hurt you if I don't realize my strength."

I nod, and we both take a second to breathe and calm ourselves.

"Will we feel it?" I ask.

"They said we'll know immediately. Their bond wasn't as developed as ours when they mated, but they said it feels like it snaps into place."

"Like a piece of your soul you didn't know was missing is found," I murmur, and Lowell cocks his head to the side. "That's how you said Luna described it the first time I asked."

"Exactly."

There's another pregnant pause while I work up the courage to ask what I really want to ask. "What if we aren't mates?"

"Doesn't change a thing," Lowell responds without missing a beat. "You're mine, *mon âme sœur*."

I smile like a fool. "What does that mean?"

"My soul mate."

"That's a human term."

"I hate to alarm you, little witch, but you are a human."

I flick his nose, and he snaps his teeth at my fingers, sending us both into a fit of giggles. It ends when I pull him into me and whisper the word back in completely butchered French. He repeats it against my lips before we close the distance again. It starts slow and sweet. He's pouring every ounce of his love into me, and it's wonderful.

And then it's not slow. It's hungry and desperate. I grip his hair, tugging him closer. His fingers slide up my thighs, hovering around the hem of my t-shirt bunched around my waist. I rock my hips against his hardening length, and the arousal pouring down the bond between us both knows no bounds.

"Lowell," I murmur, breaking away as he lavishes my jaw. "Please..."

"Please what, little witch?" He sucks my earlobe between his teeth.

"Fuck me," I whimper. "*Mate me.*"

He's on his feet in one swift motion, my legs wrapped around his waist. I close my eyes, sucking marks onto his neck, nibbling his earlobe, and nipping along his jaw. I know we're moving at Lowell's wolf speed, but it's only a breath before he's setting me down beside the bed.

"Arms up," he commands while pushing his pants off. I obey instantly, and he tears my shirt off, tossing it in the general direction of the hamper. I don't see if he makes it in before he's guiding me onto the mattress and lying over me. His tongue strokes mine with such deliberate movements that it makes me remember exactly how it felt between my legs.

"Are you wet for me, little witch?" Lowell asks, his hand skimming down my body before dipping inside me. He groans as he finds exactly how desperate I am for him and quickly adds a second finger. The heel of his hand presses against my clit, and my hips buck, searching for more friction.

"I thought you were mating me," I pant.

"Are you not enjoying this?" he teases, lowering his head to my breast and flicking his tongue against my hardened nipple. I arch into him with an unintelligible moan. "I need you ready for me. I don't want to hurt you."

"Cocky," I breathe.

"Exactly." My chuckle turns into a groan as his fingers move deeper inside me. "Let me get you ready. Let me worship you, *Ma Reine*."

"Well, when you put it like—" I don't finish my thought as he bites down on my breast, the shock of pain mixing with the pleasure from his fingers. He evades my g-spot, instead stroking my outer walls, and my body responds, opening more for him as he stretches me and adds a third finger. "Fuck, Alpha."

Lowell continues his trek lower. His tongue swirls around my navel, then his teeth nip my hips. I grab my breasts, rolling the stiff peaks between my fingers just as Lowell's mouth surrounds my clit, and he sucks on the sensitive bundle of nerves. I scream his name as my hands thread into his hair, dragging him closer. He growls in approval and gives me more, pumping and sucking all while I ride his face, using his mouth to drive me higher and higher. His fingers curl inside me just as his teeth scrape gently along my clit and I combust.

The edges of my vision go black, and my toes curl as my orgasm washes over me. Lowell works me through it, slowing as my pleasure ebbs and my breathing slows. He makes lazy circles around my clit, keeping me hyper-aware even as I cool down. Slowly, he pulls his fingers out of me and sticks all three in his mouth, sucking them clean.

"So fucking sweet," he murmurs before he places a chaste kiss on my clit and rises back up my body, bracing his forearms on either side of my head. I run my hands all over his chest and arms before tangling them in his hair and pulling him closer. I lick his bottom lip, tasting myself before he kisses me. The sound he makes as I suck his tongue into my mouth has my arousal skyrocketing again.

Lowell flips us, so I'm on top, straddling him. "This okay?" he asks, not moving a muscle as I sit astride him, my hands braced on his chest. My wonderful, strong, Alpha mate is submitting to me, letting me dictate this moment in our relationship, letting me guide the pace. It's the ultimate show of trust, and giving over that power makes me feel so incredibly sexy.

"Yes," I breathe. I lean forward to kiss him and grind my hips back. His length sliding along my slit sends shivers down my spine as it brushes my clit and then my entrance. I keep rocking back and forth, my arousal coating his cock. We kiss until I'm breathless, and I tug Lowell's lip between my teeth as I sit up, bracing myself on his chest. He's shaking as his hands fall to my hips, and I position myself over his cock.

Our eyes meet as I hover above him, his head nudging my entrance. This moment feels more monumental than any experience I've ever known. I want to savor it all, to remember every single second.

"Go on, little witch," Lowell encourages. I sink down, and he breaches my entrance.

"Fuck," we breathe in unison. He's thick, and even though I'm slick with arousal, it burns a bit as my body stretches to accommodate his girth. I'm not even halfway down, and I already feel fuller than I've ever been. I shiver as I feel every ridge, every vein, every inch of him against my walls.

I rise slightly before continuing my descent, swirling my hips as I go. "I don't know if I can—"

Lowell rises, propping himself up on one arm, and sucks my nipple into his mouth as his other hand slides between us to rub my clit.

"You can take it," he growls, and the vibrations send a wave of pleasure that shoots right to my core.

I swear as I bottom out, sinking completely down on his cock. Lowell's inhale is sharp and his eyelids flutter. "Good girl," he says, his voice raw and ragged from trying to restrain himself as I adjust to the size of him. It's so much and yet it's so fucking perfect.

He crosses his legs behind me so I'm in his lap, our chests pressed together and arms wound around each other.

"Ride me, little witch." His order comes out more like a plea. "I've been waiting too long to feel you come on my cock."

"Fucking hell." With my hands on his shoulders, I begin sliding up and down his cock, relishing the feeling of having this man inside me. My mate. The man I choose. The man I love.

Lowell keeps chanting my name as I roll my hips in long, sensual thrusts. He drives up, and my head tilts back as he hits a magical spot deep inside me. My nipples brush against his chest as he uses one arm to keep me as close as possible. His mouth is hot on my skin as he buries himself inside me, branding me every time he matches my thrusts.

It's so good it's all I can do to keep moving.

There's a sharp tug on the back of my hair, and my eyes pop open, locking with Lowell's.

And then it happens.

The mating bond snaps into place like a rubber band pulled tautly. I thought I could sense his emotions before, but they were muted. Now they're vibrant, beautiful colors that explode from his chest into mine. I can sense the underlying worry Lowell still carries over my well-being, but it's masked under layers of arousal, passion, and love. My heart feels like it's about to burst, and tears spill past my lashes as I'm bombarded with Lowell's immense feelings for me. His eyes are tearing too, and I know everything I'm feeling is only mirrored for him.

I've always hated when people say their partner completes them. It pissed me off to think people were incomplete if they were alone. Lowell doesn't complete me. His soul isn't a piece of mine that was missing. But when his soul combines with mine...it's magic. Pure and powerful magic.

"I love you so much," we say at the same time.

I start riding him again and as good as it was before, it's ten times that now. Every minute movement, every slight shift, has me shaking, and whenever something feels good on my end, my arousal is sent down the bond to Lowell in such a way that it has him shaking. And round we go, our pleasure climbing exponentially as we chase our release. It's hot and sticky and somehow so fucking romantic I could cry even as I'm about to come.

"Claim me again," I plead as I find an angle that has my clit rubbing against Lowell's pelvic bone. "Please, Alpha. Right now."

He doesn't waste a second before his teeth sink into the spot where my shoulder meets my neck. That's all it takes to send me over the edge, screaming his name as I come. My muscles squeeze Lowell's cock, and he groans against my skin as he's locked against me. My walls flutter around him, and he can't hold out anymore. His balls tighten, and he comes inside me with a feral growl.

Lowell releases my neck and captures my mouth. I can taste my blood on his lips, and I moan as he flips us over, laying me back against the pillows without ever slipping out of me. Wrapping an arm around my leg, he hoists it over his shoulder.

He hits an even deeper spot that I didn't know existed, and I see stars. "How are you still hard?" I gasp as he starts to move. My question isn't answered as he slams into me, already driving me toward another orgasm. His mouth swallows my moans, drinking them like he's dying of thirst. When he reaches between us and circles my clit, I lose it, my orgasm crashing over me in a powerful wave.

The word *orgasm* in French means *a little death*. I used to think that was a little ridiculous and maybe a touch dramatic, but I get it now. Fucking hell do I get it. I can't scream or move or do anything other than let this orgasm have full control of my body. I'm shaking and writhing, and somehow it keeps going on and on and *on*.

Lowell doesn't slow his pace but grabs my other leg and tosses it over his shoulder, bending me in half as he keeps going. I haven't even come down from the last orgasm, and I'm already building to another.

"Such a good girl, drenching me," Lowell growls, and I whimper.

"Holy shit, you're gonna make me come again."

"Give it to me, little witch," he commands with a dark chuckle. His thrusts turn wild, punishing. He's moving so fast I can barely see him. "I'm close. Come with me."

And because he owns every ounce of pleasure in my body, my mouth opens in a silent scream, and my eyes roll to the back of my head as the most powerful orgasm I've ever had knocks me sideways.

He swears. "That's right, milk my cock." He thickens inside me as he comes with a ridiculously sexy groan.

Lowell sits back to release my legs, and they fall open around him. Slumping back forward, his forearms bracing on the bed above my shoulders. He strokes my hair, and my eyes flutter closed as his brow touches mine. A flare of protectiveness washes through me as Lowell gently kisses my cheeks, temple, and eyelids like he's trying to memorize every feature.

"My mate," he murmurs.

"My mate."

Chapter Six

"Did I hurt you?" Lowell asks as he nuzzles into my neck, licking my new claiming mark.

"Not at all," I hum. I run my nails lightly over his back as his softening cock slips out of me and the evidence of both our orgasms drips down my thighs. "But you made a mess of me." Lowell's laughter brings a sleepy smile to my lips.

"We can't have that," he says, leaning over me, his hair falling around us like a curtain. He kisses me sweetly before standing and scooping me into his arms. Somehow, I have the wherewithal to throw a cleansing spell at the sheets before we enter the bathroom and go straight into the shower.

Ice-cold water drenches me for the moment it takes to get warm. I scowl comically at Lowell, whose laughter bounces around the glass enclosure, and he lowers me to the tile floor. I turn my back on him with a harrumph, facing the beautiful blue mosaic so he doesn't see my smile breaking through, even though I know he feels it through our bond. His amusement changes and a glance over my shoulder tells me he's scanning my naked, wet body. I arch so my hair tickles my lower back and rivets of water slide down my tresses. With a low growl of approval, Lowell yanks me back against him, his erection hard against my ass as his hands slide around my hips and brush against my sensitive slit.

"Is this part of the mating?" I ask, melting under his touch. "The short...rebound time? Or are you always this—"

"This is all because of you, little witch," Lowell says, his stubble brushing against my scarred skin. "You have no fucking idea how badly I want you."

"You have me," I breathe as his fingers slide through my wetness. I should be done, sore. I just had multiple earth-shattering orgasms, but the feel of Lowell behind me has me ready to go again. His breath ghosts my ear as he bites down on my lobe before licking away the hurt. I'm desperate for him to be back inside me, for us to be fused again.

I arch back into him, grinding my ass against his rock-hard length.

"You're not ready for that." Lowell chuckles, and his suggestion has my toes curling. He's right. He's about ten times the size of anything I've had back there, and I need to work up to that, but I'm certainly not going to admit it. So instead, I bend forward and push against him further.

Lowell threads his fingers in my hair and tugs me back up. "Turn around," he growls in my ear.

"You don't want me like this?"

"Later," he responds gruffly, spinning me around since I didn't move fast enough for him. "Right now, I want to look into your eyes when you come." He lifts me, and I barely have time to wrap my legs around his waist as he impales me on his cock.

"Fuck. Me," I swear. He keeps me away from the wall, with nothing to hold onto but him.

"That's the plan, *Ma Reine*," Lowell chuckles as he lifts me and slams me back down. His pace remains fast, his large biceps straining with each move. I try to roll my hips to aid his thrust, but I'm completely held at my wolf's mercy.

He moves slightly so the warm water streams directly between us, heating my blood and making my nipples pebble. The beads track down his chest, highlighting every curve of every muscle and making me want to lick him. I look down to do just that but get distracted by the sight of him sinking inside me. I'm mesmerized and so fucking turned on watching us move together.

Lowell's growl rumbles through me as a wave of lust has me clenching around him. "You see that little witch?" he asks, and I realize his eyes are also cast to where we're joined. "Look how perfectly you take my cock. Fucking made for me."

His praise washes over me as warm as the water, and I tear my eyes away from the sight of us fucking to kiss him. I can't stop kissing him. It's like we're magnetized. He devours my lips and pushes me back against the wall. His body is flush against mine, rendering me immobile, and I go pliant in his arms. The clash of his warm body and the cold from the tiles has my senses kicking into overdrive.

"This okay?" he asks, a fleeting moment of uncertainty flashing in his eyes. I take stock of my body, making sure being restrained by him in this way isn't triggering. I run my hands up and down his chest before settling them into his hair. He holds completely still, waiting for my answer.

I nod. "I need the words, Katie," he says as he slowly starts to move. It's too slow. I need more.

"Yes. Good." I can't seem to string more than a few words together as he grinds into me with renewed vigor. And the fact that I can't move and am completely at his mercy heightens the experience. "Oh my god," I moan.

"Is that my nickname now, little witch?" he asks with a cocky smile as he drives me higher and higher.

"I'll call you whatever you want. Just please don't stop."

Lowell laughs as he kisses me savagely and continues doing exactly what he was doing. He doesn't speed up or slow down. He just keeps hitting that spot at the same tempo. His grip is hard enough to bruise, fingers digging into my ass and hips, and the thought of his marks there as well as my neck sends me over the edge.

"Open your eyes," Lowell commands, leaning against my forehead, so I have no choice but to stare into those entrancing golden eyes as the pleasure washes over me. My nails dig into his back, drawing a growl from his lips as he continues to fuck me.

"One more," Lowell demands, and those two words are enough to have me right on the edge again. His hand slips between us, and his fingers rub my clit in quick circles. Lowell groans as his movements become erratic, and I know he's close again too. The sound of our bodies slapping together and our heavy breaths echo against the tiles, bouncing back to us as we're encased in this erotic bubble.

I'm worried it's too much, that I'm too wrung out, but the look on Lowell's face and my name on his lips as ecstasy overtakes him are enough to have me coming with him.

"Holy shit," I breathe when we both come down, and I throw my arms around his neck, clinging to him as my legs tremble. Lowell grunts in agreement, his breaths short and strained. "I don't think I can stand."

"You don't have to," Lowell says, and fuck if that doesn't make me feel all warm and fuzzy. His head tips back into the water, and I chase him, kissing my faded claiming mark. "Do it," he growls as he hardens inside me again. *Fucking again.* But I'm right there with him. Lowell wasn't kidding when he said that's how new mates feel. I'm insatiable. Ravenous.

"You want me to claim you, pup?" I purr, flicking my tongue out and catching a bead of water.

"Please, *Ma Reine.*"

I brace one hand against the tiles at my back and use the purchase to roll my hips while keeping his cock fully seated inside me.

I hesitate, unsure of what to do. The first time I claimed Lowell, it was an accident. I didn't even know I did it until way after the fact. Both times he's claimed me, it felt like such an intentional act, like he was tapping into his were-magic. I'm not sure I can replicate it. As if it hears me, the bond guides me forward, and I find my teeth grazing against Lowell's skin. I surrender, letting it dictate my actions and sink my teeth into his flesh.

Lowell growls loudly, but not from pain. An intense wave of arousal flushes through me, and he starts matching my movements, circling his hips in tandem with mine as I remain latched to his neck. A string of incoherent French falls from his lips, and the pleasure spikes to new levels as the coppery taste of blood flows into my mouth. I release my mate, my head tipping back to the tiles as we come together in perfect synchronicity I've never achieved before.

Lowell's eyes open sleepily, and he smiles at me like I'm the center of his world. I open my mouth to speak, but everything seems too trivial. Even *I love you* isn't enough to describe how much this man means to me. My body trembles with the sheer emotion coursing through me. I can't think. I'm reduced to this overwhelming feeling.

"Alpha—"

"I know, little witch," Lowell says, brushing his nose against mine. He brushes a droplet of water from my cheek that I'm not unconvinced isn't a tear. "I feel it too. What do you need?"

"You," I say simply. Lowell smiles and hugs me tightly, running his fingers through my hair.

My head falls against his chest, and the thumping of his heartbeat relaxes me. A gentle rumbling from his chest combines with an intense need to care for me through our bond. Lowell starts softly singing a song in French, his deep baritone warm and rich, and I sink into the safety he provides.

I must drift off because the next thing I know, I'm being lowered into a warm bath. Bubbles scented with lavender and vanilla surround me as Lowell steps into the tub behind me. His legs come around my sides, and he pulls me back until I'm resting against his chest. I sigh as his strong arms circle my middle, only to start slowly washing me with a loofah. He kisses my hair, my neck, and my shoulders. I feel revered and precious in his arms.

"Mine," I murmur, holding onto his arms and leaning into his body.

"Always." We stay in the tub for a bit, basking in this perfect moment as I try to absorb it all.

I'M FLOATING ON A raft in the infinity pool, a warming spell negating the cool temperatures outside. The day is perfect, the sky blue and cloudless, the sun strong. I'd have put on a bathing suit if I wasn't sure the magical boundary is keeping us hidden, but honestly, anytime I've put on clothes in the past day and a half they've been torn off.

I play with my Light Magic, tossing the glittering ball up in the air and changing the shape to a spear as I launch it across the yard towards the beach. It hits the magical shield with a thud just beyond the table and dissipates. In between all the sex, Lowell and I have been testing our abilities. My were-magic comes as naturally as my lightning now that Lowell and I have mated, and my Dark Magic will improve as Adriana trains me. But my Light Magic, despite being the magic I was born with, is the weakest, so I've been focusing on that.

I refuse to touch my hellfire. I don't even want to acknowledge that I have it.

I dip my fingers into the water, steering my float back into the center of the pool, and let my eyes drift closed. Lowell and I slept for maybe an hour at a time before one of us would wake the other in deliciously creative ways. My thighs clench at the thought of him waking me this morning with his head between my legs, an orgasm already tearing through me as I woke.

There's a faint pull on the mating bond before I'm blasted with intense amusement.

"INCOMING," Lowell bellows, and I shriek as he cannonballs into the water right by my float. I'm hit with the splash right before the wave he creates upends my float, sending me into the water.

I pop up, sputtering and swiping water droplets from my eyes, to find my mate missing from the surface. "Shit," I swear and spin around. I throw my Mind Magic out, but Lowell's arms lock around my legs before I can find him. He hoists me over his shoulder and stands in the pool, catapulting me out of the water. "Lowell," I squeal as he laughs. "Put me down."

"As you wish, *Ma Reine*." He tosses me backward off his shoulders, and I slam into the water again. This time I circle him, popping up and flinging my hair back, so the spray hits him in the face. We're both cackling as my quick splash turns into a serious splash fight with violent waves powered by magic.

"All right!" I throw up a temporary shield as Lowell's largest wave carries me straight into the deep end. "I yield!"

He swims to me, his werewolf speed mind-boggling even in the water. He did indeed get stronger and faster since we mated. "What do I win, little witch?" he asks, wrapping his arms around my middle and tugging me closer.

"Hmmm," I taunt as I tap my finger on my chin. "What do you want?" His gaze heats before his mouth descends on mine. I wind my legs around his hips, removing all space between our bodies.

I'm not sure how we're expected to return to normal. How I'm expected to keep my hands off my mate when he's walking around looking delectable all the time. A queen should be able to conduct a meeting without needing to mount her partner, but at this point, I don't see that happening.

"I thought you were making lunch," I say, breaking our kiss, but Lowell drags me back closer, his hands keeping steady pressure on my back so I'm unable to move away.

I was, he speaks through our reestablished Mind Magic channel while his tongue expertly strokes mine. *But someone was thinking very naughty thoughts, and I got distracted.*

Did you turn the oven off, at least?

Never turned it on. I was making sandwiches.

Thank fuck. Vlad will kill us if we burn down his house.

I realize my mistake as soon as the words leave my mind.

Lowell tosses me away, an intense protective instinct clicking into place, just before a growl reverberates in his chest. I land on my feet in the shallow end, the splash from my landing rippling around me as I keep my eyes on my mate, who is shaking violently, his bones snapping and reforming as he fights the urge to shift.

"HEY," I command, snapping his attention to me. I keep my distance but hold one hand out in front of me. "You can't shift. We talked about this, remember? You don't know if you'll accidentally hurt me if you shift."

"I wouldn't." His voice doesn't quite sound like him, and I wonder if I'm speaking more to his wolf. I swim forward, and he starts to turn his back.

"Alpha, eyes on me," I say. They're glowing now, bright yellow. "Why are you upset? Was it hearing another's name or that a person might hurt me?"

"Yes."

I close the gap between us, using a gentle hushing sound to put him at ease. "Look," I say softly, offering him my throat. "I'm all yours. I'm here and safe, and yours."

His breathing is fast and heavy, but the color of his eyes fades back to their usual gold. He releases a puff of air and winds his arms around me, holding me tight to his body as he buries his face in my neck.

"I'm so sorry, Alpha," I murmur, nuzzling the claiming mark I've left on him. He shivers against me. "What do you need?"

His emotions are shaken up, a desire to protect me warring with a possessive need to claim me. He wraps his hand around the hair at the nape of my neck and pulls. My head snaps back, and he follows me, kissing me savagely. I match his intensity, my growing need spiked by my desire to give Lowell what he needs from me. We're a tangle of tongues, lips, and teeth, as we swallow each other's moans.

He swims us over to the steps and uses his grip on my hair to pull me away from his mouth. I whimper at the loss of contact.

"What's your safe word?" His voice is raw and deep and makes my core clench.

"Watermelon."

He guides me to sit on the top step as he takes the one below. The water pools around the middle of his thighs, leaving his cock standing erect and completely out of the water. I don't wait for instruction before taking him to the back of my throat. He groans, grabbing my head with both hands and holding me close. I breathe through my nose, my eyes leaking as I look up and meet his, which are pleading and asking for permission.

I slide up his length and flick my tongue on the underside of his head. "Take what you need," I say.

He buries himself in my throat, fucking my mouth brutally. Saliva drips down my chin as I hollow out my cheeks, and he growls his approval. God, I love this. I love watching him unravel. There's something so carnal and heady about the way he uses me for his pleasure. It has fire zinging through my veins straight to my core, making me clench my thighs beneath the water.

I cup his balls in my hand, squeezing while one finger works its way back, my nail gently scraping the flesh between his balls and ass.

With a primal groan, he yanks me off roughly and flips me over, so I'm kneeling on the top step. Water runs down my body, and my hands fly out to brace myself on the concrete outside the pool.

My breath catches as he pins me down with a flat palm against my shoulder blades while his other hand caresses my ass. He trails a line of kisses down my spine and sinks his teeth into the cheek he was just caressing. I yelp and try to turn, but I'm held in place.

"Mine," he growls.

"Yours," I respond immediately. If I wasn't wet already, I am now.

"Don't move your hands from the edge," he orders, and I do as he says, arching my back, so my ass is higher in the air. Lowell's hand comes down hard, the sting from the slap more intense since my skin is wet.

He caresses my ass where he hit, his other hand moving between my legs, spreading my arousal up to my clit. "I think you like that too much, little witch," he says darkly, but his voice sounds much more like his own. "You're soaked for me."

"We're in a pool." Another hard spank, and my eyes roll to the back of my head as Lowell mutters something that sounds a lot like *brat.*

His fingers move faster in tight circles. "Let me hear you," he commands. I release an obscenely loud moan, and Lowell's pace quickens until he's practically vibrating against me. "Good girl."

I scream, about to have my umpteenth orgasm of the day when Lowell pulls away. "What the hell?" I demand, turning as much as I can. I'm about to tear into him when he starts stroking my sensitive clit again, his movements so goddamn *slow*. I shift against him, trying to control the situation, but he's intent on building me back up at his pace.

"Not a fan of edging, little witch?" he asks, and my eyes widen when I realize this is my punishment. I whimper, and he delivers a sharp slap to my clit. My eyes bug out of my head, shock warring with how fucking good that felt, making it impossible to form a coherent thought.

"You know better. I need your words," Lowell says. "What do you need?"

"You."

He slams into me, and I cry out, sagging against my forearms on the lip of the pool. I'm not sure I'll ever get used to the feel of him inside me, filling me so thoroughly. He stays fully sheathed in me until my body adjusts, and I wriggle against him, silently asking for more.

"You could give me excessive orgasms," I pant as he starts to move. "You know, as a punishment." His hand claps against my other ass cheek this time, and I groan as he grips the spot, using that section to pull me back further on his hard cock.

"My greedy mate," he tsks as he starts rutting into me. His pace is fast and furious. "You think you can come with me, little witch?"

My body is building towards orgasm again, but I'm still far enough away that I'll need a little more assistance. "I need—"

I don't need to finish the thought. His thumb brushes over my asshole, applying pressure but not pushing inside.

"Yes," I groan. Everything is going so fast that all I can do is hold on and let him control me. He's dominating my pleasure, my body. And I have no problem submitting to him when I have a safe word, knowing he'll stop if I say so. That security gives me all the power.

"I'm going to count us down," Lowell says, "and we'll come on zero. Do you understand?" His movements are growing erratic, and his voice is strained with the restraint he's using waiting for me. I agree, and Lowell starts counting down from five. He reaches three, and I'm shaking as the orgasm threatens to overtake me.

"Hold it," he commands, and I bite my lip to distract myself from the immense rush I'm feeling.

"Two," Lowell grits out, and my core clenches around his cock. Then his thumb breaches the tight ring of muscles, sliding inside me, and I'm screaming. "One. Zero." The last two numbers are rushed, bleeding into each other as we both fall over the edge. Lowell roars and keeps pounding as he spills into me.

When we're both spent, he slumps against my back, placing kisses up my spine until he reaches my neck. "Thank you," he murmurs.

"I feel like I should be saying that to you," I chuckle. My body is sore and probably bruised, but I'm so satiated that I can barely form coherent thoughts.

"Thank you for always knowing how to calm me down," he amends. "I love you so much, Katie," he whispers.

"I love you too."

Chapter Seven

CLOTHES ARE BULLSHIT.

After days of being joined at the hips to my mate, I can officially say I hate wearing clothing and would much rather be draped in him than any fabric.

The sun sets over the ocean, casting the room in a warm orange glow and reminding me why clothes are a necessary evil. Even though the mating frenzy has cooled slightly, we're both still easily set off, and we have company coming. So instead of lying tangled up in the sheets, we're making out on the couch like teenagers, afraid to touch anything other than each other's arms lest one of us end up on our knees in front of the other.

"Fucking hell, little witch. We don't have time," Lowell groans, hardening against me. I chuckle against his lips, teasing his tongue with mine, showing him exactly what I'd be doing if we were alone. "I will spank your ass raw if you keep this up." Everything in my body clenches as I maneuver so I'm on top of him.

"We can be quick," I whisper as the sun starts to dip beyond the horizon. They'll be here as soon as it's fully dark, so we only have a few minutes. Lowell smacks my ass, and I yelp and sit up. He chases me, kissing up my chest and nuzzling against my collarbone before lightly nipping it with his teeth.

"Get in the bedroom."

"Yes, sir," Vlad drawls from the portal entrance, and I groan in frustration as three sets of footsteps come closer. Lowell growls. "Not a sir, huh? Is it daddy? Master? Or do you go into total role-playing mode and ask her to call you 'my king?'"

"It's totally Alpha." Edina laughs and flips the light switch, and I squint until she lowers it to a more ambient setting. Now that I think about it, I don't know if Lowell and I have turned the lights on in the past few days.

Vlad stands in front of Edina and Adriana, blocking them in case Lowell loses control, but I'm still nuzzled into my mate's neck, and his body remains relaxed. There's not a hint of jealousy or possessiveness in our bond. When he realizes they're safe, Vlad runs a hand through his perfectly styled blonde hair, and undoes the top button on his suit jacket, returning to his relaxed default.

"Is that so?" he asks, and I nod sheepishly. He clicks his tongue. "How uninspired. I expected more from you, baby queen."

He shifts so I can see my best friend and sister. Edina steps forward in a simple blue sweater and leggings, looking around the room as she wrinkles her button nose.

"Where's a safe place to sit?" she gestures wildly, not getting too close to any surfaces. I laugh, burying my head in Lowell's hair as he points to an armchair closest to the television. Edina nods her thanks on her way to the chair when there's a blur of movement just as she's about to sit down. "Goddamn it, Vlad!"

"Goddess-damnit," Vlad taunts from his spot in the chair. She flips him off and opens her mouth, no doubt to release a string of profanity, when Vlad moves with his super-speed again and yanks her back onto his lap. Edina rolls her eyes and smacks him in the face with a flap of her wing, but then closes her eyes and her wings disappear. I don't get the chance to ask where they went or why she looks so comfortable in Vlad's lap before Adriana tosses me a vial of tonic.

"To prevent a UTI," she says, her gray eyes dull with heavy bags underneath. She fidgets with the hem of her sweater dress, toeing the plush gray area rug with a booted toe. "The healer wants to see you when we return to the coven, but he said to get a start on that."

I untangle myself from my mate and drink the fizzy tonic, which leaves the lingering taste of cranberries. Adriana spins around the room, her blonde curls bouncing with her.

"Lowell was kidding," I say softly. "I cleansed everything before you got here."

She sighs in relief but then shoots daggers at Edina and Vlad before sitting in the farthest chair away from them. Vlad, seeing this, wraps an arm around Edina's waist, which my best friend slaps away.

"What's this? What's happening?" I ask, leaning forward like somehow less distance will help me discern the vibe.

"Nothing," Edina and Adriana say at the same time as Vlad says, "Edina and I fucked."

"What?" Lowell and I ask in unison.

Edina's eyes start practically glowing with her anger as she turns back to the vampire and smacks him across his chest. Vlad just runs a hand through his hair like he's completely unaffected by her lashing out and Adriana's Dark Magic flares in her hands, coating her skin in a protective layer.

"It doesn't mean anything," Edina says to Adriana, who is firmly looking at the ground. "It was a one-time thing."

"Three times," Vlad amends.

"Dude!" She attempts to smack him again, but he snags her wrist this time.

"We're all adults here," Vlad says indifferently. "We're both single—" Adriana winces but remains silent. "—We have nothing to hide. It's not anything to be ashamed of."

Edina looks down, avoiding my eyes. And that's when I know there's something worse that she's not telling me. Because my best friend has never once been ashamed of her sex life.

"What is it?" I demand, and Edina looks up with a mask plastered on her pretty pale features.

"There was an incident when she was in Faerie," Vlad says.

"I'm going to freeze your dick off," Edina seethes.

"You use that threat a lot, you know."

"It's fucking effective."

Vlad chuckles. "I told you to tell them. You didn't listen."

"Because I'm not ready to talk about it!" Edina turns away from the vampire and faces me, the cracks in her façade showing. "I'll tell you everything," she continues. "But not right now. Not right after your mating."

The hurt Edina is feeling is palpable, showing on every inch of her features, from the subtle way her hands shake to the rigid set of her jaw. When she returned home from Faerie, I knew something was wrong, but so much was happening that I didn't push it. She usually needs time to process on her own, and I thought I was right to give that to her. But something in the pleading way she's looking at me makes me think I was very wrong, and even though she's asking me to drop it, I press.

"You don't have to tell me," I start slowly. "But when I was hurt, you wouldn't let me shove it down and not talk about it. Is that what you're doing? Burying your problems by sleeping with Vlad?"

"You could sound a tad less disgusted, baby queen," Vlad says.

Edina scoffs, but the sound gets caught in her throat. "Fine," she breathes and stands, crossing to the windows, not meeting my concerned gaze while she tells her story. "When I was in Faerie, the queen— my *mother*— wanted me to look for my mate." Snow starts gently falling around her, and ice creeps up her arms.

"It was Puck, the Fae I met in Salem," she continues. "The one who first took me to Faerie. Fae recognize their mates instantly. We can sense it easier than shifters. He said he suspected when we met, but he didn't know for sure because I hadn't emerged. The bond clicked when we saw each other at my welcome party."

"That's..." I'm about to say great when Vlad catches my gaze and shakes his head. Edina turns, the stubborn set of her shoulders a total contrast to her wavering bottom lip.

"He rejected me," she whispers. Lowell inhales sharply, and my mouth falls open. "He rejected the bond. That's what happened right before I came back."

I'm on my feet in a second, but Lowell is faster, and he pulls my best friend into a wordless hug. Her whole body goes ramrod straight, and the snow intensifies, but then she slowly raises her arms, and a sob breaks free. Lowell holds her as she cries, ice tears falling onto the floor between their bodies. When his golden eyes meet mine, they're shining with tears, and he doesn't need to say anything for me to know how he's feeling. My heartbreak at seeing my friend's pain became his own.

Vlad's arm brushes against mine as he stands beside me. I reach down and grab his hand, squeezing it tightly. "We had sex when I dropped Edina off in Faerie," he says to me, but his eyes are on Adriana, who is still looking at the carpet. "When she got back, we were both upset, needed a distraction, and leaned on each other."

Adriana scoffs. "You have something to say?" Vlad asks, his voice cold and scarier than I've ever heard.

"I actually need to apologize to Katie," she says. Her tone matches Vlad's, and for a moment, I'm reminded that my sister is a scary-as-fuck Dark Witch who could kill us all and make it look like an accident. "I'm sure you've figured it out, but I slept with Rodger before he died. I shouldn't have. You're my sister, and your ex should have been off limits."

Vlad growls. "It's fine, Adriana," I interject. She offers me a tight smile, before training her eyes on Vlad like she's daring him to say a word. My eyes bounce between them as they remain locked in this weird tension-filled stare-down. "For the love of God, will one of you tell me what happened the day we went to the dragon hoard?"

"Absolutely nothing," Adriana says, standing and storming into the backyard.

I wait until the door closes behind her before turning and pinching Vlad's bicep hard enough to bruise. "We left you three alone for two minutes." I twist before releasing him. "We don't have time for this messy love triangle bullshit."

"There's no triangle," Vlad insists. "Edina and I haven't had sex since Adriana walked in on us."

"She walked in on you?"

"And Adriana and I can't be together," he continues, ignoring me. "So, we can all move forward and focus on more important things. Like the fucking war. Or the fact that your best friend is breaking right now."

I glare because he has a point. Edina laughs through her tears at something Lowell says and pulls away from my mate. I'm there as soon as she's free of his arms, wrapping her into a hug of my own. Edina isn't crying anymore, but her sadness is still hovering like a raincloud above her head.

"Love you most," I murmur, and her arms tighten around me.

"You smell like sex," she responds, and the two of us laugh, not letting go even as our laughter shakes our bodies. When we finally pull apart, she links her fingers through mine. "I just didn't want you to worry about being happy in front of me. Because I'm so happy you're happy, and I'd never want to fuck that up for you, babes."

"I know," I sigh and tug her back towards the couch. She sits, tucking her legs under her body and leaning against my shoulder as Lowell sits on my other side, wrapping his arm low around my waist. Vlad sits back in his chair and clears his throat.

"Now that's done—" He swerves as Edina throws a snowball at his face. It hits the back of the chair and slowly leaks down until I wave a hand to clean it up. "We have other things to discuss before we head back to the Highlands."

"We're not going to your house?" I ask, and he shakes his head.

"No, we're not," Adriana says, closing the backdoor behind her. Her usual take-charge demeanor is back in place. Our eyes connect, and she gives me a shaky smile. I know she's okay for now, but I need to talk to her later to make sure. "The wolves and vampires will be arriving in a couple of days, and we need to have a plan."

A creak comes from the portal door. Edina and Vlad go unnaturally still, and Lowell and I jump up, my lightning bursting to life in my hands.

"It's okay," Adriana says. "I invited—" Two familiar figures walk into the living room.

"Mom." I drop my magic and run around the couch. My mother's emerald green eyes take me in, scanning me like she's looking for physical signs of injury. I barrel into her, and she hugs me back, squeezing so tightly I can barely breathe.

"Sweetheart, I'm so sorry," she says.

I break away from her to find Marcus, my larger-than-life stepfather smiling widely. Tears are in his eyes as I hug him, and he clings to me like he may never see me again. "I'm okay," I tell them both, pulling away and holding their hands.

"Mom, Marcus," I say softly, falling in beside Lowell. I wrap my arm around his waist, and his arm instinctively falls around my shoulders, tucking me into his side. "I'm sure you've already met—"

"We have," Marcus says, winking at us. "But go on."

"This is my mate and my partner," I say, beaming as Lowell kisses the top of my head. I feel warm fuzzy feelings radiating from him as he smiles at my parents. My mother's eyes narrow, like they usually do when assessing one of my boyfriends, but then she surprises me by smiling at him and nodding.

"Your mom and I worked together a lot while you were—"

"We have a lot to discuss," my mother says quickly. She's not quite slipping into her general mode, but she's close. "Let's sit."

My parents take spots on the couch next to Edina. Adriana vacates her chair, grabbing a stool from the island, and she surprises me by putting the chair between Vlad's and the one she left open. Lowell and I make our way over to the remaining chair, and Lowell sits as I drop to the floor, resting my head between his legs.

"First things first," Vlad says. "Sybil, one of the vampires under my command, owns a chain of blood banks. They relieve medical facilities and other blood banks of blood that are deemed unusable for transfusions, and she sells it to vampires to drink. She graciously offered to supply the coven with blood—"

"Upon threat of dismemberment," Lowell adds.

"—and since London is one of the largest locations," Vlad continues, "she hired armored vans to bring the supply to the Highlands."

"But they were ambushed," Marcus finishes. "Dragons officers destroyed all the blood."

"Archer knew we had an army of Magical Creatures," Lowell says softly as I put together the connection. "He saw us at the siege. It's a smart move."

"We can have some imported from Tokyo and New Orleans," Vlad continues, "but it'll take some maneuvering."

"In the meantime, we have hundreds of vampires descending on the Highland Coven with no way to feed them," I surmise, and Vlad nods. "The witches will have to pair up with them. How often does a typical vampire need to feed? I know you're different since you're old as fuck."

"Kathryn," my mother hisses, but Vlad just chuckles.

"Every day to every other day, depending on age. Will the witches feed the vampires?"

"I don't think we have much choice. I'm not sending them out to do their own hunting."

"I wouldn't either," Vlad agrees. "You'll make it happen, baby queen?"

"Yes," I say. "What else?"

"The usurpers involved in Father's coup have been wiped of their memories and returned home," Adriana says. "I also caved in the old throne room so Archer can't return. The Earth Elementals that left the palace helped me make a new one and add more barracks-style bedrooms."

"We still have soldiers at Dragons Headquarters," my mother says. "The ones who were observed helping you have been relocated to stay with us, as have their families."

"Is Deavers really dead?" I ask, and my mother nods. I was hoping that was something I had hallucinated. "He was engaged." She nods again, silently assuring me his fiancé was taken care of.

"Reports are mixed on why he died," Marcus says. "Some of the men said he was made as a spy, but Jefferson and Soto said—"

"Archer killed him for touching me," I say softly. "I'm not sure which, but I believe it's the latter."

"Speak of the devil..." Vlad fishes in his pocket and pulls out his phone, hitting a few buttons and tossing it to me. "Take a look."

I glance down at a tabloid article about the coronation. Archer is standing stoically on the dais in front of the throne. Just the sight of him has my blood boiling. Lowell starts making that rumbling sound in his chest that always puts me at ease, but even that's not quelling the intense rage I feel.

"What am I looking at?" I ask as I study his full regalia. He came to me in the same outfit, the cape, the giant crown, the sword...

The sword.

"Are you fucking kidding me?" I zoom in on the silver sword with the ruby in the hilt. "Mother fucking asshole. Cock sucking, son of a—"

"Kathryn," my mother scolds as I continue my tirade, tossing the phone a little too hard back at Vlad, who passes it to Edina.

"That's the sword you need," she accurately guesses, passing the phone to my parents. "The last piece of the blood oath."

"He had it on," I fume, standing from my spot and starting to pace. "When he...he had it on that night when he was torturing me. I saw it. I looked at the damn hilt, trying to figure out a way to get it and skewer him with it."

"There's no way you could have gotten it that night," Marcus assures me. I grab a book off the closest shelf and throw it toward one of the solid walls. I don't hear it connect, so I assume Vlad grabs it but I'm seeing red, unable to focus on anything except the rage that the last piece of that puzzle was within striking distance, and I failed to get it.

"Holy shit," Adriana says. I'm vaguely aware of a commotion, but I can't hear it as another realization crashes over me. I've seen that sword another time too. I bumped into its case the night of the ball, in the weird covered pathway that led to Archer's old room. I remember thinking it was random that there was a sword at the edge of a hedge maze, but they were hiding it. No one knew about that pathway except Archer and his father. Even as his guard, I didn't know about it. The sword has literally slipped through my hands *twice.*

"Katie," someone bellows. I look up and realize I can't see anyone. A ring of white fire surrounds me. Lowell tugs sharply on our mating bond, flooding me with calming energy, but it's not enough.

"What do I do?" I ask the room.

"For the love of magic, stop moving," Vlad commands. There's some more whispering as the flames continue to dance in front of me. I will them down, but they refuse to listen. It's like they have a mind of their own.

"For fuck's sake," Edina swears, and suddenly I'm doused in freezing water that extinguishes the flames and leaves me shivering.

"I had no control over it," I breathe as Adriana magically dries me off, and my mother sends a warming spell my way. "It took over."

"You need to be impassive and detached to control hellfire," Edina says, and all the heads snap to her. "What? I wasn't in Faerie long, but I made sure they taught me the important shit. Hellfire is the closest thing to Fae magic in this realm. Neither reacts well to strong emotions."

"Impassive and detached," I repeat, and she nods.

"We can work on it. I can put you out if you lose control," she says with a smile.

Lowell stands before me, cupping my face in his hands, his thumbs gently stroking my cheeks. "I'm okay," I assure him, and he grunts in response. "I just lost my temper. It won't happen again."

"Better not," Vlad scoffs as Adriana starts repairing the floorboard I burned. "I'm not buying you another mating present."

Lowell and I turn to him. "What?" we speak in unison.

"This is your mating present," Vlad says, gesturing to the house. I stare at him open-mouthed. "Did you really think a vampire would buy himself a beach house? I mean, sure, I built in a room for myself, but—" He's cut off as I throw my arms around his neck.

"Is that why you stocked the bookshelves with romance novels?" I whisper in his ear as we hug.

"These are the dirtiest ones I could find," he says, and I laugh as I pull away. Lowell walks towards Vlad, who holds out a hand for him to shake, which naturally Lowell ignores, wrapping the vampire in a bear hug instead.

"Well," Marcus laughs, "this regime will never be dull."

Chapter Eight

After Lowell and I are caught up on everything that transpired after the siege, he makes dinner while my mother informs me of her efforts with the Dragons. An influx of soldiers joined up following Deavers' death and are still reporting to my mother and Marcus via Mind Magic. Unfortunately, none of the other generals were included in our plans, so we won't know much until orders reach the lower levels.

Lowell makes dinner for the lot of us while we discuss the arrival of the wolves and vampires and plan our retaliation against Archer for ruining our blood supply. It's amidst a bite of couscous that I realize exactly how we should strike back.

"Mom," I start, and everyone looks up from their plates. "Do we have allies waiting for us in any of the other Dragon bases? Particularly the ones with portals."

"A few in Salem," she says carefully. "A couple in some of the smaller European and American bases. Washington, New Orleans, Paris, Warsaw. But none in Shanghai or the rest of Asia. We were planning on reaching out, but it will be harder now that our rebellion is public."

"No, that's okay," I say. "Reach out to the Americans. Tell them if they plan on traveling by portal, they need to get to Salem by tomorrow afternoon."

"Why the rush?" Adriana asks, grinning knowingly.

"Because we're going to seal the portal doors. And while the Dragons are distracted by that attack, we're going to free every witch imprisoned for the use of Dark or Light Magic." The room is silent as I take a bite of my kebab.

"Have you lost your mind?" my mother demands.

"Katie, there are some serious criminals in the prison," Marcus says softly.

"Actually," Adriana interjects, her eyes clouding over in a vision, "most are harmless and would be an asset."

"You'd be fighting against centaurs, little witch," Lowell says from behind me. "Their arrows have magical properties that affect clotting."

"And they can pierce magical shields," my mother says.

"We can approach them and see if they'll come to our aid."

"Centaurs were the only race of Magical Creatures that weren't totally fucked when the Baran line took over," Vlad says. "They won't join us."

"Then we get our people and get out." I stand and start collecting plates to bring to the sink. "There must be an entire coven's worth of witches who would join us and aren't dangerous."

"I can get names and cell numbers of the wrongly imprisoned," Adriana offers.

"Babes," Edina says cautiously. "I know you have your magic back now, and you're all gung-ho to be a bad bitch again, but let's talk this out step by step. Why are we closing the portals if I destroyed the one to the palace?"

"Because Archer had Fae working with him. Fae with hellfire."

Edina starts shaking her head. "No, there's no way. There aren't any Fae who have hellfire. Not anymore."

"There was just one. I met him," Marcus says. Edina's eyes glow softly and ice crystalizes around her knuckles before she tamps down her magic. "He trained Archer, teaching him how to control the hellfire, and then he returned to Faerie."

"But nothing is stopping him from calling him back." I sit back on the floor between Lowell's legs.

"Could Fae break into the portal to the coven? Or Vlad's house?" Lowell asks.

"When I commissioned the portal doors," Vlad says, "I had the Fae who made them provide numerous wards, anti-detection spells, and so on. They're secure."

"We're all agreed on closing the portals to the Dragon strongholds," my mother says, steering us back to the matter at hand. "But why on earth do you want to raid the prison?"

"Tons of reasons." I shrug.

"Name one." She fixes me with a withering stare.

"We need more people. Closing the portals is a stopgap. It'll delay the arrival of reinforcements but it won't stop them forever. And we're severely outnumbered."

"I'll call the American Pack Master," Lowell says. "See if they'll be willing to come to our aid. It's a little easier for them over there, but I'm sure they'll be interested in a regime change."

"We can call in more contacts, too," Marcus offers.

"We need everyone we can get," I huff, exasperated. "You know what we're up against. Most witches proficient in Battle Magic go to the Dragons, and there are only so many places we can pull people from."

"Also…" Adriana starts, and all heads swivel to her as her eyes clear free of a vision. "You need to retaliate. Hitting the prison, which is supposed to be impenetrable, makes the Kingdom look weak. And it's not as hard as you think it'd be to break in or break people out. Trust me, I've done it twice before."

"Twice?" Marcus asks, and she gives a sheepish smile.

"You only knew about one because I wanted you to."

The room grows silent, everyone looking a little miserable and not wanting to admit that I'm right, but I can feel them slowly changing their minds.

"Can we think about it?" Lowell asks, his hands resting on my shoulders. "We can make the plan to close the portals and discuss the prison raid in the morning."

Everyone clearly agrees but waits for my decision. "Fine. We'll discuss it in the morning."

Vlad clears his throat. "Are you ready to hear my plan for the post-war government? Or are you still harping on the idea of the four monarchs?"

"I've been asking for your plan since we met," I growl, but Vlad gives me a challenging stare and waits. I roll my eyes so hard you can hear them. "Please tell me your plan, oh wise and ancient vampire." He ignores the sarcasm dripping from my words.

"You're the sole queen," he says. "It makes even more sense now that you have all four magics."

"Four?" my mother asks, and without a word, I call my were-magic to my hand. Her eyebrow hits her hairline as she takes in the swirling golden magic that matches my mate's eyes. She nods curtly, and I banish the magic as Lowell leans forward and nuzzles my temple.

"If I'm the sole queen," I start, "it'll just look like a power grab. I'm already known for my ambition… and my ego, honestly. That's all the Kingdom will see."

Vlad continues. "In addition to our baby queen, we institute a cabinet of four and a council beneath them."

"How many people?" Adriana asks.

"Sixteen in total," Vlad says. "You have three representatives from each faction of magic reporting to your cabinet, which is another four."

"Like the vampires," Lowell says.

"It's worked for about five hundred years," Vlad says. "Your council members should be elected, but we'll deal with the semantics later."

"But I'll choose my cabinet," I say, and Vlad nods. "That's a fair system."

"You just can't choose me," Lowell says.

"Why?" I say, rising to my knees and turning to face him.

"I'm your mate. I'd never go against you, and the community knows it. I'm still your second for the duration of the war, but after it's over, you'll need to choose one person from each sector of magic."

I purse my lips, and Lowell steals a kiss. I sigh when he pulls away. "We're not done with this discussion." His eyes darken, and I realize I'm between his legs on my knees. Delicious warmth blooms in my core, and Lowell's breath hitches as he feels it in the bond.

"And on that note," Vlad says, standing in a flash. "We need to get back to the Highlands. Katie needs to project the image of a queen from the moment we walk there. This means no one," Vlad fully turns to my parents, "can question her in front of the other members of this rebellion."

"Understood," my mother says and offers him a smug smile. "We'll just question her in private."

Marcus laughs and pulls my mom under his arm, a move that usually makes her stiffen, but today she relaxes into his hold, and I catch the rare glimpse of what they're like in private.

Everyone starts moving towards the beach house doors, and I stand to leave, but Lowell grabs my hand, holding me in place. "We'll be right behind you," he says to the group.

"Mhmm," Edina hums, wiggling her eyebrows.

"We have work to do tonight," Vlad reminds us.

"Two minutes," Lowell promises, and I can't control the disappointed whimper that escapes my lips and makes everyone laugh as they close the portal door behind them.

Lowell grabs my hands, linking our fingers together and tilting his forehead to meet mine. The emotions flowing between us in the bond are mixed. He's upset and worried, but there's also love and gratitude.

"What is it, pup?" I ask softly as he releases a slow breath.

"Thank you for accepting our mating bond," he says. I wrap my arms around his torso, resting my head against his chest as I fold into him. He kisses the top of my head as we stand there for a moment holding each other.

"Come on," I say as I pull out of his hold. "Time to leave our mating bubble."

"After you, *Ma Reine.*" He smirks, and hand in hand, we step into the portal.

WALKING DOWN THE HALLWAYS of the Highland Coven is surreal. Everyone is...happy. Lighter. Like simply removing the toxicity of my father made it easier to breathe somehow. Witches in their black robes smile as they pass, dipping into a slight bow instead of the usual genuflecting that I begged everyone to stop.

The green light that made everything look creepy and ominous has been replaced by bright white magical orbs that float every few feet along the carved ceilings. Some of the hewn rock walls now have designs, no doubt the result of one of the Earth Elementals. If I remember correctly, Jefferson is particularly good with rock carvings, and if I had to wager a guess, this is his work.

Lowell and I follow Adriana through the halls, past the empty training area and the bustling corridors leading to the mess hall and residences. The ground rises on a slight incline before the ceiling, and the walls give way to a large cavern.

"The new throne room." Adriana beams as my hands fly to my mouth. The space is easily three times the size of the last throne room. The entire top of the mountain is carved open and encased in glass, letting in the moonlight and giving us a perfect view of the stars. "The O'Malley twins did that," Adriana says, regarding my awe at the glass ceiling. "Fire and Earth Elementals can make glass when they work together...who knew?"

The room is covered in personal touches that Adriana points out, giving credit to each of the men who made them. Most of the room is bare, left open for the masses joining us. But behind the carved-stone dais that houses my glass throne is a patch of wildflowers growing from the rocks. I approach it cautiously, stopping when I find the etched rock plaque at the front of the plot.

"For all who have fallen," I read, "and for those who mourn them." Footsteps echo in the large chamber as more people enter, but I ignore them. There have only been a few scattered battles, and already we need a memorial. I picture Deavers, the charred bodies from Sicily, and the attack here in the Highlands.

"May your sacrifice not be made in vain," I whisper as my golden magic drips from my fingertips and encases the outer edge of the garden. It glows brightly before vanishing, leaving an invisible shield of protection guarding the flowers.

I turn back, seeing the rest of my family has followed me into the throne room. They're silent, reverent. "I know you think the plan tomorrow is reckless," I start slowly, swallowing the lump in my throat. "But there is a very real chance we won't survive this war."

"Katie—" Lowell starts, but I squeeze his hand in mine.

"While we're still here and have the chance to make a difference, we need to rescue those who were wrongfully imprisoned for just using their raw magic. If we lose, they'll rot in that prison."

"If we lose, they'll be on the run anyway," my mother points out. I release Lowell's hand and walk to stand in front of her and my stepfather.

"But at least they'll be free, with their families. We owe them that. Especially since the three of us put a portion of them in there. And—" I swallow hard, "I was just in prison for three days and almost lost my damn mind. These people have been there for years...decades. We can't just leave them."

My parents exchange a glance and then nod. I turn to Vlad arching an eyebrow at him expectantly. "You're doing this now because I specifically said no one could contradict you in public," he monotones, and I smile. "Fine. There are some Magical Creatures we should free as well."

I turn to Edina and Adriana, whom agree, before looking to Lowell. He sighs deeply before nodding.

"Tomorrow night," I instruct. "We split into three teams. We'll need a few more people, so we should go to the war room and discuss before the night is over."

"We'll make it happen," Lowell says.

"Let's plan a prison break," Vlad says with a devilish smile.

Chapter Nine

Aᴛᴛᴇʀ ᴀ ɴɪɢʜᴛ ᴏꜰ fitful sleep, I walk to the brand-new medical bay Adriana built for Coleman. It's even bigger than the medical bay in the Dragons Headquarters, with ten beds, all surrounded by crisp blue curtains. The fluorescent lights are blindingly bright and reflect off the shiny stainless-steel surfaces that house all manner of tonics, potions, and salves.

I tap on the open doorframe, and Coleman looks up from his current patient, one of Lowell's nieces. Her black hair is tied in haphazard pigtails, and she has a large pink bandage wrapped around her knee.

"Hi, Your Majesty," she coos around the lollipop in her mouth. "You forgot your crown again."

"You're right. I'm sorry, AM." She lights up at the use of her nickname, and I turn my attention to the older man who steps in front of me. "Is she okay?" I whisper.

"Oh yes," he assures me. "Werewolves heal very quickly. Ava Marie just likes the bandages."

"I skinned my knee," she replies, kicking her legs. "Am I all fixed, Mister Coleman?"

"Yes, dear." She hops off the exam table and bolts out of the room with unnatural speed. "No running with that stick in your mouth!" He clicks his tongue, but his blue eyes are bright with laughter. "Her mother has her hands full with that one."

"She's too cute for her own good," I agree. He gives me a small smile, but I can tell he's already assessing me.

"How are you feeling?" he asks, nodding for me to take a seat on one of the beds. He stares me down until I sit. "Are you sleeping?"

"No, but not for the reasons you think." Coleman doesn't laugh at my attempted levity. "This will sound like a cop-out, but I think my anxiety was worse last time because I didn't have my magic. It made me feel helpless. But it's back now."

"You were still tortured," he says gently.

"But I survived," I assert. "I'm not hiding from it; I'm not shoving down emotions. I know I still have a lot to unpack about my time down there, but you'll help me through that. If we can still have our sessions."

"Of course, Katie." He beams with pride, his smile wrinkling the skin around his eyes. "That's a big step, admitting you can't handle your trauma alone. You've come a long way in a short time."

"I'm an overachiever like that."

Light Magic illuminates his hands. "May I?" he asks, and I drop my hands to my sides for his scan. He immediately places the magical light on my lower stomach.

"Archer's infusions broke apart the hellfire holding my magic hostage."

"That's not what I'm checking." The blood drains from my face, and a lump rises in my throat. *There's no way.*

He waits an eternity before nodding and pulling his hands away. "You're not pregnant," he says as he grabs a vial from a glass cabinet.

"Oh, thank fuck," I breathe, scraping my hands through my hair. "You just scared the shit out of me."

"Luna told me to check on you immediately," Coleman explains. "Werewolves are notoriously fertile, apparently even more so when they're mated. Take the tonic twice a month from now on." He hands it to me. "And avoid sex while you're ovulating until you're ready for a child. If Lowell was a witch, I'd also tell him to take the tonic, but I'm not sure of its effects on werewolves."

I barely get the stopper off before chugging the liquid. Lowell and I haven't talked about a family yet, but there's no way I'm getting pregnant while we're in the middle of a war. I need to be on the front lines, and I know Lowell wouldn't let me lead if I was carrying a child.

"I have a favor to ask," I say as Coleman takes the now-empty vial and begins washing it out. "Would you be willing to help me learn some basic healing? After the vampires and wolves arrive, and we have a spare minute."

"Of course. We can do it after our therapy sessions."

"Deal," I smirk. "I'm off to train with Adriana. Did she tell you we'll need you and the other healers on standby for tonight?"

"We'll bring supplies to the war room as soon as you leave."

I hop off the bed and head toward the hallway. "Your Majesty?" he calls, and I turn back. "Give 'em hell."

I smile confidently and snag a lollipop on my way out.

I saunter into the training arena with lightning covering my purple sports bra and leggings combo, making my body look like a stormy sky. The few people sparring stop and stare as I skip over to Edina and Astor, the Fae assigned to train her, who are talking in hushed tones and working on hand motions for some Fae spells. Lowell, training with his sister and a Beta, Lyra, tracks me with a hungry expression that instantly switches to pain as Lyra uses his distraction to get the upper hand. She tosses her head back in a hearty laugh but still parries the rebuttal attack my mate launches, and they begin moving in a blur of dark hair and tanned muscles as they tap into their werewolf speed.

I add an extra flourish of magic, and my best friend rolls her eyes emphatically. "I was worried the months without magic would humble you," she taunts.

"You should know better." I send a small bolt of lightning her way, which she blocks easily. She motions for me to give more, taking up a defensive position. Edina was the only one in school who could ever come close to matching me in Battle Magic, so we were always paired together. It's a familiar feeling, getting ready to advance on her while she prepares to defend.

Iridescent wings snap out, the navy razorback tank top she wears allowing their access to be unhindered. Her eyes flash with an excited gleam that promises this will be a match unlike any we've had before, and then she attacks first, launching an icicle at me.

"Oh, that's how it is?" I laugh as I barely dodge it. Edina's never been the aggressor, but then again, her magic wasn't what it is now.

"Bring it, babes."

We trade blows, neither of us pulling any punches as magic combines and explodes. It's so fucking fun. Every time she clips me, freezing my fingers or drenching me in a torrent of cold water, Edina cackles gleefully. And every time I get the jump on her, frizzing her hair with little licks of lightning, she screams obscenities until I cast a silencing spell.

After a while, when we're both sweating with exertion and panting from laughter, Edina freezes the floor beneath me, sending me slipping and sliding closer to her. The witches in the training room, who have abandoned their sparring matches to watch, gasp as she circles a lasso of water around her head and tosses it in a large arc. She's trying to bind my arms so I can't cast, which would end the match.

Right before the lasso descends around me, I harness the element, bending the water to my will and sending the lasso back at Edina.

"Fuck me," she growls as the freezing water wraps around her middle and pins her arms to her sides. "I forgot you can do that." I tighten the lasso and let lightning dance across my eyes in a challenge. "Yield! I yield! Don't actually electrocute me, you psycho."

I laugh as I drop the magic and wrap her in a hug. "You almost beat me," I whisper.

"I know, right?" She pulls back, beaming. "I'm coming for you, one day soon, babes."

"Hell yeah, you are."

"How did you do that?" Astor asks. His long arms are folded across his chest, and his eyes are narrowed. "How did you take Edina's element?"

"I'm not really sure," I answer. I created this technique, but it was something that came to me naturally. "It feels almost like Mind Magic, like I'm harnessing the intention of the element and changing it to fit my needs."

"Have you taught anyone else to do this?"

I shake my head. When I learned this was something I could do, I tried to teach Marcus, but Mind Magic was never his strong suit so he wasn't able. And when I tried to show my mother, we wound up in a fight because Mind Magic was in a legal gray area, and she didn't want me pushing my luck.

"You will show Princess Edina," Astor declares, and I arch an eyebrow.

"Ignore him," Edina says, making the male bristle and open his mouth to protest. "But yeah, if you don't mind, that's freaking badass."

Satisfied with my compliance, Astor begins to point out every moment where Edina went wrong in our sparring match. I'm still not sure of Astor's role in Edina's life. When I asked, she said he's 'her father, but not actually her father.' I didn't get any more information, but I can't help hunting for similarities between them. He has similar coloring and a similar build, but there's no warmth to him, no sign of the sass and mischief that lights up my best friend. And the eyes are different.

There's a trickle of something down the mating bond before I'm hoisted off my feet, hanging upside down off Lowell's shoulder as his laughter fills the training room. I screech his name, but he does a full lap before finally setting me back down and assuming a sparring position.

"You were looking overconfident there, little witch," he teases. "Let's see how you handle a werewolf now that you have your magic back. Unless you're afraid to lose in front of your soldiers…"

I'm about to launch myself at my mate when Adriana enters the room and snaps her fingers. "Everyone out," she commands. She waits by the door, her chin lifted as everyone except Edina, Lowell, and Astor scatter from the training room.

When the last person leaves, her cold façade fades into a bright, eager smile. "Ready to teleport?" She gathers her blonde curls and ties them into a messy bun on the top of her head.

"So. Fucking. Ready," I whoop. Those of us left gather in the center of the training room. Edina is bouncing from foot to foot, her wings fluttering excitedly.

Adriana nods. "Astor, I may need your assistance translating this for Edina if there are any discrepancies with Fae magic."

"Certainly," he responds with a terse smile.

"Katie, call your Dark Magic," Adriana instructs. I shake away the distractions and reach into the pit of my power in my stomach. I'm bombarded with all my different forms of raw magic, and I struggle for control as they all fight for dominance. My lightning is second nature, but separating the Light and Dark is like trying to diffuse a bomb while hanging upside down off a moving train.

"You'd think I didn't practice at all." I release a frustrated breath.

"Separating the magic will be the most difficult part," Adriana says. "I assume you did that part quickly and worked with each faction individually when you practiced on your vacation." I grunt in acknowledgment. "Remember, they're here to serve you. You control your magic, not the other way around."

I latch onto my darkness and draw it forward. "Beautiful," Lowell murmurs from across the room. I let the pitch-black magic coat my hands and snake up my arms, marveling as it sparkles with a prism of colors as it hits the light.

"Good," Adriana praises, her own gray form of Dark Magic similarly sweeping over her arms. "Teleportation is a pretty simple concept. Raw magic responds to your intentions, so all you need to do is be explicitly clear about whom you're moving, where you're going, and then focus on that destination, whether towards a person or place."

"*Person* or place?" Edina asks.

"Let's say you're teleporting to a place you've never been before," Adriana explains, "but you know Katie will be there. If you set your intention to teleport to Katie, your magic should do the rest."

"Will that work if we don't know where they are?" I ask, and she nods.

"The only time it won't work is if your person is within a ward that prevents teleporting, like the coven or Vlad's house. If you tried to teleport to someone within a ward, you'd get redirected and could wind up lost in space."

Edina and I gape at her before exchanging a *what the hell* look.

"Same goes if your intention is muddy," she continues. "If you have a vague idea of where you're going, like a country or large city, it won't work. The best-case scenario is ending up in the wrong place. The worst is your body gets severed between multiple locations. I knew a witch who tried to teleport to *the US,* and we found his head in Chicago, his torso in Savannah, and his limbs in Albuquerque."

"Great," Edina deadpans. "And I'm assuming teleporting between realms is a no-no?"

"Correct," Astor confirms. "Use the portal for that."

"You can also let others set your intention by using Mind Magic, but let's try something simple first," Adriana says and points to the doorway. "Katie, we're going to teleport there first. Me and you. I modified the wards here to allow the four of us to teleport at will. Ready to give it a shot?"

"Are you kidding me? I could end up *severing* us."

"With such a short distance, it would only be a flesh wound. Most likely."

I swear but take Adriana's arm the same way she's taken mine so many times before. I release a shaky breath and imagine my magic taking us to the doorway. The darkness swirls around us and begins squeezing. I close my eyes, using every ounce of brainpower to imagine our destination.

The pressure subsides when it feels like my lungs are about to pop, and I tentatively crack my eyes open. Adriana and I are both whole and standing in the doorway. A second later Edina and Astor pop up behind us. The two of us whoop in excitement. Impulsively, I will my magic to teleport the four of us to Lowell, focusing on his signature rather than his exact location.

We land in front of my mate, and I topple forward into his waiting arms as everyone behind me starts yelling about being reckless. Lowell just laughs and kisses me deeply, pride radiating through our bond and warming me from the inside out.

"My brilliant mate," he murmurs against my lips. "The world isn't ready for you." I shift slightly in Lowell's lap, feeling him harden beneath me.

But you are, Alpha, I send through our mental channel, and his eyes darken in a predatory way that has fire shooting straight to my core.

"Dude," Edina exclaims with a huff. "You get that I can smell arousal, right? Don't be gross."

Lowell and I laugh as I pull away, and Adriana fights to hide a smile. "Teleport us all outside, Katie," she says.

I take hold of everyone's hands and teleport the group out into the bright spring sunlight. Lowell scoops me in his arms when we land and spins me in circles until I'm dizzy and my head is light.

We spend the next few hours teleporting short distances, one hill to another. Adriana shows me how to let her set the intention of our teleportation by allowing her past my shields, and Edina allows me in so I can do the same.

"Okay," Adriana says. "Final test before we should rest and get ready for our missions tonight." The sun is starting to set, coloring the sky with its dying rays, and I know we'll have to get going once the vampires rise for the evening.

"Where to?" I ask.

"Marcus's country cottage." My eyes widen as I try to calculate that distance. Longer distances require more energy, and we'll need all the energy we can get for tonight. "You'll be fine," Adriana says, reading my thoughts. "One of you will teleport us down, and the other will bring us back. Who's starting us off?"

Edina and I exchange a glance, and I reach for everyone's hands. "I'll take us there."

"There are wards around the immediate house," Adriana instructs. "Visualize the street just outside."

The group circles around me, touching me in some way. I picture Marcus's perfect country cottage, the rough cobblestone walkway, and the daffodils that should be poking out of the fenced-in garden. The last time I was there was when Edina emerged and destroyed the guest room. When we left, I never thought I'd be back. One look at my best friend tells me she's thinking the same thing, and she grips my hand tightly as Lowell's arms wrap around my middle.

The Dark Magic wraps around us, and the squeezing starts. It lasts longer this time than in previous times, and I can almost feel us hurtling through space toward our destination. My feet touch down on the rough rock walkway a moment later, and my breath leaves my body.

"Holy shit." I stare at the home that provided me with countless Christmases and summers. It's completely engulfed in flames.

"What are the chances that's a natural fire?" Edina breathes.

"Slim to none," Astor replies. "Only one type of fire can break through this kind of shield. Not to mention burn stone." *Hellfire.*

There's a loud crack, and something inside gives way, sending a torrent of sparks out the front windows. Adriana shields us from the blow, but I still feel the heat as the embers catch the grass and flowers on the lawn before us.

"Is this a message for you or Marcus?" Lowell asks.

"Yes," I respond, staring at the smoldering house. My anger spikes. My own hellfire calls me in the darkest way, egged on by my Dark Magic. I suppress the intense desire for retribution. I can call on it later when we're attacking the prison.

"Why didn't I see this?" Adriana asks no one in particular, and her gray eyes cloud as she sifts through visions, looking for an explanation.

Edina lets loose a wild scream, and a torrent of ice magic explodes from her fingertips, extinguishing the fire with a deafening hiss. "My favorite sweater was in there," she seethes. She may joke, but I know she's as upset as I am about the loss of this place.

"We need to go," Lowell insists. Sending my Mind Magic out, I search for anyone who may be near but only find a few mortals in the house down the road. They mention checking on the commotion, and I know Lowell is right.

"Get us out of here," I instruct, and everyone places a hand on Edina. Her magic envelops us, wrapping our group in an icy embrace.

Just as we're about to disappear, there's a scream in the distance, and a speck that looks suspiciously like a man on a broom flies in the direction of London.

Chapter Ten

Lowell and I stand in the doorway of the war room, watching as all thirty people on the three missions awkwardly carve out an inch of free space for themselves. Adriana is rigid with protocol, so everyone is standing in small groups, waiting for their queen to sit first. Edina and Astor are talking with Lyra and her girlfriend, Alaina, whom I learned is also a Beta in Lowell's pack. A few other wolves are chatting with the witches who helped me escape from the palace, and my mom and Marcus are riveted by tales of centuries past from some of the vampires I met at the council meeting, including Vlad's brother, Aleksander.

The energy in the room buzzes with anticipation. Everyone seems excited and ready to land a blow on the opposition.

That used to be me.

I was rarely nervous before a mission and could always quiet my mind and retreat into my military calm. Tonight, there's a weight in my gut.

"What are you thinking?" Lowell asks, his hands falling to my waist as his chin rests on my head.

"I'm thinking..." I start slowly. "That this is only going to get harder. Sending everyone into danger."

Lowell hums and holds me tighter, kissing my scarred shoulder. "Crown feeling a little heavy?"

"That about sums it up."

"Game face on, *Ma Reine*," he says. "You've got this." I release a sigh before pulling out of his arms and clearing the doubt from my mind like cobwebs in an attic.

I walk in, and all conversation stops. "Sheesh, way to make a girl self-conscious," I tease. Most people in the room know me well enough to laugh, but there are some uneasy looks. I slide past the masses and take my seat at the head of the table. People who've been given a leadership role in this mission then take seats while everyone else hugs the wall.

"I know this was last minute, so let's go over the plan again before we leave. Vlad, keep an eye on the time?" He nods.

"Our goal is to cause chaos and disable the portal entrances," I continue. "The portal in the palace is thankfully disabled from the rescue mission, but that leaves two others that the Dragons are aware of open for transport.

"We'll attack three locations simultaneously. Hopefully, the disturbance in the Dragons' strongholds will keep the focus off the prison break."

"The Shanghai mission will be under my command," my mother says, her green eyes hard as she looks over the group that's gathered. "The O'Malley twins and I will head for their airfield and destroy as many brooms, planes, and other transport as we can while Sybil and Alaina lead the vampires and omegas to meet Sybil's contact bringing the bagged blood. They'll get as much as they can through the portal until it needs to be sealed by Astor."

"I'm leading the American mission," Lowell says, and I can tell he still isn't happy about being separated from me. It took a lot of arguing to convince him we needed to split our leaders, but it goes against his Alpha instincts to not protect his mate. "Our goal is to transport the Northeast sector of the American Werewolf Pack and any Dragon officers that Misty and Marcus have converted to our side."

"Our contacts in Salem are waiting for my go-ahead," Marcus adds. "Once we leave, they'll begin the disturbance to give people a chance to get to the portal. Those who can't get to us in time have an evacuation plan. After Edina seals the Salem portal, she and I will travel to the backup portal in Boston and wait until everyone arrives before closing that as well."

"No vampires are on the American mission, correct?" I confirm. We couldn't make sure it was dark in all time zones, so the vampires are sticking to Shanghai and the prison missions.

"Correct," Aleksander, Vlad's brother, confirms, pushing his hand through his shoulder-length blonde hair. "The vampires in America have been in touch with any witches and wolves too far from Salem to tell them the location of the closest portal."

When Vlad told me exactly how many portals were hidden in the Americas, I spit out my water. There are enough that all our allies coming from the Western Hemisphere could come via portal without raising the suspicions of the Dragons, so our American mission is now mostly about transporting the soldiers we've flipped and the packs in New England.

"We should go in five, baby queen," Vlad says.

"Queen Kathryn," Adriana hisses.

"Once Astor and I are done with the other portals," Edina cuts off their bickering, "we'll head straight to the prison to help Vlad and Queen Kathryn with prisoner transport and sealing up that portal."

"She gets a title, and I just get Vlad?"

"You don't hear me bitching about not getting titled."

"Is that an invitation to call you princess? Because the other night—"

"And that right there is why you don't get titled," I tease, and the vampires all go on alert until Vlad laughs.

"I'm leading the prison break," I say, and rush through the details as fast as I can. "Does anyone have any questions?"

"Just one," Sybil says, and I fight the urge to roll my eyes. I'm still a little salty that she attacked me the first time we met. Her dark eyes narrow, drawing further attention to her pinched features. "What are the orders regarding the opposition?"

"Meaning?"

"She means do we kill, capture, or are we just blocking attacks?" Soto asks softly, and Sybil nods. I swipe my hand down my face and sigh.

"These people will still be under our rule should we win this war. I don't want to start by killing off a bunch of their friends." I look to Lowell, and he nods in agreement. "No unnecessary violence, but I want to see each one of you back here at the end of this mission. Do what you have to defend yourselves."

Everyone nods solemnly, and I check the international clocks. It's just passed three a.m. in Shanghai, which means we need to get a move on if they're going to get back before sunrise. I stand, and everyone follows suit.

"All right," I say, smiling confidently. "Be safe out there."

The Shanghai mission is leaving first since they're the tightest on time. There are a few quick goodbyes. Astor hugs Edina, Lyra and Alaina share an extremely sloppy kiss, and my mom pecks Marcus and gives me a soft smile from across the room before disappearing into the swirling mist.

"Little witch." Lowell tugs my hand and pulls me off to the side. He leans down and rests his forehead against mine.

"I love you," I whisper as we link our fingers together.

"What happened to *no goodbyes?*" he asks with a smirk.

"Fuck that. Every time I said that one or both of us almost died."

Lowell laughs and pulls me into a real embrace. "In that case," he nuzzles my hair, "I love you more than anything else on this earth, *Ma Reine.*" I tilt my head and kiss him, pouring all my emotion into our kiss.

"Come home to me," I murmur, pulling apart and staring into my mate's eyes. We take a simultaneous inhale, and when we release it, I feel his strength fortifying me, seeping into my bones. "Thank you for trusting me to take care of myself."

"Always," he responds before stealing another quick kiss. Before I can say another word, he zips into the portal and is enveloped in mist. Edina mouths *I've got him* before she and Marcus follow my mate to their mission.

Adriana meanders closer to me, and I grab her hand. "You've been quiet about this plan," I murmur. "Should I be worried?"

"It's not that," she says, her gray eyes clouding. "I think the magic suppressant makes things harder for me to see. It was like that the first time we broke into the prison too. But the plan is solid. We just need to trust it."

"Did Seth use magic suppressant to hide his plans to break the fealty vow?" I ask. My father somehow hid his entire plan to kill the king from Adriana. Which is what accelerated our timeline and ultimately landed me in that dungeon.

"None of his cronies would tell me," she says. "But I think so."

"And what do you see about the other missions?" I prod. Adriana worries her bottom lip.

"If I say, it'll go differently."

"Fuck, that's annoying," Lyra complains.

"Lyra," I bark as Adriana hangs her head.

"Not you, Adriana. Just the fact that saying something aloud could literally jinx us."

"It's not a jinx—"

"We really need to go," Vlad presses, ending our conversation. Adriana gives me a weak smile and tugs me forward. Vlad and Lyra go in first, followed by Jefferson, Soto, and the rest of the vampires. When they're all gone, I say a prayer to whoever could be listening, and Adriana and I step into the portal.

THE PORTAL LETS US out in a condemned house in a port town. When something so close to the prison was abandoned, Vlad swooped in and hid it from mortal eyes with the help of some witches, but he hasn't put any effort into fixing the place up. The only functional room is the living room, with its peeling seashell wallpaper and cracked white windowsills. Remnants of furniture lie in a heap in one corner, and cabinets hang off hinges in the destroyed kitchen nook. The entire back half of the house is caved in. The only thing that looks cared for is the closet door, which serves as the portal entrance.

I cross to the grime-encrusted windows and look out over the quaint town. It's suspiciously quiet, considering it's one of the first mild days we've had in Scotland. I hold a hand out, motioning for everyone to wait as I send my Mind Magic into the town, sweeping the rows of little white houses in search of life. All I encounter are mortal minds going about their evening routines. No sign of any foul play.

I've only been to the prison once before, and we flew on brooms directly to the gate. I don't think I registered the severity of the island that houses the Kingdom's most notorious villains the way I do now, staring at it across just a few miles of ocean. The island has no beach and no place for a boat to dock. It's a solid wall of rock that extends from the gray water straight into the clouds at a ninety-degree angle. The rocks are carved so that not even experienced climbers would dare scale the beast. And then there are the wards, which make even looking at the island for too long difficult. The place is ominous and perfectly hidden in plain sight.

"Are we breaking the wards?" Vlad asks, and I shake my head. Breaking the wards completely would draw too much attention. Instead, Adriana will carve a hole large enough for us to fit through, and we'll enter that way. "You'll need to get back through the wards before teleporting."

"We'll be able to teleport on the island itself," Adriana sneers. "But not past the barrier, which is why the vampires will be waiting for us to help transport prisoners across the water."

"Why can't we teleport past the wards if a section is open?" Lyra asks.

"It's too risky," Adriana says. "If we're a fraction of an inch off with our intention, we could get hurt. We'll teleport everyone to the island's edge and fly through before teleporting back here."

She nods, appeased. I'm defecting to Adriana on this plan. She's the only person to successfully break into this prison and live to tell the tale. Twice, apparently.

"Get in position," I instruct. Jefferson, Soto, Lyra, and I all find a way to hold onto Adriana. "Alek, you said you have a way out there?"

"We'll have a boat at the base of the island."

"That's your plan?" Lyra demands. "They'll see a boat approaching, you moron."

"Maybe if we were as slow as wolves, they would," Alek smirks, flashing his fangs. Lyra growls.

"Enough," I snap, and they both backdown. "Alek, if you're seen, we're all dead. You get that, right?"

"I have a thousand years of practice being invisible, Your Majesty," he vows with sudden seriousness. "We won't be seen."

"Vlad," I say, and he steps forward. "You're up. Do you need one of us to teleport—"

"Don't worry about me, baby queen." He salutes before bolting out of the door, leaving me gaping out the window after him. When he gets to the water, I expect him to stop. But he keeps running, his feet moving so quickly it looks like he's gliding along the water's surface.

"Fucking vampires," I swear, and the Magical Creatures all chuckle. "Let's do this, Adriana." She nods quickly, and the familiar sensation of teleporting takes over as we disappear in a puff of smoke.

We reappear in freefall, and my stomach drifts into my throat and steals my voice so I can't scream. As I'm about to flail, my feet touch down on a gray cloud of Adriana's magic. Our group steadies each other as she slowly floats us closer to the island and the wards.

"You need to teach me this one," I tell her, and she agrees as I put a cloaking spell around us, making us invisible, inaudible, and masking our scent.

Immense power radiates off the shield surrounding the island. It feels like witches have added layers and layers of protection for centuries. We stop our approach, and I wait for something to happen, but nothing does.

Katie, I don't think I can break through these, Adriana says, sounding panicked even in my mental channel. *They've added a lot of magic since the last time...*

Tell me what to do.

Imagine your magic like a machete. It needs to be precise and go all the way through. And don't touch the barrier, or it will give away our position.

I call forth my Dark Magic, wrangling it into a thin, long blade as Adriana guides me to stand beside her. As soon as my magic connects with the shield, it becomes visible to me. I send the mental picture of the little chunk of shimmering magic trying to hold on against my onslaught.

My jaw tics as I finally pierce the outer shell. My magic slides through layers and layers and layers of magic, so many that I lose track. Each layer puts up a fight, trying to force me out. Finally, the resistance stops, and I release a sigh of relief.

I drag my magic machete into a square large enough for Jefferson, the tallest of our group. As soon as I'm done, Adriana's magic sweeps in, and together, we peel back the shield like a curtain opening across a stage.

Adriana guides us through the shield with her magic and continues to transport us until we touch down on soft green grass. I take a moment to mentally confirm our location with the remaining vampires before looking across the large lawn to the prison.

The structure is made of the same stone that forms the cliffside, and I imagine it looks like part of the island in the distance. Up close, it's a fortress. A wall surrounding the building is thick enough that the centaur sentinels can comfortably stand in any direction. Their hooves click loud enough for me to hear them even at this distance, and their bows are drawn tight, their strong arms not wavering even once.

The centaur closest to us stops, ears twitching. He slowly pivots to our location and stares, his brown eyes, which match his flank boring into our party. We hold extremely still, but so does the centaur.

Can he see through the illusion? Soto asks.

I don't think— A shout has everyone, including the centaur, turning towards the front gate. He abandons his post, cantering along the wall toward the disturbance.

Let's move, Adriana says and starts tugging us in the same direction.

Why are we going toward Vlad? Jefferson asks.

We're going in through the main gate.

Chapter Eleven

WHAT DO YOU MEAN? I hiss, my hand gripping Adriana's shoulder to keep her from moving forward. *You said you had a way in.*

I do, she responds. *The main gate.*

I pinch the bridge of my nose, making sure I send my exhale of frustration through our channel. This is my damn fault for delegating such a large part of the mission.

How are we getting prisoners through the main gates? I ask, my anger unhidden.

Soto and Jefferson are turning off the magical suppression, Adriana reminds me. *That part of the plan is the same. We'll still be able to teleport everyone to the edge of the island.*

Fine, let's move.

Blindly, we grope around until everyone has one hand on one person's shoulder like some kind of twisted, invisible conga line. We move as fast as we can across the open stretch of the lawn, making sure our steps are light so we don't leave divots in the grass.

I send my Mind Magic out in a golden web, but the magical suppressants around the building don't let me feel anyone other than the handful of centaur guards in front. Luckily, they haven't updated their inner security since Adriana's break-in six months ago.

We reach the wall and slink along in the shadows. Adriana stops abruptly, causing Lyra to bump into me and grumble in our channel about being invisible.

"You should reconsider," Vlad's voice carries to us, and we inch forward at a snail's pace.

"Why would we help you?" a deep voice booms as we round the corner. As I suspected, the gate is locked, with a line of centaurs in front of it.

How the hell are we getting in there? I ask Adriana through our private channel. The witches with us don't need to hear my doubts.

Vlad's distraction. Trust me.

Vlad looks bored. Like he knew this part of the mission was a waste of time. The centaur he's speaking to, on the other hand, looks like he's thirty seconds from charging and knocking Vlad off the cliffside.

"Oh, you know," Vlad says, tugging on his suit jacket, "Magical Creature loyalty and all that."

Ready? Vlad asks, and we confirm. I feel everyone brace for the sprint we'll need to take to get inside the prison.

The centaur scoffs and opens his mouth when there's an earth-shattering *boom.*

Move now, I order, and we all start at a run. Lyra breaks off from the group to scout ahead, and Jefferson's hand replaces hers on my shoulder as we sprint toward the gate.

Are they closing the gates? I send to Lyra and Vlad, unable to see through the smoke bomb Vlad detonated.

They won't be able to, Vlad's mind floats through mine with a hint of amusement.

He blew up the fucking gate, Lyra responds, her voice laced with equal parts fear, respect, and delight.

Never underestimate the power of a grenade, baby queen.

You said you were using a smoke bomb! I yell.

I changed my mind.

Grenades were not a part of the plan. The plan was to sneak in unnoticed, not flash a giant glittery sign saying *we're breaking into the prison*. Now they'll expect intruders, which makes our job that much harder.

I'm about to tear Vlad a new one for going off-script when Lyra calls for us to wait. Centaurs pour out of the gate in droves, charging for the spot where Vlad was just standing. They keep coming, herds and herds of them. We would have been trampled if we were in front of the gates.

Will they find the hole in the wards? I ask, but as I do, another explosion rocks the island opposite from where we entered.

Not now, they won't, Vlad responds as the centaurs stampede in the direction of the newest bomb.

All clear, Lyra says, and we finish our sprint along the wall and walk through the destroyed iron gates. We continue past the abandoned prison yard, basically just a patch of dirt between the building and the wall, right to the front door.

Adriana steps through first and becomes visible. We worked through a couple of strategies for this part of the plan, and we agreed it'd be faster to send Soto and Jefferson to disable the magical suppressant than to try and break it from the outside. This is the part where we need to be fast.

Lyra shifts before she crosses the threshold and lifts both Jefferson and Soto, who make horrified expressions as they're plastered to her naked body. She takes off in a flash of speed and a yelp from Jefferson as they head for the control rooms. Once Lyra delivers them, she'll run back and wait for the suppression to be lifted to free some of the Magical Creatures.

Adriana and I run in the opposite direction, finding the stairwell and charging up. The top levels are all the "lesser" criminals, people locked up for political crimes and illegal use of Dark or Light Magic, so that's where we'll start.

The fortress reminds me a lot of the Dragons' headquarters, all thick somber stones and dim lighting. There are no windows even though we're above ground, and I know all too well how disorienting that must be for the prisoners. We continue winding up the spiral staircase until Adriana finally stops in front of me and pushes a door open.

We proceed slowly into a corridor that's filled with cells. "Huh," Adriana muses. "I would have thought after my last break-in that they'd up security on the individual floors." She flashes me a smile that promises they'll regret that decision, and I can't help but agree.

"Keep their cuffs on," she reminds me. We decided transporting people would be easier if they weren't trying to fight us along the way. "You're freeing this entire floor. I'll be right below you. When you're done, meet me two floors below this one."

Adriana leaves, her footsteps echoing in the staircase as I turn to the rows of cells. I walk tentatively down the aisle, peering at the people inside. Everyone looks defeated, broken. Not only are they filthy and thin, but they've lost their spirit. Most of them are older than my mother, and I can't imagine how long they've been here.

I clear my throat, and several faces tilt up to look at me, but most stare blankly at the walls or the ceiling of their cells. "My name is Kathryn Carmichael," I announce to whoever is listening. "I am Queen of the Dark Magic Covens, and I'm here to break you out today."

Silence. I swallow hard and try again. "In a moment, the magic suppressant will be turned off, and I'll open your cell doors. I need you all to follow me down two flights of stairs so we can teleport you past the wards."

There's a scoff from the darkness. "Why should we believe you?" a man asks. I follow the voice, which is rough from disuse, until I find the speaker. A tall man with long white hair that hangs limply to his waist stands at the cell doors. His blue eyes pierce through the darkness, full of malice. "Do you remember me, Kathryn?"

I stare back at the man, searching for some sign of recognition. "I was friends with your father," he continues. "Lived next door to you in Salem."

I nod, connecting the dots. He was always a kind man; Adriana and I played with his daughters. "Want to know why I'm here?" he asks, amusement lacing his words but not reaching his eyes. "After your father was arrested, the Dragons rounded up anyone with Dark Magic within a five-mile radius of your house and jailed us. Never used my raw magic, but they didn't care. Thank goodness the girls were Elemental Witches like their mom.

"We get a little news here," he continues. "But we heard you followed in your mom's footsteps and became one of them."

"I'm not anymore," I say simply. "And I'm sorry you were arrested. That's not right and one of the things I plan to correct."

"As queen," he sneers. "Why shouldn't I just rat you out? Call the guards? Get time taken off my sentence."

"Because they won't take time off your sentence," I respond. "But if you come with me, we can provide sanctuary. Or help you hide until we win the war."

"You're going to war?" an older woman behind me asks. Even at her age, I can see her formidable strength.

"Against the Elemental Witches," I respond. "Well, against the current monarchy. My goal is to make the Kingdom safe for all forms of magic. To restore the balance that was upset during the Four Kings War."

The hum of the magical suppressant ceases. I breathe a sigh of relief as my magic wakes up, jumping in my stomach like it's excited to get to work.

"Aren't you gonna open the bars?" the woman calls from the end of the row.

"Step back," I say, flashing her a smile. I call my lightning to my hands, letting it skitter across my skin and some of the murmurs of excitement reach my ears. Once I'm satisfied everyone is at a safe distance, I release a bolt from each hand. It blasts the lock of the first two doors, and they spring open. I continue to do this down the line until every cell is unlocked.

"Follow me," I call to the prisoners. Most tentatively look around before slowly exiting their cells, but a few are obstinate and stay put. "Come on now. I can't leave you here."

"Well, I'm not going with some half-assed plan created by a fake queen," my old neighbor says.

"Katie, what the hell is taking so long?" Adriana appears at the entryway with a scowl on her face.

"They don't want to come," I tell her, and she rolls her eyes. The scent of Dark Magic permeates the air and everyone, even our neighbor, falls into a straight line.

"There," Adriana says, satisfied, and starts to walk back down the stairs, the inmates following her like ducklings following their mother.

"Adriana," I scold, falling in step next to her. "We don't Mind Control our allies."

"My Katie," she sighs heavily. "At some point, you started to see us as the heroes. But we broke into a Kingdom prison, and our friends are attacking military bases. We're not the good guys."

"We're not bad," I protest. "We're...rebels."

"So, what's one more little rebellion?" She winks.

"I'm genuinely concerned that you don't see the difference between using Mind Control on innocent people and fighting for a better future."

She shrugs. "We have two more floors to hit. Open the cells, and I'll get them to the floor where we're meeting Lyra."

"Every cell on these floors?" I ask as we approach the third floor down. Adriana nods, and I walk in without a word and blast open all the cell doors before heading down another level. They all follow without complaint, puppets on Adriana's strings.

We hit two more floors with more hardened criminals. We get the non-threatening ones, people that were falsely imprisoned, and head back to the ground floor. The crowd behind us is massive, so I use a cloaking spell to turn them invisible and silence their steps in the echoing stairwell.

I extend the web of my Mind Magic, the golden light trickling over every mind, ensuring they're not fighting the Mind Control and that they're still with us.

When we reach the bottom level, Lyra is in her wolf form, growling at a few vampires. Their fangs are extended fully, and they look at the cloaked group behind us like it's their buffet.

Adriana fixes them with a glare and ensnares them in her Mind Magic. They go slack, their mouths hang open, and their fangs return to their usual points. "Lyra, go to Alek. I'll make them run alongside you."

Lyra nods her large wolfish head before taking off in a sprint. Every Magical Creature follows her at the same pace, leaving me dizzy as they flee the prison. I toss a cloaking spell at them just as they pass the doors.

Katie, Soto's voice echoes down the channel. *You've got company. We saw centaurs coming your way as we were on our way out of the gate. Do you want us to double back?*

No, I insist. *Go, get out of here. We'll be okay.* The Elemental Witches can't teleport, so there's no reason to have them here for this next part.

I turn to Adriana and grab her extended hand as I remove the cloaking spell from the first ten or so prisoners. "Can you take this many?" I ask, and she nods. She calls them forward since they're all still under her thrall, and she disappears in a puff of gray smoke.

Any word from Edina and Astor? I ask the group and am met with negative responses. In retrospect, we really should have just teleported everyone from their cells, but we figured the closer we could walk them to the gate, the easier it would be on our magic stores. Teleporting this many people to the barrier will take a lot of magic.

Adriana reappears, and I uncover the next group while she erects a shield to ward against the impending centaurs. Once ten witches are around me, I focus on the edge of the barrier, pouring all my energy into that spot as my Dark Magic swirls around us and squeezes. When I open my eyes, Alek and some of his other vampires are there.

"Quickly," he instructs, and the three vampires each grab a few witches, taking off at top speed towards the cottage, running across the water just like Vlad did. We need more people for this to work. *Where the hell are Edina and Astor?*

I teleport back into the fortress, using Adriana's magical signature to call me back. I appear in front of her, and she takes off immediately, just as the sound of hooves clicking against stone reaches my ears.

"I'm not walking up those stairs," one of the centaurs gripes, and I hold my breath in anticipation as they close in.

"Rosamund is letting the power go to his head," another says. "But we still have to go."

"Then he should drag his fat-ass up the stairs," the first centaur says. I look around frantically for a place we can hide, but we're blocking the stairs. They won't see us, but they'll run straight into us if they turn the corner.

Adriana pops back into view, and I grab her arm, yanking her behind the shield. *What do we do?*

I need you to teleport them all, she says. *I can hold them off with Mind Control, but Magical Creatures are harder to control than witches. I won't be able to do both.*

I don't know if I can teleport that many, I admit.

You can, she insists. *Half at a time. As soon as you give me the all-clear, I'll teleport to you, and they'll be none the wiser.*

It's harder to gather all the witches underneath the cloaking spell. I'm not sure how to do this, but I know they must be touching me. I wait until I feel hands on every inch of my body, and when there's no available skin left, I teleport to the edge of the island and drop our spells.

"Holy shit," Alek swears as he sees the new group.

"Centaurs found us," I tell him. "Adriana is holding them, but hurry with this group."

"What can I do?" Lyra asks, back in her human form and completely naked.

"Get out of here," I tell her. "Your brother will kill me if anything happens to you."

She opens her mouth like she's about to protest, but I make myself invisible before teleporting to Adriana and heading into the fortress again. I land, and Adriana is visible, fighting with magic against the centaurs, who have broken past her mental assault.

Get the rest out, she says, sensing my presence. I want to protest, but Adriana's magic explodes out of her in a show of power I haven't seen. Gray strands wrap around each of the centaurs' legs, tripping them up and keeping them immobile. They roar in defiance as she batters them with magic that somehow isn't killing them or making them pass out.

I run to the group still waiting, and invade their Minds, forcing them to move closer to me. Adriana releases them, and I practically feel her sigh of relief at not having to divide her magic.

More power streams from her fingertips in sharp blasts, finally cutting into the flanks of the Magical Creatures

As soon as all the prisoners have a hand on me, I teleport us to the opening in the wards. Centaurs are everywhere, and sirens are blaring. They must know there's been a break-in, and now they're swarming, looking for the source of the leak.

Alek and his vampires are back, and I remove the cloaking around us so they can gather the last of the prisoners, including my old neighbor. As soon as the three vampires have everyone loaded into their arms in a show of their magical strength, I cast a cloaking spell after them.

"Straight to the portal," I command, receiving mental confirmation that they heard me.

Katie, where are you? a voice I don't have time to identify echoes in my mind. I teleport directly to Adriana, who is backed against a corner, her magic looking much weaker than it was moments ago.

"Katie, go," she insists. But I grab her hand just as two centaurs knock arrows into their bows. I close my eyes as my magic envelops us, and we disappear just as an arrow grazes the tip of my ear.

We land at the edge of the island, and Adriana falters. I wrap my arm around her, stepping to the edge of the island and looking at the sheer drop of pure rock that ends in jagged boulders that break the surf.

"Can I teleport to the shack from here?" I ask. If we're close to the edge, maybe—

"No." Adriana is panting. She summons a weak-looking magical cloud, and we fly off the island's edge. Straight into a magical shield. Adriana barely gets us back to land before her magic sputters and disappears. She's running on empty. "They must have put up another layer."

I send my magic out, and it connects with a thin ward. "How?" I demand. That's when I hear it. In addition to hooves, footsteps are pounding on the island. "Dragon officers?" Adriana nods.

"The centaurs who attacked us said a few were on staff since I broke in the last time."

"What do I do?" Her eyes close. I swear and shake her, but even when her eyes open again, they're glassy. "Okay, we'll just shred the ward and get out of here. Stay with me."

My hands are shaking as I cast the Dark Magic against the ward. It's thick, not as thick as it was the first time, but too thick to do this quickly. "How did the vampires get through the wards and we can't?" I ask, slashing at the ward in sharp jabs instead of elegant lines.

The sound of hooves gets closer and closer. In every direction I turn, there's a new clump of centaurs charging toward us, weapons bared.

"We're out of time," Adriana whimpers.

"Fuck no, we're not," I growl. *The vampires got through the wards. They took the prisoners out.* There must be some type of loophole in the shielding spell that allows Magical Creatures to transport people off the island.

"Freeze! Stay right where you are." The centaurs are twenty feet away. I can smell the smoke from the Fire Magic in the hands of the Dragons officers.

VLAD, I call down our mental channel. *I hope you're close otherwise this is gonna hurt like a bitch.*

I take a running leap toward the edge of the cliff, pushing off as hard as I can, and we start plummeting.

I start to flail, dropping like a freaking stone toward the churning ocean below. Jagged rocks reach for us, and I cast a cushioning spell, hoping at least this magic can be used in the thick of the wards. The spray of water kisses my face and the smell of the salt invades my senses. I try to turn mid-air so I'll take the brunt of the fall and, hopefully, Adriana will survive.

Strong arms grab me, and all of a sudden, we're falling sideways, zipping horizontally over the water at a speed I can't even register. I look up and see Vlad's stern face focused solely on my sister. He's whispering something in her ear that I can't hear, and when his blue eyes connect to mine, he scowls.

"Anytime you want to teleport us out of here would be fucking great," he hisses, and I realize we've breached the wards. I teleport us back to the front stoop of the cottage and without missing a step, Vlad runs us into the swirling mist of the portal. The angry screams of centaurs follow behind us as the door slams shut.

Chapter Twelve

WE LAND ROUGHLY IN the war room, which has been turned into a triage center. Coleman and his team of healers rush around checking on several patients and ordering less severe injuries into the hallway, where more healers wait to patch them up with Light Magic or administer tonics.

I disentangle myself from the weird hold Vlad has on me and Adriana, but he's not paying attention to me. He rushes over to a cot, grabs the hair of the vampire lying on it, and throws him into a wheelchair. "Check her," he orders no one in particular, gently laying Adriana on the vacated bed.

"Vlad," I scream and check on the discarded vampire, who insists he's fine. Alek appears, handing the vampire a blood pouch, and steers the wheelchair out of the line of fire.

Vlad paces back and forth, his eyes murderous. "She's fine," I assure him. "She's just drained." I try to stop his pacing, but he hisses at me, his fangs extended.

"You don't know she's fine," he snarls, getting so close that I need to crane my neck up to see him. "She's unconscious. There's blood."

"The blood is mine." I gesture to my ear, which is wet, sticky, and still bleeding. "She used a ton of magic. She was holding off centaurs and teleporting and using Mind Control—"

He ignores me as a healer approaches to look her over. Vlad snaps his hand out and grabs her by the throat. "I want Coleman, not some half-rate—"

"Enough!" My magic rises to my skin. He turns back his attention to me, a feral look on his face. "You need to take a step outside right now."

"I'm not going anywhere," he growls but releases the witch, who runs off.

"Yes, you are," I say, my voice laced with power. "I won't have you terrorizing my healers and the other witches who need help. You need to take a breath and get your shit together."

Vlad moves to come at me, but I've wrapped him in my lightning. He looks down in surprise when it holds him tight, and when his eyes meet mine again, some of the darkness has faded.

"Katie." His voice breaks, chest heaving. A vein in his neck pulses as he tries to look back at Adriana, but I snake the magic up to his chin, keeping his attention on mine. The fear I see in his eyes is so raw it slices through me.

"I know," I soften. "I promise I'll stay with her until Coleman can check her out." He huffs but nods. "Thank you. Now I need your help organizing this mess."

I slowly release him from the magical binds, and he looks past me like he's seeing the scene for the first time in the war room for the first time.

"SYBIL," Vlad bellows, and in the blink of an eye, the vampire is in front of us, looking worse for wear. Her usual impeccable blonde bun is loose, with tendrils of hair escaping. Her clothes are askew, and she's much paler than usual. Vlad ignores it. "I need your help getting the new arrivals into rooms."

"Adriana left me a copy of her intake form in case things went badly on your mission," she says, her dark eyes darting to my sister's unconscious form. "We've started but with the influx of the prisoners—"

"Send the prisoners to the throne room for now," Vlad instructs. "Tell me you got blood." Sybil starts telling him about the Shanghai mission as they head down the hallway to continue organizing the new coven members.

As soon as they're gone, I call Coleman. He runs over and immediately starts assessing Adriana.

"How bad is it?" I ask. "Keep in mind, I just told an overprotective vampire she's fine, and I have no doubt he'll kill us all if something happens to her."

"When did she lose consciousness?" Coleman asks.

"I think on our way back. I was—" I don't want to say hurtling towards my death, but also...

Coleman keeps working, brow furrowed, but then nods. "She's fine. She just needs to recharge. Can I get a restorative tonic here?" Coleman calls, and a female healer approaches with the vial. Coleman carefully lifts Adriana's head. She stirs, and he whispers until she opens her mouth, swallowing down the tonic.

The female healer comes over to me, white light in her hands.

"I'm fine," I assure her, batting her hand away. "It's just a scratch."

"You're bleeding," she says.

"Let her heal your ear," Coleman says.

"I'm—"

"Kathryn, what were you hit with?" He raises his voice in a way I've only seen him do with his granddaughter. "Because you know centaur arrows affect clotting. Let Ashley fix your damn ear."

I give him an amused arch of my eyebrow and nod to the witch, who starts running her Light Magic over the scrape from the arrow.

It takes her a surprising amount of time to get my skin to stitch back together. While she works, I survey the room filled with people from the prison. Vampires administer tonics while healers run white light over the more severe injuries, but overall, everyone seems okay. There's nothing life-threatening, which is more than I could have asked for.

When I'm finally healed, I walk into the hall, where two Water Elementals have created a shower area in an alcove in the rock. One witch helps with shaving and cutting hair for those who want it, while another checks for lice and other bugs. When I asked, they said Adriana gave them these orders before we left. The girl thinks of everything.

I keep searching for someone to update me when I see two familiar mops of red hair.

"O'Malley," I call, and they both turn immediately and dip into a hasty bow which I wave off. "My mom?"

"She's in the mess hall, organizing the blood issue," Jared says. "Sybil was being very particular about who handled it. She said if the vampires have unfettered access, they'll drink it all."

"Thank you. Is the American mission back yet?"

"Not yet." I nod my thanks and head down the halls in search of my mom.

The mess hall is relatively empty, only occupied by several small clusters of witches gathered at the cafeteria-style tables. The cavern is as large, if not larger than the throne room, but the lower ceiling and the sheer amount of seating make it feel cramped. I don't come down here often. The few times I have, everyone either scattered to let me have privacy or wanted to talk so much that I couldn't eat.

I walk straight to the back, slipping between the rows of tables and into the opening in the rock that leads to the kitchen.

"Sort them by type," my mother barks. "And do not let them spill. The last thing we need is blood in the chicken marinade."

The kitchen is the only place in the coven with electricity, courtesy of a generator that Adriana stole along with enough gas to run it for a century. It's impeccably clean. The large stainless steel prep tables that occupy the center of the space gleam under the fluorescent lights, and even the rock floors have a subtle shine from the countless scrubbings they've received. The back wall is lined with grills and fryers, and professional-grade ovens and stovetops are along the right wall.

My mother is to the left, standing in the doorway of the giant walk-in refrigerator. Her ponytail is undisturbed, not a hair out of place, as she orders around some witches in their black robes. The only sign that anything is amiss is the tension in her shoulders. As far as she knows, Marcus and I aren't back yet.

"Mom," I call, and she whirls around, her emerald-green eyes latching to mine. She breathes a sigh of relief and rushes over to hug me. I balk at the outright show of affection but return the embrace.

"How did it go?" she asks as she pulls away. Her eyes skate over the blood on my shirt, but I wave her off. "Where's Adriana?"

"Adriana is drained, but Coleman said she'll be fine," I tell her, and her brow furrows. "Did you know the Dragons are stationed at the prison?"

"What?"

"Yeah," I breathe. "Looked like one battalion, but it was hard to tell. They found our hole in their wards and patched it. It made escaping...problematic."

"They must have added them recently. Unless—"

"Unless?"

"Unless I was left out of that decision for a reason." My lips part on inhale. My mother and Marcus were two of the highest-ranking officers in the Dragons. If information was hidden from them, then someone suspected foul play.

My mom shakes her head as if banishing the very thought. "It's probably nothing, but I'll see what we can find out. Did you get everyone out?"

I nod, taking her cue to drop the subject. Even if the Dragons suspected their treachery, my parents are safe now, they're with us. "How did it go for you?" I ask.

"Extremely well," she says with a smile. "Jared and Justin lit up the airfield and all of their RVs, and Sybil got a large portion of blood through the portal before we had to seal it. We should be okay until she can risk leaving to get more."

"Good," I say. "Any idea where Astor is?"

"He just passed us," a gruff baritone voice behind me says, and my body crumples. Without looking, I turn and fling myself into Lowell's arms, letting the mating bond guide me. He snatches me out of the air and buries his head in the crook of my neck. "Hey, little witch."

"Hi, pup." We sigh in tandem before I pick my head up and kiss him. He scowls at the blood crusted on my shirt and trickling down my scarred skin.

"What happened?" he growls. I try to kiss him again to calm him down, but he sets me on my feet and levels me with a stern stare.

"Arrow to the ear," I say, flashing a smile. "It's already been cleared by medical."

Lowell's eyes narrow but must be appeased because he says, "Astor was going to close the portal entrance by the prison."

"Good. Now, what happened? Why were you so late getting back?"

"There was a leak," Lowell says, and my mom's eyes widen. "They knew we were coming and attacked our allies stationed by the portal. We lost... a lot. Not the people we brought with us but the soldiers on the ground. The wolves needed to reroute to the Boston portal, which took time."

"Where's Marcus?" I ask for my mom. I know she's panicking but won't show weakness in asking.

"With a friend of his," he says to my mom. "The American general you were able to flip. He was the one who discovered the leak and handled it, but not before he was struck with an arrow."

"Earth Magic or centaur?" I ask.

"Earth Magic. He'll be fine, just needs to be patched up."

"How many of the Dragons did we get out?"

"They're tallying them now. Marcus thinks it's two-thirds of the force we expected. Edina is waiting at the portal for any stragglers.

Said she'd give it another fifteen minutes from when I left...so she should be back—"

"Now," my best friend says, floating into the kitchen before retracting her wings. "Can we take this debrief to a table? I'm allergic to anything that resembles cooking."

"Same," I laugh, and we grab the table closest to the kitchen so my mom can keep an eye on things. Lowell zips off and returns with coffee for everyone before sitting beside me.

"I ran into Vlad on my way down here, and he was shitting a brick," Edina says. "I think the recruits are terrified of him."

"He's being dramatic," I say and repeat the update on Adriana.

"He's not dramatic," Lowell says, wrapping his arm low around my waist. "He's just an idiot who won't admit he's in love with your sister."

"Facts," Edina says with a smirk. "You remember what Lo-Lo was like when you were hurt, babes—"

"Lo-Lo?" Lowell asks, and I dissolve into a fit of hysterical laughter.

"Please only call him that from now on," I get out between breaths.

"Traitor," Lowell chuckles and nips my non-injured ear. My mother shakes her head, but even she can't hide the lift in the corner of her mouth.

After the laughter subsides, fatigue replaces it. "I need to speak with all the prisoners and see if they want to join us."

"I thought that was a condition of us rescuing them," Edina says.

"No," I insist, downing the rest of the coffee. "You didn't see it in there, E. It made my cell look like a suite in a five-star resort. I'm not keeping them as prisoners after everything they dealt with. If they don't want to stay, we'll portal them as close as we can to their homes and alter the memories, so they think they escaped on their own."

"I think most will want to help," my mother says. "I'll come with you when you speak to them."

"They didn't trust me and I was only a captain. They're not going to want to speak to a former general." My mom purses her lips but nods. "Can you and Edina help Vlad and Sybil get everyone set up in rooms?" I ask. "There's a communal space Adriana was saving for overflow. If we don't have time tonight, get them set up there."

We all stand, getting ready to go our separate ways. But as soon as Edina and my mom leave the mess hall, I grab Lowell's hand tugging him into me. "Next time we stay together," I insist. I don't like that my mate was in such grave danger and I wasn't there to keep him safe. Just the thought of him in an active battle without me has my heart pounding in my ears.

"You worried about me, little witch?" he asks, wrapping his arms around me. I inhale his earth and rain scent and relax in his hold.

"You know better than to ask that." I smile, and Lowell kisses the top of my head.

"One condition," he murmurs, and I pull back to look into his eyes. "No cliff diving."

I grimace. "Heard about that, did you?"

"Yep." He fixes me with a hard stare. "No unnecessary risks."

"Yes, Alpha," I add a little extra purr to my voice to soften him up and am met with a blast of arousal down our mating bond.

"You're cruel," he whispers and kisses me longer than before, full of so much promise it has me aching.

"Come on," I sigh, pulling away, but keeping our fingers laced together. "I want to wash the blood off before we talk to the prisoners."

Chapter Thirteen

The prisoners unanimously agree to work with us to topple the monarchy. Unfortunately, many of them are too old to fight or their Battle Magic is just too weak. Even so, they're excited to help, offering to run surveillance or even just cook and clean. Most Light Magic users are experienced in healing, and Coleman has already arranged refresher courses. If last night taught me anything, it's that we don't have nearly enough healers.

My old neighbor asked if we could send for the prisoners' families, assuring us that they would want to help. Lowell's eldest sister, Luna, and her mate Cyril overheard his request and jumped right in, taking names, cities, old phone numbers... any way the prisoners could think to contact them. They'll start the search tomorrow.

Between talking to the prisoners and getting everyone set up in rooms, Lowell and I finally return to our room around dawn. The rest of the packs and vampires will arrive by this evening, but with Adriana out of commission, we can only afford a minute of sleep.

I barely get my boots off before I flop face-first onto the mattress.

"I have never been this tired," I grumble, my voice muffled by the pillows. Lowell chuckles as I hear him undressing. He slides under the covers and brushes my hair off my face.

"Is that so?" he asks, his fingers drifting up my arm, then sliding to my rib cage. His touch is light, barely there, but it still leaves goosebumps in its wake.

"Pup..." I warn as I roll over to face him.

"Yes, *Ma Reine*?" He moves to my hip, toying with the waistband of my leggings. My breath catches as he connects with bare skin. He's just playing, switching from rubbing circles with his calloused fingertips to gently scraping his nails, and somehow I'm suddenly wide awake.

"We only have a few hours to sleep..."

His hands slide back up, this time under my shirt, making it ride up as he reaches the underside of my breast. "I'm just making sure you're relaxed," he feigns innocence. "Wouldn't want you to be wound up after your mission."

I groan as he palms my breast over the lace of my bra. He's barely touching me, and my entire body is lit like a Christmas tree. "Lowell—" It comes out a breathy moan.

"I love how responsive you are," he murmurs, shifting to hover over me.

And then he waits, holding himself off me and making those ridiculous muscles bulge.

"Like I'm gonna say no," I answer his unasked question, and Lowell laughs as he closes the distance between us and kisses me. He takes his time stroking my tongue with his. His hands roam over my curves at an impossibly slow rate that has me panting in anticipation and frustration. "Alpha, I have about ten minutes of energy left. Get to the damn point."

"So demanding," he tsks, but yanks my leggings down to my knees, not even bothering to push them off. I wait with a smile on my face until I hear him inhale.

"You've been walking around without panties on?" he growls, biting my inner thigh hard enough to make me yelp. With no warning, his tongue swipes the length of my core, and my back bows off the bed. "I should punish you for being such a bad girl."

I whimper, and he teases me, building me up until I'm squirming but not getting me there. The third time he drives me close to my orgasm, only to pull away, I scream. "Damn it, Alpha."

"You have a request?" he says, blowing air against my sensitive clit. Goosebumps erupt over my entire body. I'm hot and cold, and I need *more*.

"I want your cock, not your tongue."

"Is that so?" He rises back up my body, taking my shirt with him and tossing it aside. "Maybe I should tease you more. Make you beg for it."

"Hah." I take my middle finger and stick it in my mouth, making a show of sucking on it before releasing the digit with a pop. I slide it through the valley of my breasts and down my stomach, leaving a shimmering trail straight to my center. Lowell's eyes are transfixed, his jaw ticking as I roll my finger over my clit.

"I don't beg, pup." I moan a little dramatically as I slip my finger inside my entrance. "So, if you're not gonna finish this—"

I'm not even sure how it happens, but in the next breath, my hands are ripped away from my sex, and my legs, still bound by my half-on leggings, are thrown over one of Lowell's shoulders and he slams into me. We both swear, and my eyes roll back in my head as he fills me so completely.

Lowell grips my jaw in his large hand, holding me immobile. "Don't think for a second that I would ever leave you unsatisfied, *Ma Reine*."

"I know," I smirk and bite my lower lip. "Now fuck me, Alpha. *Please*." I lay it on thick with the begging and Lowell's laugh shakes his whole body.

"Such a fucking brat," he teases, and starts thrusting, instantly hitting the spot inside me that makes my eyes roll to the back of my head.

"Every time," he breathes.

"What?"

"Every time feels better than the last." He quickens his pace. "So fucking warm and wet and—" He breaks off with a swear as my muscles clamp down around him.

"You drive me damn near insane," Lowell growls.

"Feeling's mutual," I pant. My nails dig into his shoulders just as he rolls my clit between his fingers. I come with a silent scream. A thousand lightning bolts ignite my blood, shooting down my spine, and making my toes curl.

Lowell follows me, his cock thickening as I grip him, and he spills inside me with a groan. He collapses, giving me his weight and burying his head in my neck.

"How's your magic?" he asks.

"What?"

"Are you low?"

"Umm..." I shake my head, clearing the post-orgasm fog enough to reach into the pit of my stomach where my magic resides.

The multiple forms are like excited puppies when I reach within myself, all jumping at the chance to be used. I don't feel a lack of power at all...which is odd because I used a giant chunk of magic teleporting as much as I did today. "I'm good. Why?"

"Clean us up so we can go to bed," he says, and I laugh hard enough that I shake him.

Lowell draws out of me and flops over onto his back as I cleanse the sheets and the both of us before shimmying my leggings back into place. I relax into him, nuzzling his bare chest as his arms encircle me. I love this almost more than the sex. Okay, that's a lie. But I do love falling asleep in my mate's arms.

"What time is it?" I ask.

"We have a few hours still," Lowell says, a yawn lifting his chest before he settles back down.

"Thank god." My eyes drift closed. "Love you." I feel his love mirrored in our bond, but I'm asleep before I hear him utter the words.

"KATIE."

The door is thrown open, and all the protective spells encasing the room are obliterated.

I jackknife up in bed, but Lowell is faster and uses his body to block me from the door. My sister runs inside, curls sticking up at odd angles and face entirely too pale.

"Adriana, what the hell—"

Vlad appears in a blur, looking just as haggard. His usually impeccable hair is a mess, his suit jacket is nowhere to be found, and his shirt is half hanging out of his pants. "Damnit Adriana, get back in bed," the vampire huffs.

"Were they in bed *together*?" I whisper-shout.

"I know as much as you know," my mate replies in the same tone.

Adriana screams like a toddler and runs around the bed, heading for the bathroom. Naturally, Vlad is faster, and he heads her off and throws her over his shoulder. She starts raining punches down on his back, but he doesn't even flinch.

"Aww, you used to hold me like that when I was being irrational," I murmur in Lowell's ear, nipping his earlobe.

Vlad, clearly unamused by the situation, growls. "Adriana keeps slipping past the guards I've assigned to her room."

"Why does she need guards?" I ask.

"Because she won't rest."

"Tell him there's too much to do," Adrianna shrieks, trying to wriggle free. "People are arriving, and they don't know where to go, and the wolves only served meat for breakfast, so the vegetarians are starving and—"

"You almost died," Vlad bellows.

"She really didn't." The glare Vlad gives would make a lesser person crap their pants. "Adriana, can you dictate from a bed?" I ask. She huffs and nods. Or at least I think she does. "Then delegate. You have an entire camp of soldiers. Use them."

"Fine," she grumbles, and Vlad leaves with her still slung over his shoulder.

Lowell lies back down, pulling me with him and cocooning me in his arms. I'm about to drift back to sleep when the door opens again.

"Your shields suck," Edina says, and I groan as I hear her pad over to my side of the bed. The mattress dips at my back, and her cold hands land on my biceps, making me yelp as she snuggles into me.

"We may need to have a conversation about boundaries," I grumble, and she laughs melodically. "Lowell's naked."

"Eh, I've seen it." I turn over my shoulder and glare. "Come on, don't get bitchy on me." She starts hysterically laughing, releasing me and lying on her back. "Get it? Cause you're mated to a wolf...so you're—"

"Yeah, I got it." I turn in Lowell's arms, so he's spooning me, and I can see my best friend. "Why are you in my bed?"

"I lost my fuck buddy," Edina sighs. "Which is fine because I was just gonna sleep with his brother, but either Alek isn't into women or he just has no interest in me."

"I'm sorry." Lowell's breathing evens out behind me as he falls back asleep.

"It's fine," Edina says. "We have thousands of people arriving today. I'm bound to find one I can pass the time with." Her smile doesn't reach her eyes.

"E—"

"Are you ready for everyone tomorrow?" She's deflecting. That's not what's on her mind. That's not why she's in my bed instead of alone in hers.

"Yes, we're ready. But—"

"I'm worried they won't cooperate," Edina continues. "Not with you, but with each other."

"I know, but we'll deal with it," I say. Her hands start to shake, but when she notices me looking, she shoves them under the blankets. "E, talk to me."

She shakes her head. "It's nothing."

It's not nothing. Icy tears are sliding down her cheeks. I knew from the moment she arrived back from Faerie that something was wrong, but since she told us about Puck, I see it all the time. There's a layer of melancholy she tries to hide beneath sarcasm and a light laugh.

"Scale of one to ten, how bad does it hurt?" I ask.

She scoffs, about to deflect again, but then the fight slips away. "Eleven." I swipe the newest tear away, and she shudders. "It's constant, babes. I can't even describe it, but it's like a throbbing ache right here." She thumps her hand against her chest. "The only time it's any better is when I'm drunk, fighting, or fucking."

I hate seeing her like this. My indestructible best friend who has helped me through so much is hurting, and I can do nothing about it. I've asked everyone about rejected mates, the wolves, Vlad, and even Astor. It's so rare that none of them had any answers on how to help lessen Edina's pain.

"You wanna fight then?" I ask, and she rolls her eyes. "I'm serious. We can do it. We've had some pretty epic blowups that we can recreate. Or, hear me out—" Edina is chuckling, "—we can get drunk, and then fight. Two birds, one stone."

"Are you gonna offer me makeup sex after?"

"I would, but I don't want it to ruin our friendship." Her laugh is genuine this time, and I roll out of Lowell's arms enough to hug her. "Love you."

She gasps in feigned horror. "Babes, your mate is right there." I laugh too loudly, and Lowell grumbles behind me. We both snap our lips closed to hold it in, which only makes us laugh harder.

"No need to stop now." Lowell's words are stern, but pure amusement flows down our bond.

"Sorry, Lo-Lo." It sends us into another fit that has him joining in.

"What are the chances of us getting any sleep?" I ask.

"Very slim," Edina sighs. I sit up in bed, throwing the comforter off Edina and me but keeping Lowell covered.

"Let's go help Adriana," I say. "She's supposed to be resting, and Vlad shouldn't be up either."

"Good luck getting him to leave her side," Edina scoffs. "How long do you think it'll take for them to get over themselves and have sex?"

"There's a calendar pool outside the mess hall," Lowell smirks, sitting up, but keeping the blanket on his lap. "I told you I'd get him back." I laugh as he kisses me.

Edina hops out of the bed and lights up the room with a flick of her hand. "I'll start heading over." She fixes us both with a serious stare. "This is not an open invitation for you to fuck again. I expect you in the war room in five minutes. I'm only leaving so the wolf can get dressed without you killing me."

"Love you," I say as Lowell kisses my shoulder.

"Love you most," she says, turning around at the door. "Love you a moderate amount, Lo-Lo."

"Feeling's mutual, E," Lowell says. My heart goes all warm and fuzzy at their budding friendship. Edina leaves, and Lowell gently bites the skin on my shoulder.

"How mad will she be if we take...six minutes to get there?" he asks.

"I think it's worth the risk." I push Lowell's shoulders so he flops back on the pillows before straddling his hips and kissing him deeply. "Definitely worth it."

HOURS LATER, ADRIANA SIMPLY refuses to sit any longer and takes total control of the incoming soldiers. Lowell and I take a long shower, only ten percent actual showering before we exit the bathroom in a tangle of limbs and towels.

"Fucking hell," Vlad grumbles, and I jump about ten feet in the air, clutching the towel to my chest. "Baby queen, I've been alive for a thousand years. Do you think your breasts are anything special?"

"Ouch."

"I think they're spectacular," Lowell says, his breath warm against my ear, and I let out an honest-to-god giggle.

Vlad groans dramatically. "Are you ever not fucking?"

"I mean...we're not right now," I tease.

"But in all fairness, we would be if you weren't here," Lowell says, and the corner of Vlad's mouth twitches in amusement.

"Did Adriana banish you?" I ask, moving to the closet to grab my clothes for the meeting in the throne room. Everyone will be there tonight to hear me greet them and begin training. I'm not nervous about the training part, but motivating everyone, getting them to put aside centuries' worth of prejudices to work together...yeah, that's fucking terrifying.

"She's infuriating," Vlad growls. I pull out a simple but ridiculously nice tunic and leggings. Lowell stands between Vlad and me, even though Vlad is looking anywhere but at me.

"You're too old to be acting this stupid," I tease.

"People have died for lesser statements, Kathryn," Vlad intones.

"I'm pretty used to death threats. You're gonna need to do better if you want to stop me from telling you to get your head out of your ass." I throw a little lick of lightning at him.

"That was hot, do it again," he laughs.

When I'm fully dressed, I emerge around Lowell, who darts forward and dresses entirely too quickly. I'm only partially embarrassed that I pout once he has pants on.

"What the hell are you wearing?" Vlad asks me.

"Clothes?"

"I have a dress in your wardrobe set out. And the crown, locket, and scepter are—"

"Yeah, hard pass," I say, putting my hands on my hips. "Toting that shit around isn't going to make them respect me. And I want them to view me as their commanding officer, not a queen who will sit on the sidelines and watch as they're slaughtered. They need to know I'll be leading the charge."

Vlad purses his lips. "Fine. But you wear that dress to your coronation. It cost a fortune."

"You can afford it," I tease, and Vlad shrugs but doesn't disagree. "One more thing." I drift off, my gaze darting to my mate, whom I know won't love this next part. "I need you both to back down today and let me handle whatever they throw at us. If the vampires or wolves think I'm weak—"

"They'll challenge you," Lowell finishes as he cuffs the sleeves of his button-down and rolls them up his forearms. "We're right behind you, but we'll let you handle it."

"Really, baby queen, you act like we're controlling assholes."

"Protective," I amend, "not controlling. But thank you for letting me handle this."

Lowell comes over, wraps an arm low around my waist, and kisses my temple. "Ready?"

"As I'll ever be."

Chapter Fourteen

THE MAGICAL ORBS THAT light the throne room brighten upon my entrance, illuminating every single person as their eyes turn to me. I'm no stranger to crowds, but this is daunting. Despite the expansion Adriana orchestrated, there are people as far as the eye can see. Some of the witches have taken to brooms so they have a better vantage point.

Keeping my head held high, I walk up the steps to the dais with Lowell and Vlad flanking me. Edina, Adriana, my parents, and Lowell's entire family stand behind the dais in front of the memorial garden. It looks like they're there because of the space issue, but I know better. They're being cautious and bracing for an attack from behind. It's the same reason the rest of the people who made up our small missions are directly in front of the dais.

Before losing my magic, I'd laugh at the sheer number of people who think they needed to shield me. I would have said I could handle any threat. Now, it's comforting. Not on a power level, since I'm still stronger than any of them, but as a show of friendship and solidarity.

I take a moment to survey the crowd. Even with the lack of space, people are separated into three distinct vertical groups.

That won't work at all.

"Vampires," I address the far right of the hall, "find a witch. Do not bite them."

No one moves, but I stand strong, staring them down. A small smile creeps over my face as lightning dances across my skin and I hear gasps. Most of the vampires hadn't heard the rumors I had lightning magic at all, and those who did assume my magic was still impaired.

To my freaking shock, Sybil moves across the room first, finding Cecelia, my friend from the Chicago Coven. When she's beside her witch, she gives me a slight bow.

She's such a kiss ass, Vlad says in my head, and I have to work hard not to laugh out loud as the rest of the vampires start moving around the cavern.

"Werewolves, please join one of the existing duos," I command.

"No." The man who speaks is standing on the left side of the hall, at the very front of the lines of werewolves. He reminds me of a lumberjack. Broad muscles strain against a flannel shirt, and his thick, chocolate beard is untamed enough to be rugged without looking sloppy. He cracks his knuckles like that's a threat. This is the American Pack Master. Lowell warned me he might put me through my paces.

I meet his brown eyes as they glow a soft amber color. His power is unmistakable, but I can tell he has too much control to shift in a room so full. So, I stand my ground, holding his gaze in a silent challenge. The rest of the wolves, the betas and omegas, shuffle nervously, looking between us like they're trying to figure out which Alpha to stand behind.

I expect the bond to be overloaded with emotion. I expect Lowell to react possessively or protectively, but I only feel quiet pride. He's already sure I'll win this stand-off, which I will. I have no other choice.

The American Alpha growls low, causing several pack members to whimper. I respond by letting my were-magic surface on my skin. His eyes widen a fraction of an inch, but he still doesn't move. Not even as I use the magic to flow over the empty floor to where he stands. Not when I guide it gently up his legs until it's encasing him in place, keeping him from moving.

My magic continues to crawl over the pack master's body, leaching upwards until it's surrounding his shoulders, his neck, and his ears. When it finally sweeps up over his beard, I see it. A tiny dip of his head, a submission. I drop my magic, and the Alpha smiles widely before going over to where Aleksander stands with Adriana, completing their triad.

Nicely done, baby queen, Vlad says.

Once everyone is more or less teamed up, I address the crowd again. "The time for being separate is over. Honestly, it's never done us any favors.

"As many of you know, last night, we struck a blow against the current monarchy." I recount our tales of the individual missions, and everyone listens with rapt attention. Once I'm done, I say, "We have a victory under our belts, but that doesn't mean we get to rest. We begin training immediately because I do not doubt that the king is planning a retaliation while we stand here talking."

"When we fight," Lowell says, taking up the reins, "we'll be fighting in trios. The witches stationed here have been working on one-sided shields, which will allow us to attack while remaining safe."

I step to the side of the throne, and Lowell and Vlad follow, stepping in so we're in a tighter version of the formation we were just in. "Please assume these positions," I instruct. "Vampires on the right, werewolves on the left, and witches in front."

As everyone moves, I put up a one-sided shield, sighing as it comes easily. A month ago, I couldn't do this at all. It shimmers before becoming invisible.

"Witches, erect your shields." Most are flawless, but a few flicker and sputter. "If you have not mastered these, I expect you to do so. Practice it like the life of your entire group depends on it."

I thank and dismiss everyone who won't be fighting before going over various strategies, movements, and ways vampires and werewolves can take the attack while remaining shielded. Once questions have been asked and answered, I instruct everyone to line the throne room, leaving the center open in a makeshift sparring ring.

Four groups at a time, trios square off against each other. It's an assessment, a way to see where we're starting. I catch sight of Jeremy, a lanky teen who served as a spy for me when my father was still alive, skirting around the fighting and taking notes for us to review later.

Each "battle" only lasts a few minutes since we have a lot to cover tonight. Vampires and werewolves test the bounds of their new shields as they land deafening physical blows on their opponents. Several times, Vlad and Lowell had to swoop in to stop a vampire from biting a witch, but we expected that. Edina randomly hops in the ring and attacks shields, some of which hold up, but most don't.

We still have a lot of work to do.

"All right, everyone!" I call about halfway through our training session. "We're going to move this party outside so the wolves can shift—"

The most obnoxious ringtone I've ever heard echoes in the stone walls of the caverns. Everyone shifts uncomfortably, but I just slowly turn over my shoulder and arch an eyebrow.

"Apologies, baby queen," Vlad says, flashing a smile. "This is important. I'll meet you outside."

I shake my head, unable to stifle my chuckle, as Vlad disappears outside. "He's lucky I'm not a total asshole," I mutter to Lowell. The witches closest to the dais laugh along with us, and I wink in their direction.

"Apparently we're taking a break," I announce to the cavern. "Grab some water and meet outside the coven doors in ten minutes." Everyone disperses, and the crowd stays mixed this time, making me smile.

Lowell slings his arm around my waist and tugs me to the edge of the dais, where the American Pack Master is standing with Alek.

"How'd it feel getting your ass kicked by a witch, Butch?" Lowell taunts. The American Pack Master scrubs a hand across the back of his neck but is all smiles.

"No hard feelings, Alpha," he booms.

"You should be apologizing to my mate," Lowell responds, and the man's eyebrows arch for a second before he dips into a bow.

"My apologies, Your Majesty," he says. "I needed to ensure you were fit to deal with Alphas."

"Lowell's recommendation didn't matter?" I ask, not offended but intrigued.

"Not once you claimed each other." He smiles. "He might as well be an omega when it comes to you. As it should be. My husband is a Beta and runs the show in our family, not that I'll ever admit it."

"Is he here?" I ask. Butch shakes his head.

"Back home, keeping an eye on the children and elderly of our pack. He didn't want to leave our baby girl." Butch pulls out his phone and shows us a picture of him holding a baby in one of his oversized hands. "Jack just about killed me after this was taken. Acted like I'd drop her or something." He accompanies the statement with another one of those infectious laughs.

"So, should we be expecting pups by the end of the war?" he asks, his eyes dipping to my stomach.

"No," Lowell and I say forcefully in unison. Our eyes catch and pressure I didn't know I was carrying eases. I hadn't had the chance to tell him I've been doubling up on birth control tonic. Part of me was nervous that he'd be upset, but I should know better.

"Someday," I add with a smile at my mate.

"When we're not in a war," Lowell finishes, tugging me closer and leaning down to brush a kiss on my lips. Hope for the future lights up the mating bond as I nestle under his arm.

"Wow," Butch murmurs. When I narrow my eyes in question, he elaborates, "I've never met fated mates before. None of the packs under my jurisdiction have a pair. You can see the love between you like it's tangible. To see it in person, it's..."

"Magical," Lowell says, and he nods. The bond between us gives another tug.

Vlad appears in a blur, looking frazzled. He swipes a hand through his blonde hair and stares down the Pack Master until Butch excuses himself. Edina, Adriana, and my parents appear from the crowd as soon as he's gone.

"We have a problem," Vlad says, his voice barely a whisper. Adriana casts a spell, and magic shimmers encasing our little group before becoming invisible again.

"They can't hear us now," Adriana says. "But they can see us, so keep your reactions neutral."

"They'll know soon enough," Vlad says, glancing at the emptying cavern. "Someone's coming."

"Who?" I ask.

"All I know is that it's one person." Vlad's jaw tics. "On a broom."

One person. On a broom.

Only one person knows the location of our hideout and can fly long distances on a broom. And there's only one person crazy enough to face off against an army of Dark Witches alone.

"You saw this?" I breathe. Lowell tightens his hold on me.

"No," Vlad replies, still glancing around the cavern even though the few people remaining can't hear us. "I have spies stationed throughout the country. They've been tracking the person's progress since they left Edinburgh."

"From the safehouse, probably," my mother says, her lips pursed.

"How far?"

"Should be here any minute," Vlad says.

"Adriana, can I still teleport within the coven?" I ask.

"Yes," she says. Without hesitating, my parents reach out and touch Adriana while Edina takes Vlad's hand, and Lowell tightens his grip on me. Simultaneous swirls of magic in different colors wrap around our groups, and we teleport outside.

Some of the witches startle when we arrive in a patch of open grass at the mouth of the tunnel, but most are consumed by their own work. The witches have taken it upon themselves to light the valley with floating magical orbs that cast a soft white glow on the lush green grass. Wolves are clustered to one side of the hill as they strip and shift, the vampires surrounding them, ensuring they don't accidentally hurt anyone. I'd be touched by the teamwork if I wasn't entirely focused on Vlad's message.

"Mom, get everyone into formation," I instruct. "That training might come into play much sooner than anticipated." She and Marcus run off to organize the troops, and I turn to Lowell. "I need you there too."

"Little witch—"

"I know I promised we wouldn't be separated, but I need you to get the wolves ready. They won't listen to my parents, and you know it."

Lowell cups my face. "I was going to tell you I love you and to kick ass."

"Oh." I kiss him quickly. "Love you too."

"Keep them safe," he murmurs before pulling away and shifting. I scratch behind his ears, and he makes the low rumbling sound that always makes me calm. He barks loudly, and every wolf in the clearing freezes.

"Why do you want them in formation?" Edina asks. "You think the one person is a decoy?"

"We need to be ready for anything. Adriana, how far did you extend the ward?"

While Lowell and I were mating, one of the improvements Adriana made was an extra magical barrier around the entire valley. She wanted another layer of defense, but we also wanted an outdoor space for drills and for the wolves to run and sleep during the full moon. Every witch in the coven has helped fortify the wards, but I'm still unsure how they'll hold up against hellfire.

"Just beyond the stream," she says.

"Take us, quickly." We all fall into formation around Adriana, grabbing hold of her as her gray magic encases and takes us to the other side of the small stream.

Standing just feet away from the barrier is a figure shrouded in darkness. A dark cloak makes it hard to see details, but I can tell they're tall and have a boxier build.

"Katie?" the voice calls. The breath leaves my body, my shoulders sagging in relief.

It's not Archer.

"I'm here to see Kathryn Carmichael." I know that voice. I've heard my name said in that timbre before. Who the hell—

Recognition floods me. "Jai?" I breathe. He can't hear me on the other side of the barrier, but I'm positive it's him. The cloak comes off his head, revealing the tightly cropped curls and bright green eyes of Archer's best friend.

"Another one of your ex-boyfriends?" Vlad intones.

"Nope, that's one of mine," Edina grumbles. "I'll deal with him."

She walks past the wards and Jai's mouth drops. "Can I help you?" she asks, but he just stares, his eyes bouncing between her wings and her ears.

"It's true." He laughs under his breath. "I'm not gonna lie; I was a little pissed when you didn't call me after our night together."

"Yeah, I wouldn't have called you anyway," Edina says, and Vlad barks a laugh so loud I'm half convinced they hear it through the wards. "Why are you here?"

"I need to speak to Katie," Jai says, turning and looking directly at me, even though we're invisible to him. "And I assume if she sent you, that means she's close."

"Maybe, but I'm not sending her out here until I know what you want and that you're alone."

"I'm alone." Jai takes a phone out of his pocket and extends it to Edina. "And she needs to see this." Edina tentatively reaches out and grabs the phone, not taking her eyes off Jai.

"Archer's gone insane," Jai continues. "He's angry and feels betrayed, but he still thinks Katie is being coerced."

"She's not," Edina says.

"I know," Jai says. "I heard her say she has a mate. I grew up next to a wolf pack. I know what that means, but Archer won't listen to me. And then Marcus left...he was like a second dad to Archer. He stopped trusting anyone. Which brings me to this." He jabs his finger at the phone in Edina's hand.

Edina finally looks at the screen, and I watch as her mouth slowly parts and her breathing increases. I tug on the mating bond, flooding my concern and worry to Lowell so he'll know to get his ass back here. He arrives in the blink of an eye, staying in his wolf form.

"Come out," Edina breathes. As one unit, the four of us step beyond the wards. Jai blinks at the entourage and shrinks back in fear as Vlad and Lowell snarl and bare their teeth.

"Down," I command, and the men back off, but Adriana's magic stays coiled around her arms.

Adriana, can you check his mind? I ask. *Make sure he's telling the truth.*

On it.

"Look," Edina says and passes me the phone. It's open to a list of names, mostly male. I'm about to ask the meaning when I zoom out slightly and see it. Ranks ranging from private to colonel.

"Holy shit."

"Archer launched an investigation of the Dragons," Jai says softly. "He did it quietly. Just a handful of officers knew it was happening. This is what they came back with."

What is it? Lowell asks through our mental channel.

"A list of every officer we turned," I say and hand the phone to Adriana.

I'm confirming it with your mom, Edina says.

"Tonight, he told me his plan," Jai says, swallowing. "He's evacuated everyone stationed at Headquarters who isn't on this list. It was done under the guise of a mission to the prison, but really, they're headed to a new safe house nearby."

"Where?" Vlad asks.

"I can't tell you that."

That's all of them, my mom says.

Tell them to evacuate, now, I relay to her as I ask, "What does he have planned?"

Jai's eyes bounce back and forth between us. "There are bombs. I don't know when they detonate, but..."

"The stones that make up Headquarters are built to survive bombs," I tell him. "They're protected by magic. Not even Earth or Fire Elementals can damage them."

"The generals disabled the protective spells before they left," Jai says. "It's just regular stone now."

"Fuck," Vlad breathes.

"I couldn't sit by while he killed—" Jai's jaw tics. "Archer has lost so much of himself; I couldn't let him murder this many people. He called it treason, and I guess it is, but how he's going about it…"

"Do you have a timeline?" I ask, and Jai shakes his head.

They've started evacuating, my mom says. *We'll need to bring them here, but there aren't many transportation options. The first men said they cleared out the brooms and most RVs.*

We have brooms, Adriana replies and looks at me. I nod, and she teleports away to help my mom gather supplies to help get everyone out.

"Vlad, go with her," I say. "You have at least one unknown portal in London, right?"

"Obviously."

"Good, show everyone where it is and meet us at Headquarters. Have the vampires bring people from there to the portal as fast as possible."

Vlad disappears in a flash of vampire speed, and I turn to Lowell and Edina. "We're going straight to Headquarters," I say, and then turn back to Jai and offer him a small smile. "Thank you for telling us. Do you want to stay here? We can keep you safe. We'll get any family you want safe too."

Jai shakes his head sadly. "I can't leave Archer any more than you could leave Edina," he sighs. "I need to try and keep him on this side of sanity."

He mounts his broom and flips his cloak up. "Jai," I call. "Offer stands. Anytime you need sanctuary."

"Thanks." He kicks off the ground and disappears into the night just as my Dark Magic wraps around me, Lowell and Edina, and the Highlands begin to disappear.

Chapter Fifteen

WE LAND IN FRONT of a dilapidated building in London and run towards it. The shield shimmers until the magic floats over my skin, revealing the Dragons Headquarters and the pure chaos that is the outdoor pad of the compound.

The small group of witches that Adriana teleported here are spaced out along the shield's edge. As soldiers exit the compound, Marcus directs small groups to one of the witches, who then step beyond the border and teleport away, probably to the portal. Knowing Adriana, she brought every witch who knows how to teleport, but they're not as strong as my sister or me, and they'll run out of energy fast.

My mother is yelling instructions to the soldiers, telling them to remain calm but move quickly as they march through the narrow doorway and onto the landing pad. Some higher-up officers are starting up the few RVs remaining, and witches pile into them, shoving as many members in as possible before driving off. Aerial units are flying two and three to a broom, which is definitely not safe.

"Katie." Adriana is pale as she emerges. "The bombs are magical, and they're everywhere. I can't disable them all."

"Where's Vlad with the vampires?"

"They just left with a group, but there's only so many they can carry." Massive amounts of soldiers pour from the narrow doorway, two at a time.

"Tell everyone the location of the portal," I instruct. "Have them get in cabs, busses, tandem-fucking-bikes, whatever they need to. Just get out of this area before it blows."

"You're sure you want to reveal the portal's location?" Edina whispers. "Vlad said it's the last one in London."

"Once everyone is evacuated, there's no reason to come back. Archer is in the Highlands; we'll have no soldiers here. We can seal the portal and wash our hands of the city."

"Your Majesty." Butch arrives with Lowell's sisters and a pack of wolves in their human forms. "We can help. Tell us where to go."

"Take as many witches as you can to the portal."

"We can take more in our wolf forms, but—"

"One of the witches can cloak you. Just don't run into anyone." Butch nods, and the wolves peel off to fill in the gaps along the shield's outer edge. They shift, and without a word, Marcus starts directing people to them.

I release a breath, shutting out all the chaos around me and formulating the rest of my shaky plan. We can't wait until all the soldiers get out from the bottom of the compound, it's too many stories, and the halls are too narrow. There won't be enough time, and soon people will ignore all their training and start panicking.

"We need to open a portal here," I say aloud, looking at my best friend. "Have you learned how to do that?"

She considers for a minute, and I recognize the tell-tale signs that she's using Mind Magic. "Astor can help me," she says finally.

"He says there needs to be a doorway or an archway to make it work."

"Good, let's get to the pit."

"No teleporting in the building," Adriana says. "I was working on the bombs, so I didn't disable the wards yet—"

Edina salutes her and flies over everyone's heads. "Get those wards down!" I tell Adriana as Lowell shifts into his huge white wolf, and I jump onto his back before he takes off into the throng of people exiting Headquarters.

When we finally make it through the doors, the terror is palpable. The cold gray stones which once provided me such comfort are now ominous. I can feel them closing in on us, trapping us all beneath the earth. The halls are too narrow, and even with the open center that gives the illusion of space, it's claustrophobic. Soldiers march in varying states of unease, constantly moving forward as quickly as they can, forming a wall of bodies that I don't know how we will get through.

Hang on, Lowell instructs and dives over the center barrier. I clutch his fur as we free fall through the center of the helix, spinning down and down towards the pit. Just before we get to the bottom floor, I throw a cushioning spell at the ground below us so that when Lowell hits the ground, he gently bounces. I slide off his back without breaking our momentum.

"Damn, that looked fun," Edina whines, where she stands in the middle of the raised sparring platform. She walks to the edge and points to the doorway that leads to the sloping hallways. "Can we use that for the portal?"

People practically leap over each other to cram into the small space, and I shake my head. "It's the same problem we have now. It's too narrow."

I turn away from the crowds to look at one of the black stone walls. It's hard for me to believe that these stones meant to suppress magic are now just rocks. An idea takes shape, and I launch my lightning at one crack between the stones. Nothing happens. I try again, this time narrowing the magic to one spot until a tiny hole appears.

"Okay, so now we just need—"

"Captain?" I turn and find a clump of soldiers who aren't even trying to get near the doors, resigned to their fate. A man pushes to the front of the group, his blonde hair in disarray. "Are you really here?" Kyle, a private and my one-night stand from what seems like lifetimes ago, asks.

I ignore the question. "I need all the Earth Elementals," I instruct, running to the wall I was just battering with my magic. "I need an archway the size of this wall."

The Earth Elementals from Kyle's group and those that hear me from the end of the line immediately do my bidding. Stones start chipping and breaking off under their onslaught. Dust flies in the room, and the Air Elementals clear it away so their comrades can keep working without losing visibility.

Edina flits off, and I hear her voice echoing in the helix, calling for more Earth Elementals seconds before even more soldiers come through the doorway to help clear the archway.

Kyle approaches, brow crinkled. "Why did you come for us?" he asks. "Why not save the officers?"

"I'd love to say I knew who'd be down here," I say with a laugh. "But honestly, it didn't matter. I'm not letting you all be slaughtered."

He nods, looking between me and the gigantic wolf at my side. "If it gets too late, promise you'll get her out of here," he says to Lowell, who barks in response. Kyle nods and joins the other group as we wait for the wards to break.

"Is there anyone who's not in love with you?" Lowell's voice is light as he shifts back into his human form.

"Jealous, pup?" I tease.

"Nah." He smirks and pulls me in. "You're in my bed tonight, little witch."

"If we survive."

Lowell hums in agreement just as the ground around us begins to shake. All movement stops as everyone collectively holds their breath.

Sorry! Adriana says down the mental channel. *Some Earth Elementals tried to blast another hole through the concrete up here. I tried to tell them the halls are the same size, so it wouldn't matter but—*

We're working on the lower exit. Tell everyone to keep moving but have the lower half of the line stand by for instructions.

"Let's move this along," I call to my Earth Elementals, who are struggling with the formidable rocks. Other Elementals get closer to the archway, trying to help with spells or any other way they can.

Edina lands beside me. "Astor is ready. I just need to send him the location of the door, and he'll help me through the inside."

"Faster," I call as the men and women hit a particularly stubborn patch of rock. There's a chorus of voices in distress as they realize they can't break through the rock with magic, and some start tearing at it with their fingernails.

"It's not deep enough," Edina confirms.

"Katie," Lowell says, his gold eyes crinkled. "We need something stronger than their magic."

"My lightning didn't do anything, and I don't know that Edina's ice is going to—" An eyebrow arch is all it takes to discern his meaning. I swipe my hand down my face. "Shit."

I grab Edina's hand and step closer to the witches. "Everyone, stop and get behind me." They all scurry out of the way, leaving me and Edina standing in front of the slight indent in the stones. "E, I need a wall of ice between me and everyone here."

Edina nods, not questioning me for a moment before erecting the wall. I briefly hear Lowell scream at being locked on the other side, but Edina holds fast, her sapphire eyes glowing with the use of her power.

I reach deep within myself, finding the kernel of magic I've neglected, and release all my emotions. The worry, the love, the anger at Archer for threatening so many lives, all of it. When I'm a blank canvas, I grab onto the magic and open my eyes.

White flames dance across my vision, and my head spins with the power. It's intoxicating, controlling this raw force, and I can see how someone would get addicted to this feeling. It's stronger than my lightning and any magic I've ever felt, including when I was supercharged on the throne when I became queen. The hellfire is destruction and devastation wrapped up in flames. I could end worlds, crumple empires, and destroy civilizations.

I keep my emotions in check, not allowing myself to be seduced by the power surging through my veins. It feels like a sentient being that wants to control me, but I remind it through my relaxation that I am its master. Finally, it submits, ready to do my bidding.

I send the hellfire in a targeted blast. Stone explodes, and the earth around us shudders as the fire blasts through layer after layer of rock. When it's deep enough, I send the fire wide until the entire wall is engulfed in flames that bury deep into the stone.

"That's good," Edina calls, and I feel the gentle brush of her magic against my skin, reminding me to cool off. I release another breath and banish the hellfire, absorbing it back into my skin as Edina douses the wall in water, making it hiss.

Lowell is there immediately, hands cupping my face as he searches for any sign of distress or injury. I smirk, even though I'm panting from the energy it took to banish the flames. "That little bitch made it look hard." Lowell's laughter echoes in the cavernous space as he pulls me in for a passionate kiss. There are some whistles from the crowd, and I think it might be about us, but when I pull away, Edina opens a doorway, and Astor is on the other side.

"Go on," Edina says, rolling her eyes in exasperation. "Follow the nice Fae before we're all blown to pieces."

The soldiers start advancing in organized lines, group by group disappearing into the portal.

Send the lower levels of soldiers down, I instruct my mom, but Lowell must have given the command already. Wolves appear in the pit, ushering massive crowds toward us as more and more people head into the portal.

Anyone left? my mother asks as the last soldiers go through the portal. *Everyone up here is gone.*

I breathe a sigh of relief. *We'll do a final check.* Lowell shifts back and barks something to the wolves, who yip in agreement before taking off in the direction of the helix.

"E, get out and close the portal. Anyone else we find, we'll bring out the front."

Wards are down, Adriana says.

A little late, but thanks, I chuckle.

I hop on Lowell's back, and he starts running. We spiral through the hallways, sticking to the main path as I search for any remaining stragglers with my Mind Magic. We're almost to the top when Lowell whines and skids to a stop.

Lyra found healers. He takes off down one of the longer hallways off the helix. *They're not aligned with your mom but missed Archer's evacuation order.*

Tell the wolves to get out. We'll get them.

The medical bay is blindingly bright and smells like sage and antiseptic. I jump off Lowell's back and fling back the curtain, finding two healers and one very ill patient on the bed between them. The younger one, a mousy brown witch whom I remember from my trips to see Deavers, screams when she sees Lowell in his wolf form. Her hands are shaking as she raises them, and Light Magic sputters and fizzles, making her whimper in fear.

"We have to evacuate," I order. "There are bombs placed throughout the entire building."

"We can't," the other healer, a young man, says, looking at their sick patient. "He can't be moved. He could die."

"He's definitely gonna die if you stay here, so let's go." They hesitate one second too long so I take a page from Adriana's book and reach into their minds, spearing past their fragile shields and seizing control. I have them lift the patient between them and start walking towards me just as the earth quakes.

Katie! Adriana's voice rings in my ears. *It's starting. Where the hell are you?*

I hasten my mental hold on the healers, and they run over to me. They grab onto me as I place a hand on Lowell's furry body and the sick patient. The black smoke of my teleportation spell envelops us just as an explosion blows open the medical bay doors. Smoke and fire and the sheer volume of the *boom* distract me from my destination for a moment, but I refocus with all my might, bringing us up and out of Headquarters.

We land in a heap at the edge of the compound, and I abandon my hold on everyone as I step closer to Headquarters. I send out a shield, willing it down to the depths of the pit and the length of all the underground tunnels, encasing the entire structure in a bubble of magic.

The earth trembles beneath our feet, and the underground helix collapses like a giant sinkhole. Debris flies, hitting the edge of my shield before falling back into the crater. When the last of the bombs detonate, and all that's remaining of the explosion is the dust trapped under my shield, I sink to my knees, staring at the hole in the world that was once my home. This is where I met Marcus and watched him and my mom fall in love. Where I learned how to fight and use the excess power I have for good. A hand squeezes my shoulder, and I reach for it, knowing I'll find my mom watching the destruction with me. She may not have lived here as I did, but this was her home too.

A whine of pain draws my attention away from the smoldering rocks, and I turn to find Lowell shifted and curled in the fetal position. "What's wrong?" I demand. He's holding his side, both hands splayed wide across the length of his torso. Gingerly, he removes one, revealing a gash.

Gash isn't the right word. There's a chunk of skin missing.

I can see his ribcage.

He presses his blood-soaked hand back to the wound. "Why isn't it healing?" I ask, running over to him. His breaths are shallow and too fast; even though he looks calm, the bond is teeming with fear and pain.

"Get over here," I scream at the healers we saved. "Is that from teleporting?"

"I've never—" the mousy witch starts, her hands shaking.

"We've never teleported before," the other healer replies. "We've never seen an injury like that."

Adriana barrels past them, practically knocking them over like two bowling pins. "We need to get him back to Coleman," I implore.

"He can't teleport like that," she replies. "He's not healing fast enough. You need to put concentrated Light Magic on that wound."

"There are mortals—" the healer starts. My eyes leave my mate long enough to see a crowd of mortals lingering, looking between us and the blast site, but the snarl that escapes my lips is enough to stop them from protesting any further. As they work, I slip into the minds of every mortal in the vicinity and give them the overwhelming urge that they left the stove on in their flats. They scurry like rats in multiple directions away from the smoking crater in the city's center and my mate lying on his side.

My were-magic reacts to Lowell's cry of pain, surging to the surface and dripping down my hand. I caress his cheek and will the magic to take some of his pain. When it touches his skin, I wince as it hits me in the side, exactly where Lowell's injury is, but his brow relaxes as the pain fades, and that makes it worth it. He huffs a small chuckle. "You're going to be the death of me, little witch."

"It's a very solid possibility," I admit, worrying my bottom lip. He reaches up and removes my flesh from my teeth, his thumb brushing across my lower lip.

"Worth it," he murmurs as I lean down and kiss him gently.

"He should be good to move now," the female healer says. "But maybe not...umm..."

"No teleporting," Adriana says.

I reach out to the channel I share with Vlad and ask him for an escort back to the portal. "Listen," I direct at the witches, "you have a choice. You can come back with us, joining our side in this rebellion against the man who just tried to blow you up, or I can erase your memories, and you can go home. You have about thirty seconds to decide."

"You said Mister Coleman is with you?" the male asks, and I nod. They exchange a glance. "This is our brother." He gestures to the man on the stretcher. "We don't have the supplies or resources to help him, but Coleman should."

"He can come too," I tell them. "And any other family you have."

"It's only the three of us," the woman replies as Vlad arrives.

"Fucking hell," he says, looking at the giant hole. "I leave you alone for ten minutes." He turns to Lowell, assessing the damage before heaving my wolf into a cradle in his arms.

"I wish I had a camera," Adriana breathes next to me, regarding the sight of the giant werewolf in the vampire's arms. My laugh is only thirty percent hysterical and is made worse when both men scowl comically and take off in a blur of speed.

Adriana grabs hold of the healers. I hold out a hand for my parents, but she waves me off. "Maybe I should handle the teleporting." My parents immediately grab onto her.

"I love that my humor is rubbing off on you," I deadpan as we all grab onto my sister so she can take everyone to the portal.

Chapter Sixteen

"THE ATTACK ON THE Dragons Army Headquarters in London comes just days after the attacks on the bases in Shanghai and Salem."

Someone raises the volume on the laptop in the center of the war room table as the blonde witch is replaced by pictures of explosions in Shanghai, carnage and bodies in Salem, and the collapse of the Headquarters in London. I drum my nails against the table as the newscaster continues talking about casualties and destruction.

"It's been confirmed that these attacks are the work of a rebel uprising of Dark Witch Covens and Magical Creatures. These rebels are led by none other than former Dragons Captain Kathryn Carmichael." A picture of me kneeling amidst the rubble at Headquarters flashes on the screen. "Sources say Carmichael deserted the army in December after officials discovered her infamous Lightning Magic was, in fact, Dark Magic."

"Shit," Edina breathes.

"They're thorough," Vlad comments, swiveling side to side in his chair.

"Our reporter sat with King Archer Baran today in an undisclosed location to hear his opinion on the matter and to discuss his strategy for dealing with the Dark Witches."

The feed cuts to a brunette witch wearing pearls and an honest-to-God pants suit, sitting in a director's chair. She fluffs a stack of index cards.

"Your Majesty," she purrs, and the camera flips to Archer wearing his full regalia. The fucking sword is on his belt, the ruby winking under the lights, mocking me.

Edina hisses. Vlad boos.

"So far, the terrorists have only attacked military bases. Do you think this will change?"

"Terrorists?" Adriana fumes.

"I don't believe so, but everyone should be vigilant. Especially those who live in areas highly populated with other witches." Archer's voice is serious, but there's no conviction behind it. It feels like he's reading from a prompter.

"Do you recommend evacuation of those areas?"

"Not at this time."

"It must have been quite the shock to hear Kathryn Carmichael was leading this charge. Especially since you were...close. I admit, most of the women in the Kingdom were envious when we saw pictures of the two of you from the Solstice ball." The brunette makes a high-pitched screeching sound that I think is supposed to be a laugh. She plays with the ends of her hair and bats her eyelashes.

"Anyone else feel like we're about to watch low-budget porn?" Lyra asks from her spot over my shoulder.

"She's about thirty seconds away from dropping to her knees," Vlad says.

"Do you think if Archer gets laid, he'll just let us have the Kingdom?" Edina's laugh covers Archer's answer.

"Enough," my mother barks, silencing the room.

"Did you suspect she was in league with the Dark Witches when you attended the Solstice Ball? Sources say your relationship was fast, and the timing does seem coincidental—"

"No," Archer snaps, plucking the crown off his head and running a hand through his blue-black hair. "Katie is the love of my life, and I do not doubt that she's been brainwashed by the Dark Witches. I tried to save her, but I was unsuccessful."

"But—" The brunette pauses, looking behind the camera for guidance. This was clearly not something they expected Archer to say.

"Don't misunderstand me," Archer says, turning his hazel eyes to the camera. "Kathryn Carmichael is dangerous. She's incredibly powerful and should be avoided at all costs. If you see her or any of the other wanted witches, do not engage, but please call the Dragons' direct hotline." A phone number flashes on the screen alongside pictures. It starts with me, my mom, and Marcus and continues going until most of the people we've recruited have been named.

Edina snaps the laptop closed, plunging the war room into silence. "Well, I've never been a wanted criminal before," she snarks. "That's a fun new development."

I lean forward, pressing my hands into my eye sockets. "How bad is this?"

"He made you seem unstable and fanatical," my mom responds.

"We have a good number of soldiers now," Marcus says, softer than my mother's no-bullshit response. "But he made it impossible to recruit anymore."

"And we don't know where *he* is now," Adriana says, hissing the pronoun like it offends her to even think about the prince.

"The interview was at the safehouse in Edinburgh," I tell them. "I recognize the god-awful wallpaper. But Jai said they have another location, so I assume that was a decoy in case the news crew was on our side."

"Did he say where?" Marcus asks.

"Just that it was close."

"We can scour the country," Vlad says. "How many soldiers are decent in Mind Magic?"

"The building will be warded," my mom says. "Mind Magic will only work if they can sense shields."

"We have a few who are proficient," Adriana offers. "We can send them on scouting missions."

"And you can't see a location?" I ask. Adriana shakes her head, her gray eyes welling with tears. "Hey, it's fine." I reach across the table to hold her hand. "Is there anyone we can ask about your visions and how Archer is blocking them?"

"I..." Her eyes cloud over, and she breathes a huge sigh of relief. "I can talk to Rodger's teacher. If I take the portal to Tokyo, I can teleport from there."

"Go. We're almost done here," I tell her, squeezing her hand. "Take someone with you." My mom stands to go with her.

"Be careful," Vlad says, his eyes latching with my sister's. Adriana gives him a shy smile, and the air between them turns palpable.

Then Vlad clears his throat. "The Dragons gave our pictures to the mortals as well. If anyone sees you—"

Adriana's face falls, and she disappears into the portal without letting him finish, my mother on her heels. Edina chuckles. "You're an idiot," she says to Vlad. "I would have thought that you'd have better game since you're ancient."

"Thanks, Tinker Bell." He pinches the bridge of his nose.

"You should have left it at 'be careful.'"

"I got that," he snaps.

"Did you, though?"

Everyone in the room averts their eyes until I clear my throat. "I want every witch to continue to add to the outside wards," I say, moving us forward. "The full moon starts tomorrow night, and I don't want any accidents."

"We should move the witches who can't fight," Marcus offers. "Archer already broke through these wards once."

"They can go to my house," Vlad offers, still slightly dejected. "Archer was next door and didn't realize it exists."

"Our pack will be there too," Lyra says. "We're running there tomorrow, so there's a little more space beneath the wards here."

"Is that safe?" Edina asks.

"It has the same shields that surround Vlad's house. We'll be fine."

"Then that's settled," I say. "Let's get the children and elderly set up to move today. How are we doing space-wise?"

"My progeny and some of the baby vampires still out in the world are bringing coffins with the latest shipment of blood," Sybil says. "We should be able to consolidate to a few rooms during the day."

"And my pack prefers sleeping outside," Butch says. "So even after the full moon, we're good to stay out there."

"Thank you both," I say. "I'll have some Earth Elementals create a structure, so you have some shelter above ground." The Pack Master laughs but expresses his thanks as I dismiss the extra members to begin their tasks.

"How's Lowell?" Vlad asks when they're gone.

Lowell's wound was harder to heal than it should have been. We stopped the bleeding in the field, but the actual stitching together of muscles was tough. Luckily, werewolves heal faster than humans, so he should be fine in a few days. But not in time to shift for the full moon without tearing open the wound.

"Losing his mind," I sigh. "It hasn't even been a day, and he's already going stir-crazy. It took his mother and Luna tying him to the hospital bed to keep him out of the meeting tonight."

"Why didn't you want him here?"

"Because I mention Archer's name, and he practically blows a gasket," I huff, blowing a stray hair away from my face. "Seeing him on screen would be a recipe for disaster. I have no idea how we will survive the full moon tomorrow."

"He should stay in the cells," Vlad says. "The magic suppressant might take some of the edge off." I nod my thanks.

"What are we going to do about Archer's interview?" Edina asks softly. "If we win this war, the public will need to trust you."

"You could go with the mad queen angle," Vlad offers, and I level him with my best death glare. "No? I think it would be hilarious."

"Not going for comedy here, Vlad."

"Fine." He smirks. "How...legal are you looking to keep things?"

"I'm already a wanted criminal."

"Great." He leans over the boardroom table. "I have hackers. We can tap into every screen registered to every witch in the Kingdom and release a statement."

"I'm sorry. You have *hackers?*"

"Witches mostly, a few vampires," Vlad says. "They specialize in keeping magical information out of the hands of mortals, but I'm sure they'd be up for a challenge."

"They wouldn't turn you in?"

"Not if I pay them enough."

"Fine," I say. "Call them."

"Your mom and I will make statements also," Marcus says. "It will help to see two former generals speaking about the injustices of the government. Especially since your sanity is in question."

"You'd do that?" I ask, suddenly sounding like a small child.

"Of course, Katie. We'll help in any way we can."

I thank him, and he leaves me alone with Vlad and Edina.

"Now what?" Edina asks, squeezing my hand.

"We get through the full moon," I say, "and then we get our troops ready for war."

THE SLAP OF BARE feet on stone floats down the hallway before I even get close to my destination. I wince as I round the corner and the bars of multiple cells come into view. Somehow this secluded corner of the coven is a little more depressing than the rest. The magical lights aren't as bright, the stones seem a little damper, and the hum of the magical suppressant makes my skin crawl.

I pause outside the cell where Lowell is pacing. His eyes are wild, darting in every direction. I hate that this is what we had to do to keep my mate safe tonight.

"Hey, Alpha," I coo, and he turns to bare his teeth. When his gaze lands on me, he sighs, his shoulders rounding and his whole body sagging just a bit. Lowell breathes heavily, his entire body heaving with the motion, but he stops his pacing and waits. For good measure, I cast a barrier spell around the door and one to both ends of the hall. I learned the hard way that my mate is a flight risk. Well...Vlad learned when Lowell tackled him trying to escape.

Full moons are a fun time.

I take the key from my pocket and unlock the door, sliding in quickly. The magic suppressant washes over me, making me shiver as my power goes dormant. When the door is firmly locked, I turn back to my mate.

"Little witch." My nickname turns into a wolfish whine, hitting me like a punch in the gut. Lowell runs his hands through his already mussed hair. His whole body is trembling with the desire to shift.

"Oh, pup," I breathe, rushing over to him. He buries his face in my neck, whimpering as I rub his back. "I know, I know."

"I miss my pack," he cries into my skin, and my heart breaks for him. I tug him over to the bed Adriana set up in the cell and sit with my back against the wall. He rests his head on my stomach, and I run my fingers through his hair as he buries into me. "I hate this."

"I'm sorry," I murmur, kissing the top of his head.

"It's not your fault."

"Kinda is." He tilts his head up to look at me. "You still love me even though I sliced your stomach open?"

"Always," he says, nuzzling back into me. I knead the tight muscles of his shoulders, watching as he relaxes under my touch.

"Would it help to tell me what you'd be doing if you were with your pack?"

He hums in agreement. "We run, mostly. Sometimes we hunt. But my favorite part—" He swallows thickly. I hate how much this hurts him. I knew shifting would be a problem, but I wasn't anticipating how much being separated from his pack during the full moon would hurt.

"Tell me," I encourage.

A heavy sigh. "We sleep in a pile."

"A dogpile?" I ask, unable to contain my smile.

"You tease, but under the stars, surrounded by my pack... It's unlike anything you've ever felt." Lowell's voice is dreamy as he tells me all kinds of things about where everyone sleeps and how, since they were born, the twins claimed the spots next to him.

"When all this is over, I want you to come with me."

"I can come?" I ask.

"Of course," Lowell says. His hands start tracing patterns along my stomach. "You'll want to be there when we have pups..."

My heart rate picks up. Lowell lifts his head. "You said you want kids one day," he murmurs.

"Yes..."

"We hadn't talked about that." He props his chin on my stomach.

"We hadn't." I smile, running my fingers through his hair. "It's a good thing we had Butch bring it up in front of a crowd."

Lowell chuckles. "We've been busy."

"That's the understatement of the year." I seriously can't believe the whirlwind that's been the last four months. If you told me last autumn that by the spring, I'd be a wanted criminal mated to a werewolf, I would have called you crazy. Well, I would have been excited about the werewolf part.

But there's still so much ahead of us. We're not even close to being done with the threats facing us. We may never be.

"What is it?" Lowell asks, not even needing the bond to read my emotions. He maneuvers us, pulling me flat onto the mattress and turning me on my side so we face each other. His nose brushes against mine in that tender gesture he does that promises I'm safe and cherished.

"It's hard to think about that," I whisper. "It's hard to dream of a future."

Lowell wraps his hand around my neck and pulls me into a kiss. "We'll survive this war," he says against my lips.

"And when we do, I'll be a queen with a ton of responsibility."

"So, no pups for a while," Lowell says with a smile. "But one day."

"One day," I agree. He kisses me deeply, slow and coaxing and full of promise.

"You realize I'm not going to be able to keep my hands off you when you're carrying my child, don't you?"

"In a sexual way or because your protective instincts will be in overdrive?"

"Yes." His laugh soothes my soul, even as he snaps his teeth at my lips. "Do you need me to take a tonic?" he asks, kissing the corner of my mouth as he pulls away.

"Won't work on wolves," I say. "But thank you, pup." He brushes his nose against mine again before tucking me into his chest.

"Thank you," he murmurs, kissing the top of my head. He squeezes me tighter, pulling me in even more.

"For?"

"Being my pack tonight."

I tilt my head up and kiss the stubble on his chin.

About an hour later, after I found some very effective ways of keeping Lowell's mind off shifting, he sits straight up in bed, jostling me off his chest. "What is it?" I ask.

Before Lowell can answer, Vlad appears with five wolves in tow. Lowell lets out another whine as he searches the pairs of eyes identical to his.

"It seems some of the pack missed their brother," Vlad says. One wolf barks. "And son." Another bark. "And his mate. If you want the message delivered correctly, Lorraine, shift and tell them yourself."

I laugh, but Lowell is deathly still, like moving one muscle might scare them away. "Can they come in the cell with the suppressant?" I ask.

"We'll have to turn it off. But if Lowell can promise not to shift, we can allow his pack in. What do you say, Lowell?"

My mate nods slowly. Vlad grabs a key from his pocket and unlocks the door, holding a hand out to keep the wolves at bay until I hear the magic suppressant in our cell turn off. The familiar feeling of my magic and the mating bond rush through me, and Lowell sighs in relief.

"You can't shift," I remind him gently.

"I'm good, little witch."

His family bound into the room, surrounding us. They each take turns licking our faces, which is gross and sweet at the same time, before clambering onto the mattress. Lowell pulls my back into his chest, and the wolves surround us. Like he told me, the twins fight for the spot next to their brother, eventually lying perpendicular so both heads touch his back. Lyra nestles in front of me and nudges my hand with her nose until I scratch behind her ears. I lose track of Lyra and Lorraine, but there's a heavy weight on my feet.

Lowell's whole body relaxes, and unrestrained joy filters down the bond as he drifts off to sleep.

Chapter Seventeen

I WALK INTO THE training room, tightening my ponytail and slipping my phone into my leggings pocket. It's been three weeks since the bombing at Dragon Headquarters. Three weeks of radio silence from Archer and his people.

Adriana confirmed that there is a spell others can use to hide from clairvoyants, but short of teaching the spell to her, the man she met in Japan didn't offer a way to reverse the effects. It hasn't stopped Adriana from looking for a workaround, but so far, Archer has remained invisible to her.

While we keep waiting for the other shoe to drop, we've been training mercilessly. The days blur together in a sea of exercises and tactic meetings, broken only by my own training in Light Magic and hellfire. Coleman taught me more effective healing spells that can be used in a pinch on the battlefield, and my mother showed me how to hone my Light Magic as Battle Magic.

The hellfire has been trickier, especially in high-pressure situations. If I have any emotions, the hellfire seizes control of my body and aims for destruction. I was doused more times than I can count in Edina's ice magic while I fumbled with control. In the end, we decided I wouldn't use it if it could be avoided.

I toe the mats laid over the expanse of the training room, wondering what my tutors have planned for me today. Adriana is in the center of the room, speaking in hushed tones with Cecelia Andrews, Edina, and Astor.

"Oh good, let's get started," she calls, bouncing over to me, her ringlets moving in time with her steps.

"Why did we baby-proof the training room?" I ask. The mats covering every square inch of the floor are standard, but the ones lining the walls, not so much.

"Trust me," Edina laughs. "You'll be happy for the padding in a minute."

"We're learning to fly," Adriana squeals. A slow smile creeps across my face. *Finally.* I've been begging Adriana to teach me the damn cloud-flying magic since the prison break-in, but something has always taken precedence.

"Call your Dark Magic forth," Cecelia instructs, and my iridescent black smoke coils around my arms. "Instead of fashioning it into a weapon, you want to form a cloud that stays around your feet."

"That's important," Adriana says. "If it's higher than your knees, you'll fly sideways."

"Or upside down." Cecelia grimaces. My magic slides down my body, pooling around my ankles. "Good, add some more. More cushion is never a bad thing."

"Don't I know it," I joke, adding more magic until the cloud billows around my calves.

"From here, it's pretty simple," Adriana says. "Treat it like Battle Magic, and it'll do your bidding. Instead of attacking, you want it to carry you forward."

I nod and will the magic to raise me off the ground. Nothing happens. I try again, and this time my feet leave the mat, only to come back down a second later. I grunt, and this time imagine flying forward. My magic listens and drags me along the floor, scraping my toes against the mats before depositing me in heap a few feet away.

Edina snickers, and I glare. "I'm sorry, babes. I've just never seen you not succeed at something on your first try. It's fascinating."

"You're a terrible friend," I grumble as I finally lift off the ground...only to fly straight into the wall. "Fucking hell."

"Don't let Edina's comments discourage you," Astor says. "Her first attempts at flight were awful."

"Thanks, Astor," Edina snipes.

"You're welcome." His reply is completely sincere. Even with the extended time spent with Edina, poor Astor still doesn't recognize sarcasm.

I grit my teeth, determined to get this before I have to get ready. We're hacking into everyone's electronics tonight, and I need to convince them I'm not a brainwashed psycho. I could use a win before that.

I crash. Hard.

I'm not sure how it happened, but I somehow embed myself between the mats and whack my shin against the rock wall. I scream obscenities as Adriana and Cecelia run over to help dislodge me.

"What the hell are you doing to my mate?" Lowell bellows from the training ring. I'm pried free of the wall mats only to land on my ass on the floor mats. A trickle of amusement comes down our bond when he realizes I'm okay.

"I hate each and every one of you," I groan, standing as Lowell runs over to me and drops to his knees, kissing my injured shin and draining the fight from me.

"You're trying too hard, *Ma Reine*," he murmurs, rising and kissing the sensitive spot beneath my ear. "You need to relax."

"Easier said than—" He wraps my ponytail around his fingers and yanks my head to the side, giving himself access to my neck.

"Umm...guys?" Adriana says, but I ignore her in favor of the warmth spreading from my belly up my spine and to the tips of my toes.

"You worry too much," Lowell says against my skin. "Breathe. Your magic knows what you want."

"Katie—" It's Cecelia's voice this time. Lowell gets to my collarbone and gently nibbles his way toward my shoulder. A soft moan escapes my lips.

"Kathryn Isabelle Carmichael!" Edina screams.

"Did you just middle-name me?" I growl, opening my eyes. My frustration fades to wonder.

Lowell and I are in the air, floating in slow, lazy circles around the center of the training room. "How did you know what to do, pup?" I ask.

"Instinct." Lowell gives me a sexy smirk. I hold onto him as we start to lower back to the ground. "And I could feel you overthinking."

"Helpful." We touch down on the ground, and I do a little happy dance before grabbing his hand and towing him over to my trainers.

"Did I learn faster than Edina?" I tease, and she sticks her tongue out at me.

"Yes," Astor says. "Although she learned to fly distances as well. I won't be able to properly compare until you've flown outside this room."

"Excellent idea, Astor," Adriana says with a too-wide smile. "Let's go get some coffee."

"That sounds great." I take a step, and Adriana stops me with a hand on my chest.

"Let's fly to the mess hall. And try not to kick anyone in the head...they get mad about that."

I SIT PERFECTLY STILL as Edina curls my hair around the ruby tiara. I tried to convince everyone to let me address the public in street clothes, but I was massively outvoted. *They need to see you as a queen. They need to believe you're ready for this position.* I think going on screen in a gown and crown will make me look as crazy as Archer said I am. But what do I know? I'm only leading a rebellion.

The cerulean gown has a high neckline that extends into cap sleeves and is unembellished satin that flows in one long line. No one will see the bottom since I'm sitting, but Vlad insisted clean lines would make me seem more imposing. The color was debated for a solid hour. I couldn't wear red since that was reminiscent of my dress at the Solstice Ball, and black was out because of Dark Magic. And while everyone went back and forth on what colors were acceptable and would still look good on camera, all I could think was that this will be my life if I become queen. An endless series of small choices that shouldn't matter become of the utmost importance. It's daunting.

I tug on the locket at my neck that thumps with Lowell's heartbeat. It's calm, reassuring…and the total opposite of my own which is racing. My mate is currently standing behind the camera with Vlad because, in all the practice runs of my speech, my voice was warmer when I spoke to Lowell.

"Two minutes," Vlad says. Edina places one curl strategically across my shoulder while Adriana spells the enchanted mirror to show my speech.

My mother and Marcus take their spots on either side of me. Generals of the Dragons aren't celebrities by any means, but they have been seen with the late king enough that people know who they are. They're respected in the community, so having them behind me is a strong statement.

Especially since my public persona was questionable at best, even before Archer's accusations.

"How are you doing, babes?" Edina asks as Adriana hands me a glass of water.

"Nervous as fuck."

Ninety percent of the Kingdom of Magic is comprised of witches who are living amongst mortals. Witches who use their magic in minimal ways to make their lives easier. Some use it to make mortals' lives better, all while being virtually unknown except to the other witches they see.

How do I relate to people like that? I've lived exclusively amongst witches for my entire life. I went from school to Dragons Headquarters to the coven. I've never had to hide my magic, to know the fear of being discovered.

"Stick to the script," Vlad says. "These are people you're helping."

I take a sip of the water Adriana gave me. In reality, most Elemental Witches won't be affected by the change in power. They'll continue living their lives under a new regime. Yes, my goal is to make sure we help them all and make the Kingdom a safe place, but will I actually affect their lives?

"Hey, *Ma Reine*," Lowell murmurs, suddenly right in front of me. "You're doing a good thing. Your reign will help every witch you're addressing."

"Will it?" I breathe. "How do we know that? Because some ghost told me this is what was supposed to happen?" Lowell steals some of my anxiety, his eyes flaring yellow as he uses the bond to keep me on solid ground. "I feel like such a fraud."

"You're not," Vlad says. "I've met a lot of frauds in my lifetime. You're not it, baby queen. Now get your shit together 'cause we're live in thirty seconds."

"We should have just recorded this." Everyone starts scrambling back to their spaces.

"Probably, but it's too late now because we're live in five—" Vlad counts down and then gives me the signal to start speaking.

I smile, locking eyes with my mate as he nods encouragingly. Calming energy floods the bond. "Good evening, citizens of the Kingdom of Magic. My name is Kathryn Carmichael, and I'm here to set the record straight.

"You may have heard of me before. You've heard stories that sound more like legend than reality. You've heard tales of lightning magic, whispers of a prophecy, and more than enough gossip about my romantic life." I chuckle under my breath, and Vlad rolls his eyes at my deviation from the script.

"Most recently, you've heard stories that I deserted the army I spent my entire life training to be a part of. You've heard tales of attempted coups against the monarchy that I swore to protect, whispers that I have Dark Magic, and rumors that I've been brainwashed and attacked innocent soldiers.

"This past winter, I discovered that my Lightning Magic is not a rare form of Elemental Magic, but rather two magics that have merged." My Light Magic illuminates my skin, and I watch in the mirror as it wraps around me like a blanket of sunlight. Then, I call my Dark Magic, letting the iridescent black smoke be seen on its own before letting the two combine into my lightning.

"When I learned I had Dark Magic within me, I was scared. I heard the stories, the claims that Dark Magic was inherently evil and could corrupt even the gentlest souls. But the first time I used my Dark Magic was to save the life of a soldier, a very dear friend." I swallow thickly, willing my emotions to stay down at the thought of Deavers.

"When it worked, I should have been elated. Instead, I was terrified. Not only because the use of Dark Magic was illegal but because everything I thought I knew about this magic was obliterated. It was supposed to be evil. But it didn't destroy or taint or corrupt. *It saved.*"

Lowell gives me an encouraging nod as I let my magic drop, absorbing it back into the pit of my stomach. "I began to question everything around me, everything I knew to be true. And in that questioning, I found centuries of injustice that began with the Four Kings War.

"History tells us that King Baran saved witches from a lifetime of infighting. In reality, he created a rift where there was once harmony. Since acquiring this knowledge, I have made it my mission to restore balance in the Kingdom of Magic.

"I come to you tonight not to place blame but to open your eyes. I hope you can see that I have not been brainwashed and am not looking to hurt civilians. I am looking to bring the Kingdom of Magic back together. To create a world where all voices are heard and all forms of magic are celebrated.

"Thank you."

I smile warmly again, and Vlad waves his hand to acknowledge that the feed has been cut. "Thirty seconds."

Everyone springs into action, moving around to prepare for my mother and Marcus's speech next. I vacate my seat while another is rolled in. I excuse myself to the hallway just as I hear Vlad counting down for the next broadcast. Leaning against the wall, I take deep breaths until I hear Lowell's footsteps against the stone floors.

Warm arms encircle me, and I sag into the comfort, the tension bleeding from my shoulders. He presses a kiss on my temple, just below my tiara. "You did beautifully, *Ma Reine*."

I nod, swallowing thickly. "Now we wait for the fallout."

Chapter Eighteen

Another moon cycle passes, and there's no word from Archer or the Dragons. We were sure that my message would have some sort of backlash. We fortified shields and have soldiers stationed outside around the clock waiting to sound the alarm, but there's been nothing. They've gone completely underground...literally. We can't even find their hideout, which means they must have copied our use of the hills for their new headquarters.

Vlad's spies out in the wild have heard mixed reactions to my address. Most witches are cautious, like even mentioning the war will bring it to their doorstep. Some are firmly on our side and believe our mission is just. Others don't see the reason for a change.

None of it matters until we win the war, so we're back to training. A lot of training. *So much fucking training.*

The atmosphere in the coven is tense. Not only are people scared, but the close quarters and the extended downtime are getting to everyone. The entire situation is a powder keg ready to blow. I'm not one to wish for fighting, but if we don't get some sort of intel soon, our army will riot.

Today we have a meeting to discuss letting people leave for some secured locations, like Lowell's pack or Vlad's safehouses.

We can't let everyone go, but it might help morale to have some extended time above ground and for some of the soldiers, their own room.

I'm procrastinating. As soon as I wake up, I have to put out whatever fires have occurred while I've slept, so I roll over, resigning myself to just five more minutes. I pat the mattress next to me, finding empty sheets where my mate should be.

"Pup?" I call sleepily before a feather-light touch brushes my calves. Lips skim the sensitive flesh of my inner thigh before bypassing my sex and landing on my stomach. A warm tongue trails up my torso, pushing the oversized t-shirt up with it. "Good morning," I moan as stubble bites into the soft skin of my breasts.

Lowell pushes the blanket away so that I can see the smile lighting up his face. I brush the curtain of his dark hair aside as he smiles and places a chaste kiss right above my heart. "Happy birthday, little witch."

I hum as he sinks back down slightly, his mouth surrounding my nipple and gently sucking. We've been restricted to quickies for the past three weeks, but today Lowell is taking his time. He's savoring every inch of my skin, memorizing the swell of my breasts. His fingers play along my other breast as his teeth scrape my sensitive bud in his mouth. I can't control the groan that escapes as the heat builds in my belly, traveling lower as he continues his ministrations.

"I didn't tell you it was my birthday," I hum as he works his way back down my body, sliding off my now-soaked underwear as he goes.

"Edina told me." His breath is hot against my core as his fingers gently glide through the slickness that's gathered there. Fuck, I need him. I'm not going to last very long at all. "Lie back," he instructs, naturally making me prop myself up on my elbows to watch.

His eyes lock on mine, the glint in them promising he'll find fun and interesting ways to punish me before his lips close around my clit. I inhale sharply as he easily sinks a finger inside me as his tongue switches to gently teasing circles. "Please don't edge me," I whine and lie back as requested. "I can't take it, Alpha."

Lowell smirks in that sexy way that makes me want to spontaneously combust. "Since you asked nicely." He adds another finger and returns to my clit. His fingers instantly find my g-spot as he pistons them in and out of me just the way I like it.

"I love how you taste," Lowell groans, licking a long line from my opening back to my clit. "I could stay here all day. For the rest of our lives."

My hips thrust up on their own accord, and Lowell's arm presses on my lower stomach, holding me still while he brings me closer and closer to orgasm. The pressure from the weight in that spot adds to the sensation.

"Please don't stop."

Lowell's lips form a seal around my sensitive bundle of nerves while his tongue flicks against it. *I'm not gonna stop, little witch,* he sends to my mind. *Not until you come. All. Over. Me.*

"Fuck," I scream as I approach the edge.

That's right. Give it to me.

The door flings open, and Edina, Vlad, and Adriana stand there with presents and balloons. "Happy Birthday!" they all shout, and I'm powerless to stop the orgasm that rips through me.

"Oh god!" Adriana shrieks. Balloons float to the ceiling as she starts yelling something about her visions and runs away.

Lowell doesn't stop. And Edina and Vlad don't leave.

"Pup." I turn away from the door and throw a pillow over my face while simultaneously trying to bat him away.

I promised I wouldn't stop.

"Shit. Watermelon!"

He pulls away with a chuckle that's positively feral and places a kiss on my inner thigh.

"Aww, we have the same safe word!" Edina coos, clutching her heart.

"That's...something I'll need to unpack in therapy." I pull the pillow away from my face. "Now, please, get the fuck out." Edina laughs and waves as she walks away, leaving Vlad leaning against my doorway. "Vlad, I'm not kidding."

"Not an exhibitionist, baby queen?" he asks, and I launch the pillow at him. "I'm going. I'm going. But here—" He tosses a package, and it lands on the mattress right beside Lowell's head. "Trust me. You want it now. Happy birthday!"

He leaves, closing the door behind him, and I throw a spell at the hunk of wood that will keep it locked. "We really need to have a conversation with them about boundaries," I grumble.

"Good luck with that." The arm pinning me down eases, and Lowell swipes my birthday present. "Are you ready to continue?" Lowell's voice is low and thick with arousal, and fuck if it doesn't make me shiver.

"Yes," I breathe, and instantly his tongue is back on my sensitive clit. I hiss at the overstimulation, but he works me in slow circles until my body relaxes into the pleasure. A bow is tossed out of the covers, quickly followed by the top of the box.

"What could Vlad have possibly gotten me that we'd need right—" I gasp as something cold and metal brushes against my asshole. Lowell flings the covers back and shows me a velvet box filled with sex toys.

"Any preferences?" He removes a tickler and brushes the feather across my breasts before returning it to the box.

"Hang on," I murmur, sanitizing everything in each sealed box, even hitting the item Lowell is hiding. "What's in your hand?"

"Do you want to see it, or would you like a surprise for your birthday?" he asks. I consider for all of a second before declaring surprise. He places the item I'm pretty sure is a plug beside my leg under the covers and pulls a blindfold from the box. "What's your safe word, little witch?"

"You already heard it today." His teeth sink into the tender flesh of my stomach, making me yelp. "Watermelon." My breathing increases as he licks away the hurt and slips the silk over my eyes and secures it tightly.

"Good girl," he murmurs before ensnaring me in a searing kiss. "I'm going to bypass the restraints and handcuffs in here, but I expect you to stay still. If you don't want anything, use your safe word."

"Yes, Alpha."

A light touch grazes across my chest, swirling around my nipples. I whimper as the feather from the tickler continues its pace before switching to the other side.

"Think I can make you come just like this, little witch?" Lowell asks and my pussy clenches.

"Probably," I pant.

Lowell groans. The feather trails down my body and brushes against my clit, and it takes all my concentration to remain still and not arch into him. "So fucking beautiful," he says. I hear him digging around in the box as he continues the light touch. The feather is removed, and I wait quietly for whatever is next.

The buzzing starts right before a vibrator connects with my clit. I scream out as my body bucks off the bed. It feels like suction on my clit in addition to the buzzing and *holy shit.* I explode in seconds, coming with a scream loud enough to rattle the walls. I'm still in the throes of my orgasm when I hear the unmistakable sound of a cap opening. Cold liquid drops onto my asshole, the lube quickly warming as he pushes a finger inside me. He works it in and out before more lube is applied and another finger added as he stretches me out. The pressure combined with the vibrator on my clit is enough to almost make me come again.

Lowell removes his fingers and the same cold metal from before, now coated in lube, brushes against my hole. "Ready?" Lowell asks, and I nod. "I need words, little witch."

"Fuck yes, please," I moan, and he slides the plug inside me painfully slow. It burns slightly, but my body is warmed up and ready and I quickly adjust to the fullness. Lowell ups the speed on the vibrator until the plug is completely inside me and I'm seconds away from coming again before he pulls away, leaving the plug in my ass.

"Perfect." The mattress shifts as he stands, leaving me lying there.

"Wait." I tug on the mating bond as I feel him leave for the bathroom. The water turns on and I release a breath of frustration.

I know I'm not restrained and could follow him, but I wait until I hear his footsteps entering back in the room.

"Look at you," Lowell preens, and grips my jaw possessively. I expect him to kiss me, but he doesn't; he just holds me there. "Laid out so beautifully for me." A finger gently strokes down the side of my breast. "What does my perfect mate want next?"

"Kiss me," I moan, and he claims my mouth savagely. It's wet and dirty and has me dying to squeeze my legs together, but I keep perfectly still.

"Good fucking girl," Lowell growls, shifting so his hot breath is in my ear, flicking his tongue against the lobe. "What position would you like? Show me." I immediately flip over onto my hands and knees. Lowell chuckles darkly. "You love this."

"I could point out the irony that you don't," I say, turning my head over my shoulder.

"It's because I like watching your face as you come around my cock," Lowell says before kissing his way down my spine. His cock nudges my entrance, and he moves his hips forward, his pelvis bumping the plug and pushing it in further. I try to grind back to gain more friction, but Lowell pulls away, and his hand claps down on my ass.

"What did I say about moving?" he asks.

"Sorry, Alpha," I breathe.

"Damn right you are." He grips my hips in his massive hands and slams into me with one thrust.

"Holy shit," I cry as he gives me a minute to get used to the fullness. Lowell fills me to the brim on a normal day, but now with the plug in my ass... "I can't—"

"Relax. You can move how you need to." My body melts, and my head falls forward, pushing my ass up higher. Lowell's hand connects with my ass again, and I scream as my muscles clench around the plug and his cock. He groans and spanks my other cheek.

"Please," I whimper.

"Please, what?"

"Move." I can feel Lowell's desire through our bond, and I know he won't last long once he gets started. Which is why I'm not surprised when he moves so slowly I could scream.

"You should be more specific, little witch," Lowell says, his voice strained as he keeps up his slow pace.

"Harder," I command. "Faster. Fuck me like you mean it, pup."

Lowell responds with another smack to my ass, sheathing himself to the hilt. His control snaps as he starts rutting into me, using my body for his pleasure. I chant his name as he fills me, and between him and the plug, I feel fuller than I've ever felt. It's so fucking much but so fucking good.

Lowell releases one hand that's gripping my ass. When it appears again, the vibrator is pressed against my clit. My orgasm barrels into me with the force of a train. And then it keeps going, rolling in wave after wave, never losing intensity. My entire body is being broken down and reformed over and over again, and I never want it to stop.

I'm still screaming and spasming over his cock when he wraps his other hand around my hair and hauls me upright, so my back is against his chest. This new position puts him even deeper as he holds my body close, banding his arm around my breasts.

"Give me one more," Lowell orders and rolls my nipple between his fingers. It's so overwhelming I'm not sure if I can. Every point of contact is buzzing, and between the vibrator, the plug, his cock, and his fingers, I can't focus. It's too much.

Because he always knows exactly what I need, Lowell lifts the vibrator and begins pulsing it, so it presses against my clit in short bursts that are timed perfectly with his thrusts. That's enough to send me over the edge, and I shout his name as my walls clench, pulling him over the edge with me. He comes with a roar that I'm pretty sure is heard above ground, clinging to me as he rides out his release.

Lowell removes the vibrator from my sensitive clit and guides me back to my stomach so he can slowly work the plug out of my ass. I lift the blindfold, tossing it to the side as Lowell somehow scoops me into his arms and kisses me sweetly. He murmurs praise as his lips caress my cheeks and my neck.

"Happy birthday, *Ma Reine*," he whispers.

"Thank you, Alpha," I mumble, and Lowell carries me into the bathroom, where he fills the bathtub.

Chapter Nineteen

After we bathe, I stand in front of the wardrobe in my room, staring it down like it's personally offended me. I release a heavy breath, staring at an array of clothes, none of which I purchased myself.

The bond pulses, releasing some of the tension in my shoulders, and Lowell steps up behind me, his calloused fingers gently brushing against the bare skin at my waist. "If you don't get dressed soon, we may never leave the room," he murmurs in my ear, stepping closer to me until I feel his erection tenting the towel slung over his hips.

"At least then I'd know what to wear," I grumble, spinning and letting him get a look at my matching scarlet bra and panties set. His eyes drink in the lace hungrily as a rumble in his chest shoots directly to my core.

He cages me into the edge of the wardrobe, his heat warming me through the flimsy fabric of my lingerie. My nipples pebble as my breasts graze his sculpted chest. He leans down and pulls my bottom lip between his teeth before handing me a navy maxi dress.

"I need to change my bra," I laugh, and he flicks open the clasp in a movement so fast I barely catch it. I laugh as I dig out a strapless one, and Lowell moves across the room, removing the temptation of his body. I swear I've never been this insatiable before, but anytime I'm near Lowell, I want to be on top of him. Or underneath him. Or up against a wall.

"Heels?"

"Flats." He smirks, and I purse my lips.

"And we're leaving the coven?" I ask for the hundredth time, hoping my mate will slip and spill whatever secret plans he's made for my birthday. He nods and puts on a pair of dark jeans. "Are we going out in public?"

"With our faces on the mortal and witch's 'most wanted'?" Lowell asks, raising an eyebrow as he starts to get dressed. *He's got a point.*

I slip on the dress, the lightweight cotton gathering at my waist before flowing gently to my feet. I select a pair of flats, marveling at the fact that they fit perfectly. Vlad is seriously thorough when outfitting a wardrobe. When I turn, Lowell is dressed in a dark dress shirt, a few buttons popped open to reveal his tanned skin. His eyes rake over me hungrily before he extends the blindfold.

"I thought you wanted to leave the room," I tease, grabbing the silk mask from him.

"You're gonna have to trust me, little witch," my mate smirks, and I slip the mask over my eyes. I set my makeup with a spell, so I'm not worried about it, and my hair is simply down in waves so it's not like it'll be ruined.

Lowell takes my hand and guides me down the hallway. I cast my mind out simply on habit, noting a few people when we walk past, but they make themselves known, all wishing me a happy birthday. Everyone seems lighter today, more relaxed than in the past few weeks, and I wonder if Lowell threatened everyone to behave tonight.

"Twenty-one," he says in my ear as his hand slips around my waist. I fit against his side seamlessly as I hum in confirmation. Edina and I always had grandiose ideas for our twenty-first birthdays, which were only slightly modified when I moved to London and could drink legally at eighteen. Her birthday was nothing like we planned, though the party was stellar before the shit hit the fan.

Lowell guides me through a doorway, and there are more murmured 'Happy birthdays' before he pauses. "I'm going to hold you while we're in the portal," he says.

"Are we going to the beach house?"

Lowell just laughs and lifts me into his arms. I huff and rest my head on his shoulder as he carries me over the threshold and mist kisses my skin.

When we exit the portal, I immediately recognize the scent. "We're at Vlad's?" I ask as he sets me down and guides me out of the library into the marble foyer. I half expect him to lead me to the backyard, thinking we may be headed to the pack, but we turn the other direction and go out the front. It's spring now, and the scent of flowers and fresh-cut grass tinges the balmy night air as we head off the front porch and onto the lawn.

Outside, I completely lose track of where we are because I'm pretty sure Lowell walks in circles to confuse me. The texture of the grass changes to sand, and Lowell pulls my mask off, revealing the almost-full moon that illuminates the lake.

"Should we be here—"

"I bribed some of the water sprites to keep Delmare busy," Lowell says, tugging my hand. He finally stops a bit away from the lake, and he grins, his smile so infectious that I can't help but echo the motion.

"Right…here," he says, moving me by the shoulders so I'm facing the woods. "This is where I saw you for the first time."

Warmth blooms in my chest as I stare up into those golden eyes. "I think you were closer to the water, Alpha."

"The first time I saw you, you were there." He tilts my chin at the sky above us dotted with stars. "You were on a broom, flying like a madwoman."

I tear my eyes away from the brilliant night sky and back at my mate, who spins me around and tugs me closer to the water. "This is where I first spoke to you," he says, stopping a few paces away from the water. He circles me, wrapping his arms around my waist as I lean back into his chest. "And I was completely enchanted."

"Because I was naked."

Lowell nips the exposed skin at my neck before replacing the hurt with a tender kiss. "It was your eyes, little witch. And then you sassed me."

"What did I say?" I ask, leaning far enough to the side to see his smile.

"I asked what you were…even though I already knew—"

"Because of Vlad's spies?"

"Because of Vlad's spies. And you said, 'I'll show you mine if you show me yours.'"

I scoff, leaning back further into Lowell as his laughter rumbles through me. "God, I was an asshole."

"You were bold." I arch an eyebrow, but he's already pulling me a little way away. "And here...is where you claimed me." He kneels and tugs me down so I'm sitting on his lap the same way I was that night. We had just met and I trusted him so completely and felt so comfortable in his arms. I should have known then.

I rest my head in the crook of Lowell's neck as we sit silently for a moment.

"Blindfold on one more time," he murmurs into my hair, and I sigh as he secures it over my eyes. He gives me a quick kiss before standing with me, still cradled in his arms as he starts walking.

The scent shifts to that of the forest, and I know by the crunch of Lowell's feet that's where we must be headed. I relax into his hold, nuzzling him as we walk in silence. A wave of nervousness passes through our bond, but just as quickly as it's there, it's gone, and he's setting me on my feet.

Lowell pulls off my blindfold. The light of the moon is obstructed by the leaves, so it's hard to see where we are, but Lowell looks at me expectantly. "Do you recognize this place?" he asks, and I shake my head. "Maybe this will help." He snaps his fingers, and little fairy lights spring to life, creating a magical glow over the clearing.

"How—"

"Adriana helped just now," Lowell says. "But don't worry, she can't hear us." I'm about to question it when I feel the familiar sensation of a shield being slid into place. "Do you know where we are?"

I look around the clearing, and my eyes fall upon a familiar tree that my sister magically tied my mate to when he was convinced

I was in peril. "This is where you first kissed me," I whisper, and Lowell is there, his lips descending on mine again.

My heart is bursting as I jump into his arms as I did during that first kiss. Even then, I knew this man was different, that he would ruin me for all other men. He doesn't kiss me long but sets me on my feet and steps back.

Another wave of nervousness flits through our bond. "Why are you nervous—"

Lowell drops to one knee.

I gasp, my hand flying to my mouth. Tears are instantly in my eyes.

"*Ma Reine, mon âme sœur,*" Lowell starts, taking my free hand in his. "Even if we weren't mates, I would choose you. Every minute. Every day. Every lifetime."

My entire body is vibrating with emotion. I'm trying not to cry so I can savor this moment. So I can memorize the look in Lowell's eyes.

I'm failing tragically.

"Kathryn Isabelle Carmichael," Lowell says, a smile breaking across his beautiful face, lighting up his golden eyes. A strangled mix of a cry and a laugh escapes my lips. "Will you marry me?"

"Yes."

There's no hesitation. No doubt. It's the easiest decision I've ever made.

Lowell sighs, and I fling myself into his arms where he's kneeling. Our lips collide as his arm circles my waist, and his other hand cups my cheek, brushing away the tears that have started freely falling. We break apart, and Lowell reaches into his pocket and pulls out a small velvet box.

"This was your grandmother's," Lowell says. "Marcus's mother's ring. When I asked his permission—"

"You asked my parents' permission?" My eyes water all over again. Lowell nods as he slides the ring on my finger, and I look down at the beautiful canary diamond. "It's perfect," I breathe, and Lowell chuckles as he secures it and kisses me again.

"WILL YOU LET US THE FUCK IN?" My best friend's voice pierces the air.

"They can see us, but they can't hear anything," Lowell murmurs. "Are you ready to see them?" I nod emphatically, and Lowell makes a hand motion. The shield falls away, revealing Vlad, Adriana, and Edina waiting with bated breath.

Edina waits half a second before tearing across the clearing and tackling me from Lowell's arms to the ground. She squeals loud enough to wake the dead as we hug and laugh. When we pull away, she immediately grabs my hand.

"Fuck me, that's gorgeous," she says. She turns to Lowell, who is now in an embrace with Vlad. The vampire has a rare beaming smile, and I think I might catch a glimpse of blood tears brimming on his pale lashes.

"You did good, Lo-Lo," Edina says, standing and launching herself at my fiancé. *My fiancé.* I get myself to my feet only to have Adriana almost knock me over again.

"My Katie," she whispers as I feel a sob shudder through her. I pull away, and she cups my face in her hands. "I'm just so glad I got to be in your life for this moment."

My emotions are raw, and any control over them slips, and I break down, clutching her back in my arms. My big sister. My first real friend.

"Will you be my maid of honor?" I ask. "Well, co-maid of honor."

"I was gonna say, babes," Edina says, breaking from her conversation with my fiancé. *Yeah, I'm gonna say that a lot.*

"Yes, of course," Adriana says, her gray eyes welling with tears again. "I assume the date will be after...everything."

I look at my mate, whose eyes find mine like he already knows the answer. "Tomorrow," I say, and he crosses the clearing to be by my side. "There's no reason to wait."

"I agree, little witch," he says, kissing me passionately.

"Are you out of your damn mind?" Edina shrieks as Adriana says, "We need to plan a wedding in one day?"

"Less than that if we go to the party set up in the house," Vlad intones. I look at the vampire, and he tosses me a wink.

"It doesn't have to be big. We can do it outside in the hills, just after sunset. Family and close friends only. Twenty people max."

"Oh, fuck that," Edina says. "You need to invite everyone; they all know this is happening. And I've been planning your bachelorette party since we were sixteen. You're not depriving me of that."

I exchange glances with Lowell, who is biting his lip in an attempt not to laugh.

"Fine," I say dramatically. "Will three days be enough for all of you?"

Vlad, Edina, and Adriana all exchange glances before Adriana nods. "We can make that work."

Lowell leans down and kisses my head, making me warm and fuzzy.

"Let's go tell the group inside," Vlad says. "Your mom is likely to have opinions on your dress that I should get before I call my contact. It's a good thing she's a vampire and fucking fast with a pattern."

Edina and Vlad start discussing lace over tulle while Adriana skips along beside them, asking about candles or flowers. I lean into Lowell's side, wrapping my arms around his waist and just breathing in his scent.

This, right here. This is what we're fighting for. A world where a witch can marry a werewolf, where a Fae and a vampire can become friends and bicker with a Dark Witch about a wedding that has all four magics invited.

For the first time, I let myself envision a future world where that's possible.

Chapter Twenty

THE STEADY THUMP OF bass greets me as I walk into the mess hall. Except it looks nothing like the cafeteria. Podiums with a mix of cages and stripper poles magically float above the ground, close enough to jump onto but high enough to be visible over the throng of women dancing. I should probably be surprised that Edina found men to dance shirtless in the cages, but I learned a long time ago never to underestimate my best friend's power with the opposite sex.

Magical multicolored lights flash, casting the whole room in a darkened rainbow glow. Music blares out of giant speakers, and the dance floor is packed. Like fire hazard packed. I enter slowly, taking everything in with my mouth on the floor. My eyes fix on one of the poles in the center of the room, where my best friend is currently hanging upside down with her legs open in a split.

When she sees me, Edina screams and uses her wings to float off the podium and over the crowd. "Babes! You look hot!" She surveys my little black dress, nodding in approval like she wasn't the one who picked it out for me. "Hang on. I've been working on this."

She holds her hands in front of her and takes a deep breath. From out of thin air, she procures a bride sash and a furry tiara.

She squeals in delight at her trick, throws the sash over my shoulder, and plops the crown on my head.

"You realize I'm supposed to show some decorum in front of these people, right?" I ask. Edina tilts her head back and laughs as she tugs me through the crowd.

"Everyone knows what a bachelorette party is!" she bellows. "And if they don't, Adriana will just wipe it from their little memories."

"E!" Her cackle is barely heard over the music.

"Let's get you a drink, Your Majesty!" The crowd around us lets up a chorus of 'woos,' and Edina tugs me across the room, stopping once we reach the back edge of the dance floor, pointing proudly at our destination.

A gigantic penis-shaped ice luge.

"Edina, oh my god." The ice sculpture is at least ten feet tall...maybe more if you count the balls. Lyra is at the top of the—well, the scrotum—pouring amber liquid down the shaft where it flows to the tip and into my future mother-in-law's waiting mouth. When the shot stops flowing, everyone cheers as she sits up and adjusts her bun. She winks as she walks past me and out of the mess hall, leaving me wondering if she was really just there.

"This way we can do blow-job shots without all the nasty whipped cream and shit." Edina cuts the line to the luge and shoves me onto my knees in front of the statue. When I glare at her, she grabs my hair and tips my head back until I open my mouth for the descending shot.

"I knew you liked it rough," she laughs as I sputter around the never-ending stream of alcohol.

"YEAH, KATIE! TAKE IT!" In my peripheral, I can barely see Luna cheering as she's half-held up by Lowell's twin sisters.

When I can't take anymore, I jump out of the way for the next witch to drink from the giant penis. I stumble slightly as I get up, and Edina wraps her hand around my waist. Lyra joins us, her girlfriend Alaina hanging onto her waist. "Are we dancing?" she screams over the music.

"Where's Adriana?" I ask, and Edina points behind a full bar, where Adriana is hovering in the corner. I motion for the rest to go on without me, but Edina sticks to my side like glue as I make my way over to my sister.

"You're not drinking?" I lean against the wall next to her, and Edina takes the spot on her opposite side.

"No...I think one of us should be—"

"Adriana, everything is covered for tonight," Edina says. "You should let loose. Let your hair down!"

"My hair is down." She fluffs her curls, and Edina rolls her eyes before disappearing behind the bar.

"As my Maid of Honor, you're required to have fun tonight," I say, flashing her a smile. She runs her fingers along the *Maid of Honor* sash she's wearing over her red wrap dress. "The boys are on security tonight, right?" She nods.

Edina returns with a tray of nine shots and three larger mixed drinks. "If we're doing this, we're going all in."

Adriana worries her lip but then conjures a cloud of Dark Magic to hold the tray. I laugh and pass her three shots, arranging the others in front of us.

"Are we toasting?" I ask.

"Obviously we're toasting to you, babes!" Edina holds her shot aloft. I laugh but take my first shot, the alcohol burning on the way down despite my previous shot. "This one is in memoriam of our single party days." We all take another shot.

"And this one," Adriana pipes up, "is for the love that you and Lowell have."

"Don't get all sappy on me!" Edina screams.

"Let me finish," Adriana says. "And for locking down that ridiculous cock." I spit out the chaser I'm drinking, and Edina throws her head back in laughter.

"Well...here's to that then," I laugh, and we each drink our final shot. Grabbing the larger drinks, which taste like cherry but I'm sure pack a punch, I tug the girls onto the dance floor.

I AM THOROUGHLY TRASHED. That's what happens when you drink with witches who know how to perform a refilling spell: your cup is literally never empty.

Luna, the twins, and I are all sitting in chairs that line the room, our heels long since discarded in the sea of bodies still writhing on the dance floor. My main source of entertainment at this moment is Adriana, who is working a stripper pole like a freaking pro. She's drawn a crowd, too, everyone cheering and throwing shit onto her podium.

"Hypothetical question," Edina flops down next to me, sloppily leaning too close. At some point, she lost her dress and now she is in her lacy underwear and Maid-of-Honor sash. "Scale of one to ten. How bad would it be if I had a threesome with Lyra and Alaina?"

"Bad," both twins answer in unison.

"Really? They seemed open to a third tonight," Edina pouts.

"They probably are," Luna answers. "But whenever they bring another woman in, Alaina gets jealous. And when she's jealous, she gets..."

"Stabby," the twins supply.

"Fucking hell." Edina plucks the drink from my hands and takes a swig.

"I thought you were..."Leanne trails off.

"Heterosexual?" Edina asks, and she nods. "I can see how you'd think that based on the sheer amount of dick I pull," Edina says, and I am unrestrained in my hysteria. "But I'm down for anything. Girls usually want to wife me up, though, and I'm not about that life. No offense, babes."

"None was taken until just now," I laugh, and she kisses my cheek.

Lyra and Alaina stumble over and replace my drink. "So, since you're marrying our brother," Lyra says. "I feel like it's our duty as his sisters—"

"Am I gonna get the 'you hurt him, and you die' speech?"

"—for us to tell you, he's an asshole." All four girls crack up, and Edina and I join them.

"No, seriously though," Luna says. "We're so happy for you both and that we can call you a sister tomorrow!" She leans over and brushes her nose against mine in the same way that Lowell does.

"Come on, kiddos," she says to the twins. "It's past your bedtime, and this mama needs to find her mate."

"Ew," the twins cry but follow her out of the mess hall. Lyra and Alaina salute us and head back to the dance floor.

Edina's smile slips when she doesn't think I'm looking. I grab her hand, linking our fingers, and she tries to put her façade back on, but I've already seen past it.

"Scale of one to ten, how bad does it hurt today?" I ask.

She leans her head against my shoulder. "Six. Five if I can have the rest of your drink." I hand it over, and she takes a long sip. "I just wish I knew why," she whispers, fiddling with the plastic cup.

"I know."

"I keep going over it in my head. All of it. The night we spent together, the moment he—" she takes another, much longer drink. "And I keep wondering if things would have been different if I stayed until I emerged."

I kiss her temple, wishing I had answers or knew what to say to give her comfort.

When she sits back up, all traces of vulnerability are gone. "But fuck him, right? If he doesn't want all this," she shimmies her half-naked self in the chair, "then it's his loss. And that guy in the cage's gain." She gestures to a ripped blonde in the cage closest to us. "You wanna come dance?"

I start to stand, but Adriana comes over. Her cheeks are flushed, and her eyes are as wide as saucers. "I think I did something..." Edina turns to her with intrigue, and I arch my eyebrow. "I was talking to Vlad—"

"Just now?" I ask.

"Mentally. And I...said some stuff."

"Oh my god," Edina laughs. "She magically drunk texted him."

I bite my lip to hold in my laugh. "What did you say?"

"Umm...well, you know how I borrowed those romance novels from you?" I do not, but I nod anyway. "Just ...things I learned from those."

"Adriana, you are a constant surprise," Edina breathes.

"Did he respond?" I ask. Adriana's blush tells me enough. "So, are you going over there?"

"I..." Adriana sighs. "I want to."

"Fuck yeah, you do!" Edina cheers.

"But it's bad—"

"Oh, it won't be bad."

"E!" I slap her arm.

Adriana sighs again. "I practically threw myself at him...on multiple occasions. He's always been the one stopping it. I don't think my ego can handle it."

"It's his hang-up," Edina says, reaching out and grabbing Adriana's hand. "Trust me. You're hot. There's no way he wouldn't want you."

"You think I'm hot?" Adriana asks, her spine straightening a bit.

"Hell yeah," Edina and I cheer at the same time.

"You should go over there," I tell her. "Make him listen to the many ideas you've received from reading my books." Adriana chews on her lip before striding with purpose out the door, wobbling slightly on her heels.

"Was Vlad really that good?" I whisper to Edina.

"Good enough that I went back three times." We both erupt in a fit of giggles. "Seriously, Magical Creatures...who knew? We should have started fucking them ages ago."

"Here's to that!"

"Well," Edina stands and extends her hand to me, "now it's your turn to be my wingwoman. Come help me score cage-boy."

"Please, like you need help," I scoff but stand and link my arm through hers as we make our way back onto the dance floor.

I'M GETTING MARRIED TODAY.

The impending bridezilla-style freak-out I'm sure everyone is expecting from me is quickly dampened as Lowell's lips tease mine apart, his tongue playfully flicking against them until I open for him. I sigh, content, not even bothering to open my eyes as we kiss, cocooned in blankets. I got about another hour into the bachelorette party before Lowell showed up and threw me over his shoulder to bring me to bed. There wasn't a single complaint from me.

Lowell groans as I slide my hand down the hard planes of his stomach, and he moves to kiss my neck.

"There's only one problem with having the wedding today." He hisses when I slip my hand beneath the elastic of his sweatpants and grip his cock firmly at the base.

"What's that?" I groan as he bites down on my earlobe, his breath tickling the shell of my ear as I continue pumping his hard length.

"I only got a few days to call you my fiancé."

"That was weak, pup." His deep laugh rumbles through me as I bury my head in his chest, continuing to work him in my hand.

The door opens with a clang.

"NO!"

Lowell is thrown off me, and I'm surrounded by gray magic. The same magic quickly blinds my eyes so I can't see a damn thing.

"Holy shit, Adriana," Edina's voice cuts through Lowell's snarling and the crackling of my magic against my skin. "I said to wake her, not hold her hostage."

"It's bad luck to see the bride on the wedding day," my sister shouts. Lowell growls again, mumbling something about our eyes being closed.

"Lo-Lo, your pack has something planned for you before the ceremony," Edina says calmly. "Go meet them at Vlad's house. Your suit is there."

"Out," Adriana commands. "We have to get ready!"

I absently wonder how long they think it'll take us to get ready when we have magic, but I don't open my mouth.

"Sorry, pup," I call, still unable to see. "I'll finish what I started later."

"Damn right you will," he says, his voice dipping in a way that makes my toes curl. "I love you, little witch. I'll see you at the altar."

I smile like a freaking idiot as I repeat the sentiment. When the door closes, Adriana removes my magical bindings. I plan on glaring at her, but she's smiling so widely that I find it hard to be mad.

"How was *your* night last night?" I ask, and she looks down, toeing my carpet.

"Fine." She sighs, but the smile is still in her eyes. "Well, nothing happened because I threw up the minute I got there."

"Oof," Edina breathes.

"But it was good after that," Adriana hedges. "I stayed the night, and we just cuddled."

"That's freaking adorable," I tell her, and she blushes again.

"Anyway, since we didn't have much time to prepare, we didn't get to throw you a shower."

"You managed the bachelorette just fine."

"So, we're doing it now!"

Lowell's sisters all barrel through the door, each carrying platters of food, presents, and champagne. My mouth pops open. I'm literally only wearing Lowell's shirt.

Luna chuckles. "Let's do this in the mess hall, maybe," she says with a wink.

"A much better idea," Lyra chimes in, ushering the twins back out of the room.

Adriana tosses me white sweatpants with the word Bride across the ass in rhinestones, and I look to Edina for help. "Oh, we're doing this," she says, giving me a matching tank top. "Get dressed. We'll have Coleman meet us in the mess hall for your hangover."

"You're a goddess," I mutter, and then mentally ask, *How much more of this should I expect?*

It's an all-day affair. Get ready, bride! I groan as she and Adriana leave me to get dressed.

MY BRIDAL BRUNCH IS small, just my maids-of-honor, Lowell's sisters and mom, and my mom. They made it into a lingerie party, and I spent the day sending mental pictures of the items to Lowell, who in turn tells me all the dirty things he plans to do to me in said lingerie.

After the party, we all traipse into the throne room, which Adriana turned into a giant fitting room for all of us to get ready while she disappears to oversee the final touches of the ceremony. She solicited coven members to take care of all the arrangements but wants to check that they did everything to her exact specifications.

My dress isn't in yet, but I'm assured it will be by the time I walk down the aisle.

Everyone leaves to finish their hair and makeup in their rooms, leaving me with Edina as she elaborately pins my hair, leaving a few curls down around my face and neck. My makeup is subtle, just a fine shimmer of gold powder on my eyes and light mascara.

"Are you nervous?" she asks. She's fully dressed, her lavender gown perfect against her tanned skin. It's tight against her bodice, held by thin straps before tapering off in a sea of tulle. She looks like a Faerie princess, even with her wings retracted.

"Not about the wedding."

"About the war? We're ready for whatever comes."

"I know." I shake my head, trying to push away the impending worries. "I just feel like I'm waiting for the other shoe to drop."

"Try not to dwell on it. Tonight is about you and your mate." Edina laughs breathlessly. "I can't believe you're getting married. I knew you'd take the plunge first, but I expected to at least have you a few more years."

"You always have me." I grab her hand, stilling it. "Love you."

"Love you most." Edina's eyes get misty. "You should hear how excited everyone is about tonight." She curls a hair that was already in a perfect spiral. "It's helped morale a lot. I know that's not what this is about, but everyone's thrilled for you and Lowell."

My mother comes in wearing a deep royal purple gown that's simple and understated but compliments her so well. Her hair is in a slightly more elaborate bun than she usually wears, and her makeup perfectly frames her emerald-green eyes. Her arm is hoisted up, and a brown dress bag is hanging down beside her.

"Edina," my mother says warmly. "May I have a moment with my daughter?"

Edina squeezes my hand. "I'll see you out there, babes."

When she leaves, my mom hangs the garment bag on the back of the door and hands me a pair of dainty sandals. "Vladimir said, and I quote, 'heels will be a disaster in the grass.'"

I laugh, and my mother's eyes sparkle. "So that's it?" I ask, gesturing to the dress bag. "Can I see it?"

"Not until it's on," she instructs, motioning to turn away from the mirror. I slip my robe off until I'm just in the lingerie I was instructed to wear. It's a white corset with satin panties that match.

I hear the zipper slide down the garment bag and my mother's gasp. "Is it bad?" I ask, not turning around.

"No." Her voice is choked with emotion. "No, it's perfect."

She clears her throat, and fabric rustles. "Eyes closed." I close them and at her suggestion, lift my legs, sliding the smooth material up my body. The dress fits like a glove, and I can already tell it's a formfitting silhouette.

She slides delicate straps up my arms and then zips up the back. "Kathryn," my mother says. "I just want to tell you how much Marcus and I love Lowell. He's a perfect match for you."

"I didn't have any say in that," I chuckle. Fate is funny, but it drew us together that night at the lake, and I don't think it could have kept us apart after.

"I also..." she trails off, sighing heavily. "I want to tell you how proud I am of you." She slowly spins me back towards the mirror. "After everything happened with your father, I kept you on a short leash, and I'm sorry. I knew you were destined for something wonderful, but I was worried."

My brow creases, but I keep my eyes closed. "I was worried you'd turn into your father," she continues. "I should have known better and given you the space you needed to find yourself. In the few months since you left the Dragons, you've flourished. And it's...it's a pleasure to see you become the leader I always knew you could be."

I bite down on the inside of my lip, trying to keep the tears brimming in my eyes from sliding down my cheeks. "Thanks, mom."

The familiar weight of Aldonza's necklace settles on my chest, and my mother does the clasp. "Open your eyes," she says, taking a step away.

For the first time in months, my eyes don't immediately go to my scar.

The dress is trumpet-style, hugging my figure, fitting every curve like a glove before gently fluttering out at my thighs. The v-neckline is subtle but provides a tasteful amount of cleavage. The thin straps are covered in ivory lace, so they look like vines draped across my shoulders. But that's not what takes my breath away.

It's gold. Not a chintzy, cheap gold. But a perfect, shimmery pale gold that's just past nude.

Ivory lace lays over top gold satin, delicately twisting in a gentle floral pattern. My mother bends down and fluffs out the train covered in the same ivory lace that ends in a scalloped edge. It's ethereal, simple, yet elegant.

It's exactly what I would have chosen if I could have picked any dress in the entire world.

The sound of leather shoes against the stones is the only warning I get before Vlad appears in a navy tux with black lapels. His mouth parts when he sees me, his blue eyes shining.

"Lowell is a lucky son-of-a-bitch," he says with a wink, and I laugh before crossing to hug him. "Do you like it?" I nod emphatically, unsure if I can get words out without crying.

"So, don't freak out," Vlad starts.

"That's a surefire way to make me freak out."

"I'm marrying you."

"You're not my type," I tease.

"Adriana got a vision about the minister that was..." He shakes his head. "Anyway, I'm ordained. I had a feeling when Lowell met you that I'd need to be."

"You didn't even know me then."

"When you're immortal, you realize that life is cyclical," Vlad says. "History repeats itself. You're a lightning wielder, the one to complete the prophecy. You claimed a werewolf on your first meeting. Finley's story was similar, so I assumed it would be close."

"So, you got ordained," I surmise.

"It's gonna be beautiful," Vlad says with an evil smirk. "Are you ready, baby queen?"

I look back at my mom and extend my hand. She steps up and grabs it. "We're ready," I say.

"I'll get Marcus," my mom says, but I pull her to a stop. Marcus is supposed to walk me down the aisle. But something about that just doesn't feel right.

"I think you both should walk me down the aisle," I say, and my mother grants me a very rare, very full smile.

"I'd be honored," she says softly.

Chapter Twenty-One

Everyone is already outside for the ceremony or preparing for the reception, so the halls are deserted. We round a corner and see my stepfather dressed in a black tuxedo and a purple tie that matches my mother's dress. He rocks on his heels as he looks towards the hidden door, where the sound of an acoustic guitar trickles through the walls. When he hears our approach, he turns and makes a noise that sounds a lot like a choked sob.

"Hi, Dad," I murmur with a big smile. I should have started calling him Dad ages ago. For a while, using his first name kept some sense of formality when it came to work. But after I left the Dragons...I'm not sure I ever made it clear to the man in front of me how much he means to me. Has been since the moment he started training me, even before he and my mom got together.

He brings a large hand to his jaw, scraping his fingers through his neatly trimmed beard. "Katie." His voice breaks, tears brimming in his warm brown eyes. "Are you determined to make me cry?" he asks, and I laugh as tears spring to my own eyes.

I release my mom's hand and step into Marcus's embrace, his warm arms enveloping me. "You're stunning," he replies as we break apart, and he spins me to take in the full effect of my dress.

He looks over my shoulder, and he and my mom share a look that is nothing but love and pride.

"Vlad did good." I toss a wink over my shoulder at the vampire, who is doing his best not to interrupt the moment.

"We should get going," Vlad replies. "Your bridesmaids are just outside. The ceremony is around the corner so Lowell won't see you until you're ready to walk down the aisle."

Marcus and my mom take a quick moment to kiss while Vlad presses his hand to the blank wall, opening the hidden doorway. Lilac petals and small votive candles form a pathway from the door to the valley beyond, but hushed conversation mixed with soft instrumental music and a soft glow is all I can see of the ceremony area. Adriana and Edina turn the corner, bickering over toasts, and stop dead when they see us.

"Fuck, I said I wasn't gonna cry today," Edina exclaims before bounding towards me and wrapping me in a hug. She pulls back, looking at the dress, which shimmers in the candlelight. "Babes—"

"I look hot, right?" I ask, and she laughs through her tears.

"Everything's ready," Adriana says as she embraces me. "The only thing I couldn't find is the rings."

"We don't have rings—" A high-pitched squeal cuts off my explanation as Lowell's sisters appear.

Luna gets to me first, speaking a thousand miles an hour and crying as she adjusts a few curls disrupted by all the hugs. The twins are next in matching mauve dresses with high necklines. Their hair is styled back in a way that makes it almost impossible for me to tell them apart, and one look at the smirk in their eyes tells me they did it on purpose. They appraise me with their heads cocked.

"Remember how we didn't threaten you last night?" Laura asks.

"Well," Leanne continues. They pause, looking at each other before looking back and me and speaking in unison.

"If you hurt our brother, we'll tear your intestines from your stomach and feed them to some actual unsuspecting wolf while we watch you die slowly."

Vlad whistles low. "I'd expect nothing less," I say, and their expression shifts to surprise. "I swear on my life I'll never hurt him."

They exchange another glance before Lyra steps up and smacks them both on the head. "Don't be little shits," she growls before turning her back on them and looking at me. "Lowell is lucky to have you."

"Thanks."

The music picks up in volume. "That's our cue, ladies," Vlad says, zipping around them and waiting until the music swells before following the curving path of candles around the hill. The girls arrange themselves into a line, so their dresses create a purple ombre effect.

"Hold this by your belly button," Adriana says, thrusting a bouquet of lilacs into my hands.

"And push your tits up and out," Edina says, fluffing my train before they link arms. She winks over her shoulder as I laugh, and then she and Adriana disappear around the corner.

"Ready?" my mom asks, laying her hand on the crook of my elbow holding my bouquet. Marcus links his arm through my other arm, gently squeezing in reassurance. I take a deep breath, nerves finally kicking in. A flood of warmth and love floods down the mating bond, making me smile as I push back the same level of love.

The music changes to a French song Lowell sang for me right after we mated. I smile, nodding to my parents as we walk around the hills to my wedding ceremony.

The sight takes my breath away. The entire field is lit with candles. Small votives line the perimeter and the aisle, which is strewn with white and lilac petals. Candles are bewitched to hang overhead, showering the sky in golden sparks that dissipate long before they reach the heads of the guests who have gathered in their finest. They all stand from gilded chairs when I approach the aisle.

My mate is standing beneath a golden archway wrapped with purple and white flowers. He's wearing a black tuxedo with a lilac sprig pinned to the lapel, his hair in gentle waves kissing his shoulders. Our gazes lock, and I move in a daze as my feet start carrying me toward him, the mating bond tugging tight like it wants us to hurry up. He's grinning unapologetically, and I know I'm mirroring the expression because my cheeks begin to hurt. A single tear tracks down his cheek, but he lets it fall.

We reach the end of the aisle, and Lowell steps out to shake Marcus's hand. My stepfather has descended into full, blubbering tears and my mother just shakes her head as Lowell releases his grip and kisses her on the cheek. While she says something to him, I turn to the front row, finding Lowell's mom and wrapping her in a hug.

When we part, I take Lowell's hand and let him guide me to my place under the floral archway. Edina takes my bouquet as Adriana casts a spell that makes my train lay perfectly. I'm aware of it all, but my mate entrances me. I want to lean in and kiss him or hug him or something. He reads my mind and leans forward, his forehead meeting mine. My eyes drift closed, and we steal this moment together.

"*Ma déesse*," Lowell whispers.

"What does that mean?"

"My goddess."

When we break apart, we leave our hands clasped and look at Vlad standing between us with an amused expression.

"Baby queen, give me some volume?" I roll my eyes, knowing he can speak loud enough to command an entire army, but I wave my hand to amplify his voice. He clears his throat at full volume.

"When you've been alive as long as I have," Vlad says to the crowd. "You have a lot of time to observe people. You learn to pick up on cues and emotions they try to hide.

"I was there the night Katie and Lowell met," he continues. "And from the first moment they saw each other, I knew there was something. Which was unfortunate because we were trying to kidnap Katie and hold her for ransom."

The crowd erupts, a mixture of laughter from those who knew the story to outrage to those who didn't. Lowell and I just laugh, and I throw a silencing spell at the crowd so Vlad can continue.

"A dozen words was all it took," Vlad continues like nothing just happened. "Katie and Lowell barely exchanged two sentences before I saw the resolve in his eyes to abandon our plan. I watched as he saved her life, as she claimed him without knowing, as Lowell exchanged in a pissing contest with her boyfriend whom we won't talk about."

Lowell's brow furrows, and I run my thumb along his knuckles until he relaxes. "And by the end of the night, I knew that was it," Vlad says. "They didn't know it. Lowell worried about what would happen between his pack and the mermaids. Katie assumed she'd never see him again. But I knew."

Vlad clears his throat again, and I catch a glimpse of him composing himself out of the corner of my eye. "Are you crying?" I whisper.

"Shut up, baby queen."

"You can't tell a bride to shut up on her wedding day," Adriana hisses.

"Just did." The shoulders of the crowd shake beyond the silencing spell, and I know they're laughing at our little exchange.

"In all my years," Vlad continues, his voice serious and thick with emotion, "I've seen love like theirs only a handful of times. It's the stuff of legends. The kind of love that can change the world with its purity. And we are so lucky to be able to witness it firsthand tonight when they declare to the world that not only are they fated, but that they are each other's *chosen*."

I turn back to my mate as a tear slides down his cheek, and I don't even think before I lift my hand to brush it away. He kisses the inside of my wrist as I cup his cheek before lowering my hand.

"Unmute your guests," Vlad says softly. I drop the silencing spell as I look out at the entire coven and they smile widely, tears in their eyes, and I'm struck by the sheer loyalty I feel radiating from them. These people don't just believe in our cause. They don't even believe just in me. They believe in *us*.

"Now." Vlad dabs his eyes with a handkerchief before returning it to his jacket pocket. "Since the couple got engaged all of a minute ago," he adds in an eye roll that makes the audience laugh. "They haven't prepared vows of their own—"

"Actually," Lowell and I say in unison, and the crowd chuckles again as we share a smile. Vlad laughs the loudest.

"Groom first."

Lowell pulls me a fraction of an inch closer like he needs the warmth of my body.

"There's not much I haven't already promised you, *Ma Reine*," he says. "And instead of repeating all the promises I've made you over the last few months, tonight, I promise you this."

He drops one of my hands so he can cup my cheek. "I vow to be your safe harbor and the arms you can fall into. So that when the days are hard, when we're tired and broken, you have one moment of happiness. Because, *mon âme sœur*, I didn't know true happiness until I met you. I love you so much."

"I love you," I whisper back as Vlad nods for me to start my vows. Edina hands me a piece of paper, and I unfold it, my hands shaking.

"I might butcher this," I say before I feel Adriana's magic amplifying my words. "Lowell." I look into his eyes once before I need the paper. Adriana steps forward, conjuring a stream of golden sparks from her wand.

I recite my vows in French.

Lowell's breath catches when he realizes what I'm doing, and I have to release a breath to keep going. I tell him how in my darkest hour, he was my light. How his patience and kindness healed my soul and helped me become stronger. I tell him all the hopes I have for the future, all the wonderful things I want for us.

While I speak, Adriana uses her wand to write the words in English for the guests of our coven.

When I finish and look up from my paper, tears are freely falling from Lowell's eyes, and the rest of the crowd is sniffling. Even Vlad is dabbing the corner of his eye as he noticeably tears his eyes away from my sister.

"Vlad," he says, his voice choked and rough. "I swear if you don't let me kiss her—"

"We're not at that part."

"Skip ahead," Lowell and I say together, and then we laugh.

"Fine, fine. I now pronounce you married partners. You may kiss—"

He doesn't finish before Lowell pulls me into a kiss, and the entire coven erupts in cheers.

The band starts playing celebratory music, and by the time Lowell and I break apart, the neat little lines of chairs have been pushed aside in favor of small cocktail-style tables. The entire American pack starts dragging out buffet tables for the platters and platters of food as the Dark Witches walk around with trays of champagne and shots.

"How long were we just kissing?" I ask, and Lowell laughs before pulling me into another deep kiss that has a fire brewing in my belly. A chorus of cat calls goes up again as he lifts me into his arms and pushes my dress aside so my legs can wrap around his waist.

"So much for decorum," Edina chides at my side.

"Totally overrated," I snip before returning my attention to my mate and partner.

An hour or so goes by in a blur of congratulations and trying unsuccessfully to snag hors d'oeuvres being passed around. The entire army wants to wish us well, and it's nice to see everyone so at ease, smiling and laughing together like one giant community instead of individual factions.

A sharp whistle cuts through the din, and everyone's attention snaps to Marcus, who is standing under the archway of flowers.

"As the Father of the Bride, I've prepared a few words," he begins. "Unfortunately, Katie's mother edited my speech and cut out all my embarrassing stories about our future queen. Including the first time we met, when she waltzed into the Dragons Headquarters, thinking she was untouchable—"

"Oh god," I breathe.

"—And I trapped her in an air cyclone for about thirty minutes until she admitted she still had a lot to learn." Lowell joins the rest of the guests as they laugh.

"In all seriousness," Marcus continues, "weddings are a time of hope. They make us look to the future and allow us to imagine a brighter tomorrow. I don't know about you all, but that's been a little hard for me lately."

The mood sobers. "It's been hard to think of anything past this impending war." He swallows deeply. "But somehow, these two have found hope through this sea of murky darkness. While we all run around scared and at each other's throats, these two find time to laugh."

Everyone around us hums in agreement. "They smile, and hug and kiss... sometimes too graphically for her father to witness." The crowd laughs along with my stepfather.

"And that is what we're fighting for. For a world filled with laughter in the most somber of situations. For a world run by leaders who hope.

"This wedding is just one more way that Katie and Lowell have shown us how they'll take care of the Kingdom when they reign. Because when we needed a reason to celebrate, they gave us the best one. So, if you would all join me in raising a glass—" Lowell and I are handed champagne glasses as everyone raises theirs as well.

"To my daughter and her mate. May you always have laughter, love, and hope. Cheers." Everyone clinks glasses as Lowell and I steal a quick kiss before following suit. "Now," Marcus continues, "it's time for the happy couple to share their first dance."

Adriana grabs our empty glasses as Lowell takes my hand and leads me to the center of the dance floor, where the werewolf band starts playing an instrumental cover of a Nocturn song.

"Did you pick this song?" I ask as he pulls me close, his thumb stroking the base of my spine.

"I did," he says, brushing his nose against mine.

"You know this song was written about me, right?" His eyebrows quirk up. "This is Rodger's band." He shrugs and pulls me in closer.

"Can't blame the man for having good taste," he murmurs into my hair, and I toss my head back in a laugh. We continue swaying to the love song as the world fades into a candlelight blur.

"Have I told you yet how stunning you are?" Lowell asks, his breath tickling the shell of my ear. He's whispered it about a million times in a few hours. "Then have I told you how much I can't wait to get you out of that dress?"

I laugh as the song ends, and everyone encourages us to kiss. Lowell pulls me into him, dipping me backward as he kisses me. There's nothing but love and adoration flowing through our bond, making my heart soar.

The music picks up, and soon the dance floor...area...empty space in the middle of the tables is packed. Lowell and I dance together for a few songs before Marcus cuts in, and we're passed between family and friends. One song spills into the next as we dance with everyone at the party. When Lowell's sisters steal me for a group dance, I drag Adriana into the fray, the pack of us thrashing wildly and laughing at the top of our lungs.

I'm mid-spin under Adriana's arm when she stiffens, causing me to stumble because... champagne. I follow her serious gaze across the dance floor where Edina and Vlad are dancing together, her back molded to his front as he whispers something in her ear that causes her to laugh.

"Adriana—" I start. She gives me a tight smile. "You know they're just friends now, right."

She nods stiffly. "I'm gonna do a perimeter check," she shouts over the music.

"We can have someone else do it." She shakes her head, squeezing my hand before disappearing into the crowd. I sigh deeply, looking back at Edina and Vlad, who have separated and are currently doing some sort of swing dance.

Lowell's arms wrap around my middle, and his head comes down to the crook of my neck, kissing the sensitive flesh and making me melt back into him.

"I have a surprise for you," he says in my ear, his hot breath making me shiver.

"If it's your cock, it's not much of a surprise anymore," I chide, and he swats at my ass.

"Come on." He tugs my hand, and we make our way slowly across the dance floor, and somehow, no one stops us.

Lowell leads me past the table set up and down a small path lined with magical lights. "Where are we going?" I ask as we round a curve, so we're tucked behind a mountain. I'm about to jump him when I see two men sitting on chairs, the magical light between them brighter than the rest of the party. They smile and try to hide tattoo guns behind their backs but fail spectacularly.

"Wolves don't usually exchange rings," Lowell says, which I know. It could seriously hurt them if they needed to shift in a pinch. "Instead, a lot of us get tattoos on our ring fingers."

He looks at me expectantly, excitement barreling through our bond. "Hell yes," I respond without even being asked a question. Lowell yips before kissing me and then drags me over to the men, who jump up and allow us to take a seat.

"Any specific pattern you're thinking, Your Majesty?" my artist asks, and I quickly open a private Mind Magic channel with him to tell him my idea.

They work quickly as Lowell and I take a moment to talk, ignoring the sting on our left hands. When they're done, Lowell's artist calls Light Magic to his hands as soon as they finish and heals me before healing my mate. They nod, heading to join the rest of the party and giving us a minute.

"Let's see it," Lowell smirks, grabbing my hands and holding them up. He swallows before his golden eyes meet mine.

"It's our moon," I explain. The design around my finger is the different phases of the moon, surrounded by a small string of stars that serve as the band. But the moon on the top of my finger, which will sit right under my canary diamond engagement ring, is a Waxing Gibbous Moon, the moon we met under. The same moon is above our heads right now.

"Little witch—" Lowell says, clearing his throat as tears spring to his eyes. I use the opportunity to snag his hand and smile at the incredibly intricate dark band surrounding his ring finger that's broken up with white-inked lightning.

I pull him into me, tucking my head into his chest, huffing in frustration as his shirt blocks his skin from me. Lowell tips my chin up and kisses me quickly. "I love you so fucking much," he murmurs against my lips.

"I—"

KATIE, Adriana's voice rings out in my mind before the channel goes silent.

Chapter Twenty-Two

AN EAR-PIERCING SHRIEK ECHOES across the valley, and Lowell and I exchange a panicked glance before he scoops me up and runs around the hill toward the party. The music has stopped, replaced by the soundtrack of children crying and their parents' soothing tones as they usher the young inside the coven.

My mother and Marcus shout orders, and our party guests break into rough battle formations. Wolves shift, witches summon smaller shields, and vampires zip around, extracting hidden weapons or grabbing whatever they can find.

"What is it?" I ask, but then I see the black figures on brooms streaking overhead. Magic bounces off the shield, searching for a way in with no avail. "We're fine," I assure the witches close to us. "The shield will hold—"

A blast of white fire collides with our shield and it cracks in a spider-web, slowly leaching down the side until a cluster of witches reacts, sending magic to patch the hole.

Edina lands beside us. "I can cover us, but we won't be able to see out." She's right beside me, but I can barely hear her over the commotion.

"Anyone get a count?" I ask as I nod to Edina, who covers our shield in impenetrable ice. Between both forms of magic, it *should* be impossible for Archer to break in.

"It's a small group," Marcus says. "Archer and a handful of the aerial soldiers."

"This is personal," Lowell says low in my ear. Archer would have brought an entire army if he was planning on attacking us in earnest. This is a targeted blow meant to disrupt morale and ruin my wedding.

"Fuck him," I breathe. "Did anyone see what direction they came from?"

"South," Marcus replies.

My Dark Magic coils around me, and I shoot up into the air so everyone can see me. I amplify my voice, and all movements stop. "Vampires, get the brooms from the weapons closet. Flyers, I need twenty of you on brooms and in the air in the next sixty seconds. Then I need our fastest wolves on the ground at the southern border of the shield and a handful covering the other directions in case they circled. Follow them when they retreat but stay hidden. We're finding out the location of that goddamned hideout."

"Where do you want the rest of us?" Vlad asks as I touch back down on the grass.

"Everyone else goes inside but get in formation in the halls," I say. Vlad regards me curiously. "This was an impulsive decision, I'm sure of it. We'll be prepared, but I don't think any other forces are coming. If we can, we handle this quietly."

Vlad grabs my arm and pulls me close. "If you get your shot, take it," he whispers. I swallow hard but give him a terse nod. "I'll go help Adriana inside." He zips off, leaving me with a lump in my throat.

If you get a shot, take it.

I don't have time to dwell on it. Over twenty flyers, including Jefferson, Soto, and the O'Malley twins, surround us, brooms in hand. Sybil hands my mother a broom before following Vlad like a lost puppy. My mother quickly kisses Marcus before mounting her broom, and he winks in my direction before helping with the bottleneck formed to get back inside the coven.

"Go get those wolves ready to run, Alpha," I instruct with a smile. Lowell kisses my cheek, sending a wave of love down our bond before barking orders to the wolves.

I turn back to the contingent of flyers we've assembled. "I want half of you to flank their troops. Cloak yourselves and circle around." My mother whistles, and soldiers surround her before they become invisible.

One glance at the doors to the coven tells me everyone is inside safely, but I still use my Mind Magic to ensure there are no stragglers. The only things outside are discarded plastic champagne flutes and knocked-over wedding chairs.

"I told you I had a feeling," I mutter to Edina. Then, louder, "Take down the ice so we can see what we're dealing with."

I rise again in a cloud of Dark Magic with Edina and Astor beside me and the rest of the witches ascending on brooms behind us. Edina slowly drops her magic, one glittering inch of ice disappearing at a time until we get a clear view of what's beyond the magical shield.

Ten witches in billowing black cloaks are hovering in a v-formation with Archer at the helm. They float, waiting. We outnumber them three-to-one, which is good, but I recognize these soldiers. They're the best aerial division the Dragons have, so we'll have our work cut out for us.

We fly out of the shielded area, rising until we're even with Archer. I don't want him attacking the coven shield again, so I make a show of putting up a separate one-sided shield in front of our ranks. Let them focus on us rather than breaching our carefully crafted defenses.

Archer's hazel eyes gleam in the light of the fireball in his hand. Regular fire, I note, not hellfire. I expect to feel panic, or at least apprehension, seeing him for the first time since he tortured me. But my mind is clear, and my emotions are controlled.

"Sorry to interrupt," Archer says, his voice colder than I've heard it before. His gaze tracks down my body in my dress as the train flutters behind me.

"Liar," Edina scoffs, distracting Archer as she calls ice to her hands. I use the reprieve to search for any cloaked soldiers and signal our group when I find none.

Archer turns his gaze back to me. "It wasn't too long ago when you were beside me, fighting a man who flew on nothing but Dark Magic."

"Life's a bitch like that," I hum. "Any particular reason you're keeping me from my wedding night?"

"Where is your groom?"

"Probably naked and waiting for me to join him." Not a lie, but I let the implication speak for itself.

"Holy shit, babes," Edina snorts next to me, her laugh echoing in the valley. *Maybe don't bait the psychopath.*

I'm giving the others time to get in position, I respond, watching as Archer turns a putrid shade of purple. *I want their attention on me.*

I feel a magical caress against my mental shields, a request to open an old channel. "Say whatever you want to say, Archer," I call. "I have no secrets from my army."

"I was going to say you look beautiful," he says, his eyes softening. "And propose a compromise."

"And what's that?" I ask. He hesitates. "Let me guess. Turn over my army, renounce my mate, agree not to use my Dark Magic, and come back to the palace and play obedient queen?" Archer's gaze hardens. "And what would you offer my people? Amnesty?"

"If that's what it takes."

"It's a shame I don't believe you."

Magic flares from the hands of Archer's soldiers. Most of the soldiers have Fire Magic, which seems short-sighted since they're on brooms. My group responds in kind, readying their varied forms of magic, and there's confusion on our opponent's faces as some of my witches call Light Magic to their hands. They'll soon learn that Light Magic is one of the more powerful forms of Battle Magic.

"Come with me," Archer insists.

"Showing up at the wedding and begging the bride to run away with you," I tsk. "It's a little predictable. Entirely too emotional. Tragically cliché. And overall, not a very strategic move."

In position, my mother says.

"And one more thing—" My mother drops the cloaking spell on her group. Our witches have their battalion completely surrounded, and they start swiveling on their brooms as they realize we've outmaneuvered them. I lift my hand, flashing my tattooed finger. "You're too late."

Every witch around me launches magic at Archer's shield, and his soldiers scramble to keep it up as they balk under our assault. They clearly haven't been practicing the one-sided shields I've made my army learn. Archer screams orders, unable to cast and retaliate, while the men struggle to keep the shields erected around him.

"E," I murmur, watching as Archer looks ready to explode. She and Astor fly forward the slightest amount. "Three, two, one—"

Hellfire explodes from the top of Archer's head, causing the men around him to drop the shield and scatter away from the blast. Edina and Astor waste no time shooting a heavy stream of ice at him until it forms a round sphere. They hold it as Archer continues to burn white-hot inside the ice.

"Why isn't the fire going out?" I ask as his crew starts battling our soldiers, who block and parry the attacks seamlessly.

"I don't know," Edina grits through her teeth as the ice cracks, and she focuses to reform it. "I don't know that I can hold him."

"Water, use your water," Astor commands. Edina trembles as the ice shatters, and she sends a torrent of water that extinguishes the flame. Archer snarls, dripping wet and still angry as hell but completely doused. I shoot lightning at him, but one of his men intercepts my attack.

"This isn't over," he sneers, and a line of hellfire punches a hole in the coven shield and collides with my archway of flowers. Petals scatter, spreading embers on the nearby tables.

Astor reacts quickly, putting out the fire as I watch my wedding reception go up in smoke. When I turn, Archer and his group retreat to the south.

Southern wolves, they're headed your way, I send mentally before addressing the soldiers around me. "I need some of you to follow, but keep a safe distance. I want their eyes on the sky as the wolves follow from below."

Without any discussion, a handful of witches break from the pack. The rest of us lower back to the ground, where Lowell and Vlad are waiting with concerned looks.

"Was Adriana with you?" Vlad asks, and I shake my head.

"She's not inside?"

"When was the last time anyone saw her?" Vlad growls, his whole body vibrating.

"She was doing a perimeter check," I tell him. "She mentally called me right before Archer attacked. I thought—"

Vlad takes off into the hills before I can finish my thought, and Lowell uses our mental channel to instruct the wolves still stationed around the perimeter to search for Adriana.

"We'll search from above," Edina says, motioning to the group, who mount their brooms and peel off in different directions. My mother walks over and grabs my hand as I shake.

"You don't think Archer had her." I say it like a statement, but it's a question. I would have noticed if Adriana was amongst his ranks. Unless he grabbed her before the battle and sent someone back to his hideout with her.

"Even if he does," my mom says softly, "she's escaped him before."

"He won't give her that chance—"

A bellow bounces through the valley, shaking the ground. A moment later, Vlad appears in a flash of his vampire speed with a pale figure cradled in his arms. Adriana's lilac dress is torn, and scratches cover her exposed skin. Her arm and leg are bent at odd angles, and her hands are swollen. A trickle of blood seeps from the corner of her mouth, landing in her ringlets, which are more reddish-brown than blonde right now.

"No," I breathe, grabbing her hand, which lies motionless. I send Light Magic into the extremity, but I haven't learned how to heal broken bones, so I'm not sure what good it's doing. Her gray eyes are glassy, but they blink open and closed regularly. Her breath is shallow and rattles as she exhales.

"She was on the side of the hill," Vlad says, laying her on the grass as someone calls for Coleman. The vampire brushes a twig from my sister's hair, smoothing down the wayward curl.

"Knocked...out of...the...sky," Adriana wheezes, and Coleman appears, white light already coating his hands.

"I gave her some blood when I found her," Vlad tells both the healer and me. "But it's not working. I can give more—"

Coleman's eyes meet mine, and he swallows a lump. Adriana moves her non-injured arm and places a bloated hand in Vlad's. He leans in, and she whispers something to him which has blood tears welling in his eyes as he cups her cheek.

"She has a lot of internal bleeding," Coleman says softly. "The magic...it might not work in time."

"Do it anyway," Lowell orders as he steps into me, his hands reassuringly resting at my hips.

Coleman nods and moves to my sister's head, working on the giant gash on her forehead. Two more healers join us, taking residence at her side, their Light Magic flaring around their hands as they work to reset bones and slow bleeding.

"My Katie," Adriana rasps, tearing her eyes away from Vlad. The healers move to her lungs, and she takes a deeper breath as the magic sets. "I'm sorry I won't get to see you be the queen you're destined to be."

"Adriana, stop that right now." Tears are clouding my eyes. "You're not going anywhere."

I look at Coleman for an assessment, and he shakes his head solemnly. Lowell's grip tightens on me as my stomach bottoms out. The healers are focused on Adriana's belly, their brows furrowed in concentration.

"She's bleeding faster than we can fix," the one healer squeaks. "I don't know..."

"It's okay," Adriana says, but one look from me keeps the healers going. I don't accept this. I won't.

Vlad is whispering a stream of constant words to Adriana as blood falls freely down his cheeks. "Vlad," I whisper. His body tensing is the only acknowledgment I get that he's heard me. "Turn her."

All movement stops as everyone turns to face me. "Turn her," I repeat, this time a command.

Vlad's shoulders slump. "I can't."

"The fuck you can't!"

"There are rules—"

"You're the one who makes the rules," I fume.

"You know nothing about vampire law, Kathryn," Vlad hisses. "The rules are there for a reason. Immortality isn't a decision to be made in a time of crisis. Especially not by a vampire in love with a dying human."

Vlad's admission hangs in the air, and Adriana gasps before choking, a gurgling sound that scares the shit out of me. I squeeze her hand. The healers must have fixed it enough to feel me because she rolls her head back to my side. "Adriana, do you want to fight? If you're tired, if you're done...it's okay. But if you want to live, I need you to nod."

Her eyes bounce to Vlad, a tear leaking down her cheek as she nods.

"Vlad, please," I say, my voice breaking.

He cups Adriana's face in both hands, and it's such a tender moment that I almost feel like we shouldn't witness it. She mouths something to him, and his jaw works.

"Okay," he whispers so softly I barely hear him. "Find Sybil and tell her to meet me in my room with a coffin." He scoops Adriana into his arms and slowly walks towards the coven so as not to jostle her. I follow hot on his heels through the labyrinth of halls until we reach his room.

"You need to leave," he orders, not bothering to even look at me as he walks to the bed and sets Adriana down on the black satin sheets. She's shivering now, her whole body shaking in violent tremors.

"I'm not leaving her—" I protest. Vlad turns and looms over me, causing me to crane my neck up to meet his eyes.

"I am breaking multiple vampire laws tonight," he says. "Having mortals witness how vampires are made is not going to be one of them."

"Promise me you won't let her die," I insist, not backing down. He shakes his head and returns to Adriana's side, whispering something in her ear.

Sybil appears, toting a coffin under her arm. "Want to move the fuck out of the way?"

I growl at her before slowly backing out of the room, leaving Adriana with Sybil and Vlad. Lowell appears at my side, wrapping his arms around me as the door is shut, leaving us in the hallway.

"Was that the right call?" I breathe.

"He'll take care of her." Lowell presses his lips to my temple.

"He loves her." I look up at my mate. "I knew they had something, but love—"

A blood-curdling scream comes from the door. It buckles my knees and has me gripping my chest. "Come on. We can't stay here." Lowell pulls me from my spot in the hallway, screams following us all the way to the war room.

Chapter Twenty-Three

"YOU'RE NOT GONNA LIKE this." Lyra and Alaina are standing in the doorway of the war room, stark naked and covered in sweat. Lowell and I are lounging on a sofa that Edina procured from thin air, but at their arrival, I sit upright. Lowell's arm never leaves my waist. He's been wrapped around me since we left Adriana with Vlad.

Unbeknownst to us, Adriana was getting visions of her death for weeks, but she couldn't discern the time or place. She told only Kyle due to another vision and started training him in all her duties. He jumped in as soon as we told him what happened, so the coven is taken care of, which is why our family has retreated to the war room.

I can't speak for the others, but without Adriana, I feel...lost. Her guidance and visions have always been there, steady and consistent. Our cause needs her, but selfishly, I don't want to lose my sister again. I just got her back.

"What won't I like?" I ask the wolves. The other people in the room, my parents, Edina, and Lowell's family, all sit up straighter, bracing for the news.

"We found Archer's base," Lyra says. "They knew we were following, so they stopped trying to hide it."

"And?"

"It's close. A few valleys over. Earth Elementals must have built it because it's a fortress."

"It's above ground?" Lowell asks, and they nod. "How is that possible? How didn't we find it?"

"That's not all..." Alaina trails off, looking to her girlfriend for help.

"It's surrounded with hellfire."

Someone swears. Someone else gasps.

I lean forward, propping my elbows on my knees and pressing the heels of my hands into my eyes. And I start to laugh. Tears leak from my eyes, and my whole body shakes. I can't stop. It's like my wires are crossed. I should be crying, but instead, I laugh. Everyone looks at me like I'm having a nervous breakdown, which is fair.

"I think everyone should give us a minute," Edina says.

"No." I take a deep breath and wipe the tears from my eyes, trying to regain my composure. "No, they can stay." I huff out one last laugh. "I think I need a drink."

"And maybe some cake?" Luna suggests. "The cake was still down here when the attack happened. I'll bring some back."

"Have the wolves cut the rest and serve it in the mess hall," Lowell says, and Luna motions for Laura and Leanne to follow and help. Lyra and Alaina also excuse themselves to get dressed. When they're gone, the room quiets, the weight of the announcement hanging in the air.

"Surrounded in hellfire," I scoff. "We can't get one freaking break."

One glance at Edina tells me she's just as worried as me. Her bottom lip is firmly between her teeth, and her wings are no longer retracted. "Does this mean what I think it means?" I ask.

"Probably." Everyone looks between the two of us. "There's no way Archer can hold a wall of hellfire by himself."

"You think Fae are working with him," Lowell says, his grip tightening around me.

"And I'd guess he has a good amount if he could keep the entire structure hidden from us," Edina says. I shudder. The Fae were supposed to be our ace in the hole. And now he has an army of them too.

"I'll send Astor back to Faerie and get him to light a fire under my mother's ass," Edina says.

"Not literally." I find my joke too funny. Edina and Lowell exchange concerned glances before he thanks her, and she leaves to find Astor.

"There's nothing more to be done tonight," Lorraine says softly. "Let's try and put it aside for a bit. It's still your wedding day, after all."

Everyone follows my mother-in-law's suggestion, trying to lighten the mood with talk of the ceremony. We eat cake, Lowell and I show off our tattoo rings, and my mate finally ditches his jacket and shirt, which I'm surprised made it as long as it did. When we run out of ways to avoid the attack or Adriana, we busy ourselves discussing preparations for the full moon in two days.

At some point, I must fall asleep in Lowell's arms because the next thing I know, I'm being carried into our bedroom. I'm barely awake as he slides the zipper of my wedding dress down and helps me out of my uncomfortable but sexy-as-hell lingerie. His touch is gentle, revenant, and not at all sexual. He hands me one of his shirts, and I slip it on before climbing into bed.

"Mine," Lowell whispers as he completely engulfs me in his arms. I echo the statement, pulling him as close as possible until we fall asleep.

We sleep most of the day, letting everyone else handle the aftermath of the attack. After a quick shower, I grab a bag of blood from the kitchen and camp outside Vlad's room. Lowell sits beside me, one of his hands always touching me as I chew on my lip and wait for the sun to set.

Alek is the first to appear, a beautiful vampire with black hair and tanned skin at his side. I ask questions, but they ignore me, dutifully standing on either side of Vlad's door.

My breath hitches as the door opens, but before I can catch it, I'm slammed back against the wall, and fangs sink into my neck. Lowell shifts so fast that he shreds his pants, but I'm faster. Gold magic flares around me, throwing the vampire across the hall and back into the closed door. My blood trickles down the side of Vlad's mouth as he snarls at me. Alek and the other vampire grab his arms, holding him back, and I run Light Magic over the bite mark, glaring the entire time.

"I'm sorry, did that hurt?" he sneers. "That's *nothing* compared to what Adriana went through. What *you* put her through." A stone settles in my stomach, sinking lower as he shakes off the other vampires. Lowell growls a low warning and stands between his best friend and me.

"Did it work?" I ask, my voice thick with emotion.

"Yes." My breath whooshes out of my body, my chest caving in relief. Vlad laughs without humor. "You have no idea the position you put me in, Katie."

"Because I asked you to save my sister? The woman you love?"

"Because you asked me to choose you over my people," he fumes. "The laws you asked me to break are why we've been able to stay hidden from the mortals. Why we haven't killed each other in senseless wars." Lowell shifts back into his human form but stays between the vampires and me.

"Explain," I demand.

When Vlad doesn't answer, Alek speaks. "You know Magical Creatures came from Faerie, yeah?" I nod. "Vampyres there are born, not made, so, when they turned the first humans, they didn't give us any guidelines, and it was a fucking mess."

"The lust that happens from the bite can accelerate feelings," the female vampire explains. "You'd be surprised how many vampires fall hopelessly in love with the humans they feed from, especially if there's chemistry before the bite."

"That's why you said you shouldn't have fed from Adriana," I say to Vlad, who won't look at me.

"A lot of humans were turned because the vampire was in love," the female continues.

"Turning a vampire is a commitment you'll never understand," Vlad says. His voice is low and rough around the edges. "Not even when you have children. It's not a lifetime commitment. It's an *eternal* commitment. Vampires didn't understand that and would grow tired of their lovers after a few centuries. It led to wars. Some of the wars grew so large they made it into mortal history, though the reason was always misinterpreted.

"When I became the Count, I formed the Council and created laws. You need approval before you make a vampire. The request is instantly denied if you have any romantic relationship with the human you wish to turn." Alek scoffs, drawing my attention briefly, but Vlad ignores him.

"I've been able to keep my feelings separate from feeding for centuries," he continues with a heavy sigh. "Until your sister." His blue eyes soften, a ghost of a smile crossing his face. "*That's* why I stopped anything from happening between us. I didn't want this life for her. She's too good for it. But I also distanced myself from her so that if I ever wanted to—"

"You had the option to turn her," I finish for him. "What's the punishment for turning her without permission?"

"There will be a hearing," Alek says. "But traditionally, the maker loses his fangs. They grow back, but in the meantime, he won't be able to feed."

"Except bagged blood." All three vampires shudder.

The door behind Vlad creaks open, and a blonde ringlet peeks out. "Vlad?" Adriana's voice is timid and scared as she appears in the doorway. Alek and the brunette tense like they're prepared for battle.

She's still covered in dirt, her dress from the wedding torn and tattered. Her hair is a rat's nest of knots and wayward blood-crusted curls. Her skin has that same sallow look that Vlad gets when he hasn't fed, but other than that, she's healed. Her swollen legs regular-sized. Her breaths come in regular intervals.

She cocks her head to the side and takes a deep inhale. Her gray eyes dilate, her pupils blowing as her fangs descend over her pink lips.

"Fuck," Lowell swears, shifting back into his wolf as Adriana appears in front of me in a flash, her fangs reaching for my neck. Unlike with Vlad, I don't react. I can't hurt her. It's my fault she's a vampire, how can I stop her from feeding from me when I put her in this position?

"Adriana," Vlad calls sternly, and she halts an inch from my skin. "Sweetheart, look at me."

She hisses but turns. He crooks his finger, and she walks to him like she's tethered to a string. "Your sister brought you blood," Vlad says, holding his hand out for me to toss it to him and deftly snatching the bag from mid-air. He procures a metal straw from his back pocket, pokes a hole in the pouch, and raises it to my sister's lips. She takes a deep drink and makes a face.

"It tastes stale."

"I know," he says, brushing her hair. She leans into his touch. "But you must tame the bloodlust before feeding on a human. You'll never forgive me if you kill your sister."

"You're mad at her," she says, pausing her sipping for a minute, completely ignoring the rest of us.

"Yes, but she's family. I can be mad at her and still love her enough not to want her dead." Vlad's eyes flit to me, and he offers a small smile.

Adriana finishes her blood, and Vlad pulls her in close, holding her tight to his body. Her arms wind around his torso, and she sighs. Then she fidgets, a deep primal moan emitting from her lips that has Vlad's knuckles turning white with restraint.

"I know, sweetheart," he murmurs, kissing the top of her head. "It's a lot of sensations to get used to." She nods, and it takes me a minute to realize her hands are dropping to the front of Vlad's pants as her lips start working their way up his neck.

"What's happening?" I squeak. Vlad swears under his breath.

"When a vampire is made, they emerge in a primal state," Alek explains. Vlad is now panting as Adriana writhes against him. "All you can think about is blood and sex."

"I need to get her out of here," Vlad tells me, his teeth clenching so hard he looks like he's about to crack his jaw. "I have a safe house a few miles away. We'll be there until she can master her urges. Knowing Adriana, we'll be back in just a few days."

"Do we know if she'll keep her magic? Her clairvoyance?" I ask.

"She may be the first vampire-witch hybrid," he says. "My maker might know more. He returned to Faerie, but I'll send word and ask."

"Adriana—" I start. She lifts her head and smiles.

"My Katie," she whispers, nuzzling into Vlad's neck, and I try really hard to keep my eyes up so I can't see if her hand is still wrapped around his dick. "I can't see anything about your future." She sighs. "It's a relief to see you and not see you dying."

I laugh despite myself, and she gives me a toothy smile as Vlad scoops her into his arms.

"We'll be back soon," he assures me. "Say goodbye to your sister, Adriana." Adriana waves and they disappear in a flash of movement. Only when she leaves do I crumple to the floor, followed by my mate, who holds me until I can stand again.

Chapter Twenty-Four

Lowell and I stand by the portal as a steady stream of wolves goes through. We were hoping to extend our wards a bit so that all the packs could run here, but Archer's stronghold is just too close for them to be safe. The American Packs agreed to stay, but the rest are divided between a few secured forests.

"I should stay," Lowell mutters, standing in front of me and blocking my view of the portal. I know why he's offering; we've discussed it at length. The coven will be more vulnerable without the wolves here, but we can hold down the fort for a few days. The vampires and witches are already on high alert.

"We'll be fine," I assure him.

"Lyra is staying behind with the pups—"

"Lyra?" I arch my eyebrow.

"She lost a bet," Lowell chuckles. "But I'll switch with her. She'll jump at the chance—"

"We'll be fine." I wrap my arms around Lowell's waist and bury my head in his chest. His chin dips to rest on the crown of my head, tucking me in close. "Go. Run with your pack. Sleep in the dogpile."

"I should have never told you about that," he teases. I lift on my toes to press a kiss to the corner of his mouth. "I'll come back tomorrow morning."

"If you insist."

He kisses me earnestly, pulling me tight to his body like he can wrap me away from the world. "I'd feel better if Vlad was back," he grumbles.

Vlad has sent messages the past few days, and, as predicted, Adriana is only a few days away from being able to be around humans. There was nothing but pride in his tone via our Mind Magic channel when he told us how she's already successfully learned to feed without killing someone.

"We've got it covered, Lo-Lo," Edina says, fluttering over the war room table and landing beside me before retracting her wings. She slings her arm around my waist.

"And if I need you, you'll feel it," I remind my mate for the thousandth time. "Now go, or you'll miss it."

Lowell kisses me one last time before walking through the portal, keeping his eyes on me until the mist swallows him up.

"Should we get drunk? I found a bottle of Faerie wine in Astor's room." Edina waggles her eyebrows, and I laugh.

"We've got work to do," I say, pulling her arm as she whines. "We're triple-checking the wards, then ensuring everyone is ready with the emergency plans."

"You're no fun," Edina pouts.

"I know. I'm an old married lady."

I drag Edina through the tunnels, checking the wards we erected throughout the coven. After the wedding and learning how close Archer is, we wanted as much protection as we can get, so we added extra wards in case soldiers breach our outside defenses. Now you can't make it four feet without hitting another shield.

"Have you heard anything from Astor?" I ask.

"Nothing." It's only been a few hours in Faerie since Astor left to ask the Fae to hurry the fuck up. It makes sense that we don't have news yet, but we're still on edge about Fae working with Archer. "If we don't hear from him after the full moon, I'm gonna start calling every mirror in Faerie until someone answers."

"Good."

We get outside and take off in opposite directions, flying over the shifted pack of wolves running over the hills. I check the wards, adding as much magic as possible to strengthen the protection.

When I finally finish, it's dark, and the full moon is out in all its glory. The howls of wolves are my soundtrack as I land in a cloud of Dark Magic in the doorway of the coven. I head to the training room to help my mother, who is reviewing the emergency protocol with the witches. Then I run down to the medical bay and check in with Coleman, ensuring he and his healers are ready to move if we have an attack and need them closer to the fighting.

I'm just about to call it a night when I'm bowled over by three wolf pups charging down the hallway. They circle me, darting between my legs and tripping me up until I fall to the ground, where they jump on top of me, licking my face and nipping at my hands until I pet them.

"Lorenzo, Bella, Ava Marie, I swear to all things magical, if you don't get back here right now—" The pups all yip and bolt down the hallway, leaving me sprawled on the floor as a very angry Lyra bursts around the corner.

I bite my lip to hold back my smile as she hunches over to catch her breath. Her hair is rumpled, her clothes askew, and a silver bracelet around her wrist hums with magic suppressant to keep her from shifting. "I heard you lost a bet," I tease as I pry myself off the floor.

"You could at least pretend you're not enjoying this," she grumbles.

"Where's the fun in that?"

Lyra runs her hand through her hair and releases a pained growl. "I am not maternal." The pups take that moment to charge past us, nothing more than three little blurs of gray and white fur and high-pitched barks of delight. "I may never forgive my sister for procreating."

"What was the bet?" I ask since Lyra is making no moves to chase down our nieces and nephew.

She sighs heavily. "You know Alaina and I have an open relationship." I nod. "Luna bet me that she'd bring up the topic of monogamy after your wedding. Which she did. So now she and I are in a fight, which probably would have blown over tonight, but I'm here instead of with the pack and—" she groans, and I reach out and rub her arm. "So basically, it's your fault."

"We could also blame your brother."

"I like that better."

The kids come running around the corner again, but this time I'm ready. I throw up a shield just past us, keeping it visible, so they don't crash into it. When they skid to a stop and start running back the way they came, I seal off that way too. They bark in a way that I can only interpret as laughter as they try to find a way out.

"Who wants to have a sleepover with Aunt Katie?" I ask, and all three of the pups jump up my legs. "Sit," I command, and instantly all three butts hit the ground, tails wagging. "Good boy, good girls."

I turn back to Lyra, who's looking at me like I'm the wolf whisperer. "Give me your hand," I tell her, and she does instantly. I use my magic to snap the suppressing band off her wrist, and her chest heaves in relief. "Go fix things with Alaina. I got this."

"Are you sure?" Lyra asks, but she's already stripping her clothes off. She shifts into her wolf form and nudges my hand with her snout in thanks before she takes off in a run down the hall.

"All right, it's bedtime." Three identical sets of puppy eyes bore into me, matched by a whine by the smallest wolf. "You know where my room is?" Three nods. "Want to race?"

The pups all stand and start wagging their tails, rushing over to the shield. "On your mark—" I ascend on a cloud of Dark Magic above their little heads. "Get set—" they start jumping up and down. "Go!" I drop the shield and fly as fast as I can to try and keep up with their wolf speed. They make up for their little legs with sheer energy, and I laugh as I lag behind.

I apologize to any witches caught in the path of our race as we blur past on the way to my room. When they reach the door, they barrel through and jump on the bed as I touch down. They run in circles around the mattress, kicking up the comforter before settling down into a small pile. "Goodnight." I kiss each furry head and cast a shield around the door before heading into the bathroom. I'm pretty sure they're all asleep before I close the door.

I'm just finishing washing my face when I feel something collide with my shield. Panic blooms in my chest, and I charge out of the bathroom with lightning coating my skin. I fling it open to see Lyra about to crash into the shield again. Her gold eyes look haunted. She shifts and her whole body trembles. My chest tightens as her bottom lip quivers. "Fire," she gasps.

It feels like the floor drops out beneath me as Lyra sinks to her knees in a heap.

Fire. She said fire.

"Where?" I know where. If it were here, there would have been an alarm. There would be movement in the halls, screaming and orders being shouted down mental channels. But I need to hear it. I need to hear Lyra say the words.

"Our pack."

My mind goes blank. All emotions shut down so I can think and plot on the fly. I sound the alarm through the mental channel to the entire coven and call for someone to come watch the children asleep in my bed. Then I ask Edina and any Water Elementals to go straight to the woods behind Vlad's house and order witches who can teleport to check on the other packs. I tell everyone else to be on high alert here.

Once everything is set in motion, I grab Lyra, teleport to the portal, where she shifts, and I hop on her back. I'm not sure what is on fire, so I don't want to teleport directly to the woods, but Lyra understands that without explanation. She dives into the mist, and I squeeze my eyes shut as it feels like we're hurtling down the portal at a thousand miles per hour.

We land in Vlad's office a moment later, and the stench of smoke overwhelms me. It permeates the air, only getting thicker as we run through the back door and out to the lawn. Only when Lyra slows her steps do I open my eyes.

"Holy shit."

Edina beat us here, so the flames are out, but the once lush forest is nothing more than a blackened scar across the land. Not a tree or patch of earth was spared from the blaze. It's now just a pile of ash and embers. My best friend stands panting at the edge of the smoldering remains of wood, which hiss from the onslaught of her freezing water. "I'm so sorry."

She grabs my hand as I walk up beside her, linking our fingers together as I stare into the rubble. I can't comprehend what I'm seeing. There's no way this can all be destroyed. That the pack was in the woods when this... I cast my mind out, searching for any signs of life in the area, praying the pack made it out before the fire reached them.

Lowell? I call mentally, but I know from the way Edina tenses that I've also said it out loud. The mating bond is still intact, not splintering like it did when Lowell almost died. I focus on that one nugget of hope. If he's still alive, maybe everyone else is with him. Maybe they went to the hill Lowell showed me.

Lyra charges past us, diving over the hot embers as she runs closer to the location of the werewolf camp. Edina and I follow, flying over burnt stumps that were once thriving trees. I continue searching for signs of life with my mind, not even coming across insects or birds.

I feel like we fly through the barren wasteland forever before we catch Lyra as she pauses, whining to the full moon that lights our way. The shield is torn down. I can feel the magic that guarded the little village, and it's in tatters. The stone houses once laid in perfect circles around the town square are toppled. Lowell's is miraculously still standing, but the roof is caved in.

Lyra picks her way over the remains, even though I offer to carry her in the air. The closer we get to the town center, the thicker the smoke gets.

"Oh god." Edina gags a moment before I'm overwhelmed with the scent of burnt flesh. I clap my hand over my nose, trying to ward off the smell that haunts my dreams.

And then I see it.

In the dead center of the clearing, where the bonfire once stood, is a pile of bones. They gleam white, the blackened flesh mostly melted off. Some are scattered a little way away like they were trying to escape, but most are clustered in a heap in the center.

"The dogpile," I gasp as Lyra inches closer, nudging one of the skeletons with her nose. I spin around frantically, noticing how the scorch marks that mar the ground are darker at the edges.

"He trapped them," I breathe, a single tear tracking down my cheek. "He burned the forest from the outside in. He caged them in." My breath is coming faster, the words falling on the floor like little bombs as reality sinks in.

A blur flashes in my peripheral, and then Vlad is there. He's wearing a signature suit, but his tie is loosened, and his shirt is rumpled. "I just heard," he breathes, his blue eyes raking over the devastation.

"I checked the area," Edina says, appearing back at my side. I hadn't even realized she had left. "There are no tracks. No footprints or signs of movement anywhere."

Water starts to fall from the sky. The Water Elementals must have all arrived to put out the last of the fire.

"Was this the Fae?" Edina asks. "It seems powerful...it couldn't have been—"

A glint at the edge of the pile catches my eye, and I approach it, brushing away the tears that have begun falling. I toe the item, flipping it over, and glass sprays from where the heat cracked it. It's a golden picture frame, the picture inside charred at the edges but somehow still visible amidst the destruction. The picture of Archer and me at the solstice ball. The one I gave him.

I sink to my knees, not caring that the heat seeps through my leggings. "It was Archer. I don't know if he had help, but he was here."

"He killed the entire pack?" Edina breathes, kneeling beside me and grabbing my hand again.

"The kids are in the coven." My voice is shaking. My grip on Edina's hand is the only thing keeping me together. "And I can feel Lowell. He's alive. But E, if Archer has him—"

A growl sounds behind me, and I turn. Lowell is standing there in his wolf form, his golden eyes bouncing around the town center. My chest cracks in half, and I can't control the tears any longer. The worry is gone, but it's replaced by soul-crushing grief.

Lowell lifts his head to the sky and howls, low and mournful. Lyra joins him. A hand is clamping down around my heart, making each beat painful and constricted, but it's nothing compared to my mate's wave of guilt and grief. On shaky legs, I stand and make my way to him, falling before him and wrapping my arms around his neck.

Our entire family. Luna and Cyril, Leanne and Laura, my mother-in-law.

They're all *gone*.

Chapter Twenty-Five

Lowell and Lyra sit amongst the wreckage that was their pack for hours, occasionally howling to the sky. Their grief is tangible, and I can't find words to help. Instead, I pour all my love for my mate through our bond. Occasionally, he turns and licks my hand in acknowledgment, but mostly he stares at the pile of charred remains.

Clouds roll overhead, blocking out the full moon's light as if it can hide the evidence of the atrocities committed here. Once all the fires are extinguished, I send the Water Elementals back to the Highlands, but Edina and Vlad stay, sitting beside us in our silent vigil.

"Are we sure everyone was here?" Vlad asks. "Maybe some left."

They were all here when I left, Lowell says. *And I'm bonded to them all. I would feel something if they were alive.*

He told us the story earlier via his Mind Magic channel. Two of the Alphas were fighting for dominance, and Lowell went to put them in their place. It's nothing he hasn't dealt with before, but the small amount of time it took him to portal to the woods in London was enough for him to be absent here. The guilt my mate feels is enough to clog my throat and keep a steady prick of tears in my eyes.

"But we don't know for sure," Vlad says, his jaw set in determination. "I'll call in a favor from a Fae necromancer."

"A what?" Edina breathes, the color leeching from her face.

"They can assess the remains," Vlad says. "They'll be able to tell us who was here if anyone made it out. I'll leave for Faerie now and be back tomorrow night." A modicum of hope springs from my mate like a beacon in the darkness.

"Even with the time difference?" Edina asks, and Vlad smirks.

"The Fae take favors very seriously," he says. "There will be no hesitation."

If you see Astor, tell him to get his ass back here, Edina sends mentally. Vlad salutes her and takes off towards his house.

Lyra shifts back into her human form, cradling her knees to her chest. "Alaina was there."

"We don't know—"

"I do," she says softly. "I feel it. She's gone, and I never told her—" A choked sob breaks off her words. Edina and I drop hands and circle her, each throwing an arm around her shoulders as she sobs. "She wanted a commitment, and I told her no. She died not knowing how much I love her."

"She knew," Edina says, idly stroking her hair while I rub soothing lines up and down her spine.

A keening song drifts through the air from the direction of the lake, and Lowell's ears twitch in response. *That's Delmare,* he says. Even his mental voice sounds despondent. There's no love lost between me and the Siren who lives in this lake, but the song compels me to stand.

"I'll see what she wants." I don't wait for their response as I pick my way through the forest in the dark, not even bothering to conjure a light to guide my way.

I reach the grassy knoll before the beach and wrap my arms around my middle, trying to contain my emotions. My mate needs me to be strong. I need to be there for him like all the times he's been there for me. There's no space for me to fall apart right now.

When I reach the beach, I sit, waiting as the song reaches its crescendo and Delmare glances over her delicate shoulder. She's in her half-human form, her skin and seafoam green hair somehow alight even without the moonlight. She hops off her perch, flicking her iridescent black tail above the water as she dives into the depths.

When she surfaces in front of me, she's with Marella, a water sprite whose entire body is covered in gleaming blue scales. Both sets of eyes look at me with sorrow and pity.

"Katie," Marella says, and I nod in greeting, not trusting my voice not to break. I turn back to Delmare, who looks different, her usual haughty exterior cracked. Her eyes are rimmed in red as she lifts her eyes from the water to look at me.

"We saw the smoke," Delmare says, a tear sliding down tinted green skin. "I tried—" she gasps.

"We tried to put out the flames before they spread inward," Marella says. "But we couldn't reach them fast enough."

"Thank you for trying," I say.

"Lowell?" Delmare asks.

"Alive," I respond. "Lyra is too. Everyone else—" I turn my head, stifling my sob by clearing my throat. "Vlad is retrieving a necromancer to find out, but it doesn't look good."

Magic shimmers around Delmare, and she strides out of the water on two legs, fully naked, though her hair does cover her breasts. She sits on the beach next to me and places her hand on mine, her fingers gently brushing against the tattoo on my ring finger. My engagement ring is on my nightstand back at the coven.

"We'll help," she says softly, "however we can."

I pull my hand out of her grasp. "Why?" I ask after a moment. "You hate me, and I know you're not overly fond of other witches."

"True," Delmare says, her laugh lacking the usual melody. "But standing by while this happens—" she gestures to the carnage of the forest, "—is inexcusable."

"We can't just sit by and wait while King Archer massacres us," Marella says, her voice thick with hatred. "The water sprites can't help much, but the Sirens can."

I stare over the lake as other merfolk breach the surface, silently showing their support. There are so many that they fill the entire lake, the surface a rainbow of colored scales as the other Sirens walk on two legs and ring the beach.

"What can you do?" I ask, looking at Delmare.

"How many spies do you have?"

"None," I tell her. "Our spies were made, and we had to bring them back to the coven."

Delmare smiles a slow, evil-looking smile that reveals her teeth, sharpened into blackened points. "Send us in," she says. "Our music tends to make humans...forget that we're dangerous."

"Archer has excellent mental shields," I warn her, but she waves a hand like it's inconsequential.

"We'll tell him the Sirens want to be on his side of the war," she says. "I'll make it convincing. I'll get him to barter with us. But once we're in, my friends will start mining for information, seeking out the weak points."

"I should discuss this with—"

"Yes," Lowell says, his voice low and raspy. My mate is back in his human form, and I ignore the possessive urge to block his naked body from Delmare.

"We need all the help we can get," Edina says, emerging from the woods with Lyra still tucked beneath her arm, a blanket draped over the latter's shoulders.

"Good," Delmare says, and Lowell looks out over the water, acknowledging the other merfolk who have gathered in support of his fallen pack. One by one, they nod and disappear beneath the water, Delmare and Marella leaving last. Before she leaves, Delmare promises they'll go in the morning, which is only a few hours off at this point.

Lowell sits beside me as Edina and Lyra hang back. He drapes his arm around my shoulders and grips my chin with his other hand, forcing me to meet those brilliant golden eyes.

"Don't you dare blame yourself for this," he says, reading my emotions and my damn soul.

"I baited him at the wedding," I say. "I shouldn't have. I knew he was unstable, but this...."

"I think it's pretty safe to say he'll do just about anything to get you back," Lowell says.

I balk. "You don't think this is about the army."

"No, little witch."

Unbridled rage boils in my stomach, replacing the grief and making me see red. I know Archer has proven countless times he'll sacrifice innocents, but I assumed this was a way to eliminate a large portion of the army. To think that he did this to kill my mate...

"I'm going to fucking kill him," I breathe, pushing to my feet, but Lowell wraps me in his arms.

"Yes, you will," he murmurs. "But I'm not sending you in there without a plan. You and Lyra are the only family I have left and—" He breaks off, his body shuddering with the need to shift, and I hold on tight, anchoring him to me.

"You're right," I whisper. Lowell squeezes me so tight I might snap in half, but I take it all. "He'll pay for this, but not now. I'm not leaving you." The shock wears off all at once, and I'm hit with the barrage of Lowell's emotions. It's all I can do to keep breathing. To keep my mate breathing.

We stand by the lake until the sun rises, all of us taking turns crying and feeling guilty about one thing or another as we comfort each other. The four of us lean on each other until Delmare and her Sirens emerge.

"We just need someone to allow us through Vlad's shields," she says. Edina waves her hand, and the shield closest to us shimmers as the magic is modified. "Any chance you're stationed by the ocean?" Her voice is full of longing and hope, so raw and pure that it makes me smile.

"You can afford a small detour," I say. Her whole body sags in relief. "When we win this war, you'll return to the oceans. We'll have to discuss some ground rules, but I won't keep you locked in these lakes."

"Thank you." She and her group disappear over the hill while the rest of us continue to watch the sunrise.

I convince Lowell and Lyra to go back to the coven, but they refuse to leave the war room until Vlad returns. They won't eat, and they won't sleep. They just stare at the portal with rapt attention.

Edina and I cram in on either side of the wolves on the couch she procured. None of us know what to say, so we just sit in silence. The mirror that once showed views of the palace now just shows our gaunt expressions full of terror and, more terrifying, one iota of hope.

Much earlier than expected, the door swings open, and the mist floods inside.

It's not Vlad.

A beautiful woman sways into the doorway, her dark hair bound back in a braid that's threaded with golden jewelry. The pupils of her yellow-green eyes are narrowed into reptilian slits. The last time I saw her, she shot ultraviolet dragon fire at me.

Ethelinda. The dragon queen.

She makes no move to come closer but waits until two behemoths appear at her back. Without leaving my spot on the couch, I surround the group with lightning, keeping them firmly in place by the door. One of the beefy men chortles and runs a hand through his toffee-colored hair.

"More impressive than the last time we saw you." I recognize his voice. He's the shifter who threatened to chain and burn me. Electricity licks his skin, but it only makes him laugh.

"Enough," Ethelinda commands, and he falls silent. "We're not here for a quarrel. We have come to pay our respects for the fallen werewolf pack." She turns to Lowell. "Your mother and I met a time or two. She, and all the others, will be greatly missed."

"We don't have confirmation they're gone," Lyra growls, and the dragon queen gives her a pitying look. Lowell grabs my hand and grips it tightly.

"You have a plan for retaliation?" Ethelinda continues. We don't. I haven't had the heart to bring it up until we know exactly who's gone. She nods in understanding even though I don't speak. "When you do, we would like to be of service. In addition to my dragons, I can offer the assistance of the other five dragon hoards. The shifters should be here within the next few days."

Lowell opens his mouth, and judging by the wave of irritation I feel from him, I know he's about to refute their offer. He's still angry that they planned to hold me captive after our last run-in. But honestly, if we limited our allies to people who haven't tried to kill me, we'd have about three people.

"Thank you," I respond quickly. "When Vlad returns tonight, we'll discuss working the dragons into our strategy. Will you need rooms?"

We continue discussing some minute details until Marcus comes in and greets Ethelinda like an old friend. He offers to set her and her shifters up in some of the very limited free space. The room grows silent again when they leave, and all eyes latch onto the portal.

"Maybe I should get us some food," Edina says, trying to extract herself from the couch, but Lyra latches onto her hand and squeezes until her knuckles go white. "I'll ask someone to bring food."

The portal takes that moment to start swirling again, and everyone sits straight up.

"Fucking hell," Lowell swears when it's not Vlad who enters.

The first thing I notice about the male is long, curved horns that protrude from thick, dark curls. He's tall, easily a few inches taller than everyone in the room, and his muscles are straining the button-down he's wearing, revealing a hint of black ink on his chest. And his eyes...if I couldn't tell that he was Fae from the horns, the startling teal of his eyes would be a dead giveaway.

Edina freezes. Going so still that I'm not sure she's even breathing. Lyra tenses in response, emitting a low growl as I call more lightning to my hands.

"Your Highness," the male says, dipping into a bow before rising again. "I apologize for the intrusion, but Astor sent me."

Edina scoffs, and ice starts leaking onto the armrest of the couch. Is she losing control? I haven't seen her lose control of her magic since she returned from Faerie.

"He did, I swear it."

"And you are?" I ask.

"Apologies, Your Majesty." He bows deeply again, this time facing me. "My name is Eldoris. I am the general of the Seelie Army and prince of the Summer Court." He straightens, casting a look at Edina, who looks less than amused. "When Astor returned to Faerie, he approached Summer Court first. We...hellfire has been a blight on our court, one we thought was extinguished permanently."

"In Faerie," Edina says, her eyes narrowed to slits. Eldoris cocks his head to the side in confusion. "You thought hellfire was extinguished in Faerie. Not here."

"I—yes," he replies, raising his chin, even though his tone is sheepish. "If Astor is correct, and Fae are aiding the king, it is our responsibility to help you in this war. The monarchs of the Seelie Courts have all agreed and are sending forces in the next few days. I was asked to stay to help you prepare."

"And the Unseelie Courts?" I ask.

"We're all on the same page," Eldoris assures. "Though I cannot speak to their timeline, Astor was adamant that we mobilize quickly. I'm sure both armies will cross through the portal simultaneously."

"Thank you, general." I glance at Edina from the corner of my eye. She's completely checked out, and when I try to reach her mentally, she has shields firmly in place.

"With your permission, I'm going to scan the king's fortress to confirm the presence of Fae. Your Highness, would you like to join me?" Eldoris looks at Edina expectantly, but if she hears him, there's no indication.

The silence in the room is so uncomfortable it makes me fidget. "I'll have someone escort you," I finally say, mentally asking Butch to send a werewolf to escort the Fae. Someone appears a moment later, and with a grateful nod and one final look at Edina, Eldoris exits the war room.

"Do we hate him?" I ask, whirling on my best friend. "He just offered us a crap ton of soldiers...but if you say we hate him, I'll get on board."

"No," Edina shrugs, her normal, carefree tone back in place. "I don't even know him."

"Looked like he knew you," Lowell chides, and Lyra laughs. Edina rolls her eyes good-naturedly and opens her mouth, no doubt with a quip on her tongue, but Vlad steps through the portal.

I know the answer before Vlad says anything. His face is sullen, his usually perfect hair mussed. He opens and closes his mouth a few times before clearing his throat.

"Say it," Lowell says, squeezing my hand as he sits straight up.

"I sent the necromancer back to Faerie," Vlad says. "He analyzed the entire area and the remains."

"Vlad," Lowell implores. "Just say it."

"All the pack members are accounted for. There were no survivors."

For a moment, everyone goes still, and then a stab of pain hits me right in the gut. I know Lowell has been grieving, but I also know that within his grief was the slim sliver of hope that someone made it out. One of his sisters, his mom, anyone.

I hop onto Lowell's lap, and Vlad takes my vacated seat so he can comfort both Lowell and Lyra at the same time. My impossibly strong mate is shaking, burying his face in my shoulder as he breaks in my arms. I hold him tight as his grief mixes with my own, and we both sob. His grief is all-consuming, a dark ocean of hurt that I can't save him from.

I tilt his chin up gently, allowing my golden magic to seep down my arms and onto Lowell's skin. It creeps towards his chest, and when it reaches his heart, the pain he's feeling floods into me. I grit my teeth at the extent of it, giving him a respite before his eyes flare yellow and the transfer halts.

"I'm not letting you take this from me," he murmurs, but his voice is more even.

Tears flow freely from my eyes. "Okay." I lean my forehead against his before he wraps me back in his arms.

"I left them," he murmurs against my skin as a wave of guilt threatens to capsize me.

"You couldn't have known."

"I should have been there."

"You would have been dead," Vlad says, his ice-blue eyes fixing on Lowell. Lowell doesn't lift his head; he just nuzzles against me.

"I need to do something," Lowell says finally. "We need to end this. We can't wait for him to slaughter us in our sleep."

"I agree," I respond, looking to the others, who all nod. "Three days. We'll bury our loved ones and bring the fight to them. It's time."

Lowell leans back, and the look in his eyes is feral, truly and utterly terrifying. "I know you deserve it, but I can't promise I won't be the one to kill him when push comes to shove."

"I'm not picky on how it gets done," I tell him. "We'll leave it up to fate. The first chance we have, we'll end him. Anyone who has a shot."

Chapter Twenty-Six

THE WARM, CLOUDLESS DAY doesn't make sense. It should be raining. When you're doing something devastating, it should be raining. But the sky is clear, and the setting sun colors the sky in rainbow hues when it should be gray.

Lowell, Lyra, and I are all in black, cloaked in a heavy sadness. We lead wolves and witches from Vlad's house through the blackened husks of trees that once were the forest. The sun disappears beneath the hills, but none of the witches in the back of the line call forth light. We walk by the light of the moon.

Werewolves typically bury their dead in a meaningful place, each wolf returning to the earth in a separate plot. Lowell's father is buried under the hill we went to on our first run, so that's where the remains of our family will be buried, but the rest of the pack didn't leave instructions. We're burying them in the center of their village.

We breach the rubble and halt before the large hole where the town square once sat. The European and American packs line the gravesite, and everyone else flanks them, forming concentric circles that stretch the length of the destroyed wood.

I stand behind my mate, watching his back muscles tensing and his shoulders creeping towards his ears. He shakes his head before tugging me to his side. "I can't do this." His voice cracks, his breaths come in too quickly. There's too much emotion in our bond.

Cupping his face in my hand, I brush my thumb along his thicker-than-usual stubble. His breathing slows. "I've got you," I whisper. He nods, holding onto my hand as I lower it back to our sides.

I open my mouth to speak, but the words get lodged in my throat. How do I eulogize a group of people who have had such a profound impact on my life? On my mate's life?

Releasing a shaky breath, I amplify my voice. "I always had a fascination with werewolves." Some of the group offer me small smiles. "But the stories I read, the facts I studied...nothing could live up to the reality.

"When I first came here, I thought I'd be an outcast. I thought the pack would reject me because I wasn't a wolf. But the welcome I received was nothing short of amazing.

"From the first moment I stepped within these wards, I found a family. Not just the family I would marry into but the entire pack. They didn't care that I was a witch who, at the time, didn't have magic. Or that I once served the royal family who banished them. They simply opened their hearts, passed me a drink so strong it almost killed me, and welcomed me home."

Lowell's arm wraps around my waist as I reach down and scratch the head of Luna's children, who have been so distraught that they've been in their wolf forms since they heard the news. "No pack deserves this fate," I whisper, knowing the wolves will still hear me. "But this pack—" I clear my throat and brush away a tear.

"I know we want revenge," I continue, and I get several growls of confirmation. "And I vow that I will not stop until it's ours. But tonight, we gather to say goodbye to our brothers and sisters, our fellow soldiers." I step out of Lowell's arms and call my golden magic to my hands, letting it spread down and over the bones of the pack that accepted me so freely. "May your sacrifice not be in vain."

The crowd echoes me as the magic seals an eternal shield over the remains. Lowell steps forward and, without a word, a clump of earth falls from his hand on top of my shield. Lyra follows, repeating the motion while Luna's children each kick a bit of dirt into the hole. I wait for the rest of the wolves to do the same, but everyone waits, their eyes on me.

"They're waiting for you," Lowell murmurs. "You're the last member of our pack."

My heart cracks a little further as I drop a handful of dirt into the grave. As soon as the last grain falls from my hand, everyone else follows suit. When everyone has thrown a handful, the Earth Elementals cover what's left of the hole and slowly start coaxing grass to grow over the plot. They finish by arranging fallen stones into the shape of a wolf howling at the moon.

We stare at the statue in silence until an unspoken command has them slowly leaving for the portal. When only Lowell, Lyra, the kids, and I remain, Lowell sinks to his knees and places a hand on the grass. "Our pack," he breathes. I put my hand on his shoulder as his emotions win out, and he begins to cry. "Our home is gone." He looks at Lyra, who has her arms wrapped around the pups.

"What do we do now?" Lyra asks. Lowell doesn't answer. He looks so lost it breaks my heart even further.

"We say goodbye," I say. "And then we rebuild."

"We rebuild," he agrees, pulling me down to kneel next to him. We sit for a while, just holding each other before he stands and lays his jacket at the base of the headstone before shifting and shredding the rest of his clothing.

I climb onto his back, stroking his head as Lyra helps me gather two pups into my arms. When she reaches for the third, he shakes his head and shifts into a small, tear-stained boy.

"Lorenzo," Lyra breathes.

"I want to be able to say goodbye," he whispers. Lyra sets him in front of me, and he leans back into my chest, his sisters nuzzling him as I wrap all three in my arms. The girls whimper; Lorenzo's cheeks are wet.

It's not fair. They're too young to know this grief.

"Hold on tight," I say, and Lowell takes off in the direction of the hill as Lyra shifts and follows. The wind steals my tears, making my eyes dry for the first time in days.

Four silhouettes wait for us on the top of the hill. Lowell bares his teeth, ready for a fight, but my mother throws a ball of magical light into the air, illuminating her, Marcus, Edina, and Vlad. "We understand if you don't want us here," my mom starts.

"But we wanted to be here for you if you needed us," Marcus continues.

"We're family," Edina says, a tear running down her cheek. "So, we'll give you privacy if you want—"

"I didn't agree to that," Vlad intones, and Edina smacks him across the arm.

I want them here, Lowell says. I relay the message as the kids and I dismount, and he shifts. Lowell and Lyra hug Vlad and Edina, respectively, a few condolences are whispered, and then Lowell pushes past the group to an open grave that houses our family. He sits on the grass, crossing his legs as his nieces follow him and plop in his lap, nudging him until he pets behind their ears. Lorenzo sticks to me like glue, and I tuck him into my side as everyone joins my mate beside the grave.

"You gave a beautiful eulogy, Katie," Lyra says. "But you lied about how you met the pack."

"I have no idea what you're talking about," I smirk.

"You don't remember practically mounting Lowell in front of everyone?" Vlad teases.

"Kathryn," my mother hisses. Lowell laughs for the first time in days.

"You made an impression," Lyra says, and the pups yip in agreement even though they weren't there. "Mama's exact words were, 'think I'll get more grandchildren in nine months?'"

An uneasy silence follows our laughter.

"They wouldn't want us to feel guilty for laughing," Vlad says softly.

"It doesn't feel right," Lyra says.

"It doesn't," Lowell agrees, "but we can still grieve and remember the good times. They wouldn't want us to be sad forever."

"The twins would be pissed we were grieving at all," Lyra smirks, and I can imagine their cross faces scowling with impatience.

"They'd say we're wasting time," Lowell agrees.

"And we should be looking for horrific ways to make Archer pay."

"I don't know what you did to those children to make them so ruthless," Vlad chides.

We sit out on the hill swapping stories, though my parents, Edina, and I mostly listen. Vlad tells a few stories about Lowell's mom that make even Lyra blush. After countless hours, Lowell stands, holding his handful of dirt.

"We love you," he says to the grave as I coat it in a layer of protective magic.

"We'll miss you," Lyra says, dropping her handful of dirt.

"We'll make you proud," Lorenzo says on behalf of himself and his sisters.

The hole gets filled in one handful at a time, the last added just before the sun crests the hill. With one last promise, we make our way back to the portal to get ready for the next step... getting revenge on Archer for taking them away too soon.

I KNOCK ON THE doorway to the medical bay, and Coleman lifts his head from his seat, where he's stroking the fur of a wolf pup. "Your Majesty," he says as the pup whines and nuzzles against his arm until he continues to pet her. She sniffs, and I swear I see tears trickle down her snout.

We returned from the funeral a few days ago and threw ourselves into solidifying the attack we'll launch tomorrow night. The witches and werewolves have already started marching towards Archer's stronghold, cloaked in shielding spells so their approach will be hidden. The rest of us are leaving in the morning; Edina and I will teleport the healers, and Lowell and some wolves will bring the cart of supplies. The vampires are meeting us at sundown in time for the battle.

"Ava Marie?" I ask, and the pup whimpers and trots over to me, launching herself into my arms and nuzzling my hand. The children mostly stay with Mrs. Coleman while the rest of us prepare for the attack.

"She hasn't shifted back," Coleman says wearily.

"She's been a wolf since the full moon?"

Coleman nods, sighing heavily. "The American Pack Master said an Alpha can force a shift, but it's traumatic. Pups need to shift, so their skeletons develop correctly, and if she doesn't shift soon…"

I plop down on the cold, rock floor, and hold Ava Marie in front of me so that she's suspended in the air, her little legs waving like she wants to be put down. She sniffles and whines, her blue eyes pleading. She looks so much like Luna in her human form, but her wolf form is all Cyril.

"I know, baby girl," I murmur. "I know you miss your mama. I wish I could bring her back for you."

I know what it feels like to lose a parent at a young age. My father went to prison when I was a little older than Ava Marie, but I lost him much earlier than that. I lost him during the first experiment when he laid his hands on me. It never gets easier knowing the people who are meant to always be there for you are gone.

I lean my head against her forehead and brush her snout with my nose, a motion Lowell has done for me countless times. Her bones shake in my hands, and they slowly bend and snap. Her fur fades, changing to pale pink skin, and with a final shiver, she shifts into a toddler, with beet-red eyes and snot dripping down her nose. I wipe it with the sleeve of my tunic before she buries her head in my neck and wails.

I murmur soft, gentle tones, and then I start to hum. Not the song my mother once sang to me because Archer fucked that up for me, but the song I walked down the aisle to. A simple melody, a mortal French song that Lowell loves. The one he sang after we mated. Slowly, her sobs quiet, turning to soft whimpers. And then she starts to sing. Her words wobble around tears, but she sings the French perfectly in tune with my humming.

When the song ends, I turn her so she's cradled in my arms, and she sticks her thumb in her mouth. "Mama sang that to me every night," she mumbles around her finger.

"Oh," I say. "I don't have to—"

"Again?" she asks, her blue eyes hopeful as she looks up at me.

I sing the song another five times until she finally falls asleep in my arms. Coleman sighs a deep breath of relief. He's tired; we've all been tired since the attack on the full moon. It was a blow that hit us hard. The wolves knew the Italian pack well, as did a lot of the vampires. And since living in the coven…I didn't realize how close the witches had become to their werewolf combat partners. Everyone mourned. Everyone is ready for vengeance.

"My wife will look after them while we're fighting," Coleman offers. I'm glad the kids will have someone they know to be with them while we're all gone. "Have you spoken to Lyra about staying behind?"

I nod. We were all a little shocked when we read the will and saw Luna and Cyril named Lyra the guardian, but it makes sense.

Lowell's time has always been divided between multiple packs, while Lyra has been a constant fixture in the kids' lives. She openly sobbed at the news, but we promised we'd be there to help her.

"She insists on fighting," I reply. Lowell and Lyra got into a huge fight about it. He begged her to stay behind, but she refused. She wants revenge for her sisters, her mom, and her lover.

"And you? Or Lowell?"

"We can't stay behind, you know that."

Coleman sighs, looking down at the girl in my arms. "I know. I just worry what more loss will do to this girl."

I trail a finger down Ava Marie's cheek, brushing away the remnants of an old tear. He's right. I don't see how we get out of this war with our lives if our army loses.

"A lot of people are going to die," he says. "On both sides."

"People have already died," I huff. "Everyone out there knows what they signed up for. We'll take prisoners when we can, but if it's a choice between them or us, I choose us. I choose those fighting for a change over those who are content to sit back and let this continue. I need to focus on bringing our soldiers home. On making the world better for those who do survive. And I...I can't think about who I'll need to kill to do it."

"We trust your judgment," Coleman says. "We know it's time to make a stand. But I also mourn for the girl who cried over five people being destroyed before her eyes."

"She's still here," I breathe. "I'll still mourn the death of every soldier who dies on that field. Even..." I shake away that thought.

"It's okay to be upset about the reality we're in. To regret a decision that needs to be made."

I scoff. "I'm not crazy? For hating that I have to kill him?" A tear slips down my cheek. "Because I *despise* him more than I've hated anyone, and my father was a piece of shit so that's saying something. I should want to kill him. I should be looking forward to it, plotting the ways I can make him suffer. Everyone else is. I think Edina is going to dance on his corpse. But—" Ava Marie shifts in my arms, and I still until she settles back down.

"War is an impossible situation," Coleman starts after a moment. "But I think being upset about taking a life shows strength of character, not weakness. It's what makes you a great queen."

He takes my hand and squeezes.

"Thank you," I breathe, returning the squeeze before pulling away and wiping my damp cheeks. "I came down here for a sleeping tonic."

"For you or Lowell?"

"Lowell," I say, tightening my hold on Ava Marie. "He hasn't been sleeping, and I need him sharp for tomorrow. I—" A sob chokes off my airway. "I can't lose him."

Coleman stands and hands me a bottle of the tonic. "Have him take it all," he says, opening his arms for me to give him the child. "Werewolves digest the stuff too fast for it to be effective otherwise."

I nod, and when Ava Marie is in his arms, murmuring something in French under her breath as she stirs, I leave the medical bay.

Lowell is staring at the ceiling when I return to our room. I hand him the bottle wordlessly, and he downs the contents without question. I change quickly and curl into Lowell's chest, sinking into his warmth and basking in the fact that tonight may be the last night we spend in each other's arms. We don't talk, but we hold each other tighter than before until we slowly drift off to sleep.

Chapter Twenty-Seven

Katie, we have a problem, my mother's voice travels down our mental channel, reverberating in my ears. Her voice is tense, not quite panicked, but ominous enough that I hop out of bed and immediately start hunting for the fighting leathers Vlad bought me.

What's wrong? I toss Lowell's shirt off and hit my phone screen, checking the time. The blue light makes me wince as it's bright enough to illuminate my entire half of the room. It's the middle of the night.

Archer's troops are on the move. They're about halfway between our bases.

"Fuck," I scream, startling Lowell from his half-asleep state. I could tell the minute the medicine wore off because his feelings came in full force, waking me for a moment before he decided to pretend to be asleep.

"What's wrong?" he demands, already up and tugging on sweatpants as I hop into my leggings.

I loop him into the channel with my mom. *How close are they to you?*

Close. They'll run into us in twenty minutes at the rate they're moving.

"Fuck fuck fuck," I scream as my mother asks what we want to do. "Just fucking once, I'd like things to go as we planned." I get my tunic and my leather vest on as Lowell holds out the holster for my dagger for me to step into.

What do you want us to do? my mother repeats.

Retreat a little bit. I need you to buy me an extra ten minutes. When you've settled on a location, put a large shield around the army and send me your coordinates.

Lowell wraps my sword belt around my waist, and his fingers linger around my hips. His eyes are clear for the first time in days, like the threat of battle woke him up. He uses the leather to pull me closer, and I allow the moment of comfort from my mate before we need to go.

"We will survive this day," I say, assuring myself more than I'm assuring him.

"I trust you completely, little witch." He kisses me deeply, cupping the back of my head possessively and molding me to him.

"I love you," I murmur, and open the mental channel that connects the entire army. I tell everyone our timeline has moved up, and although the soldiers keep the channel free of chatter, I can practically feel their frantic energy. Lowell orders the wolves to help bring healing supplies to the battlefield, and I tell everyone else to meet us at the front of the coven for further instructions.

Lowell and I hold hands until we have to part ways, but not before he steals a quick kiss and darts toward the medical bay. I teleport just outside the coven doors, where vampires and some of the witches remaining are gathered.

"Alek?" I call, and Vlad's brother appears in front of me, ready for orders. His blonde hair is tied back in a neat bun, much like Lowell did his hair, and his fangs are bared, ready for a fight.

"I need you to organize everyone into groups. Each group of Magical Creatures needs a witch to shield them and keep them invisible while you run." He nods and starts organizing as more and more vampires and witches pour out of the cave.

The loud thumping of wheels is heard from the cavern halls, and I order everyone out of the way of the cart that holds medical supplies and tents. Lowell and his betas pull it in their wolf form, but my mate shifts when he sees me.

"There's a flaw in this plan," he says, gesturing to the cart. "It's not meant for fast travel. We could barely get it down the halls, let alone over grassy hills."

Again, time is not our friend. "E?" I call, and my best friend flutters down beside me, the Summer Court Fae on her heels. "Can you teleport the cart?"

"Fuck if I know," she says, and begrudgingly looks to Eldoris. "You have any experience teleporting large objects?"

He winks, and I laugh, even as Edina rolls her eyes. "I'll handle it," Eldoris promises. "I'll teleport to your signature as soon as you join your troops."

"We're ready," Alek calls, and I give him the go-ahead to leave. Almost at once, the field clears as vampires and witches go invisible, leaving only wind in their wake as they begin running.

"I've got the wolves," Edina says, grabbing hold of the shifted werewolves and teleporting before I can tell her otherwise. I give Eldoris a half-shrug and tight smile as he sighs and grabs the cart before following suit.

Lowell stands behind me, his hands closing around my waist and his lips brushing against his claiming mark.

"Here we go," I say, focusing on finding my mom. I cast the shielding spell, keeping us invisible before my black iridescent magic envelops us.

We arrive in an empty field, and I send out my Mind Magic until I feel my mother's shield. The night is cool and crisp and surprisingly devoid of clouds like the stars want a clear view of the events about to happen. There's a small hill in the direction of Archer's stronghold, but beyond it, I can hear the sound of thousands of boots marching. Their impact sends vibrations through the ground, quaking the earth.

We're here, I tell the army while Lowell holds my waist. Everything I'm feeling in the bond tells me he doesn't want to let go, a sentiment I mirror completely. We step forward until I feel the magic of the shield crackle over my skin. When we breach the ward, the entire army stands in front of us, loudly talking amongst themselves as they await orders.

What are the orders, Your Majesty? Marcus asks, and everyone snaps to attention as heads swivel to my position.

Get in your formations. The vampires will be here shortly. We only have a few hours with the vampires before sunrise, but we'll take what we can get.

The soldiers who were marching are already in a rough formation, but there's movement as the vampires arrive, and the healers go to the back of the clearing and start setting up tents and organizing the supplies Eldoris brought over. There are a few hushed conversations amongst trios, a few small groups breaking ranks to hug their fellow soldiers. I hope they're wishing each other well...but I think they may be saying goodbye, just in case.

"Baby queen?" Vlad calls, and then he and Adriana appear in front of us. Somehow, Adriana looks more beautiful, like becoming a vampire took her natural beauty and dialed it up to the max. Her color is good, which means she's been fed recently, but her fangs are still extended over her bottom lip.

I bypass Vlad and pull my sister into my arms, squeezing her tight. "No biting," Vlad commands.

"I wasn't going to," Adriana pouts, and I laugh in her hold.

"Fuck, I've missed you," I say, trying not to cry.

"I've missed you," she says. She inhales deeply and sighs. "Seriously, why do you smell so good? She smells like a vanilla milkshake." She pulls away and looks over her shoulder at Vlad. "Is that what she tastes like, Daddy?"

"Oh, fucking hell." I turn to put some space between me and that super fun bomb, but Lowell holds me in place and kisses my shoulder.

"You can't tell me that surprises you," Lowell whispers.

"I mean, no, but I didn't need to hear it."

Vlad yanks Adriana back and wraps his arms around her waist, so her back is plastered to his front. She giggles as he whispers something in her ear and kisses the crook of her neck. It's so freaking sweet that I can almost forget that she called him Daddy.

"You look happy," I say, and they both nod, practically glowing they're smiling so wide.

Edina plops down in the middle of our little group. Adriana hisses, bearing her fangs. "Whoa." Edina holds out her hands in surrender and backs up to me.

"Adriana, down," Vlad says, and she glares but sinks back into Vlad's hold. "She's still a little feral. It was probably a mistake to bring her, but she wouldn't stay away."

"Aww, you're a soft daddy," Edina teases...and then squeals and uses Lowell as a shield when Adriana lurches forward. Vlad snatches her by the hair, and her head snaps back as he reels her in.

"Please don't poke the baby vampire."

"What would be the fun in that?" she laughs. Vlad chuckles, but Adriana is now growling. "Okay, fine, I'll leave! Babes, where do you want me? Since I was always the attacker in our drills, I don't have a triad."

"Can you and Eldoris work together?" She glares. "You'll join with the other Fae when they arrive, but in the meantime—"

"Fine." She flies away, presumably in search of her new battle buddy, but not before she hits me with a small deluge of snow.

"Feeling antagonistic today?" Vlad smirks.

"I hope that if I keep forcing them together, Edina will get so mad that she snaps and tells me why she hates him." I smirk

"Such an abuse of power," Vlad tsks. "I love it."

Look alive, everyone, my mother calls, and I turn towards the hill as the first line of the Dragon soldiers crest the top, just black shapes in the darkness of the waning moon.

"Playtime's over," I sigh. Vlad kisses Adriana swiftly before she disappears to find Cecelia and Lyra. *Individual shields up. No need to keep them invisible.*

Lowell, Vlad, and I step to the front as lines and lines of soldiers descend the small hill and stand across the expansive field between us.

On my signal, I command and ascend on a cloud of Dark Magic, flying straight into the sky and outside the shield. I coat my body in my other forms of magic, minus the hellfire, allowing them to mingle so that I look like a shooting star. The soldiers gasp and start pointing as I hover above them. The front lines call fire to their hands, and I watch as a ripple of elements trickles back.

Fire, water, air, earth, I tell my troops, so they'll know what elements to expect. Putting Fire Elementals in the front is an odd choice. In all the drills I ran with the Dragons, we always put Earth first so they could dig trenches and build walls. I bet they rearranged because Archer thinks I'll still react poorly to fire. He should know better. It's hard to be afraid of being burned when fire is literally in your veins.

Any sign of Archer? Lowell asks.

No.

Fucking coward.

I wait, lightning crackling over my skin as the soldiers all aim at me, their eyes averted skyward while my army creeps closer, silent in their approach thanks to the shield. I know Archer's army will have shields too, but they didn't cloak themselves in invisibility, and I'm not sure if it's born of arrogance or lack of knowledge.

"My fellow soldiers," I call out to the opposing army, using an amplification spell. "I offer you this one opportunity to surrender. Turn in your king, and you will be pardoned and welcomed into the new world we are creating."

You sound like a supervillain, Vlad says, and I have to fight to keep my face impassive.

Some of the soldiers exchange glances. I recognize a few, but most are unfamiliar, and there are even more soldiers than we expected. Not only did the factions from around the world make their way here, but it seems they've been recruiting. It's staggering. We'll need to be better than them magically because they outnumber us greatly.

Lowell must sense my unease because he sends a wave of love and support that keeps my spine steeled as I wait for the answer from the army.

One of the generals takes a step forward. He's an older man who always hated me because I was a young woman who was more talented than him. I mean, it could be because I frequently ignored his orders. But it was probably the woman thing.

He launches a fireball at me. *Asswipe.*

I don't move as the orange flames approach. Just before it's about to hit me in the chest, Edina's ice magic extinguishes it, eliciting confused looks from the opposing army. I snap my fingers, not because I need it, but because I'm dramatic like that, and the shield disappears, leaving my entire army on display behind their shields. Archer's army gasps and sputters.

With a savage battle cry that I think comes from Adriana, we attack.

Chapter Twenty-Eight

THE ARMIES CLASH IN an explosion of magic. Dark Magic is blocked with flames. Fire is extinguished with ice. Beams of light pierce the field from my mother and the other Light Magic users, blasting through shields and making lines break and scatter.

I scan the army for any sign of Archer. I'm convinced he'll be in the air, hidden amongst their aerial unit, but there are so many witches on brooms I can't tell them apart. I send out my Mind Magic in a wave, but there's no familiar presence. He must not be here, which means I need to find him. I fly forward, prepared to take on the aerial unit alone when there's a sharp tug on the mating bond.

Don't fucking think about it, little witch, Lowell growls. *Get your ass on the ground and fight beside me.*

They're grouped at the back. They have to be protecting Archer.

There are too many of them for you to handle on your own, Vlad says. *We'll deal with them later...during phase two.*

Huffing out a breath of frustration, I descend off my Dark Magic cloud and land beside Vlad and my mate, who's easily the largest wolf on the battlefield, not that I'm bragging. I surround the three of us in an impenetrable shield that immediately takes fire.

"You'd think they were trying to kill us," Vlad teases. He zips away, my shield stretching to cover him as he reaches into an opposing soldier's chest, pulls out their heart, and shoves it into his mouth, draining the organ dry. I watch in horror as he drops the bloodless muscle and meets my gaze.

"What? We're short on blood at the coven." He smirks, blood dripping down his chin, and Lowell's laughter rings in my ear. I roll my eyes and electrocute the witch who snuck up behind our vampire. Vlad regards him like one would regard a bug that's not worthy of crushing before coming back to my side.

Since Archer isn't on the battlefield, the job of my trio is to break through their lines and get to the back, where he's no doubt waiting. I was hoping we could teleport, but it's too risky with all the shields in place. I'm not really in the mood to get lost in space while my soldiers fight.

Whenever a triad of our soldiers comes close to us, they help carve a path, taking out witches in vertical rows, exactly as we've practiced. They move seamlessly, striking and shielding, helping others. And still, some go down.

Everyone behind us, I call to the army and wait until I get the all-clear that everyone has dropped back. I jump over a witch who thinks they can use this moment to attack and land in a crouch, with my fists in the earth. Lightning travels through the ground and electrocutes the rows in front of us. As they writhe on the ground, my soldiers rush forward, pushing bodies away, so there's an open hole down the middle of their battle formation.

"We should be able to see Archer from here." I hop on Lowell's back, and he and Vlad sprint through the open path. The faster we get to him, the faster this can all be over with. "Where the hell is he?"

"I bet he'd come out if you take your top off," Vlad says, and Lowell snarls at him and takes it out on the poor soldier who steps into our path. Blood splatters as my wolf tears into his victim, and I snap my mouth shut just before it hits me.

Count Orlov? Sybil's shrill voice comes through the channel as I perform a quick cleansing spell and get off Lowell's back. *We have a problem.*

A fucking huge one, Edina adds. *Adriana is on a rampage.*

Vlad swears. "Katie, take me up. I need to find her."

Lowell shifts and wraps his arms around me while Vlad holds onto my wolf. I blast us up in the air, my Dark Magic blending into the pitch-black night sky. Thankfully, my shield holds strong against the barrage of magic blasted in our direction. Vlad huffs as smoke from the Fire Elementals clouds our view until Marcus uses his Air Magic to clear it away.

We all frantically scan the field. I'm about to ask Edina where she last saw Adrianna when there's a red explosion on the left side of the battlefield.

"Fuck me sideways," Vlad swears. I start flying us over as fast as I can. "This is too slow. Lowell, throw me."

"What's happening?" Lowell asks as I say, "Throw you?"

"She's in bloodlust. She'll kill anyone in her path, no matter what side they're on. I need to get her out of here. Can you two handle it without me?" Blood blooms across the battlefield like the world's most twisted fountain display.

"We're coming with you," I insist, still flying towards the site, but I have to dodge too many attacks to make a straight approach.

"Fucking throw me!" Vlad bellows.

"Don't drop us, little witch," my mate says and lets go of me. Vlad moves in front of him and bends his legs as Lowell grabs his waist and tosses him through the air like he's a little kid being tossed in a swimming pool. Vlad puts his arms in front of him in a superman pose as he streaks across the sky.

He's not shielded, I tell the army, who somehow heed my command and deflect the magical attacks directed at him. Vlad lands in a roll right in front of the most recent geyser of blood.

Status? I demand as Lowell, and I continue our much slower approach.

This is why we didn't invite baby vampires, he bellows in my head, making me wince.

You're the one who brought her! The blood explosions stop, but soldiers are still falling by the truckload. *If you're on the left side, evacuate*, I order.

No shit, Edina scoffs.

Katie. You want to see this. Get over here, Vlad says. Lowell and I exchange glances before I put on a burst of speed.

I've been in my fair share of battles. I'm not a stranger to blood and gore. But there are no words to describe the carnage around Adriana.

Blood is hovering in the air like suspended raindrops. My sister stands in the center with Vlad, her arms raised as the droplets morph into little spears, and with a battle cry, she launches them at the opposition slicing at flesh and exposing more blood. She huffs out a breath, her gray eyes glassing over as she pulls blood from the soldiers' wounds, using it to break arms and wrists and choke off their magic.

Men writhe on the ground in pain, but somehow she's not killing them. She's just leaving them incapacitated, so her supply of blood never runs out. When more arrive, she repeats the process, harnessing the blood from the exposed wounds of soldiers and turning it into a weapon.

Lowell and I land beside them, and Adriana drops her blood droplets and beams proudly. "Did you see?" she exclaims, bouncing up and down on her toes. Vlad is looking down at her with complete and total pride.

I'm saved from answering as witches attack, and I'm about to shield us when Adriana harnesses the blood to form a solid cocoon around us. It smells great.

"How—" I gag.

"I'm a Blood Witch!" she tosses her hair behind her shoulder, smearing blood in her blonde curls. "I figured it out in isolation. I wanted it to be a surprise, so I told Vlad not to tell you."

"I had her researching some obscure forms of magic that only exist in Faerie," Vlad explains. "We realized pretty early her raw magic wasn't the same, but I had a feeling she'd still have something. I believe her Dark Magic combined with her vampire abilities, and now she can use blood as raw magic."

"But my blood reacts differently, so it has to be human blood." A fireball crashes into our shield, taking the top off, and Adriana's face morphs into a mask of pure rage. She shrieks and sends the blood surrounding us at the unsuspecting witches. They sprint away from the crimson tidal wave.

When she's satisfied they're taken care of, she goes to remake the shield. "I can do it this time," I assure her, quickly throwing up my shield.

"Isn't this great?" Adriana asks. "It's so much better than my Dark Magic!"

"That's a word for it," Lowell murmurs in my ear.

Adriana's pupils dilate, and her fangs extend. "I think..."

"Yep, I need to get her out of here," Vlad says, scooping her into his arms.

"No, I can stay," she whines. "Just let me—" She lurches in Vlad's arms like she's going to attack the closest person, which happens to be me.

"You're done, sweetheart," Vlad coos. "You did so well." He turns to me as his hold on my sister tightens. "I need to chain her up in the coven before she eats everyone. I'll be back in a minute, and we can discuss how to best use Adriana's...talents."

Adriana creates one last round of blood bullets and sends them out before Vlad runs away with her in his arms.

"That was surreal," Lowell says.

All good over there? Edina asks in my mental channel.

Adriana is a blood witch. And I think she keeps trying to eat me.

Edina cackles. *That's both fantastic and scarring.*

A quick aerial view shows us that the hole we carved through the opposing lines has now been filled as his soldiers closed ranks. Rather than flying back to the same spot, Lowell and I stay on the ground, fighting our way through.

The visibility on the ground is terrible between the smoke, the dust kicked up from the Earth Elementals, and the blood. Even when we make it away from Adriana's blast radius, there's blood everywhere. It's not something I'm used to in magical battles. Magic kills swiftly, without much excess carnage. But we have wolves who are tearing apart limbs and vampires who are slitting throats, and because of that, Archer's soldiers have turned vicious. They harness their elements into whips, spears, and swords and aim to kill.

We push forward when we can, but mostly we help our soldiers on the front lines, working sideways to give everyone a much-needed break and the ability to rotate ranks. Holding down this side of the troops are Edina and Eldoris, who rain down fire and ice on the opposition in maneuvers that are so perfect they look choreographed.

When we reach her, Edina jumps skyward and freezes an entire line of soldiers in their places. They stand unmoving, encased in ice, with just the smallest gap between them. "There's your opening, babes!" she says as she dives back into the fray.

Lowell and I charge forward, slipping through the cracks of the frozen soldiers. But where the popsicle men end, more non-frozen men wait. My golden magic reacts against the barrage of attacks, flaring out around us in an explosion of gilded sparks, stopping the attacks and protecting me and my mate.

We keep fighting, getting closer to the back of the army, but there's still no sign of Archer. The fighting gets louder the closer we get to the back of their lines. The yelling mixes with the explosions, which in turn mixes with my heart thudding in my ears. It's dizzying, but we press on.

Coleman's words keep ringing in my ears. *I mourn for the girl who cried over five people being destroyed before her eyes.* I'm still that person, the one who doesn't want innocent men who are following orders to die. All this death, all the blood, all the hurt makes me sick. But still, we press on.

"Captain," a voice to my right calls, and I'm face to face with Jacobs.

I laugh at the irony of meeting a soldier from Archer's Moment of Valor when I'm thinking about the girl I was on that mission. Of course, this is also the only soldier from that mission who stayed with Archer.

"Jacobs, have you met my mate?" I smirk. Lowell turns from his current battle, where he's been breaking wrists and incapacitating soldiers, but not killing them. I didn't ask him to do that, but somehow he knows exactly what I need. My love for this man knows no bounds.

Lowell snarls, his eyes glowing bright yellow as Jacobs pales in recognition. He goes to cast, but I have his wrists completely encased in my golden magic. "Jacobs was one of the guards who helped Archer torture me."

"I didn't," Jacobs sputters. "That wasn't what His Majesty was doing—"

Lowell leaps forward, shifting in the air and aiming straight for the soldier. Jacobs' scream turns to a gurgle as teeth sink into his jugular and my mate rips out his throat. The body falls in slow motion, crumpling as Lowell snarls at the corpse.

I swallow hard. Blood drips from his snout, staining his white fur and making him look positively feral.

"I definitely shouldn't be turned on by this," I mutter, fanning myself and blocking an attack over my shoulder. Lowell shifts back into his human form, and his eyes hold a dark promise that has me entirely too distracted for a battlefield.

A wave of freezing water crashes over us, making me shriek.

"Get it together," Edina laughs, flying over us and turning her tsunami on our foes. Lowell and I both laugh as we turn and start our fight again.

THE BATTLE STARTS TO blur, becoming a monotonous push and pull. Every time we gain a few inches, we get forced back. When Vlad joins us again, he uses our mental channel to have a running commentary on the battle like some twisted sportscaster.

Ohhh! Lyra rips a man's arm off with a vicious bite to the bicep. She had great form on that tear. That'll never heal right.

General Marcus Weatherbeak, in a surprisingly savage move, uses his Air Magic to throw a soldier into the path of Vampire King Rex Takahashi, who literally tears the man's face off.

Queen Kathryn Carmichael looks about thirty seconds away from fragging her vampire bestie just to get him to stop talking. History has shown us that he won't stop. Let's see how this plays out.

"I swear to fuck, Vlad—"

Sunrise is in five. I have never been more grateful to hear Sybil's shrill voice across our mental channel.

Phase two. Everyone behind me. My troops instantly drop back, and the witches pour our combined magic into a gigantic shield covering the front half of the army while the vampires run back to the coven where they'll stay for the day.

Hold fire, I instruct as we continue pouring our energy into fortifying the shield.

You think they're gonna break for the day? Lowell asks.

The sound of hoofbeats answers him.

The Dragons' aerial unit retreats from their spot at the back of the army, and a wall of centaurs appears on the top of the hill. Their hooves stomp the ground, kicking up dirt and grass as they take their stances. Their chests are all bare, even the females, and they all raise muscled biceps in the air as they knock arrows into their bows.

Hold your shields, I command. I'm pretty sure a centaur's arrow can pierce through a shield if it's not strong enough. Edina and Eldoris come up beside me, adding their magic to the shield to form a bubble around our army.

The arrows fly in unison, more like an attack of missiles than actual arrows. They collide with the shield, followed almost instantly by another wave that breaks through some places. Screams pierce the air as witches fall. People start scrambling to patch the shield, but more arrows fly.

WHERE THE FUCK IS PHASE TWO?

I don't appreciate your tone, Your Majesty, Ethelinda's cool voice echoes in my mind. *Look. The Fuck. Up.*

I lift my eyes to the sky that's now colored with pinks and purples of sunrise. It would be beautiful if the ground weren't stained red. Giant figures blot out the rising sun, circling in from the east with a roar that shakes the hills.

Dragons, actual dragons, not the soldiers, extend their many-colored wings as they dive, opening their giant maws and blasting ultraviolet fire at the line of centaurs. The centaurs return fire, and the two Magical Creatures fight in a whirlwind of claws, hooves, fire, and arrows. We take advantage of the distraction to drop the large shield and attack again, catching the soldiers off guard. They thought they would have the upper hand when the vampires retreated. We won't always have this element of surprise, but today we do.

We don't get very far into this second wave of fighting when a melodic voice calls my mate's name over the din of the battle. A very naked Delmare saunters down the battlefield, soldiers letting her pass with a sigh. I wrap her in our shield, and she smiles at me full of pointed teeth.

"Make it look like I'm hypnotizing you," she instructs, and I glare before pasting a sleepy smile on my face that makes Delmare cackle. "There's dissension in the ranks. If I can get them to turn, do you want the soldiers?"

"Yes," I respond just as Lowell says, "No."

"Get them off the battlefield," I insist. "We'll bring them to the cells in the coven. We won't kill those who desert the Dragons."

"Great. Also, Archer's not here," Delmare says with a shrug.

"What?" Lowell bellows and Delmare glares at him so intensely that he acquiesces and pretends to be entranced by her.

"He's not here at all?" I ask.

"He's in a tent over the ridge surrounded by Fae. I don't think he'll fight until it's necessary. And he's talking about pulling his troops in at nightfall."

"We thought he might," I murmur. We lose a huge force if we don't have the vampires with us, and they can't fight during the day. "Has he figured out who you are?"

"Of course not," Delmare says, flicking her seafoam green hair over her shoulder. "His mental shields are strong, so he hasn't fallen under my influence, but he just thinks I'm a Siren who's come to aid his army." She looks over her shoulder as though getting some imaginary call. "I have to get back. Scream at me, and I'll run away."

I scream in rage that isn't faked, and Delmare squawks as she parts the rows of soldiers like the Red Sea.

Chapter Twenty-Nine

THE DAY STRETCHES ON, and there's no end to the fighting. Our forces are large enough that we can rotate who's on the front lines, but unfortunately, their aerial unit makes a reappearance in the late afternoon while our actual dragons are busy with the centaurs. Instead of hanging back and protecting their back lines, they attack and hit the back of our army hard before our flyers can get on brooms.

Whenever someone drains their magic, they retreat to the tents Coleman and the other healers have erected, but no one rests for long. The healers are stretched thin with injuries; even the cauldrons brewing tonics are always in use. Thankfully, Coleman has been brewing energy-revitalizing tonic for months, so there's a large supply.

By nightfall, our soldiers have been fighting for about eighteen hours, and the ones marching have been awake much longer than that. I almost cry in relief when Archer's troops begin retreating.

"Should we keep pressing?" Edina asks. "The vampires will be back in a minute, fresh and energized."

Even though we're drained, I consider it. Archer's army was also marching. They didn't plan to battle us last night. Maybe if we keep going, they'll start making big mistakes. I open my mouth to ask what Lowell thinks when a wall of hellfire bursts from the ground between our armies before circling the entire expanse of their camp.

I stare at the wall of white flames with hatred in my heart. I hate that I have this fire. I hate that it lives in my veins, put there by someone I trusted not to intentionally hurt me. Mostly I hate that it's the reason for this war because Archer's attack on the Highland Coven kicked off this series of events.

Edina comes up beside me, her eyes also on the flames. "I can try to take it down," she offers, and I shake my head. I can tell it is even stronger than Archer's, which is hard enough to beat.

"This was a sign." I look back at the battlefield, which is bloody and littered with bodies and appendages. Our soldiers are covered in sweat and blood and pant while they wait for orders. "We start again in the morning."

Some people physically collapse where they stand, but most turn and head for the camp the healers set up. They'll have to share tents, but I'm positive they don't care.

Edina and I set about making a shield, adding layer after layer of magic until I'm convinced it will hold against any surprise attacks. It takes us long enough that when we're done, the vampires have arrived. Without prompting, they take up watch, help the healers by using their blood to heal some of the minor injuries, or start scanning the bodies on the battlefield for any survivors.

I can't take my eyes off the fallen.

I'm rooted to the spot as I take in all the death. So much death.

"What are we gonna do when he shows up on the battlefield?" I ask softly.

Edina slings her arm around my shoulder, and we tilt our heads together until our temples touch. "We kill him, babes."

"That simple?"

Lowell wraps his arms around us both, avoiding Edina's wings. She hasn't put them away since we left the coven, and I don't know if that's because she's too tired or afraid she'll need them in a pinch.

Vlad and a few other vampires sift through the bodies, taking a count of our soldiers and marking their names so we can inform their families before we cremate their remains. We asked a few weeks back and have a list of soldiers who wanted to be buried, but most agreed on cremation. The dragons have already ignited the funeral pyre we've erected at the hill behind us.

I take deep breaths through my mouth, trying to avoid the scent of burning flesh as the day catches up with me. My knees wobble, not from exhaustion but from the crushing grief of those we've lost. Lowell is there, tightening his hold on me.

"Head held high. Don't let them see you break."

I swallow thickly and brush tears from my eyes.

Two figures slowly approach through the darkness. When Jefferson and Soto step into the light created by the hellfire wall, the former extends a steaming cup of coffee. I nod my thanks, putting on a brave face, but it must not fool them because Soto hands me a flask. I dump a measure of the amber liquid in and toast them before taking a gulp.

"Take another sip, Your Majesty," Jefferson says.

I eye them skeptically. "Why do I feel like you're about to tell me the sky is falling?" They exchange glances and wait until I take another sip of the spiked coffee.

"We're both still in the Dragons' mental channel," Soto starts slowly. "Archer asked us to get a message to you."

"What did he say?" I ask, grabbing my mate's hand.

"He wants to meet," Jefferson says. "Alone. At midnight."

"No," Lowell says, but I hold up a hand.

"You're not considering this," Edina says.

"Do we know if he's gotten any better at Mind Magic?" I ask, and the men shrug. I switch to my mental channel between Lowell and Edina. *If he doesn't have control over his Mind Magic, we can station soldiers around the perimeter. But it won't work if he remembers how to send his mind out.*

You're sure he even learned to do that? Edina asks.

Of course, I fucking taught him.

Lowell is deathly quiet, and I know he will not like my response.

"One person each," I tell Jefferson and Soto. "Witches only. I don't want him bringing his Fae goons. Those are my terms."

Jefferson falls silent as he relays the message, and I take another sip of my coffee before handing it to Lowell. His face is impassive, but I feel his rage simmering through our bond.

"He said he'll see you at midnight," Jefferson says, and then he and Soto head back to the camp.

"What the fuck are you thinking?" Lowell seethes, his voice not raising above a whisper. "The last time you went to him alone, you were almost tortured to death."

"I'll be with my mother," I tell him. "And I have my magic now. If anything, I have the upper hand."

"Don't underestimate him again," Edina says. "He doesn't have anything to lose. People get desperate and crazy when they have nothing to lose."

"I can teleport us out if things go sideways. If it makes you feel better, we'll station vampires nearby. Their minds are different enough that Archer shouldn't be able to sense them, even if his Mind Magic has improved."

"And what do we do?" Lowell grumbles.

"You watch the camp for signs of an ambush," I say. "I wouldn't be surprised if he's using the wall to assemble his troops behind our backs. My Mind Magic won't breach the barrier."

Lowell sighs heavily, but nods. I wrap my arms around his waist, wait until he sinks into my touch, and leans down to put his forehead to mine. "We will survive this day," I promise.

"I trust you, *Ma Reine*."

"KATIE," Adriana barrels into me, almost knocking me into the wall before Lowell snags us both in his large arms and throws us back a few paces. "I need you to see this."

She raises her hands, and a wave of blood flies across the battlefield. She sends some directly into her mouth, groaning in pleasure as she drinks, but saves three drops she siphons into a small vial she must have stolen from the healers.

"Adriana," I start, but she holds up a finger as she removes a piece of paper from her pocket and reads it three times before folding it and putting it away.

"Watch," she says, closing her eyes and keeping her hands out. She starts chanting in an old language that sounds like it could be Russian before removing a silver dagger from her sleeve and cutting a long line down her forearm.

"Fucking hell," Edina breathes, but Adriana only increases her chanting as she squeezes her hand, dropping three drops of her own blood into the vial with the human blood. By the time it's done, her arm is healed.

Vlad appears at my side in a blur, a furious look on his face. "What is she doing?" he demands.

"Your guess is as good as mine."

Adriana guides the blood out of the vial, the droplets mixing in a swirl of bright red and deep crimson. She halts her chanting, and her eyes glaze over, the gray turning so pale it's almost as white as her irises. "Ask me a question about the future," she says, her voice deep and not at all sounding like her own.

"Um...how will this meeting with Archer go?" I ask.

She mutters more words I don't understand, and the blood swirls faster and faster in front of us until it becomes vapor-like. Her hands stop their movements, and a picture appears in the blood. It's Archer and I talking, my mother at my back and one of the Dragons generals at his.

I'm transfixed as we talk, his gaze murderous as mine is impassive. There's a sharp nod of his chin, and he extends his hand, which I shake. We part, and the vision fades.

"We make a deal?"

"Wait," Adriana says, and another image flares in the vision. This time both Archer and I are engulfed in hellfire, my mother and the general dead behind us as we clash.

"Holy shit," Lowell breathes.

"It's not done." The vision shifts again. This time, I slice off Archer's head with my sword. The next time it shows him killing me. The next shows our entire armies appearing behind us and descending into a bloody battle.

The visions dissipate, and Adriana shakes her head. "There are too many paths," she says. "The future is too uncertain. You could reconcile, surrender, die, or kill. It's too hard to tell."

"Helpful," Edina deadpans.

"What was that? What did you just do?" I ask.

"My clairvoyance is gone," my sister responds. "But I found an old ritual in one of Vlad's grimoires that allowed powerful witches to harness their blood to see the future. Naturally, since I'm a vampire, I need human blood, but it also requires a personal sacrifice. It took some tweaking until I could figure out the right ratio of my blood to human blood.

"What you saw just now, that's what it was like in my head," Adriana continues softly. "So many possibilities, so much death. I've watched you die thousands of times, my Katie." A blood tear slides down her cheek and drips down onto the grass.

"It's why I stayed...distant," she explains. "I wanted to be your sister so badly, but the closer we got, the more persistent the visions. Even after Rodger taught me how to control them, I still saw so much death in your future, and I couldn't—"

I cut her off with a hug, wrapping my arms around her middle and trying really hard to ignore when she licks the column of my neck.

When we separate, I look at the group. "Stick with the plan," I order. "Vlad, I need some vampires to come with me. They'll be shielded and invisible, but I want them on the lookout for spies. I'm going to get my mom, and then we need to talk more strategy for the meeting, what we're willing to concede if anything."

"I still don't like this," Lowell says, pulling me into his arms again.

"Will it help if I take my sword?" I ask, and he smiles and nods.

"I'd have you armed to the teeth if you'd let me," he mutters.

"I already am," I say, letting my golden magic flare around my skin. He doesn't say it, but I know having his magic makes him feel better. He's protecting me even when he's not there.

We head back to the camp to tell my mother and Marcus about the new plan, and I can't help but feel that this meeting will dictate whether we live or die.

Chapter Thirty

My mother eyes me as we cross the battlefield to the undisturbed grass of the neutral hilltop where we'll meet Archer. We wear matching hardened expressions, our emotions shoved deep below the surface. It's no secret where I learned to don my mask in important meetings. On the inside, I'm running a million scenarios, worrying about Lowell and the troops back at the camp, trying to calculate our next move, but outwardly, I'm calm and impassive.

The air feels clearer out here, just a mile away from the fighting. The stars are twinkling overhead, their beauty mocking the devastation we spent the day looking at, and the scent of wildflowers is almost enough to eclipse the scent of blood and burning flesh wafting from the battlefield.

I adjust the sword belt around my waist, tightening the strap, so it stops sliding down over my leathers. While my mother is wearing her military-issued leathers and tunic, I opted for a tank top showing off my scar. I roll my shoulders, bringing life into my stiff muscles. Rather than discuss concessions when we got back to the camp, we took my stepfather's advice and squeezed in two hours of sleep. Somehow, I think it made me more tired, and even the energizing tonic Coleman gave me isn't enough to keep my limbs from feeling heavy.

We're in place, Vlad sends mentally. He and a handful of vampires are stationed on our half of the hill, cloaked in invisibility. Edina is at the closest edge of the wall of hellfire, so should anything happen in either arena, she's close.

Lowell?

We're prepared, little witch. Don't worry about us. Keep your eyes on le sadique.

The sadist? I ask, and I feel Lowell's mirth down the bond. *All too accurate, pup.*

We make it to the top of the hill, and my hand falls to my sword instinctively as Archer comes into view. He's conversing with one of the generals of the Dragons, an older man with gray streaks breaking up his rusty-orange hair. The general looks up when we appear, nodding once to my mother without an ounce of friendliness. He views her as a traitor now, a turncoat.

Even though I've changed my clothes, I know I look like hell. I have bags under my eyes, my hair is still in my war-torn braid, and the lives we lost sit on my shoulders like invisible weights. Archer, on the other hand, looks fine. Normal. His blue-black hair is rumpled the way it usually is, and his skin is pale but healthy.

And that pisses me off to no end.

"Katie," he greets. He wears a black cloak that flutters down to his ankles, and when he turns to me, it opens just enough that I catch a glimpse of a red stone hanging at his hip.

He has the sword, I shout down the mental channel.

Stick to the plan, no rash decisions, my mother instructs.

"You rang?" My voice is dry, even though my mind is occupied with ways of grabbing that sword and slitting his throat.

"I assumed you'd bring your husband." I hear the unasked question in his tone. He's wondering if Lowell died in the fire.

"You'd be dead if I did."

"How dare you—" the general starts, but Archer holds up a hand for him to stop.

"I said humans only," I continue. "What makes you think I'd go back on that?"

"Wouldn't be the first time you've gone back on a promise."

I scoff. "I made zero fucking promises to you." I'm provoking him a bit, but really, I'm trying to figure out if I can shred his shield while I keep him talking. At least, I assume he's shielded. It'd be really stupid if he weren't.

"What the hell do you want?" I ask, sending my Mind Magic out and indeed finding a shield. "You called this meeting. Go ahead."

He sighs heavily. "End this. Please, Katie, you can end this. *We* can end this. No one else needs to die."

"Are you willing to surrender?" I ask.

"No," Archer snaps, fire flickering across his hazel eyes.

"So, you want me to surrender." I laugh with no mirth. "You killed my family."

"I didn't," he starts.

"You killed Adriana. You killed my pack, my sisters and brother, and my fucking mother-in-law. What makes you think I'd abandon the rest of my people? Because you asked?"

"Because you're my true love," Archer says, exasperated.

"That's not a thing!" I seriously cannot believe we're having this conversation. Hundreds of people died today, and he's holding onto some ridiculous childish notion. "Only those with direct Fae lineages have mates. You can ask your hellfire-wielding friends. Magical Creatures were brought from Faerie; witches have always been human, so we can only be mated to a Magical Creature. There's no such thing as a true love."

Archer goes unnaturally still. "How did you know I have Fae working for me?"

Fuck.

Damn it, babes, Edina swears. *You're letting him rattle you.*

Yeah, I fucking know, I snap, but outwardly, I shrug, trying to play it cool. "How do you think?" I ask aloud, but he sees right through it.

Truth is, we had our suspicions. Edina and Eldoris agreed it was most likely that Archer had Fae working for him due to the wall's strength. But we didn't have confirmation until Delmare and her Sirens gave it to us.

"Give me names," Archer demands, hellfire springing to his hands. "I want all your spies or so help me, Katie. I will kill every single person on your side."

"Well, that's one way to woo a girl," I chide, my brain working overtime as I try to figure out how to get us out of this. I look over my shoulder at my mother, whose emerald eyes are wide and staring straight ahead. I follow her gaze where a line of centaurs stand, bows drawn and aimed between the two of us.

Drop the shield around us, Vlad commands. I do as he says, revealing a hoard of snarling vampires. Archer's eyes widen as he sees my sister, who is being held back by the collar of her shirt.

Archer scoffs. "Good to see you follow your own rules."

"I knew you wouldn't fight clean."

"The names of your spies," he repeats.

"We don't have spies," Edina's melodic voice drifts from overhead as she lands next to me. "It's a Fae thing. We recognize our magic. Plus," she looks Archer up and down like she finds him lacking and clicks her tongue.

Don't mention Eldoris, she says mentally. *Archer's Fae are a part of his court. They'll recognize his name.*

Archer chuckles, dropping his hellfire. "I'm going to enjoy killing you," he says to my best friend. "I never did like you."

"Because I saw your crazy from a mile off."

"Because you poisoned the love of my life against me," Archer seethes before turning to me. "But it won't matter when your army is in tatters and you have no one else. Even if I have to keep you locked in the dungeon until you come to your senses, you'll be home. With me."

"Is he fucking serious?" Edina asks.

I look past Archer to his general. "This is who you choose to follow? A mad king."

"Better than a delusional whore," he snaps back.

It happens quickly. Edina lashes out with her Fae magic, spearing straight through the shield while my mother's Light Magic blasts after it. The general narrowly dodges their attack, and Archer bellows, a sound filled with rage and self-righteousness.

The centaurs send a volley of arrows that shred our shield and make us scatter. Edina and my mom attack the general, using a two-pronged approach of Light and ice that has him on the defensive. Our vampires rush the centaurs and draw their attention so that the hill is clear for me and Archer to face off.

I am getting that fucking sword, I tell Edina and my mom. I unsheathe my sword, letting my lightning explode from the tip as he withdraws his to block my attacks. Except Archer doesn't know how to use his sword to conduct his magic, so he quickly deposits it back in his scabbard and calls his fire to his hands.

The fight is familiar, and I know what Archer is doing before I think he does. I trained him; I know when he's giving it his all and he's not fighting back. But he's not letting me win either. It reminds me of the time we fought when we got back from the Sicilian Coven when he wanted me to listen even though I was attacking in earnest.

I pour all my energy into my attacks, and his anger spikes each time he blocks me. He's dangerously close to pulling his hellfire back out, but I can't stop. This moment is important. We need a win. And to do that, I need Archer distracted and over-emotional.

My lightning streams from my sword as I slash at him with the blade. At the same time, Dark Magic coils in my hand, and I launch an attack that hits him square in the jaw.

"Katie, enough," Archer screams. Lightning coils around his waist, and I add extra force, so he writhes under the force of the electricity.

"I thought this would be more of a challenge," I sneer.

And then it happens.

Archer's eyes glow white-hot, and hellfire springs up around him, dislodging my magic and my hold on him. *E,* I call, and she abandons my mother and douses the fire before it has a chance to go anywhere. But Archer generates more.

"I'm pretty sure this won't hurt you anymore, love," he says as I dodge the fireball he throws. "But how will it affect your soldiers?"

He launches his hellfire at my mom, but Edina gets to it first. My mother doesn't even know she was in danger as she delivers a killing blow to the general, who falls at her feet. Archer tries to strike Edina, but she swats the hellfire away with a bored expression. My best friend is a complete badass.

Without exchanging a word or even a glance, Edina, my mother, and I attack Archer at the same time. He coats himself in impenetrable hellfire. With a savage scream, the fire expands, and I get a shield in front of us just in time. The force knocks us backward, and my head hits the grass hard enough to rattle my teeth.

Shaking away the dizziness, I sit up on the grass and call more magic to my hands. A centaur is in front of Archer, blocking him with his giant haunches. I swear as I scramble to my feet, and Archer swings himself onto the creature's back. "I'll see you when you surrender," he says.

The centaur nocks three arrows and fires them before taking off in a burst of speed. The arrows pierce my shield, and I dodge the one sent at me. Edina's drops harmlessly to the earth, frozen in a block of her ice, and she bellows in rage, flying off after them. Vlad, who was at the edge of the hill, jumps up and grabs her, tugging her to a stop just as a wall of hellfire springs up where she was just standing.

"Katie."

My mom's whisper sounds wrong. Choked and frantic. She's holding her neck, and when she removes her fingers, they're stained red, and a wound in her throat starts gushing blood.

Lowell, get Coleman and Marcus here right now, I scream down our mental channel. *HURRY.*

My mom is just staring at her bloody hands in complete shock. She staggers and falls to the ground, and I run to her side, catching her and laying her on the grass. Her mouth opens and closes, blood trickling from the corner of her lips and coating her teeth. I press my hands to the wound, applying pressure and calling my Light Magic. Coleman taught me how to use my Light Magic for healing, but it's not working fast enough. Every time I try to stitch the skin up, it springs open again.

"Just hang on, Mom," I plead as she grabs my arm. "Hang on."

Lowell bursts up the hill, and Marcus leaps off his back, running over to my mom and cradling her face in his hands. "Misty," he murmurs. A terrible gurgling sound chokes off her voice.

Coleman approaches, but I can't move my hands. I just know in my gut they're the only thing keeping my mother from bleeding out. "It's not helping," I gasp, adding more magic. "Why isn't this working?"

"Was she hit by a centaur arrow?" Coleman asks, and my stomach drops. *Centaur arrows affect clotting.* A strangled cry breaks free of my lips. "We'll try. We'll keep trying." Coleman lays his hands atop mine and adds his magic. The wound won't close, and blood pours through the gaps in my fingers, even as I squeeze them together.

Marcus is leaning down, kissing my mom's forehead and murmuring things I can't hear but that bring tears to her emerald eyes. "Forever," he whispers, and her lips repeat the word without sound.

"Mom, please," I say, tears dripping off my chin. She brushes them away, forcing me to take my gaze off my bloodied hands.

"I love you so much, Kathryn," she grits out, more blood rising in her throat.

"I love you," I sob. "Please." I pray to anyone listening to stop the bleeding, to have my magic start working. Anything to keep my mother here with me.

Marcus nods at Coleman, who takes a step back. "No," I scream. My step-father reaches and grabs my hands, meeting my eyes before looking back at my mother.

"We'll be okay," he promises. She releases a grateful sigh before he pulls my hand off her neck. Blood rushes out onto the grass as Marcus keeps hold of me so I can't go back. I jerk against him, begging him to release me, to let me help my mom. I can't just let her bleed out. How does he expect me to stand by and not try to help?

"We'll be okay," Marcus whispers again.

The light in her eyes dims, her shallow breaths still, her chest no longer rising and falling.

Marcus leans forward and kisses my mom's open lips before resting his head on her chest and breaking down.

I press my bloody hands to my chest, trying to keep my heart in my ribcage. It feels like I'm being cleaved in half. I can't breathe. Lowell takes a step closer to me, but I hold up my hand for him to stop. I know my mate, and he'll try to take away my pain, and I can't.

Strong arms wrap around my back, and I turn in the hold just in time for Marcus to crush me to his chest. He holds me even through his own violent sob, squeezing me tightly until my breaths slow, and I'm left with the pressing grief. This grief has been growing exponentially since the fire at the pack, but this...

He killed my mother.

I spent so much of my life rebelling against her when she was just trying to protect me. There was so much strain and harsh words that neither of us ever meant. But even with all the tension between us, I knew she'd always be there. I knew she'd protect me and help me decide what was right.

We were finally learning to talk to each other without our tempers getting in the way. Finally learning to let the love we had for each other show.

And just like that, she's gone.

And I'll never know how close we would have become.

I want to go to Lowell, but I can't let go of my stepfather. He senses it, and my mate lays a hand between my shoulder blades, silently reassuring me that he's there.

"Katie," Vlad calls across the hilltop. "I'm sorry, but you need to see this."

I pry myself out of Marcus's arms, and the small group of us that has remained at the hilltop walk to the edge of the hill...where I can see the wall of hellfire inching closer to our camp.

Chapter Thirty-One

THE PORTION OF THE wall closest to our side of the battlefield creeps forward, sending our soldiers skittering backward while theirs remain surrounded in the protection of the flames. The shield Edina and I erected shatters, and our troops struggle to form replacements. They're devoured in seconds.

"Someone really needs to kill this asshole," Edina says as she takes off into the air, flying in the direction of the fire. Lowell shifts, and Marcus and I silently hop on his back as he takes off in a blur toward the fire, the vampires hot on our heels.

Little witch, are you...

I know Lowell can feel me hardening, sealing my emotions behind a cement wall. If I stop to think about my mother on that hill, the blood currently staining the ground, her corpse lying there...

I already asked Coleman to move your mother's body, Lowell says, reading my mind.

I can't answer, so I send my grief-tinged thanks through our bond. I'm met with nothing but love and support from my mate, even though I know he's grieving as fiercely as I am. We can't focus on that now.

Just in front of the fire is Eldoris, his shield shimmering like the sun on the ocean and halting the hellfire's progress. Edina lands beside him and extinguishes the outermost layer of the wall.

"Where the fuck is our army?" she demands.

"How should I know?" he snaps. "They were on their way when I left."

"They could still be days out," she shrieks. Marcus and I dismount Lowell and add our magic to the shield.

"We don't have days," I say. "If they're launching a hellfire attack, we have a matter of hours."

Lowell stands in front of me. His eyes glow briefly, and he steals some of my fatigue and sadness through our bond before moving directly behind me in silent support. "What do you need?"

"We need to retreat," I say softly. "When the Fae get here, it's a different story, but right now, we can't do anything but hold them back."

"Then we'll hold them back," a masculine voice says. I look over my shoulder and find Kyle surrounded by the entire army of witches. As one, they reach up and cast an array of magic, all varying power levels. The magic joins the shield, shimmering iridescent in the firelight as it solidifies and turns invisible. "We're not retreating, Your Majesty."

Lowell and I exchange a glance. "Anyone who wants to retreat should," I tell the crowd of witches. "There will be no ill will towards you. I just ask if you leave that you help secure the coven and keep our elderly and children safe." They respond by adding more magic to the shield.

"We're in this," Cecelia says firmly.

"Okay." I turn to face my mate. "Send Lyra back to the coven. Any of the Magical Creatures who want to retreat should go with her."

"She won't—"

"Those kids can't lose anyone else," I whisper. "And there's a good chance we won't be able to hold this shield forever." He studies me for a moment before nodding, going to the tents to give his orders to Lyra and the other wolves to fortify the coven in case of a siege.

"Vlad? Adriana?" I call, and my sister zips to my side, wrapping her arms around me. Vlad steps up behind her, his face etched in worry. "Adriana, I need you to find out if there's a way through the wall. If there is, I need you," I point at Vlad, "to send some vampires to wreak havoc amongst their ranks. They think they're safe, hiding, and I want them to know the fear my army knows."

"Done," Adriana says, withdrawing the vial from her pocket. I extend my finger to Vlad, who pricks it on his fang and squeezes until three drops fall into the cylinder. As soon as it's done, he heals me and drags Adriana to another part of the field to perform her spell.

"I have an idea," Marcus says. "Can you spare Edina for a moment?"

I look at Eldoris and Edina, and the former nods. Edina throws one last blast of magic to add to the shield before stepping off with my stepfather. He tells her his plan in hushed tones, and she nods enthusiastically.

"Okay, babes, don't freak out," Edina says as they come back over to me.

"That's guaranteed to make me freak out."

"We need to step outside the shield," Marcus says. "Edina will cover me, but for this to work, I need direct access to the hellfire."

"No. Absolutely not. The fire is almost against the shield—"

"Katie," Marcus sighs, his eyes heavy. "I'm not asking." He steps through, leaving me screaming his name as Edina gives me an apologetic look before following him.

"What the fuck are they doing?" Lowell demands, returning to my side.

The wind picks up, subtle at first and then turning to violent gusts. Edina's ice keeps the hellfire closest to Marcus at bay as the hurricane-level gusts tear at their hair and clothes. He starts bending the gales in the air between his outstretched arms, creating a swirling tornado that sucks up Edina's ice and some of the hellfire as it spins.

"Wow," Eldoris breathes beside me. "He's strong for a human."

"You're on thin ice already. I suggest not insulting my only living parent."

"What did I do?"

"You promised me an army that isn't here," I scowl.

"*Yet*," Eldoris says. "They'll be here."

Marcus releases the tornado. Edina casts extra ice into the swirling tempest, and it barrels straight through the hellfire. The wall is thick, but when it reaches the other side, it collides with one of the Fae who is casting. He balks, and Eldoris leaps through the shield, throwing a javelin of fire at him before he has time to react. Edina follows his lead, so as the fire distracts him, an icicle spears his chest, and he falls dead.

"Does that help my cause?" Eldoris calls over his shoulder as he helps Edina shield my stepfather. Edina gives him a quizzical look, but he just laughs.

Marcus is already creating another tempest, but the Fae replace their fallen comrade, sealing the gap and making the wall whole again. "They can't do this fast enough." I gnash my teeth as the fire gets closer and closer to my stepfather. He launches one more tornado, and Eldoris and Edina manage to kill one more Fae before they retreat, and the hellfire collides with our shield.

The witches collectively inhale as our magic is tested. The hellfire is relentless, battering our shield and slowly creeping around the sides, seeking any weak points. It's like we're trapped inside the sun, too bright and too hot. Sweat beads on my forehead and slides down my temple as I add magic to the shield.

Vlad? I call through our mental channel.

The army is stationed behind the Fae, he responds. *But Adriana saw a way in. We just need to find it.*

Do what you can.

And that's what we do. The witches hold the shield while the vampires find their way in and break through the army's ranks. Vlad keeps me updated mentally, sharing particularly gory pictures of the destruction they cause when they invade the unsuspecting camp. They cause pure chaos, which is exactly what I wanted. If this wall comes down, our people will still need to fight, and I'd much rather fight exhausted soldiers than well-rested ones.

The sun rises, and the vampires return to the coven, trading places with the wolves. Butch leads the charge since Lowell is trapped here with me. He sends far fewer updates, and I'm unsure if it's because he doesn't want to show me the carnage or if they're losing more people than they're killing.

And still, the witches hold the shield against the constant barrage of hellfire being hurled at us. Normally a shield is a set-it-and-forget-it spell. But the hellfire keeps ripping through, so our army needs to constantly be casting to fill the holes. We can't even see where the Fae are to try and take them out. All we can do is keep defending our own.

Lowell and the few wolves who remained with us help the injured, move the dead, and distribute energizing or revitalizing tonics. At the rate we're expelling magic, even tonics won't work for too long. The only thing you can do to truly replenish your magic is eat and sleep. Right now, we're hanging on by a wish and a prayer.

When I think things can't get worse, the hellfire on the top of our shield parts, revealing Archer and his aerial unit. They attack from above, battering our already dwindling efforts and forming a hole, which Archer exploits. A deafening scream sounds behind me as a ball of fire collides with a witch, and they instantly burst into flames, the fire devouring them in seconds. The Water Elementals put out the blaze now inside our shield, but it takes a long time. By the time it's out, three more have sprouted from weak points in our defenses. Witches start falling left and right.

"DRAGONS," I scream. "Get in the damn air."

"We'll die if we get hit by hellfire," Ethelinda hisses.

"Then grab a witch to shield you but take care of the skies."

She hisses at me again, and I glare until she stalks off, snatching Kyle around the waist and throwing him over her shoulder as some of her shifters do the same.

It's a slight reprieve. Archer's men don't know how to fight against the dragons, and they're pushed back. White and purple fire collide in a massive explosion as Archer aims for Ethelinda, and she narrowly misses the attack with a spectacular dive. She and her entire family blast dragon fire at Archer and his men.

The hellfire recedes around the sides of our shield, forming a true wall once again as Archer and his men retreat and seal the dragons out. Ethelinda lets out a roar of defiance, spraying her fire at the white wall of flames, trying to break in.

"We should have sent them in earlier," Eldoris says, adding more of his shimmery magic to the shield.

The wall of hellfire goes out, leaving spots dancing across my vision. The relief of cool air is euphoric until it carries smoke to our lungs. A gentle breeze swirls the blackened ash that's left behind by the wall.

"What the hell—" Edina starts.

The Fae are gone, no longer on the front lines. We have a direct view of the wolves tearing into soldiers who, in turn, are blasting them with all four elements.

Should we attack? Ethelinda asks.

I can't explain why I hesitate. Maybe it's intuition from being in the army for my entire adult life. Maybe it's someone watching over me, but I *do* hesitate.

Which is good. Because a ball of hellfire the size of a meteor is hovering over the hill beyond the battlefield. The wolves notice it at the same time.

"Fuck," Eldoris breathes.

Your Majesty... Butch says.

"EVERYONE, BACK," I scream down our mental channel and aloud simultaneously. The werewolves are gone in a flash of their superior speed, taking off for the hills and nearby forests. The dragons climb higher and flee in all directions.

The hellfire streaks through the sky like a comet headed directly for us. The white-hot flames are almost blue in their intensity. Sparks fly, igniting the remaining patches of grass ablaze.

The witches linger behind me, tentatively still casting their shields. "I said retreat," I order. "I wasn't joking. Get the fuck back." They don't need to be told a third time, sprinting back toward the cover. I grab Lowell's hand, and our little group runs behind the closest hill.

"If we run any farther, they'll just do this again," I say, stopping where we stand. "They can't hit the coven. Everyone under there will be trapped."

"Then we hold them off here," Edina says, and we both add more magic to the shield.

"You should go," I plead with Lowell, who arches an eyebrow derisively. "Fine, then just...stand behind me at least."

He gives me a quick kiss and does as I say, laying his warm hands on my waist.

It gets impossibly larger as it careens toward us. The air ripples and I can feel the heat even at this distance. I thought the wall was powerful...this is an atomic bomb.

"Can we survive this?" I ask Edina.

"I don't know. Even if we can survive the flames, I have a feeling the impact will kill us." She shakes her head as the fireball gets closer and close.

"Love you," I say to Edina. The bright fire lights up her eyes, illuminating the lone tear beading on her lashes. She reaches out, grabs my hand, and then extends her other hand to Eldoris as I place mine atop Lowell's.

"Love you most," she responds. Edina erects a wall of ice before us, and I wrap our group in my protective golden magic. Even with our defenses, we're not stopping this blast.

Just before it collides with our shield, another comet-like blast flies over our heads. Instead of sparks trailing in its wake, snowflakes flutter to the top of our shield.

Edina inhales so deeply she chokes, and Eldoris says, "Thank the goddess." Fire and ice collide with a deafening boom, ash and water exploding as neither magic wins their skyward battle.

There's a feminine battle cry, and a blonde woman appears in the sky, delicate blue wings keeping her aloft. She's in sapphire blue fighting gear and is flanked by seven men, one of whom is Astor.

Edina runs through the shield and launches herself into the pack of men, who instantly surround her.

"Her mother and fathers," Eldoris says. A line of Fae appears behind Edina's mother, each with a different form of magic. "And those are the other Fae royalty." The wall of hellfire springs up again, but Edina's mother keeps it back far enough that it doesn't hurt any of the Fae in front of our shield.

I lift into the air on my Dark Magic, and the sight takes my breath away. Fae as far as the eye can see, in all shapes and forms, stand in neatly formed rows, waiting for a signal from their commanders to attack. Our army comes out from hiding, each witch, werewolf, and dragon shifter with a fierce look of determination. We have reinforcements.

We can do this.

Edina returns to my side with Astor flanking her as Edina's mother slowly prowls in front of us, regarding the wall of hellfire with her hands raised. A heartbeat passes. Then another.

"What is she waiting for?" Edina asks Astor.

"Your mother has a flare for the dramatic," he murmurs. The other Kings and Queens of the Courts fall behind her in a perfect V like they've been working together for centuries when we know that they've been fighting for as long.

Edina's mother sends a torrent of water upon the hellfire, which is extinguished immediately. Steam hisses as the ground cools. The Fae on the other side gape at our Fae, now lined up before them. Edina's mom releases another cry, this one light and lilting. It's echoed by harsh hissing and screaming before the Fae army charges. There are waves and waves of them as they storm the battlefield.

Archer's witches meet the challenge, rushing toward the Fae with false bravado. Magic in all forms explodes, the same elements colliding in the air as the Elemental Witches parry the attacks.

The Fae monarchs stand back until the last of their people trickle onto the battlefield. Then, in unison, they turn and appraise my little group. Edina's mother gives me a nod as I sink into a bow along with the rest of the party. She could be my best friend's twin. They have the same willowy frame, the same golden blonde waves, but her eyes are such a light blue they almost look white. They're piercing, and sparkle with such intensity that I know she's the most powerful Fae in existence.

"Queen Kathryn, it looks like we got here just in time." Her voice is quiet, as if she doesn't mind if we can't hear her over the battle raging behind her.

"I'll say," Edina breathes, earning a scowl. It's crazy how similar they are. Even their expressions are the same.

"Well, don't just stand there," a queen with vibrant reddish-orange curls barks. "Go, fight your war." Edina's teeth grind, and the redhead flashes her a taunting smile.

The sun sinks behind the hills, and Vlad appears, holding the three pieces of the blood oath that we possess. "This ends tonight," he says resolutely. He hands Lowell the locket to put on me before holding out the scepter and the diadem. "Shrink these, baby queen."

"So, you don't just order around Fae royalty?" one of the Fae asks, and Vlad flashes them a wicked smile.

"Good of you to show up," he snarks. "Thank you for hurrying." I shrink both items, and Vlad slides them into his pocket.

"When you get the sword, you'll need to enlarge the other two. Put the crown on, and hold the scepter and sword in your hands," he says as Lowell puts the locket around my neck.

"How do you suggest I get the sword?" I ask.

"You kill Archer," Vlad says.

"Brilliant strategy, Count Orlov," I deadpan. *Everyone ready?* The Fae continue to combat the onslaught of magic from Archer's witches. My army braces itself, and the monarchs of the Fae community insert themselves onto the battlefield.

I kiss Lowell swiftly, and he winks before shifting. Vlad grabs my hand and squeezes. "Let's claim your crown, baby queen."

I release the giant shield surrounding our army and unsheathe my sword. Lifting it straight into the air, I send lightning down the blade, letting it pierce the night sky.

This ends tonight.

Chapter Thirty-Two

WITH A BATTLE CRY echoed from every soldier, Lowell, Vlad, and I lead our army into the fray. The first fight was relatively organized, everyone sticking to the plan we had drilled into their brains over the weeks and weeks spent in the coven. But we've lost a lot of people, so triads have become pairs or groups of four or five. Even with all the chaos, our army works together seamlessly as they charge at the opponent.

My little group falls into a familiar rhythm. Both men seem determined to let me save my energy for Archer, and they end every enemy that crosses us before I can even call my magic to my hands. After Vlad snaps a soldier's neck in my path, I flick him in the ass with lightning.

"Ooh, do it again; I liked it," he teases and kills another man before he can approach me.

I eventually give up my attempts to attack and focus on finding a way through the crowd while keeping Vlad and Lowell shielded. My mate is savage tonight, no longer worrying about disarming the soldiers but going straight for the jugular. What Lowell and Vlad don't see, Edina handles from the air as she and her fathers drop their Water Magic over the heads of unsuspecting victims.

Across the field, Adriana is harnessing the blood of her victims into weapons that slash through the throats of their comrades. The Fae fight centaurs and witches, but most of them attack the Fae who were casting hellfire. Eldoris leads a charge of hundreds right to the heart of their line, causing them to disband. They still throw out their tainted magic, but it's not as concentrated with them separated the way they are. The copper scent of blood is everywhere, and the night air is thick with smoke.

"Katie." Delmare skips forward, surrounded by a small army of dazed men who defend her from harm. "Deserters!" She jumps up and down, her hair bouncing with her and revealing her naked body, which several of our soldiers definitely take note of. "My Sirens have already led loads of them off the battlefield. Where do you want them?"

"Back to the coven," I instruct. "Lyra will show you the holding cells." She mock salutes me, and she and her soldiers saunter off.

There's a hole, Edina calls. Sure enough, a large opening appears, leading right to the back of the army where Archer is flying. Dragons circle above him, dive-bombing with ultraviolet flames spewing from their throats.

Don't kill Archer, I snarl. *He's mine.*

Jumping onto Lowell's back, he and Vlad sprint through the opening. A few soldiers stagger into our path, but I push them aside with powerful blasts of Dark Magic. I can't even see if they're our troops or the opposing side, so I don't aim to hurt, simply to get them out of our way.

Archer somehow turned the tables on the dragons, flying above them, attacking their witch riders, and blasting them with a combination of regular and hellfire. Kyle falls off Ethelinda's back as she swerves to avoid him being burnt, and I throw a cushioning spell in his direction as his blonde hair careens toward the battle, but he disappears into the throng and out of sight.

Centaurs surround Archer's position on the ground, shooting arrows into the sky at the underbelly of the dragons. Their bellows of rage and pain feel like a sonic boom rattling my teeth.

I maneuver into a crouch on Lowell's back, using my grip on his fur to hold me steady as I place my feet flat against his flank. *Promise me you'll leave when hellfire starts flying,* I send to both Vlad and Lowell.

No, they respond simultaneously.

I go where you go, little witch, Lowell says, bounding to the right and dodging an arrow. I grip tightly to his fur so he doesn't dislodge me.

If this is the end, Vlad flashes me a toothy smile, *I'm honored to die alongside my best friends.*

Stubborn assholes.

You ready for this? Edina asks, breaking away from her fathers and flying in a wide circle to the right.

Ready, Adriana says and runs with her newfound speed to the left.

Here we go. I pat Lowell's head and kick off his back, springing into the air. I use the momentum to propel me far enough to get a cloud of Dark Magic under me as my mate and Vlad continue streaking toward Archer on the ground. I close the gap between us, my magic hurtling me closer.

When Archer sees me coming, he retreats. I angle my body into a superman pose, my magic fueling my flight like a jet pack. We soar away from the battle, back toward Archer's new hideout. He's faster than me. I knew this going in. He's one of the best flyers in the Kingdom.

I launch lightning at his back, hitting the broom and causing him to spin, giving me the advantage I need to close the gap. Instead of fleeing, he throws regular fire in the shape of a spear at my head. It sails harmlessly past my ear, not even close enough to singe my hair.

I stop my approach, and we hover in the air for a minute, staring at each other. We've flown far enough that no one is on the ground beneath us. No soldiers fly beside us. It's just him and me.

And only one of us will come out of this alive.

Even as far away as I am, I can see Archer realize this. His jaw tics, his eyes harden, and any hope he had of me going back to the palace with him drains from his face. Because I won't go back with him, willing or not. I won't be kept in that dungeon until he breaks me. I'll die first.

I release all the emotions I've felt over the past few days on an exhale. My mind quiets, and my heart slows as hellfire ignites in Archer's hands. The white-hot flames grow, and he heaves them toward me.

Keeping myself calm and devoid of emotion, I extend my hands.

The hellfire halts.

Archer's mouth pops open.

The immense power floods my body, making me groan as it tries to get me to react. It feeds on fear and anger and betrayal. It wants me to give into those feelings and use them to destroy Archer. But I don't give it any more power than it already has. I am its master. As soon as it realizes that, the magic bends to my will.

I give him a small smirk as I turn his element back on him. I didn't even tap into my hellfire. I just used his in the move I invented. Archer's seen it before, and when he realizes what I've done, it's too late. The hellfire washes over him. It doesn't leave a single mark on his body, I knew it wouldn't, but it incinerates his broom. There's a gasp, and his eyes connect with mine before his body falls from the sky.

Arms and legs flail as Archer hurtles toward the ground. But this isn't the way he dies. I won't let it be this easy. I cast a cushioning spell at the ground, and it catches Archer, bouncing him before it dumps him unceremoniously on the grass.

When I land, my lightning is ready, spilling from my hands and securing Archer's arms behind his back before he can even stand. My golden were-magic comes next, coating his torso in thick, honeylike magic. He thrashes against his restraints, but my magic is stronger. Hellfire explodes around his entire body, but we were anticipating that. I harness his magic again, keeping my emotions impassive as I take control of the flames and extinguish them.

When they're out, Vlad is there, snapping a pair of magic-resistant handcuffs onto Archer's wrists. He screams as he's caught in my snare. Lowell runs to my side, his white fur stained with the blood of our enemies, and Edina and Adriana appear from opposite sides of the field, where they were waiting in case Archer slipped away.

"He's not wearing the sword," Vlad says, and a vicious growl rips from my throat. Lightning blooms from my hand as I rush forward and grip Archer's jaw. He jerks from the bolts of electricity before I stop it.

"Where is it?"

"Why would I tell you?" he scoffs. "If I don't tell you, you'll have to keep me alive."

"You overestimate us," Edina deadpans.

I fight the urge to snap his neck. "You know," I start, tilting his chin higher so he's forced to look into my eyes. "Once upon a time, I was the most talented Mind Magic user in the Kingdom," I chuckle darkly. His mouth parts. "Oh wait, I still am."

I spear my Mind Magic through Archer's shields. The multiple layers I painstakingly taught him to erect around his mind shatter under my force like they're the most delicate glass. Archer cries out in pain. I could do this in a way where he wouldn't feel it, but that would be too generous.

I move through memories as he tries to bury the sword's location, another tactic I taught him. My life would be so much easier if I hadn't taught Archer how to handle his fucking magic.

The memories shift from random ones to memories of us when we were happy. He shows me when we got drunk and played the piano together, sitting around the fire playing truth or dare, our first kiss, and dancing at the ball.

A beautiful illusion. A string of happy moments I clung to, ignoring the red flags.

I stop my search and show him different memories. I show him the moments of possessiveness, the arguments, and countless images of people falling to his hellfire. I show him the funerals, the memorial gardens, and the bones of my incinerated pack members. And finally, I show my hands lifting off my mother's neck and Marcus breaking down beside me as she dies.

"Stop," he croaks, and because I'm in his brain, I can feel him lose the will to fight. His despair as the weight of his actions sinks in is crushing. He was so addicted to the thought of us that he didn't realize the hurt he was causing. It doesn't excuse any of it.

A picture floats to the forefront of his mind. A hidden tent not far from here, unguarded. The sword lies on the bed. I send the location to Vlad, who runs off in that direction and extract my mind from Archer's. Tears streak down his face.

"I really do love you," he whispers.

"This isn't love," I say, gesturing to the war that still rages behind us. "This was an infatuation that turned to toxic obsession."

Archer swallows thickly. "Can I ask a final favor?"

"You think you deserve one?" Lowell hisses as he shifts.

Archer looks pleadingly at me and takes my silence as permission. "Please don't take this out on Jai. He's the only family I have left, and he tried to stop me."

He's silent as he waits for my answer. "I won't hurt him," I promise.

Got it, Vlad says.

I unsheathe my sword. The sword Finley used on the battlefield during the Four Kings War, the one that was present during the collapse of balance in our Kingdom.

"You know, you were the first person to tell me I'd make a good queen," I say as my magics intertwine on the sword. The citrine gem in the hilt glows bright gold as it's illuminated with my were-magic. The Light Magic shines as brilliantly as sunlight and intersects with my sparkling Dark Magic, causing my lightning to flare down the length of the blade.

"You already are." Archer thrusts his chest forward, exposing his ribs. "Go ahead, love. End this."

I will my emotions to quiet, and hellfire, the final facet of my magic surrounds the others on the blade of my sword. The effect is dazzling. Archer watches all four of my magics before his eyes scan me, a sad smile crossing his lips.

"My god, you're stunning," he murmurs, echoing the words I first read from his mind. I thrust the tip of my sword into his ribcage, angling up, so it pierces his heart. The magic spreads, attacking him from the inside and speeding up the process.

I can't help the tear that falls down my cheek.

The blood drains from his face and pours from the wound as I extinguish my magic and remove my blade.

"Wow," he whispers. The light in Archer's everchanging hazel eyes goes out, and his lifeless body slumps forward.

A breath wooshes from my lungs that's both relief and extreme sadness for all the lives we lost during this war. Lowell is there, holding me up. I bury my head into his chest, the metallic odor of blood and sweat overshadowing his typically calming scent.

"*Ma Reine*," he whispers into my hair, kissing my head. My emotions are going haywire as if the time I spent suppressing them made them come back stronger. I tremble in my mate's arms. He doesn't say anything. He's just there.

When I break away, Vlad has rejoined us on the hilltop, the sword hanging limply from his wrist, dragging in the grass. Understanding shines in his blue eyes, the understanding of the pain of taking a life, even when it needs to be done. On the other hand, Edina is beaming, which is just as reassuring. Adriana isn't looking at me at all. Her pupils are dilated, eclipsing the gray irises as she watches the blood pool from Archer's fatal wound.

"Adriana, no," Vlad snaps, and she whines something about wasted food. When he's satisfied my sister will stay put, he lays the sword at my feet and removes the scepter and the diadem from his pocket. I cast the enlarging spell and, when they're the proper size, grab the scepter while he puts the crown on my head.

"This will feel like the throne," Adriana says as everyone backs away a step. "She'll be in pain, but no one can touch her." She levels a stare at Edina and Lowell.

"There were extenuating circumstances last time," Edina shrugs.

"She can do this," Lowell says, smiling so wide that I'd feel his pride even without the mating bond.

I release a deep breath and look at each exhausted member of my little family. Finley promised these items would help end the war, and we're more than ready for it to be over.

I bend down and pick up the sword. The overwhelming sensation that it's meant for me is only there for one second before pain lances through me. A thousand pins and needles stick my skin. My magic rages inside me, roaring like the most destructive storm over the ocean. My back bows and I'm vaguely aware that I'm screaming as my vision goes black.

When the churning, violent storm inside me ebbs, leaving me swaying on a gentle tide, I blink, my eyes slowly adjusting to the surroundings. I expect to be in that dark room where I last met Finley. But I'm not. I'm still on the hilltop, facing my family, who are staring open-mouthed at the space behind me.

Vlad's hand goes to his chest, and a blood tear slips past his lashes. "I've missed you."

Spinning around, I come face to face with the images of two women. They're not quite solid, their spectral visages flickering in and out of view. Finley's armor is resplendent in the moonlight. Her helmet is under her arm, and her brown hair is bound in a battle-ready braid. She looks so much like my mom that it chokes off my air.

The other woman is petite, her long dark hair unbound and wild. Her dress is modest, a gauzy black material that cinches at her waist before flowing down to her feet. Red-painted lips tilt up in a smile as her dark brown eyes crease at the edges.

"You did beautifully, Kathryn," she says, her voice lighter than I anticipated from her sharp features.

"Katie, this is Queen Carman," Vlad says as he and the rest of my group step closer. "And you already know Finley."

"Your mom is okay," Finley says. Hope nearly cracks my chest at the thought that I can call her here. Finley gives me a sad, knowing smile. "She's moved on, but she's so proud of you."

"As are we," Carman says. Finley wraps an arm low along Carman's waist, and the queen tilts her head onto her shoulder. They both look at me fondly.

"Are you ready to end this war?" they ask and I nod enthusiastically.

"Use your magic to fly to the edge of the fighting," Carman instructs. "We'll guide you from there."

Dark Magic surges to my fingertips with such force that I'm blasted into the sky. My yelp of surprise turns to laughter as I gain control of the cloud of magic.

"Right, your magic was amplified," Finley says. "We suggest going in easy until you get the hang of it."

We soar over the valley that Archer and I traversed in our chase. When I'm at the edge of the battlefield, looking over the fighting that's still in full swing, I get the overwhelming urge to use my protective magic. I let it flow from my fingers, and it quickly spreads over the entire field, immobilizing all our foes just like it did that day in the coven.

My entire army, including the Fae, look up, and I follow the deep-seated intuition to let my Light Magic illuminate me against the night sky.

"My name is Kathryn Carmichael." The voice that comes from my throat isn't entirely mine. It's Carman's influence, her mind speaking to mine on a magical level that's much deeper than Mind Magic.

"I am the heir of Carman, descendent of Darius." My Light and Dark Magic intersect at my feet, and lightning dances around my ankles. "I am the mate of Lowell Dubios, Pack Master of the European Werewolf Packs." Golden were-magic joins my Light Magic.

"And—" Hellfire erupts from my back in the shape of two fiery wings so that I look like a phoenix emblazoned in golden fire. "I am a keeper of hellfire."

The collective gasps reach my ears even at my altitude.

"Archer Baran is dead. It is time to correct the imbalance in the Kingdom of Magic that began when his line seized control of the throne two hundred years ago."

I extend the sword and the scepter and use my magic to illuminate the rubies on all four pieces of the blood oath. "Through the pieces of the blood oath, the four monarchs of long ago have given their blessing over my rule.

"As a representative of all four magics, I will strive to lead the Kingdom into an era of peace and create a place where all magics are recognized and treated equally.

"There is room for all in this new vision of our Kingdom. All I need is your surrender."

I loosen the hold on my were-magic the slightest amount, and the answer is almost instantaneous. Over three-quarters of the army drops to their knees. Those who don't are rounded up by the Fae before I completely release them from my thrall.

A euphoric cheer goes up from my army as they release magic that pierces the air like fireworks. I join their revelry before Carman and Finley guide me back to the hill where my family awaits.

Edina jumps into my arms, and we tumble to the grass. She barely retracts her wings before Adriana jumps on top of her, joining our little pile. Finely and Carman watch us, and then exchange a glance before they bullrush Vlad, practically floating through him as he laughs.

"You look half-dead," Finley teases, her spectral hand brushing the air against his chin.

"Oh, you're one to talk." Vlad blows the air where she's hovering, and her whole image shutters. Carman's laugh is light and lilting as they try to hug our vampire again.

When Edina and Adriana finally let me up, Lowell slowly prowls over to me before hoisting me into his arms. I shriek as I'm weightless from his toss before he snatches me from the air and kisses me deeply.

"I love you so much," he whispers between kisses, and I repeat the sentiment about a thousand times.

A large sigh draws our attention. "I miss my mate," Finley gripes to Carman, who abandons Vlad to pull her into a hug of their own.

"Soon, darling." Carman kisses her temple.

"Are you...moving on?" Vlad asks, and the two of them nod.

"Our business on this plane is done," Finley replies and then looks at me. "Though for you, the hard part is just beginning."

"You'll be fine," Carman says reassuringly. "You were made for this, after all."

They nod before their forms flicker and fade into the night sky.

We stand watching the space Carman and Finley vacated for a long beat.

"Anyone else get major sapphic vibes from them?" Edina asks, breaking the tension and sadness and making us all laugh. "I'm serious!"

"You're ridiculous," I laugh, burying into Lowell's side.

"What do you need, little witch?" he asks, and I peer up into his warm, golden eyes.

"We have to deal with all that." I gesture back to the battlefield. He brushes the hair from my face before kissing my forehead.

"E, talk to the Fae," Lowell commands. "Ask them to stay and help round up any prisoners and contain them in the holding cells. Adriana, we'll need to know if any of them harbor ill will."

"I'm on it," she says with a salute before skipping off.

"Vlad, we need a list of all the casualties. Both sides. Can the vampires—"

"I'll put Sybil on it. When do we want to address the citizens of the Kingdom?"

"Tomorrow," I say. "We need to figure out a plan for elections of the sixteen seats in the council first. I can choose my inner cabinet later."

"You got it, baby queen." Vlad and Edina head off, leaving me alone in my mate's arms. He scoops me into his arms, cradling me close to his chest.

"You just delegated all my work for me," I murmur, toying with the ends of his hair that have escaped his bun. "Now, what do we do?"

"First, I'm going to feed you—"

"You do love that." He flicks my nose.

"—then I'm thinking I show you all the ways I've concocted to worship my queen." I hum, completely on board with that idea. "And then we create our new world."

Chapter Thirty-Three

I FLOP INTO THE chair at the head of the table in the war room, and Adriana hands me a cup of black coffee. My little family sits around the brand-new, giant cherry-wood table that could, and will, easily fit sixteen people once the council members are selected.

It's been three months since I killed Archer and ended the war. The Fae lingered long enough to help us clean up the battlefield before heading back to Faerie to hunt down the hellfire-wielding Fae, who somehow escaped through a portal during the mayhem. Those who wouldn't surrender, and those whom Adriana sniffed out as potential threats, were sent to the prison. Ethelinda and I brokered a deal to have the dragon shifters be the guards since the centaurs can't be trusted. Or found, for that matter. They seem to have disappeared as well, but we have eyes everywhere looking for them.

We addressed the Kingdom the day following the battle and were well-received from the get-go. I think everyone was happy that the war never spread to their doorstep. When we arrived in London a few days after the final battle, the courtiers were instantly up my ass. I shocked them all by announcing our plans to relocate to the States. A pack near Salem lost their Alpha during the war, and when they asked my mate, it made the decision to leave London that much easier. For the first time in werewolf history, Lowell resigned as Pack Master, passing the torch along without death being involved. When I asked if he was sure, he winked and said, "You're not the only one who gets to change how things are done."

The courtiers protested the move, naturally, and since I hadn't been coronated, I couldn't contradict them. But then, a very unfortunate fire burned the palace to the ground. Luckily no one was inside, but someone said the flames were so hot they almost appeared white. It's purely a coincidence that the fire happened the same day they finished building a castle nestled in the Salem Woods Highland Park.

I glance over the latest reports from the army, which is in the process of being renamed. Having a Dragon army and working with dragon shifters is entirely too confusing. Headquarters successfully transitioned to Salem, and all the damage we did to the base here and in Shanghai has been repaired. We decided to leave the London location caved in and instead moved that branch to the Highland Coven since it's already equipped for an army and has portal access.

I'd like to say things have been perfect since the war, but that wouldn't be honest. About two weeks after I killed Archer, everything caught up with me. My father's betrayal, Archer torturing me, and all the death, especially the death at my own hands, hit me one morning. I remember feeling despondent, spending a day in bed, but I actually unconsciously encased myself in my golden magic. Lowell and Edina were able to get me out, and Coleman adjusted my tonic and increased my therapy sessions, which I had been missing in favor of all the work that needed to be done.

Coming to terms with the fact that I wasn't fine, but was pushing down my feelings again was hard. Really hard. I thought I had everything under control, but I didn't and admitting that I actively need help is something I struggle with daily. I still slip into that mode sometimes, pushing aside my grief to take care of those around me, but I've been working on it. And, as Coleman gently assures me in each of our sessions, taking care of my mental health is important so that I *can* take care of the Kingdom.

The past few weeks have been spent trying to contact everyone in hiding to get them ballots for an initial nomination for spots in the council. From there, we'll select the top ten of each section of magic, and have the community vote to determine the four seats of the council. Surprisingly, the Light Magic users are the hardest to track down. Adriana spent most of her youth in contact with Dark Witches, so they came forward pretty quickly, and between Lowell and Vlad we found the Magical Creatures fast as well. Though the Harpies succinctly told us to fuck off, so we decided to leave them to their chosen isolation in the mountains.

"Why am I always exhausted when we have conversations in the war room?" I ask, putting my stack of papers down and looking up at the mirror that currently has feeds of the palace and each army headquarters in separate little panes.

Beside the mirror, the warm cream walls are covered in maps with little pinpoints of magical communities, where witches have gathered in mass amounts to live by each other. Salem, London, and Shanghai are obviously hubs, but there are also large concentrations in Washington State, New York, New Orleans, and Tokyo which plays host to most of the vampires in the Kingdom.

"I think it's something to do with the *war* description," Edina snarks.

"We need to choose your cabinet," Vlad says. "It's past time, and we need them assembled for the coronation tomorrow."

There's a pregnant pause as we all refuse to acknowledge the elephant in the room. Two of the people I initially chose are no longer with us or can't serve in their positions anyway.

"Let's start easy," Vlad says. "I'm your representative for Magical Creatures."

"Says who?" I tease. "Maybe I want to pick Sybil since she doesn't technically have a position of power in the vampire council—"

Vlad flicks a balled-up piece of paper at me. "You better be joking."

I roll my eyes. "Fine," I drag out the word for about five syllables. "I'll pick you. And the Light Magic representative should be Coleman. The soldiers respect him, and he's not shy about voicing an opposing opinion to mine."

Lowell nods in approval, and I hear him call the healer through our mental channel, asking him to meet us in an hour in the throne room, where we'll inform those appointed.

"Are you choosing your stepfather for the Elemental Position?" Adriana asks. I look up and meet Marcus's eyes before I shake my head.

"I—" he starts, pulling at his beard. "I'm not staying."

Edina gasps and looks between us. I reach across the table and take my father's hand in mine. Marcus came to me a few weeks ago and told me he accepted a teaching position at a magical academy in Washington as the Battle Magic instructor. He said stepping back into the role as general without Mom would just be too hard. He's leaving after the coronation to be there in time for the fall semester.

"Who then?" Vlad prompts, pulling us back into the room.

"Jared O'Malley," I say. "I gave Jefferson, Soto, and the O'Malley twins the option to be promoted to general or take the cabinet seat. They all agreed it should be Jared with no hesitation."

They nod in approval. "That leaves Dark Magic," Edina reminds me.

"Cecelia Andrews," I tell them. Cecelia was the easiest choice. Adriana technically isn't a Dark Witch anymore, but since she's not just a vampire, that automatically puts her out of the running for any position. She claimed the role of my personal advisor, but Vlad told her she needs to control her urges before taking on any position of importance.

"Any other updates?" I ask the team.

"I heard from my mother," Edina says softly. "She expects me back the day after your coronation."

The room falls silent. I knew this was coming, but it doesn't make it hurt any less. I was hoping we'd have a few more months before she was forced to hold up her end of the bargain with her mother.

"Stop that," she says as tears spring to my eyes.

"I'm fine. I'm not crying." I swipe the tear away before it hits my cheek. "Totally fine. I'm actually glad you're going back. I'm sick of your face."

She squeezes my hand, her own eyes welling. "I'll be back once a year your time. Which will be way easier for me since it's like a month in Faerie."

"Thanks," I grumble.

"And we have the mirror. We'll be fine." I bite my bottom lip and nod. Lowell squeezes my thigh beneath the table as I release all the emotion in a long breath.

"Any word on the hellfire Fae?" I ask, and Edina shakes her head.

"I haven't spoken to anyone since they left, but I know the Summer Court is pissed and want them dead."

"That's fair," I say. I was worried the Fae would view me as a threat since I'm the only person left in the mortal realm with hellfire, but they said since I was given the hellfire, I'm more likely to pass along my Light Magic. As long as the hellfire dies with me, they're unconcerned.

"Ready for coronation updates?" Vlad asks, entirely too cheerily. Vlad said we had to invite the courtiers to the coronation, but I drew the line at having them for a ball. Instead, we're having the formal ceremony and then a party for all the soldiers.

Vlad snaps his fingers, and Kyle wheels into the war room. When he fell off Ethelinda's back, I was able to lessen the impact of his fall with my cushioning spell, but he landed hard and is paralyzed from the waist down. He's no longer a soldier but has proven himself invaluable around the palace, mainly taking on Adriana's role from the coven, keeping everything organized.

Kyle and Vlad run over the final details for the coronation tomorrow, and when they're done, the room falls into silence again.

"I keep waiting for the other shoe to drop," I murmur, and Lowell grabs my hand.

"Well, our enemies are quiet for the time being," Vlad says, and Lowell growls in his direction. "She knows we have enemies. I'm not saying anything new. But the strongest people in the Kingdom are in this room, so I think we'll survive."

The words barely leave Vlad's mouth when Lowell goes still. "Oh no."

"What?" We all jump to our feet; magic is called as everyone braces for whatever Lowell heard.

The door bursts open.

"We're under attack!" Lowell calls as three children come screaming into the room, diving across chairs and knocking things to the ground. Lowell snatches Ava Marie, who squeals in delight as he tickles her. He snaps his jaw at the other two, who shriek and hide behind my legs as an exhausted-looking Cecelia and Lyra appear in the doorway.

"They're so fast," Cecelia says, a smile breaking over her face. While technically Lyra is their guardian, Cecelia has been helping since she's been living with us in the palace for the restructuring. Which is such a blessing for everyone involved.

"Come on," Lyra says, wiping her brow from the layer of sweat that's collected, which means she definitely has been chasing them for a while. "Bedtime."

"Aunt Katie," Ava Marie says from Lowell's lap, where she's now snuggled. "Can you play us our lullaby before bed?"

"Of course," I say. "Want to see if you can beat Uncle Alpha upstairs? We'll give you a head start." They shriek and take off at a run to their rooms.

"You have thirty minutes before the meeting in the throne room," Vlad says sternly.

"It's not like they can start without me," I say, standing and tossing my hair behind my shoulder. "I'm the queen."

"She's going to be insufferable," Vlad says.

"I could have told you that," Edina chuckles.

"We should have thought this through," Lowell says before standing and looping his arms around my waist.

"Come on, pup," I whisper, and Lowell takes a minute to kiss me passionately before he scoops me into his arms and runs at his full speed after the kids. I laugh as I bury my head in the chest of my mate, listening to his calming heartbeat and knowing that we'll have a lifetime of this. Together.

Epilogue

"Please," I whimper, thrashing back and forth against my restraints. My arms are immobile behind the throne, the cuffs biting into my skin. Today is my coronation. It's supposed to be one of the best days of my life. But now...

"Was that a safe word I heard?" Lowell picks his head up from where it's positioned between my thighs. He waits just long enough for my orgasm to recede before thrusting his fingers inside me roughly and flicking my clit with his tongue.

"Just like that," I whisper as tingles erupt at the base of my spine, spreading down my legs and making my toes curl. "I'm going to—"

Lowell stops and rises so fast that he's kissing me before I can even scream my frustration to the hall. He's been edging me for at least an hour. I mean, it could have been five minutes, but damn it, it's my day, and I'm pissed that I'm being denied an orgasm.

"Yes, little witch?" he asks, hovering an inch from my face.

"Make me come," I moan, and he tugs my bottom lip between his teeth.

"Is that an order from my queen?"

"No, it's an order from your fucking mate."

Lowell chuckles darkly and skinks back to his knees. "In that case—" His mouth closes around my sensitive bundle of nerves while two fingers sink inside me. I scream as he pumps them faster and faster, and when his teeth scrape against my clit I explode.

He doesn't stop because Lowell is never satisfied with just giving me one orgasm. He works my oversensitive clit until I'm panting and coming again. And again. The waves of pleasure are so close together that I can barely tell where one orgasm ends, and the other begins.

Finally, Lowell slows his pace, coaxing me through the last bits of ecstasy until my body goes limp. I may never get enough of this man. My magic flares, snapping the cheap metal cuffs he used to tie me to the throne. He lifts me into his arms, taking my seat and draping me across his lap, where I sink into his bare chest. Murmured praise that I can't quite comprehend in my post-orgasmic bliss washes over me, and I sigh in total contentment.

"I think you like me on my knees for you," Lowell says, and I laugh softly.

"Maybe just a bit." I kiss the corner of his jaw, breathing in my scent on his skin. "Not as much as you like me on my knees, Alpha." I grind into his erection, and he groans.

"Today isn't about me," he says, scootching me onto his thigh so I can't torture him.

I sigh heavily. My feelings about tonight are so mixed. Am I ready to be crowned officially? Yes. Am I ready to party tonight with the soldiers? Hell yes. But tonight also marks the last day that Marcus and Edina will be in the palace with us, and I'm not ready to lose more of my family members. It's a double-edged sword.

The door to the throne room clatters open, and my best friend walks in, her nose scrunched in disgust. She crosses her arms over her chest, pinching the fabric of her thin robe. Her makeup and hair are already done, which means I'm very late getting ready.

"Can you two keep it in your pants for three seconds?" she laughs. "People need to sit in this room in an hour, and now it smells like sex."

"Open the windows," I say with a wave of my hand.

"It's hot as balls out there," Edina says, and Lowell laughs heartily. "Come on. You have to get ready. Your stylist left specific instructions on how you're to look today, and I think if I stray from that, he'll let Adriana eat me. And not in a fun way."

I motion for her to get started while I kiss Lowell, rocking my hips against his erection again and causing him to moan. "To be continued."

He growls in appreciation as I stand, adjust my flimsy robe and follow Edina out of the throne room, flinging a cleansing spell at the dais as we go.

LOWELL

Katie is the perfect picture of a queen. Her white ballgown is topped with black lace on the bodice before it trails down the large skirt and rims the hem. The whole thing is subtly dotted with gems in all the colors of the elements that sparkle in the light whenever she moves, and her eyes are dusted with gold that mimics the shine of her were-magic. It's perfect.

She's perfect.

She sits on the same throne I spent the afternoon ravishing her on, and I catch her sly smile as she feels my arousal spike down our mating bond. This is the throne I first saw her on, the one we had moved from the Dark Magic Coven. The courtiers lost their minds when Katie said she didn't want the Baran's throne, but she literally had it dumped in the ocean, so it became a moot point. Supposedly, Delmare is making use of it, playing the Siren queen, even though there's no such thing in mer-culture.

I stand at Katie's side in my black tuxedo, marveling at the woman I get to call my partner. This picture of grace who somehow, against all she's faced, kept her optimism and bravado. Every day I think I can't fall in love with her more, yet I do.

Her cabinet members stand behind us, all dressed in their finest. As the officiant continues his ceremony, the three witches look seconds away from tears. Vlad catches my eye and winks in that way of his that says he knew we'd end up here, standing behind the most powerful witch in existence. In the front row, Marcus sniffles, and Edina pats the large man on the bicep, even though tears are shining in her eyes as well. Adriana is on his other side wearing a smile so wide that her fangs must be splitting her upper lip, and just behind them is Lyra, holding Ava Marie while Lorenzo and Bella stand on their tiptoes to get a better look. When they wave, I catch my mate winking at them, ever poised but still unable to deny her nieces and nephew.

The weight of those absent is almost suffocating, and yet, there's something I can't seem to shake. I feel them here today, Katie's mother, along with my mama, Luna and Cyril, and Leanne and Laura. Their love is like a gentle breeze in the overcrowded throne room. I can practically hear my mother's deep voice whispering, "you married up," in my ear. Wherever they are, I know we've made them proud, and I hope that they're at peace.

Katie's nerves spike even as her face remains calm and collected. I flood our bond with my love and awe of her, and her shoulders come down the slightest bit as she leans into the comfort I can offer her.

I love you, she says, and I echo the statement as the officiant turns back to face her. He slowly walks closer to the dais with her crown on a pillow. Katie had the circular crown fashioned after Carman's diadem, with rubies inlaid in each spike.

She steps off the dais, switching places with the officiant. He continues chanting, and she dips her head, allowing him to set the crown atop her curls, perfectly styled to fit the headpiece. The room goes silent as Katie stands in front of them, looking out into the crowd filled with witches and Magical Creatures.

"All hail Queen Kathryn Carmichael," the officiant calls.

"Long live Queen Kathryn," the crowd responds in one booming voice. We all sink to our knees, bowing to our queen.

Ma Reine. Mon âme sœur. My little witch.

Queen of the Kingdom of Magic.

The End

Author's Note

Man oh man, where do I even start?

This series has been so life-changing for me, and I am so grateful to each and every one of you for picking it up and letting Katie and Co distract you from the real world for just a little bit. Is it weird to say I'm going to miss these characters? Because I abso-fucking-lutley will. Most of the stories I have planned exist in this world, or a certain (ahem) adjacent realm, so you may see cameos of this crew. But for the most part, I think Katie and Lowell deserve their chance to ride off into the sunset and for a certain author to leave them be.

You may have noticed that some stories have left themselves open-ended, and all I can say is I have lots planned, but I'm a slow writer so bear with me! The best way to stay up to date on future releases, and get first dibs on future ARCs, is by joining the GrossBooks 2.0 Readers Group or by following me on Tiktok and Instagram.

That being said there is one tinyyyyyy announcement about a certain best friend who is still a bit broken and set off to find a new life in a new realm. That's right, Edina's full-length novel, Of Ice and Heartbreak, will be available this December and will be the first book in the Fae Romance Series, a series of interconnected standalones, where each book features a new couple in each of the Faerie Courts. You can preorder the ebook now!

IF YOU MADE IT THIS FAR: Reviews are so important to Indie Authors, and it would mean the world to me if you would post your thoughts to Goodreads, Amazon, and wherever you like to review books.

OH! One final note. Remember how at the end of Made to Conquer I said the cliffhanger could have been worse? It originally left off after the incident at the werewolf camp. So....you're welcome.

Thank you all from the bottom of my heart for taking a chance on this series and a new author, and for making my dream a reality.

About the Author

Marianne A. Scott is a Sagittarius and a Ravenclaw...which should tell you all you need to know.

She enjoys writing fantastical stories adjacent to our world because she's secretly hoping that one day a rift will open between realms and magic will be real.

Also by Marianne A. Scott
The Made from Magic Series

Made from Magic

Made to Conquer

Made to Rule

Need to know what happened while Edina was in Faerie during Made to Conquer? Check out A Court Where I'm Freezing My A** Off (A Made from Magic Novella).

Coming Soon: A Fae Romance Series

Of Ice and Heartbreak (coming December 2023)

Acknowledgments

First and foremost, I'd like to thank all of you who have made it this far. Thank you for helping me realize this dream.

To the best husband in the entire universe of the world, thank you for always supporting me, and for always comforting me when the imposter syndrome hits. Thank you for being a sounding board when I need to talk through plot points, even when I don't listen and just need to talk at you. And thank you for taking care of all the behind-the-scenes things I wasn't prepared for when I went into self-publishing.

To my amazing parents, thank you for being excited every time I tell you page read numbers and Amazon rankings. You're my biggest cheerleaders and I thank you so much for your never-ending support. And for John, thank you for reading and providing me with up-to-date texts to let me know what you think. PS: I hope you all collectively skipped some sections.

To my writing partner/sounding board/plot-hole canon Rachel, thanks for listening when I talk about this series every single week during our chats. Thank you for every note, every hour spent listening to me dissect the magic system only to scream "there's a spell for that" when I couldn't answer your question and every creativity check-in.

Thank you to my first beta reader and audiobook narrator, Rosemary Adler. I am so excited to hear you bring these characters to life.

To all those who have helped me along the way, including my amazing editor Paige Lawson who made me sound way smarter than I am, and Cassidy Townsend for listening to my ramblings about the cover and turning it into something truly stunning.

Thank you to my family who are literally the most supportive people in the entire universe. I'm seriously so lucky to have you all rooting for me. I hope you know how invaluable your support has been.

And last but not least, thank you to the amazing readers who have taken a moment to reach out and tell me how much you love these books and characters. You have no idea how much your comments brighten my days and keep me going through the worst of the imposter syndrome. A huge mega shoutout to the readers in GrossBooks 2.0, for your overall positivity and willingness to talk all things book related!